Shades of Silver City

Silver City 1

Miranda Joy

Spellbound Souls

Contents

Content Warning

Please be advised that this book is intended for mature audiences, and reader discretion is recommended. *Shades of Silver City* is a dark, gritty, adult, urban fantasy with elements of mystery and romance.

Content warnings include, but are not limited to, an excess of vulgar language, sexual content, violence, assault, and brief/vague references to abuse, death, alcoholism, casual drug use, and more. Please read responsibly.

You can also email the author directly at authormirandajoy@gmail.com if you have questions or concerns.

This is for anyone who has ever felt like they don't fit in.

Being different is a beautiful thing. Who wants to fit into their cramped little boxes anyway?

> *"Color is merely light refracted through a prism—energies perceived by the naked eye. At the intersection of metaphysics and chromatics, the study of soul-shades, or auras, coalesces. Exploring further, the evidence of soul-shades suggests a deep connection between energy and consciousness, with colors providing new insights into the mysterious nature of the soul..."*

> -Excerpt from the personal journal of Dr. Claude Foster, Director of Faeology at Mesmeric Labs

CHAPTER 1
FANTASIA

"Shit, I'm late!"

I jump up from bed, quickly throwing on my work clothes and slapping on a layer of makeup.

I type out a quick message to Mellie, letting her know I'm on my way to relieve her at the bar. With a grimace, I glance at the time and stuff my phone in my back pocket. I throw my hair into a bun, exit my room, and snatch my keys off the counter. My roommates' curious eyes follow me, but we say nothing to each other. My boots are barely on my feet before I'm flying out the door and down the steps.

I overslept during my nap—a nap I wouldn't have even needed if my idiot boyfriend wasn't up all night—and morning—partying with my damn roommates.

The humid summer air weighs me down, fighting against me as I pick up my pace. The pungent odor of hot garbage assaults my senses. Sweat pricks the back of my neck. I'm rethinking my dark makeup. The cheap shit I buy—the only shit I can afford—is already melting off my face.

Someone bumps into me, making me slam into a wall. My shoulder scrapes against the rough brick, and I hiss in pain.

"Watch it, asshole!" I shout into the mass of people moving along in an anonymous, colorful blur.

A few people retaliate by shooting back vulgar names of their own.

Wincing at the tenderness in my shoulder, I brush the dirt off it.

Around me, people crowd the sidewalk. They're all in a point-less hurry, assertively pushing ahead as if competing for their place.

But they wouldn't be in this part of the city, in this sweltering temperature, if they were important.

Everyone is on edge because of the heat, which ratchets up the normal, cranky energy a notch. As much as I loathe my job as a bartender, I can't wait to sneak into the beer cooler for a reprieve when I get to work.

People rush past me, a kaleidoscope of hues, while the sun disappears behind towering buildings and casts long shadows.

As I scan the crowd and wait for a chance to cross the street, the whirl of colors momentarily flusters me. No one else has to deal with this issue, though. The color that radiates from each person—an extension of their essence, the shade of their soul—is visible only to me.

Lucky me.

I hate crowds.

Too many people.

And the darker it gets, the brighter their soul-shades appear. My head begins to ache, growing in intensity and summoning a wave of nausea. I grimace, working to keep the bile down.

Keeping my gaze downward, I try to focus on the pale cobblestone underfoot instead of the swirling fog of colors.

I wish I could turn it off. Although I haven't found a way to do that, over the years I've learned how to repress my ability—keeping my mouth shut about this useless magic.

I harrumph to myself.

Magic—if that's what it can even be called. It's magic I didn't ask for. Something that will only get me killed if the wrong people find out.

It's easier to ignore the colors when there are fewer people, but on a crowded pedestrian street and during the transition from day to night, it all becomes more overwhelming.

Keeping my elbows up as a shield, I jostle through the crowd, making my way toward the alley on the opposite side of the street. Carefully, I step around a pile of shattered glass, then break out into a jog. My skinny jeans are almost too tight to be comfortable, and my combat boots weigh me down, but I push on, swerving around a few pieces of rotting wood, some trash bags, and a couple of sleeping bodies.

I stop at a cross street, listening to the distant honking of car horns and the faint hum of city life. The scent of exhaust lingers in the air. With a quick glance in both directions, I dart across the street.

As I navigate the twists and turns of the narrow alleyways, the shadows cast by the fading light create an eerie atmosphere. The walls, worn and graffitied, tell stories of the city's lurid history. The ground beneath my feet is uneven, neglected.

The streetlights come alive and illuminate my path, an occasional flickering neon sign adding a splash of vibrant color to the growing darkness. Now that I've left the crowds behind, I can breathe a little easier.

My footsteps reverberate through the alley. With every step I take, the city's energy pushes me forward, guiding me through its maze.

Veering to the left to avoid a few trash cans, I end up tripping over a man hunched in a corner, smoking.

"Watch it, bitch!" he yells as I run away.

Gritting my teeth, I restrain myself from voicing my thoughts.

I wouldn't be in a hurry to get to work if Mellie didn't have to get home to her son. Because of me, she's already been stuck working for an hour past the end of her shift, and it weighs on my heart.

Relief washes over me when I catch sight of Pub Path, the bustling pedestrian street in the city center known for its bars. My pace quickens, and my lungs start to burn as I make a beeline for it, only for my boot to catch on something.

My arms flail as I go flying.

I slam into the cement, my knees and palms taking the impact. The collision causes a surge of pain to shoot through my body, and tears prick my eyes.

After taking a few deep breaths, I sit back on my haunches and wipe my palms on my jeans. When the pain lessens, I glance back to see what I tripped over.

Sprawled facedown on the pavement is a girl.

There's a serious drug problem in the city.

"Hey," I say. "Wake up."

Standing up, I nudge her with the toe of my boot.

She doesn't move. I reach down to shake her shoulder.

Nothing.

Dread creeps up my spine as I crouch down, ignoring my sore knees, to inspect her.

"Hey," I repeat.

I brush her hair away, uncovering a face that's too pale, with purple lips and bloodshot eyes.

Screaming, I jolt backward and fall on my ass.

My hands shake as I take in her appearance. She can't be older than fifteen or sixteen. A smoky haze surrounds her body—a grey soul-shade—indicative of her demise.

I missed it initially, so used to vibrant colors that the grey blended right in with the cement. And I've only seen grey once before.

The only other time I've seen a dead body...

An image of my parents flashes in my mind.

Squeezing my eyes shut, I shake my head.

I should call the Silver Scouts. Report the death. Clearly no one else has.

But I can't.

My stomach roils. I jump up and run to the closest dumpster, deeper in the alley, barely making it before spewing my stomach's contents.

The sobs come before I can swallow them down.

"Hey!" a deep voice calls. "Are you all right?"

My legs threaten to give out—wobbling from exhaustion and shock. Someone gently cups my arm, steadying me and rubbing my back in soothing circles.

"I'm fine," I say hoarsely. "There's a..." I swallow, glancing toward the girl. "She's—"

"I know."

The hand on my arm gives a reassuring squeeze, and in the fading light, I notice ink on the back of the hand: a dark skull with a worm crawling out of one of the eye sockets.

A damn Nightcrawler.

Yanking free of the stranger, I swallow the thick ball of fear in my throat. "I have to go."

When I glance back at the man, he's looking past me, at the dead girl. His eyes widen before narrowing into angry slits.

I spin around, ready to bolt, but the sight of a tall, shadowy creature hovering over the girl roots me in place.

My heart clenches, and for a moment, I stop breathing.

It's happening again.

Just like with my parents.

The mysterious figure, hidden beneath a cloak, releases a chilling, gut-wrenching moan that echoes through the air as it leans over the young girl. As its hands hover over her, a sense of dread permeates the atmosphere. It inhales deeply, its raspy breathing filling the silence. Slowly, deliberately, it draws the girl's foggy grey aura into its mouth.

Shivers trail down my spine.

I glance behind me, pondering my next move. Bolt past the Nightcrawler or past the creature devouring the girl's soul?

Behind me, the Nightcrawler watches the scene, remaining quiet and motionless.

"You see him, too?" I whisper.

The Nightcrawler shifts his attention to me, then reaches out, abruptly yanking me against him as he covers my mouth. He jerks me into the shadows of the alleyway, out of sight of the thing consuming the girl's soul.

Not a thing.

Fae.

With his own twisted magic.

"Don't let him see you," the man whispers in my ear.

The city's roar fades to an eerie murmur. My heartbeat pounds in my head while we stand there breathing heavily.

The gangster's muscular body presses into me from behind. He keeps one hand over my mouth, and his rings bite into my skin. His other arm wraps around my waist in a protective gesture.

I struggle against his grip, trying to pry his palm from my mouth.

He clutches me tighter, whispering for me to stop moving.

My low back presses into something hard, and my eyes widen as I reach between us, my finger brushing against metal.

A gun.

Of course this gangster has an illegal weapon on him.

A few beats pass while I consider my next move. For the love of Gods, I only want to get to work, but I really don't want to go past the monster and the dead girl. As sad as the situation is, it's better if I stay out of it. Especially if she was tied up with these two—a fae with magic and a gangster with a gun.

I need to get out of here before someone notices something amiss and calls the Silver Scouts. Their orders to protect the city mean nothing to me. I don't trust them.

The seconds tick by as I sweat.

Finally, the gangster's arm drops from my waist. I jerk away.

"Wait." He reaches for me, his other hand going for the gun in his waistband and pulling it free.

"I'm out," I say, putting my palms up in a placating gesture, but I hesitate. Even in the dim lighting, I can make out how vibrantly, stunningly golden his eyes are...just as gold as the aura radiating from his body. For a second, I'm stunned silent. But that can't be right. It's just the lighting. "Please, just let me get to work."

"You saw him." His eyes narrow.

I shake my head. "I saw nothing. I won't call the Scouts either. Swear."

"You saw the Reaper."

"Nope." I shake my head. "Didn't see—"

"Quiet," he orders in a low voice, staring at me.

"Really," I whisper, "this isn't my business."

He cocks his head, then rakes his eyes over my body, scrutinizing me.

"Can you please put the gun away at least?" I nod to the weapon in his hand, fear freezing me in place. Yeah, there is no way *his* soul-shade is gold. No way. Am I hallucinating? "Okay, okay. I'll be quiet."

He blinks a few times, as if trying to understand my words. I shrug, pressing my lips together and adhering to his command to be quiet.

"Come with me," he demands. His intense, unblinking gaze bores into me, on the verge of being creepy.

Glancing at the gun in his hand, I back away.

"Yo, she ain't breathing!" someone nearby yells. "Call it in."

"Fuck this," I mutter.

I turn toward the alley's entrance, eyeing the girl's body. At some point, the thing devouring her soul disappeared. I take my chance to turn and flee, betting on the fact that this Nightcrawler won't shoot me in front of witnesses.

And if he does, well, it's been real.

But no one will miss me.

Not even Reed.

The thought leaves me hollow.

Not even *Reed* will miss me.

I take off and leap over the poor girl's prone body, wondering if anyone will miss her.

A couple of people standing near the girl stare at me in disbelief as I burst from the mouth of the alley onto Pub Path. They call for me to stop, but I ignore them.

"We're calling the Scouts!" one of them shouts after me.

I glance over my shoulder, locking eyes with the gangster as he joins the couple beside the dead girl.

Why isn't he running, too?

Don't care.

I pump my arms, running as fast as I can to The Rising Star.

When I get there, I practically throw myself through the door, doubling over to catch my breath. A few curious eyes turn my way, but with all the strange shit that occurs in this city, my frenzied entrance ranks low on the list of unusual things.

The place is bustling, with each booth and high-top table occupied. The bar is devoid of any vacant stools. The weathered, beer-stained wood beneath my feet evokes a comforting sense of familiarity. My anxiety is eased slightly by the chatter and laughter of customers.

"Tasia!" Mellie's stern voice reaches my ears over the clamoring of the patrons and crooning music.

She's at my side in an instant, and when I catch my breath and glance at her, her annoyance fades into concern.

Throwing a bar towel over her shoulder and gripping me by the shoulders, she peers up at me. "What the hell happened to you?"

I use my thumb to swipe at the makeup I know is smudged beneath my eyes. "I'm so sorry I'm late."

"Not worried about it. I owed you one anyway."

"Would you miss me?" I ask.

"What?"

"If I died?"

She pauses, staring at me for a few blinks. Then she wraps her fingers around my wrist and pulls me toward the bathroom. What she lacks in height, she sure makes up for in strength—mentally and physically. "Clean yourself up. Take a minute or ten."

"I'm good," I reassure her.

She snorts, swatting me with her towel. "At least look in the mirror before trying to bullshit me, Tay. You look like a raccoon's ass." She crinkles her nose. "Smell like one, too."

"I—"

"Go." She uses her firm, motherly tone with me, shoving me toward the bathroom. "The bar ain't going anywhere. Neither am I."

"But...Axel..." I protest, worried about her getting back to her two-year-old son.

"With Nana."

My arms itch to reach out and pull Mellie into a hug, but I refrain, not wanting to taint her with my sweatiness. She returns to the bar, so I adhere to her instruction, entering the single-stall bathroom and locking the door.

Facing the mirror, I grimace at how awful I look. My lavender soul-shade wavers around me, taunting me. It's a reminder that I can't escape my ability, no matter how much I try.

With a sigh, I wash my face, scrubbing off all the makeup. After tonight's events, I don't care about my appearance.

But I realize two things.

One, there isn't anyone in my life who would miss me if I died.

Two, I wasn't hallucinating the Nightcrawler's soul-shade. It wasn't a trick of the light. It wasn't poor eyesight.

His soul-shade wasn't a grungy, murky color like dark brown, or even a vivid primary color. No, it was unlike anything I've seen before.

It was stunningly bright, vibrant.
As golden as those eyes of his.

CHAPTER 2
ARCHER

After getting rid of the nosey couple, I stare in the direction the blonde woman ran, wondering how she saw the Reaper.

Based on her Rising Star T-shirt, the bottle opener in her back pocket, and her comment about getting to work, I assume she's a bartender.

Finding her later shouldn't be difficult.

Death's sweet scent fills my nose.

It's cloying, nauseating.

It's not the usual stench that decaying bodies acquire after an extended period on the street. This scent is exclusively reserved for my nostrils. It's a natural ability of mine, some may say.

It's how I found the poor teenager here.

"What the hell?" Godric rounds the corner into the alley, his imposing frame dominating the space.

He carefully kneels beside the body, running a hand over his hair and shaking his head. "Not again, man. This ain't the shit I signed up for."

"It's exactly what we signed up for," I growl.

"This is the third one this week."

"We need to get ahead of it."

"Hard when we don't know what the fuck's going on around here."

I grunt. "Called Zeke?"

"He's on his way."

"Scouts, too," I say. "Glamoured the people who called it in."

"Too fucking young," Godric says, bowing his head and scrubbing at his face with a meaty paw.

"Any apparent trauma?" I ask, then turn away to poke through a couple of empty boxes nearby, looking for evidence. Unlike Godric, I'm not good at swallowing down my emotions.

Each lifeless body discovered in the streets signifies another person we let down. A testament to our negligence. Recently, the streets have transformed into a cemetery of untapped potential and muted voices.

Each of them is another Sofia—a death that arrived too soon and too cruelly.

"I don't see any." Godric sighs while I rummage through a bag of trash, causing flies to scatter chaotically. "Arch..."

My jaw clenches at the pity in his tone.

"Don't say it," I warn.

"I know you don't want to hear it, man, but it's possible that the dust is—"

"Zeke hasn't found a single trace of it in their systems."

"But if—"

"Have you seen it around? Have any of the other Night-crawlers?"

"No," he admits.

"Speculation should not be mistaken for fact. It gets us nowhere."

"Hey!" a stern voice shouts as the clamor of boots approaches. "Under direct order of the High Chancellor, Scouts forty-six and eighty-four command you to your feet. Hands up."

"Fucking clowns," Godric mutters.

I grimace. This is a recurring pattern with the Scouts. Once they spot the Nightcrawler tattoos, they'll accuse us of having committed every crime within a forty-mile radius and then call for our immediate execution. Meanwhile, without any consideration for the truth, they'll dispose of the poor girl's body in the city incinerator.

A true shame.

And a gross misinterpretation of events.

Gritting my teeth, I give Godric a subtle nod. We raise our hands, slowly rising before the Scouts. I'm careful not to move too quickly, as I don't want to reveal the gun strapped to my side. That's a sure way to meet death. It's well-concealed by my leather jacket and should remain that way unless someone looks closely.

We're mostly obscured in the shadows of the alley, but that changes when one of the Scouts activates the light in his headgear.

Silently cursing, I squint against the bright beam.

"Is that necessary?" I ask, buying time for my eyes to adjust.

The Silver Scouts wear identical protective uniforms made of pliable leather and silvery nylon. The insignia of a handprint with a swirl on the palm takes up most of their chests, marking them as government officials. Onyx helmets cover their heads but not their faces.

"Shut your gap, scum," one of them says.

Both Scouts slide their guns free of their side holsters and aim at Godric and me.

I just need a minute, not a bullet to my chest, so I heed the Scout's words and blink a few times to adjust my vision. In a matter of seconds, I'll be able to tap into my enhanced vision and see clearly, regardless of the blinding light.

The image of the mysterious bartender flickers in my mind. She expressed a desire to stay away from the Scouts. That was odd, considering most city-dwellers are loyalists. They refuse to let go of the dream of protection.

The farce of freedom.

Her lack of disillusionment is intriguing.

"—both are under arrest."

The Scout's movement catches my attention as he approaches me.

"Gentlemen," I start, keeping my tone casual enough so as not to provoke them into pulling the trigger but firm enough to keep their eyes on me.

Now that my eyes have adapted to the excessively bright light, I shift my gaze between the two of them.

"Keep your damn gap sh—"

"Quiet," I say with an eerie command. "Both of you."

The first Scout obeys me and shuts his mouth. The ease of it would make me laugh if the situation wasn't so dire.

"Don't bother looking around," I order. "There's nothing to see here. In fact, the call you received led you north, to Sweetcreek. To the ashberry fields."

Lowering his weapon, the second Scout mutters, "Ashberry fields." His eyes glaze over.

"You were never here. Never saw us," I say.

The Scouts return their weapons to their holsters, swiftly turning and running away from the alley.

Godric confidently approaches me once we're alone again.

"The ashberry fields?" he asks, humor lacing his tone. He rubs his jaw, and my eyes roam the skull tattoo on the back of his hand—the one that matches my own, branding us as Nightcrawlers for life.

I shrug. "Anywhere but here."

The ashberry fields mark the city's northernmost boundary. The Wilds lay just beyond, separated from Silver City by an iron wall meant to repel fae.

Sending the Scouts there will buy us time, keep them from asking too many questions around here. Coming to the wrong conclusions is a dangerous habit they possess.

Unlike the Scouts, the blonde bartender did not adhere to my commands, which only adds to my intrigue. She can see the Reaper, and she's unaffected by glamour.

I picture her in my mind: dark eyeliner, septum nose piercing, and a pile of white-blonde hair on her head.

"If it isn't the elusive Phantom!" a much-too-jovial voice calls out.

Turning around, I spot Zeke entering the alley. He stops beside the body, his overgrown green mohawk flopping to the side, a few strands falling into his left eye. He blows them away, his bracelets jingling as he bends down and reaches for the girl's wrist to check for a nonexistent pulse. His neon-green nails and warm skin tone contrast with the girl's pale flesh.

"Hello, Zeke," I say.

Godric grunts. "She's gone."

"Aye, Ricky," Zeke says as he stands and wipes his hands on his skinny jeans. "Nice to see you as always, you cheery bastard."

"Fuck yourself with that nickname," Godric mutters. Scowling, he crosses his muscular arms over his broad chest. "Stop wasting time and get your crew. You wouldn't be here if she had a pulse."

"Or would she still have a pulse if *you* weren't here?" Zeke raises a brow, then whistles, summoning two guys with a gurney a second later.

"Imply shit like that again, and I'll rip your nuts off, you son of a—"

"Quiet," I say. There's no glamour infused in my command. Not that it would affect Godric anyway, but both men shut their mouths. The lower-level Nightcrawlers ignore us and swiftly remove the girl's body from the alley. "We've been having some serious issues lately."

"Don't we always?" Zeke asks, pulling a joint out and lighting it up. He takes a puff and holds it out to Godric. "Want?"

Godric smacks Zeke's hand away, causing the joint to fall to the ground. "I'm working, asshole."

"And?" Zeke remains unfazed as he picks up his joint, making sure it's still lit, and takes another drag without bothering to remove the dirt. He casually leans on the brick wall.

Used to their antics, I cut to business. "Rush the results. Slash the wait time in half, and I'll double the pay."

Zeke salutes, his joint hanging crookedly from his lips. "Got it, boss."

As I straighten my jacket, I spot a long strand of white-blonde hair sticking to the leather. A spark of intrigue flickers inside me.

I pluck the hair off and stride over to Zeke, holding it out. "Bag it. Run it. Deliver the results. Quietly."

He takes another drag from his joint, coughing into his fist before pulling a small, empty bag out of his back pocket. He opens it, and I slide the strand of hair inside.

He raises a brow but says nothing. For all his faults, Zeke's one of us. A Nightcrawler. As a medical examiner, he's severely underutilized by the city. They pay him to clean up bodies and send them through the incinerator. Gods know there's never a shortage of work for him, but we pay him a healthy salary for his loyalty. His grasp of anatomy, access to pathology center resources, and authorization to utilize the incinerator are invaluable.

Plus, he enjoys the opportunity to showcase his education and expertise.

Zeke flicks the roach onto the ground, and I sigh, rubbing the scruff on my chin.

"Pick that shit up, you green-haired twat!" Godric calls from behind me.

"As if it makes a difference," Zeke mumbles. But he obliges, picking up his litter. "Look at this shithole." He waves a hand toward a mountain of trash piled high against the brick wall beside us. He kicks it, and a rat scampers out, drunkenly searching for new cover.

"Be part of the solution, not the problem," I tell him.

He rolls his eyes, muttering something about no one giving a shit as he strides out of the alley, likely headed to wherever he parked his city van on the street.

Godric scoffs in disbelief. "Piece of work, that guy."

"He's good at his job. Reliable."

"Still."

"He's as good as it gets," I say.

"Long as he has our back, guess that's what matters."

"By the way, what did you give him back there?" he asks.

"A hair sample."

"Whose?"

"Add it to the ever-growing list of mysteries around here," I say as we stride toward the street—back toward the city's beating heart. "Also...the Reaper's back in the city."

"Shit." He goes still, stopping in his tracks. "You sure?"

I nod, cracking my knuckles. Godric groans and swipes a hand over his face.

"Saw him myself."

Worse, so did *she*.

Whoever *she* is.

> *"FROM MY EXPERIENCE WITH CHROMATICS, GREY IS THE ABSENCE OF COLOR. PERHAPS THAT IS WHY I HAD NOT SEEN A SOUL-SHADE IN GREY. UNTIL YESTERDAY. I WITNESSED A HIT-AND-RUN, AND AS I HELD THE MAN'S HAND WHILE HE BLED OUT, HIS SOUL-SHADE FADED FROM A SKY-BLUE TO GREY, LEACHED OF ALL COLOR..."*
>
> *-EXCERPT FROM THE PERSONAL JOURNAL OF DR. CLAUDE FOSTER, DIRECTOR OF FAEOLOGY AT MESMERIC LABS*

CHAPTER 3
FANTASIA

"Yuh tryna strip da wood, Tasia," a gruff voice says from further down the bar.

I ignore Fredrik, the barfly that's impossible to swat away, and continue to scrub the bartop with feigned attention to detail. I wish time would hurry so I can finish and go home.

Maybe once I'm there—with Reed, in bed—my mind will stop

replaying tonight's unsettling events.

Every time I blink, I see that teen's face in my mind—her pale skin, her bloodshot eyes. It isn't unusual for people to turn up dead on the streets, but I've never been the one to find a body before.

More than anything else, though, it was her grey soul-shade that rattled me.

I hate the color grey. Not because it's a bland, low-saturation tone that offers absolutely no aesthetic appeal, but because of what it represents, the memories it dredges up.

Grey was the color of my parent's soul-shades in their last moments, thirteen years ago.

Silver Scouts.

Silver guns.

Silver City.

Silver is just as bad as grey.

The only difference is that one reflects light while the other absorbs it—but they're both the same color, reflectivity aside.

Maybe that's why I hate this forsaken city so much. Silver City is as terrible as the color it's named after. It's a low-saturation, shamble of a city.

I shudder, vigorously scrubbing the worn wood, the rough texture scraping against my fingertips. The pendant lights overhead provide only dim light, and they cast shadows, making it difficult to spot the stubborn beer stains. The thick air is stale with alcohol fumes and cigarette smoke. Even with the lively chatter and pulsating music, my thoughts continue to echo in my mind.

Only one more hour until last call.

I can do this.

Holding my breath for as long as possible, I try not to inhale the musky, bitter stench coming from the bucket of dirty water beside me while I attempt to clean. It's impossible not to think about how many bacteria are on this grimy rag. It's the last one I have, though. All the rest are dirty, sitting in a burlap sack, waiting for Jeremiah, my boss, to take them to the laundromat.

"Jus tryna have a friendly talk, Tasia," Fredrik mutters when I don't respond. He hiccups, shaking his empty glass at me. "Fine. Another Sharp Wing at least."

A brown haze hovers around his body like always. It's a bland shade, one that's easy to ignore, unlike some of the brighter colors around the room. I keep my gaze lowered, afraid the wavering colors will nauseate me.

Huffing, I toss the rag back into the bucket. Why do I even bother trying to clean this damned place? It's not like health inspectors come to this side of the city, and folk like Fredrik certainly don't come here for the atmosphere.

We might serve local craft beer, but hell, it's our low prices that lure these deadbeats in, not the quality of the beer itself. I've told Jeremiah before that if he raises his prices, he might draw a better clientele. He scoffed at me, claiming that if he did that, he'd have no patrons at all.

I don't love The Rising Star, but it's a comfortable job. I've been here six years now, and sure, the pay is shit, but it's better than the alternative. I've searched for other jobs in the past, and the only options were to sell my skin to the rich from Sweetcreek or clean up after them. Neither sounded particularly enjoyable. At least here I can serve those I understand—those like me.

Muttering under my breath, I grab a frosted mug from the concealed cooler below the counter, position it under the tap, and fill it with brown-red liquid.

"Come on, any day now." Fredrik belches, and I turn, catching him as he uses the hem of his soiled shirt to swipe away the slobber from his chin.

My nose wrinkles.

Even six beers can't distract him from my purposefully slow pace.

The air in the bar is hot and sticky, made worse by the poor air conditioning and crowded space.

An outdated rock song plays on the jukebox, one that I've been sick of hearing since my first week here. At least the other patrons seem satisfied with their drinks and conversation. They pay me no mind.

I don't like to drink—a harsh irony for a full-time bartender. My ability becomes harder to ignore when I'm intoxicated. Even so, I've sampled our Sharp Wing. It's a high-malt amber with a delicious caramel aftertaste that even I can appreciate. But people like Fredrik will never value it for what it is. The people who visit this place want to drink as much as possible for as little money as possible, hoping to escape their miserable lives for a few hours.

Suppressing a bitter laugh, I lock eyes with Fredrik. Although he mumbles something rude at me, he gives me a grin. I slide his mug across the counter toward him, intentionally letting it slosh around. A good amount splashes onto the counter, and he swears at me.

"I ought to not tip ya for that."

"Shame," I say with a sigh.

He sits at my bar five nights a week, orders seven Sharp Wings a night, totaling fourteen silver even, and tips a single silver every time. But that's not even why I dislike him so much. It's his predatory, thin-lipped smile. The way his beady little eyes roam my body with open interest.

I turn my back to the patrons, and my eyes snag on a sketch tacked to the bulletin board behind the bar.

My breath catches.

I've seen it every day for the last six months but never paid it any attention until now.

With a shaking hand, I reach for the flyer and pluck it from the bulletin board.

The noise from the bar fades to silence as I stare at the sketch.

It's a man not much older than me, with a sharp jaw, prominent nose, and tattoos on his neck. He wears a hoodie that covers his hair. The drawing is in black and white, and it's more of an exaggerated caricature than an accurate depiction, but I recognize those eyes.

They're colorless in the drawing, but in real life, they're an ethereal golden hue—almost cat-like.

Underneath the drawing, in scrawling handwriting, it says:

Wanted for murder

By order of the High Chancellor

The Phantom

Reward: 5,000 Silvers

The notorious Phantom of Silver City.

Leader of the Nightcrawlers. I knew he was in the gang when I saw the tattoo on his hand, but I hadn't expected to run into the Phantom himself.

It's the name given to him by the media, for how elusive he is.

As I stand there, mulling over his name, my chest constricts.

Shit.

We've all heard of him and his horrible lack of morals. He and the other Nightcrawlers manufacture and distribute drugs on the street, incite violence, and purposely flout the city's edicts. They constantly challenge the Silver Scouts, step all over the cityfolk, and steal with reckless abandon.

Fear courses through my veins, quickly followed by rage. *He* killed that girl. Whether or not it was intentional, if she died from an overdose, he and his stupid fucking Nightcrawlers are responsible.

"Feckin fae sympathizer!" someone booms from across the room, snagging my attention. There's a collective gasp, a loud crash, and then a few drunk patrons cheer as a scuffle breaks out.

Closing my eyes for a second, I take a breath to compose myself.

"Not again," I mutter.

Instead of tacking the sketch back on the bulletin board, I hesitate, thinking of the golden aura around the Phantom's muscular frame.

Even in the shadows, dressed like night himself and standing ten feet away from a corpse, his soul-shade glimmered like the brightest gold. Something about that image gives me pause, and I decide to go with my gut and trust him. Crumpling up the flyer, I turn around and toss it in the trash beneath the bar.

"Screw you! You don't know what you're talkin about!" someone else yells back over the music.

"Love those dirty feckers, do ya? I betchur wife does too. Betcha she's out there right now in the Wilds, suckin em reaaaaaal good."

"You sonofa—"

Bam.

One guy ruthlessly whacks another with a chair. A crowd rushes over to get a closer look, obstructing my view of the two fighting men.

Everyone's soul-shades blend and writhe, like a confused rainbow. I strain my eyes to stay focused on the fight, the vibrant colors making me more anxious than usual.

I need to defuse the situation before it becomes violent and someone calls the Scouts.

I suppress a shudder.

I've had my fill of close encounters with them tonight.

"Ya gonna deal with that, Tasia?" Fredrik, who is still at the bar nursing his beer, snorts and points with his thumb.

Of course the jerk finds this funny.

"Shut up, Fredrik. I'm not in the mood for your shit tonight."

Reaching beneath the bar, I grab one of the bats propped up against the mug cooler. Not the one with nails poking out, no, just the regular one for now.

"There goes your tip, ya mouthy little—"

"Ask me if I care."

Now I'm seething. My vision clouds, and my clenched fists tremble. The thick tension in the room suffocates me.

Normally, I can deal with Fredrik. And I'm used to breaking up fights, but everything that happened tonight has left me disoriented.

In the midst of the swirling blues, pinks, purples, and other colors, one smoky aura catches my attention.

No.

Squinting, I notice a man in the fight whose soul-shade is grey. He didn't come in here like that; I would've noticed.

"Oh, wait till I tell Jeremiah about this one, ya—"

I block out Fredrik and all other surrounding noise, completely absorbed in watching the two men fighting on the other side of the crowd.

"Move!" I shout as I tuck the bat under my arm.

I place my hands on the bar. With some effort, I swing my feet off the sticky, grimy floor and leap over the counter, clearing it smoothly. I never thought I would be in such good shape from bartending. It's not a matter of choice, for sure.

The regulars, who are still lucid and not yet fully intoxicated, give me a wide berth as I push my way toward the jukebox. They're as used to this as I am.

Sweat forms on my palms, and my knees start to wobble.

As I get closer, I realize that both of the patrons involved in the disagreement have grey soul-shades. A moment ago, only one guy did.

What the hell?

I hadn't seen a grey soul-shade in thirteen years. And now, three in one night?

The main aggressor, a beefy, red-faced man, grabs the other by the neck. "I oughta kill you for that, you son of a—"

Crack.

I bring the bat down on a high-top table beside them. It startles the larger man, and he releases the other, stumbling backward as he squints at me with confusion.

"Get the hell out of here." I shake the bat at them. "Both of you. Now! Or the next hit will land on your balls."

It's a bluff. I've never actually hit a patron with a bat before. But then again, I've never needed to. Threats normally do the trick.

A bead of sweat slides down my cheek as my eyes roam the muted cloud of grey surrounding the two drunkards.

My hands shake so hard I almost drop the bat, but I maintain a neutral expression on my face.

"I said get the fuck out!"

Instantly they stop and straighten. They both spit curses at me, then scurry through the small crowd and out the open front door.

I close my eyes and pinch the bridge of my nose. My lungs ache, on the verge of bursting. Normally, it only takes a few steady breaths to regain my composure, but I can't calm myself tonight.

Why did those men have grey soul-shades?

They're still alive.

The same song plays on repeat from the jukebox. The lead singer goes on and on about drinking beer and partying all night long. I've heard the lyrics enough times that I could recite them in my sleep.

I snap.

Crack.

Crack.

Crack.

I bring the bat down on the jukebox until my arms are weak and tingly from the impact. I'm out of breath and sweating. And the worst part of all?

The damn thing keeps on playing.

The people nearby chuckle behind their drinks, apparently highly amused. I glare back at all of them. "Play a different fucking song, for the love of Gods!"

By the time I hop the counter, return to my position behind the bar, and replace the bat to its resting position, Fredrik is standing, ready to leave. He shakes his head at me before chugging the rest of his beer. He counts out fourteen silvers, leaving nothing extra for a tip this time, and drops the stack on the counter with a *clank*.

"Jeremiah's gonna hear bout thissss," he slurs before he leaves.

As if I care.

My mind can't let go of the two men and their grey soul-shades.

Anxiously, I tap my fingers on the counter.

Before I can overthink it, I snag my phone from my back pocket and shoot Mellie a text, asking her to come down and watch the bar while I take a quick break. She can be here promptly; she shares a kid—but no love—with Jeremiah, and he houses them both above the bar in a small apartment. As bad as I feel about burdening her, this is important.

Without waiting for her to reply, I grab the bat—the one with nails this time—and bolt from The Rising Star.

"Move!" I shout as I jostle my way through the crowd on the street, glancing around desperately for the men who just left.

According to my dad's research, grey soul-shades represent the lack of a soul. His journal is the only insight I have into my magic. It showed up about two years after his death and it explained much about my ability.

Most of his entries are from After Reclamation 370.

The year they killed him.

So, grey soul-shades? They're only seen in death.

But the two men from the bar? They were filled with vibrant, angry life—very much alive.

Comprehensive Surveillance Protocols and Vigilant Oversight

Silver Edict #12

"...Ministry of Surveillance may monitor public areas to ensure the security, safety, and freedoms of Silver Citizens, thus deterring wrongdoing and upholding order."

CHAPTER 4
ARCHER

Hours after sending the Scouts on their way, the terror-stricken face of the blonde bartender remains fresh in my mind. As Godric and I walk downtown, my fingers twitch at my sides, desperate to pluck my phone out and check to see if there's any word from Zeke.

About the dead girl we found in the alley.

And the woman who can see the Reaper.

My phone volume is on high though, and it hasn't made a peep, so I know he hasn't relayed word yet.

We move farther away from the bustling city center, toward the slums on the outskirts. The congested skyscrapers slowly give way to stout buildings and massive rundown warehouses that sprawl across entire city blocks. Soon, the hum of the cars and bars and chatter fades away.

I adjust the oversized bag on my shoulder, clutching it tight. The aroma of steamed vegetables and chicken wafts into my nose, and my stomach grumbles. I'll eat later—after we've dropped off food for the street dwellers. Despite the prevailing beliefs about them, not everyone who lives on the streets is an addict or criminal. Most are victims of the system—kids who left broken homes and became adults without education and opportunities. For a few years now, it's been on my mind to build some kind of facility for those living on the streets, a shelter of sorts.

I've thought about renovating my mother's old building—it's a high-rise downtown with good bones and plenty of space—but many of the street dwellers live on the outskirts of the city and are reluctant to make their way downtown permanently.

"Pixel found a location for sale—two streets away from here," Godric says.

"Price?"

He rattles off a number. It's not too bad.

"Have her place a bid," I say. "Price is doable. We need to snag it before Arlo Osiander does."

That rich bastard has been snatching up property all around the city, and I don't like it one bit. I especially don't like that we can't find any background on him.

"I hate that guy," Godric mutters, echoing my sentiments. "You think you can convince them to trust you and move in? Not everyone *wants* to change, brother."

Holding up the bag of food to make a point that I'm *trying* to get them to trust me, I shrug. My goal is to get the people on the streets—especially the youth—into a safe, secure place, help them clean up their lives since the city refuses to acknowledge them.

"You can lead a horse to water and all that," he says.

Jaw tight, I face forward and continue trudging toward Ruin's Edge—as it's disparagingly named.

Tufts of dead grass battle their way through cracks in the pavement. Broken glass and bottles litter the area, and a few tents sit in a row off to the side. Here, many of the forgotten are left to rot.

"Remy?" I call out when we're closer.

A few people peek out, but none are the man I'm looking for.

A girl with messy black hair and nervous eyes strides up to me. I recognize her once she's closer, and I smile softly at her.

"We brought dinner, Siobhan," Godric says.

"Seen Remy around?" I ask her as I slip the bag off my shoulder and place it on the ground.

As I pull out the biodegradable containers one by one, people start filtering out of the tents to get their food.

"Nah—he went back to the city."

I grind my teeth. Stubborn ox. He refuses to stay with me, despite me having plenty of space, yet he'll frequent the alleys.

I'll have to look for him later.

Siobhan takes a small box of food and opens it, digging in with her hands.

"Have you considered my offer?" I ask.

"Yes," she says through a mouthful of chicken. "We're staying."

I share a solemn look with Godric. "It's only a matter of time before the Scouts come to relocate you."

"We'll deal."

"I'm setting up a new shelter, regardless," I say, mimicking her stubborn tone.

She merely shrugs, continuing to tear into her food. The dozen or so other people who came to get their own meals have already wandered back into their shelters, not interested in interacting.

Godric steps away to make his rounds, checking on those who might need medical assistance and making a list for our doctor on retainer. We'll send him out if we need to.

"I'm staying clean," she says. "We appreciate everything you do for us, Phantom—or at least, most of us do—but we can't owe you anything else."

"You owe me nothing, Siobhan." For a moment, I consider using glamour to convince her to take me up on my offer, but then I shove that idea aside. That's not what I use my ability for. "Think about it."

"Always do."

"What if I get a new building nearby—instead of in the inner city?"

She pauses her chewing, tilting her head as if considering my words. "Might be able to convince them. Depending."

"Try," I say.

"Fine." She sighs, but she smiles at me, and her initial anxiety washes away for a moment. "You're a pain in the ass."

"So I'm told."

It's a shame all the space in my ma's old building is going to waste, but like Godric said, I can't convince anyone to come with me.

When Godric finishes his rounds, we say our goodbyes and

head back toward the inner city.

Two blocks away, a desperate, high-pitched scream rings out.

"Help!" the voice calls. "Please, someone, help me!"

"This fucking city," Godric mutters.

We share a look, then break out into a sprint. As we run toward the cries, I pull my leather gloves out of my back pocket and slide them on.

Just in case.

I'm not a fan of getting my hands dirty, in the literal sense.

Farther down the street, the buildings give way to a mostly empty lot. A few makeshift shelters line the fence, and a couple of people mill about. The nearest streetlight buzzes loudly as its fluorescent hue flickers.

"Help!" the voice cries again, hoarser this time.

Godric smacks my shoulder. "There."

My eyes adjust, and I catch sight of someone pinning a woman down on a piece of plywood. She struggles against the attacker. He crushes her thin body beneath his, his jeans pulled halfway down. None of the nearby people move to help her.

A roaring in my head silences everything else around me, and spots of red color my vision.

In four strides, I reach the man, gripping him by the shirt and ripping him off the woman with a growl.

"Hey—"

I slam the toe of my boot into his ribs, then quickly press the heel into his throat, precariously close to crushing his windpipe.

Before we can check on the woman, she's up and bolting, sobbing as she flees.

"Let her go," I tell Godric through clenched teeth, locking my eyes on the pale loser beneath my boot. As much as I want to ensure she's okay, two notorious gangsters chasing after her in the night might only traumatize her further.

The assailant coughs and sputters beneath me, eyes wide with shock as he flails around, desperately trying to pry my boot off him. His manhood hangs out, making it clear what he was attempting to do a moment ago.

My body trembles with rage, and it takes every fiber of my control not to reach for my gun and end his despicable life.

This isn't how it should be.

"Arch," Godric whispers. "You can't take him out like this. You can't help Sofia if you're locked up."

It's too late to help Sofia.

Just like it's too late to help my ma.

I press my boot down a little harder, and the man's face begins to turn purple, his movements slowing.

"Archer." Godric's strong hand lands on my shoulder, and it's enough to ground me.

I can't do it.

Lifting my boot from the man's neck, I glower at him as he scrambles to sit up. Then I kick him, forcing him back down. His skull smashes into the uneven concrete, and he cries out in pain.

With a frustrated grunt, I step away from the man, letting Godric do his thing.

Squatting, Godric stares right into the man's dirt-streaked face. He keeps eye contact without blinking.

"Climb the fire escape"—he jerks his head toward the building beside us and leans in closer—"then jump. Headfirst. Don't scream."

The man's eyes glaze over, and he nods jerkily, but he presses himself up, yanks up his pants, and stumbles toward the building.

Without a word, Gdoric and I watch as the man mindlessly follows the orders.

Pulling a trash bin beneath the fire escape, he drags himself up the stairs and to the highest platform, at least ten stories up.

Without hesitation, the man dives off headfirst, cleaving the air with a bone-chilling silence. I turn away as his body lands, wincing at the sickening *thud*.

Bile rises in the back of my throat, but I choke it down.

No one moves for a moment. No one speaks.

A few tents rustle as people slowly crawl back into their shadows. Gagging and retching noises fill the air as someone yells out, "Gimme ya phone, Ferris, or call the damn Scouts yaself to clean this shit up!"

"We should go," Godric says.

Nodding mutely, I stride away from the lot without a backward glance.

"You saved her." He matches my pace. "She's fine. She's alive."

"*Fine*?" A disbelieving laugh bursts from me. "She is not *fine*, Godric. No one in this wretched city is *fine*."

"She's a lot better than she would've been if you hadn't gotten there."

My chest rises and falls vigorously as I swipe a leather-clad hand over my jaw, shaking my head. "Not enough. It's never enough."

Today we were in the right place at the right time, but we can't be everywhere all the time.

"I know you don't want to hear it, man, but we need to look at the facts," Godric says. "This ain't normal. People are acting fucking crazy. Young people turning up dead. With no signs as to why—"

"I'm not assuming anything until Zeke gets back to us."

"If it's the dust again, man—"

"Then we clean it up again."

A short while later, the shrill tone of my phone rings out, and my entire body softens in relief.

"That's him." I yank off my gloves, then whip out my phone and answer, listening raptly to his update.

"Ran the hair," Zeke says. He chuckles. "Found some photos. Your mystery woman is *bad*. Why didn't you mention she was so h—"

"*Zeke.*"

"Sorry, sorry, boss." The clicking of a keyboard filters through the phone. "Eh, anything useful? Not really. Basic shit. The hair belongs to one Fantasia Foster, born AR three sixty-two to Claude and Amelia Foster. Parents died when she was only eight. She was lost in the foster system after tha—"

"Claude Foster?" I repeat, processing this information.

"Uh—" Zeke pauses, andmore clacking noises fill the silence. "You got it. *Doctor* Claude Foster. Looks like he was the—"

"Director of Faeology at Mesmeric Labs," I mutter.

"Oh?" The telltale flick of a lighter reaches my ears, and a few seconds later Zeke coughs. "You know the man? His file is sealed. Can't access it on my—"

"Thanks."

Squeezing the phone so hard my knuckles ache, I hang up while Zeke is still rambling. I clench my jaw, rubbing the scruff on my chin and contemplating what this means. The file might be sealed for *him*, but Pixel—our resident hacker—can surely break through.

"Godric," I call, snagging his attention. "You'll never guess who our new friend is."

My phone buzzes with an incoming message.

I glance down at the screen.

Zeke.

I open the message. Godric and I peer down at an image of Fantasia laughing behind a bar. My phone buzzes again with another message, and a slew of heart-eyed smiley faces pour in from Zeke.

Beside me, Godric's body shakes with quiet laughter. I scoff, turning the screen off and stowing my phone away.

When I meet his eyes, he's smirking. "I see why you wanted to know who she was now," he says.

"I wanted to know how the hell she can see the Reaper."

"The real question is: she single?"

"She's *Claude Foster's* daughter."

The smile slips from his face as he presses his lips together. "Son of a bitch." He crosses his arms. "I knew it. The fucking dust is back."

"Still don't know that for sure." Striding away from Godric, I continue toward the city center.

"You're telling me Claude fucking Foster's daughter just randomly showed up *and* she's immune to glamour?" He snorts. "I might not have your ability, but this smells like bullshit."

"Not agreeing with you"—I pick up my pace—"but it'd be wise to keep her close for a bit. See what she knows. Especially with Mesmeric Labs under new ownership."

"Hey, boss," Godric says, halting beside me.

I pause and frown at him. "Don't call me that."

"Needed your attention." He smirks, shrugging a broad shoulder, then points up. "UIS got your girl."

I follow his line of sight to the closest Urban Information Screen.

The massive electronic screens are mounted on buildings every couple of blocks, continuously blasting critical news high above the city streets.

A picture of Fantasia floods the screen. I didn't get a good enough look at her earlier to see the resemblance to the late faeologist—and the pale, bleached hair threw me off—but I see it clearly now. She has his complexion, the same almond-shaped pale blue eyes, and her dark brown brows—likely her natural hair color—match the shade of her father's hair.

They have the same high cheekbones and plump lips.

Shock and sorrow lines her face as she stares down at the teenage girl we found earlier. Behind her, reaching out for her, is me.

My face isn't visible from the angle the photo was taken, but the skull tattoo on the back of my hand is easily identifiable.

Wanted for murder, by order of the High Chancellor.

"What the hell—" I glance at Godric. "Tell Pixel to get this down."

He shakes his phone at me. "She's already on it."

A moment later, the picture flickers out, replaced with an almost identical photo. Except, instead of Fantasia's white-blonde bun and pale olive skin, it's a girl with strawberry-blonde pigtails and tan skin. The Rising Star tee has been replaced with one that says Maverick's Ales. Instead of horror, the girl's face is lined with rage.

My hand is nowhere to be seen—successfully edited out.

Photo alteration courtesy of Pixel, tech genius.

I exhale a heavy sigh of relief, confident that the photo in the city's system has been replaced with this fraudulent one. Similar enough to not raise red flags, but different enough to throw people off Fantasia's tail.

I'm all for justice—even vengeance, under the right circumstances—but it wasn't her who murdered the girl. Other than being born to a jackass scientist, she's innocent in all of this.

At least I think she is.

She might be.

Either way, I'll find out myself.

> *"After injecting the mRNA serum into myself, I've unlocked the capability to visually detect electromagnetic radiation surrounding humans, represented in color form. From my previous research in the Wilds, these colors appear to be reflective of one's innermost energy—their soul."*

-EXCERPT FROM THE PERSONAL JOURNAL OF DR. CLAUDE FOSTER, DIRECTOR OF FAEOLOGY AT MESMERIC LABS

CHAPTER 5
FANTASIA

I tighten my grip on the bat, hissing at people to get out of my way. The lot of them move lazily, in slow motion, delayed to my warnings as I dart past.

At this hour, only tipsy barhoppers mill around Pub Path. The air is sticky, ripe. People stumble about the street, laughing and mingling in small groups. A few individuals scream into their cell phones or take videos, unbothered by the lack of privacy. Different tunes spill out into the street through open doors and windows, and I cringe at the hodgepodge of melodies.

Despite it being night, the city blazes with light. Pulsing colors pour out of various bars and clubs, making it hard to distinguish between the soul-shades wafting around the people as I search for the duo from the bar.

A dozen shades of blue. Various shades of green. Dusty pinks and royal purples. Some soul-shades are as bright as spitting flames, some as bland as a murky glass of Sharp Wing. And everything in between.

But no grey.

My eyes sweep over the congested street and overflowing bars, bouncing through the crowd. In the distance, a siren goes off. The aroma of fried food and sweat fills my nose, overpowering the stench of trash and musk.

An elbow jostles me out of the way, and I scowl. Then I spot them.

Just ahead, rounding into an alleyway between two towering, angular buildings, is the pair from the bar. Their grey auras are hazy and pale, as if their soul-shades are slowly fading away.

An image of my father's face in his final moment pops into my head—the sadness, the guilt, the acceptance that shifted through his kind eyes before they went blank forever.

The day it happened, a knock on the door came, and he shouted frantically for me to hide. I dove into the closet but peeked through the louvered door in time to catch the men with palm prints on their chests storm our apartment. My mother screamed. My father shook his head in my direction.

I stayed quiet. Even as a stranger's finger pulled a trigger, shattering my father's skull.

Then they pulled the trigger once more, taking my mother, too.

Everything around me falls into a bleak silence.

My hands shake.

The bat starts to slip from my hand.

White-hot anger courses through my veins. My parents should still be alive.

Gripping tighter, I push thoughts of them aside.

I surge after the men, squeezing through the throng as I make my way to the alley. Slowing down, I step over a stack of soggy cardboard boxes, almost losing my balance in the process. My free hand meets rough brick as I use the wall for support to navigate the alley. Once I'm clear of the stacks of trash and a puddle of grease, I quicken my pace.

Within seconds, I catch up to the drunkards. But without the blazingly bright lights of the bars and clubs, the alleyway is a breeding ground for shadows, and I'm barely able to make out the dimming soul-shades of the men. About ten paces ahead, the two men stumble past a mountain of black trash bags. Before they can hang a right and go out of sight down another alleyway, I open my mouth to call out to them.

A leather-clad hand presses against my mouth, silencing me. I'm jerked to the side, held hostage behind an overflowing dumpster.

My chest tightens. Instinctively, I swing my bat backward, attempting to hit the asshole while I try to jerk out of his grip.

It doesn't work.

My attacker digs his fingers into my wrist, hitting a pressure spot that causes my hand to spasm and the bat to fall from my hand. He catches it with preternatural speed before it hits the ground, then tosses it onto a pile of trash beside us. It lands atop the plastic with a soft whoosh, releasing a burst of rancid air.

I continue squirming, forcefully bringing my heel down onto his toes. But it seems to have no effect on him.

Throwing my elbows backward, I flail around desperately. The pressure against my mouth builds as his other hand wraps around my waist. I'm pulled against a firm body. He hugs me close to him, tightening his arms around me like iron chains. The scent of leather and grass fill my nostrils.

A newly familiar scent.

My heart drops.

"Quiet," a low voice whispers in my ear. "Trust me."

"Trust you?" At least, that's what I try to say. Instead, it comes out as a muffled "shush shoo" against his leather glove.

"Stop for one second," the voice says, growing irritated.

As I continue squirming, my captor sighs heavily. His warm breath tickles my ear.

The man's body is solid with muscle, and I'm not strong enough to disentangle myself from him, even with my scrappy upbringing.

It doesn't stop me from trying though. I flail, jerking my head back and trying to slam my skull into his nose. He outmaneuvers me.

A dark, hooded figure steps seemingly out of thin air and starts sauntering toward the men from the bar. My body melts, temporarily giving up the fight as I watch.

The figure moves unhurriedly toward the two drunkards.

The Reaper.

A long, dark robe covers his entire body, and a hood encases his head, making it impossible to get a look at his face. From this distance, he almost appears to be nothing more than an ominous shadow.

"Will you be quiet now?" my captor asks.

When I nod, he slowly removes his hand from my mouth. My

breaths come in rapid, silent gasps as I watch the scene before me with wide eyes.

When the Reaper reaches the men, he pauses, turning his back to us. He tilts his head forward, and a faint hum fills the air. I squint, barely able to make out what's happening. The grey fog surrounding the men wafts toward the hooded figure.

The Reaper is taking their souls...while they're alive.

My body goes slack, and my knees give out. If it wasn't for the stranger's arm around my waist, I'd be on the ground. But he holds me steady.

Not again.

Bile rises in my throat. I swallow it down. He's going to kill them. I can't let that happen.

"Sto—!" The hand slaps back onto my mouth right as the Reaper pauses and looks in my direction. I'm yanked backward into a dark doorway, out of sight of the alley. I thrash against the man restraining me.

"For the love of Sirius," my captor hisses. An annoyed grunt escapes him. "Believe it or not," he mutters, "I'm sorry for this."

There's some rustling and a tiny clatter—like a piece of plastic hitting the floor.

"Muhh ah—" I try to respond through his leather-covered hand, using my fingers to pry it away. But there's a prick on my neck, and my arms fall limp at my sides.

The world—already dark around me—melts into a void. The vigorous thumping of my heart fades to something shallower, steadier. And then I'm scooped up into strong arms while a stern voice mutters something that sounds like "Would've been easier if my glamour worked."

The first thing that hits me when I wake up is how much my

shoulders burn. When I try to move my arms, I find them bound behind my back. A weight surrounds my midsection and my ankles, tethering me to a steel surface.

Fear tiptoes up my spine, bringing me back to full consciousness.

I crack open my eyes, flinching at the bright orange light gently swaying overhead. Scanning the room, I desperately try to make sense of what the hell is going on. Brick walls surround me, and a dirt floor sits beneath me. I'm bound to a steel chair—alone—in what seems to be a basement or some small underground room.

"Hey!" I call out, relieved that there's nothing covering my mouth. My tongue is dry, and my throat aches for water. I shudder. How long have I been out? "My boyfriend is looking for me. He's going to find me, and he'll fuck you up."

It's an empty threat, a desperate one. Anyone who knows my boyfriend, Reed, knows he's probably partying with my roommates. I doubt he'll even notice my absence.

Tears prick my eyes.

"Please!" I call out, my voice cracking.

Behind me, a door creaks open and clicks shut softly.

"You're awake," the same velvety voice from earlier says.

"No shit," I mutter. "Let me go!"

"Thought your boyfriend was coming to save you?" he mutters.

"You're a huge piece of—"

I trail off as the man steps into view.

The Gods-damned Phantom.

I groan, squeezing my eyes shut. When I reopen them, I get a good look at him. In this light, I can fully make out his features.

He's not at all what I expected. The muscles and tattoos, yes, but not the head full of thick, dark, golden-blond hair. With the way it's longer and messier on the top, he appears younger, more boyish than I'd expected. Maybe mid to late twenties. Barely any older than me.

The wanted sketches make him look older, rougher, and less appealing than he truly is.

His lips tighten with annoyance as he scrutinizes me.

It's not the man's attractiveness that gives me pause. I learned at a young age never to judge a book by its cover. My first foster father was a handsome man, too. But his fondness for beating up his wife and children revealed his cruel heart.

Pretty bindings sometimes hold together ugly interiors.

No, what strikes me is the genuine concern that takes over the Phantom's eyes as he takes me in. His lips pull into a frown as his eyes roam over the position of my arms and the bindings around my ankles.

"That's excessive," he mutters, scratching the thin layer of scruff on his chin with his tattooed fingers.

"No shit." I narrow my eyes at him. Where the hell does he get the right to act concerned?

He cocks his head, curiosity replacing the annoyance. "You're just as feisty as you were in the alley earlier."

"I'm fed up. I'm tired. I'm hungry. And I told you, I didn't say shit to anyone about what I saw."

"And what exactly did you see?"

"Nothing." I clamp my lips shut, inclining my chin.

He studies me for a moment before kneeling and letting out a sigh. He eyes the ropes for a second, and then his fingers start working one of the knots. The light glints off his rings as he struggles with the rope. "For Gods' sakes, Godric," he mutters under his breath. "This isn't what I had intended."

I grunt. "Oh, so the whole shooting me up is fine, but *tying* me up is where you draw the line?"

An image of the last time someone injected something into my veins flashes through my mind. It was a few weeks before my parents' deaths.

Our little secret, my Fantastic Fantasia, my dad said after giving me a shot.

I grit my teeth and stare at the Phantom with disdain. "What did you inject me with?"

His brow scrunches, but he doesn't look at me. "A temporary sedative."

My spine tingles with unease as I thrash against the bindings.

Finally giving up on the knot, he stands, sliding out of his black leather jacket and tossing it aside. His dark, V-neck T-shirt hugs his body, showing off his muscular chest—and his handgun. The prospect of danger sends an alarm blaring through my body. Still, I find this man less terrifying than the Scouts.

The Phantom pulls a matte-black knife out of his pocket, flicking it open. I flinch, but the ropes hold my limbs in place.

"Hold still," he warns as he squats down in front of me. "Relax."

His gaze finds mine, and I notice how deep and warm the golden coloring of his eyes is. It matches the gleaming hue surrounding his body almost perfectly.

How the hell does *he* have a golden soul-shade?

Racking my brain, I sift through the various colors mentioned in my father's journal—it's how I learned about my ability and what some of the auras mean. Sadly, he was killed before he finished his research, but gold was one of the few colors he confidently interpreted.

Golden hues represent a pure soul; they're as rare as stars in the city sky. We might never see them, but they exist.

The Phantom leans closer, inspecting the ropes around my ankles. The muscles in his forearms flex in a mesmerizing manner as he starts sawing the bindings aggressively.

"Shit," I mutter, turning my head away and squeezing my eyes shut. "Be careful."

"Do you always curse this much?" he asks.

"Only when I'm kidnapped by a knife-wielding asshole."

I make the mistake of glancing back down at the asshole in question. He pauses his slicing, resting back on his haunches, and a gleam of curiosity lights up his features. My stomach knots itself again, and I scowl. The corners of his lips turn up slightly, as if he's amused.

"You're not afraid of me."

"No," I say, narrowing my eyes.

"Earlier—in the alley with the dead girl—you weren't afraid of *me*. It was the Scouts you feared."

He holds my gaze, and the air between us becomes charged with something dangerous. He waits for my confirmation, but I force myself to look away, breaking the tension.

I blink and I'm eight again. The Scouts storm our apartment. They scream at my parents to get on their knees. A gun is raised to the back of my dad's head.

Bang.

My body trembles. I'm stuck in that closet again, a prisoner to fear.

Alone.

With no one to call.

Nowhere to go.

Alone.

Even after the bodies were toted away, until the landlord came to pack up our stuff three days later and found me.

Alone.

Even in the overpopulated foster home in the city center.

I don't remember time, and I don't know what I did other than cry and sleep. But I will never forget the deafening silence and eerie numbness. It was as if my body shut down to protect me.

The Phantom continues sawing at the rope, and I count the timeworn, exposed bricks jutting out of the wall on my left to distract myself from the haunting memories.

Anything to distract myself.

Clearing the thickness from my throat, I force myself to ask, "Where are we?"

"Believe it or not," he says, "I was saving your life. Then and *now*."

"I don't need your saving," I mutter. "I needed you to *not* get me in this situation in the first place."

"You think *I'm* the reason why you're in this position?"

"No shit." I frown. "You're a serial killer. You killed that girl, and now you're after me for catching you."

It sounds ridiculous even to me.

He scoffs. "You're a terrible liar. We both know you don't really believe that."

"Fine," I say, gritting my teeth. But it's only because of his soul-shade that I *know* he's not the one who murdered the girl. I'd be hard-pressed to believe he's hurt anyone...but then again, the fact that he knocked me out and had a crony tie me up is questionable.

Can I really trust the colors of the soul-shades after all? What if my dad's interpretation was wrong?

The rope finally gives, freeing my legs. He grunts with success. I have half a mind to knee him right in his pretty mouth. I'm sure I can get the right angle and summon enough power to knock him out. Maybe even take a few of those pearly whites out in the process.

Fuck it.

I launch my knee toward his face, but he shoots up and takes a step back, getting out of reach right before I can make contact.

I growl, squirming in the chair—my arms still bound behind me.

"Savage," he says exasperatedly. "You do realize I'm trying to free you, right?"

Without waiting for a response, he rounds the chair and tugs on the rope around my wrists. Every time his fingers skim my skin, it sends sparks through me.

And each spark fuels my burgeoning fury.

"Hurry up," I command.

"Savage *and* demanding." He exhales a heavy breath and tugs a bit more forcefully.

The rough scraping sound of blade on rope fills the air, but it's not enough to drown out the thumping of my pulse in my skull.

The longer I'm stuck here, unable to move, the more I feel like that broken little girl in the closet. The one I've spent the last thirteen years trying to heal.

He stands, but instead of moving to cut my arms loose, he leans his head to the side and regards me carefully. There's a lengthy pause before he says, "You saw the Reaper."

"Don't know what you're talking about."

He sighs. "No sense in lying."

My lips tighten. When the Reaper inhaled my parents' souls, I was the only one who saw. The room was flooded with Silver Scouts and other unnamed authorities that day, but no one noticed the dark, hooded figure hovering above my parents' bodies.

No one saw their souls being stolen.

It was easy to repress the memory of the soul-sucking creature, considering I didn't see him again.

Until tonight.

"I'm not going to tell anyone," the Phantom says softly, pulling me from my thoughts. "That's what you're worried about, right?"

My brows shoot up in surprise before I neutralize the expression on my face.

Magic is banned in the city; I'd be executed just like my parents if the Scouts knew of my *ability*. It doesn't matter that it's artificial magic—injected by my faeologist father.

My heart squeezes at the thought of the betrayal from the man I loved. His final gift to me was a death sentence.

"Don't act like you know me," I say.

"I *don't* know you. But I do know you're one of the only other people who can see the Reaper."

"How exactly can *you* see him?" When he doesn't reply, I say, "Are you working with him? You keep showing up at the same time as him."

"Of course I'm not."

"You both have stupid nicknames, break the law, wear dark clothing—"

"I am *not* working with the Reaper." He snorts, and it sounds half-annoyed, half-amused. "Work with me and you'll see that for yourself."

Work with *him*?

Despite his golden aura and our shared ability to see the Reaper, helping him would be helping the Nightcrawlers. I'm trying to stay off the Scouts' radar. This is the last thing I need.

"Fuck that."

"Eloquent. Your vocabulary reflects your intelligence, you know."

I blink, processing the roundabout insult. "Excuse me if my *intelligence* isn't up to your standards."

Education is a luxury I can't afford. Though, compared to most patrons I serve, I find that my intelligence is above average. All thanks to my father's teachings. During the years I spent with him before his death, he would read me scientific journals and other research papers as bedtime stories.

The Phantom mutters under his breath and saws more force-fully. He tugs the rope, pulling my shoulder at an awkward angle. An electric tingle courses through my right arm.

"Ow! Watch it."

"Do you want me to release you or not?" he asks. "Stop mov-ing."

I grunt in response. A second later, the ropes give, and I'm freed. A sharp pain lingers in my shoulder from being confined in an awkward position, and I shake out my arms, hugging them in front of me.

A giddy warmth floods through me at the realization that I'm no longer contained. I'm one step closer to getting out of here.

When the man steps back into sight, I quickly bring my knee up, connecting with his junk.

"Sirius A!" he swears, taking the North Star's name in vain. "My balls!"

Without hesitation, I bolt around the chair and spring toward the door. But there's no doorknob. No handle. No hinges to take apart. Just a solid slab of steel built into the brick.

I pound on it. What the hell is this place?

Whirling around, I find the man doubled over, his tan cheeks flushed a deep red as he cups his crotch.

With a quick lunge, I scoop up his abandoned knife, angling it toward him.

"Let me out of here," I demand.

He clenches his teeth, glaring at me. "That's what I was doing!" He releases his privates, waving his arms up in the air with disbelief. "I asked Godric to keep an eye on you, not tie you to a damn chair. You're not a prisoner."

I grip the knife so hard my knuckles go white, then put my back against the door, keeping as much space between us as possible.

He adjusts his jeans, shaking his head at me.

"Yet you were the one who injected me with—whatever it was that knocked me out," I say.

"To save your life, woman!" he yells in exasperation, running a hand through his blond waves. His face scrunches in a way that makes him appear almost conflicted. "I wasn't going to let you die."

I fucking hate this guy.

Squeezing my eyes shut, I block out the memory of the needle piercing my skin. I have no desire to explain to this gangster how he has managed to somehow dredge up all of my past traumas in one evening.

Instead, I say, "But you let those men die!"

"They were already dead."

"No they weren't. Their soul-shades were—" I clamp my lips shut, my stomach twisting.

A beat passes, and he raises an eyebrow quizzically. "Soul-*what*?"

"Never mind."

He steps closer to me. When I recoil, he frowns and releases a sigh of resignation before retreating to his corner on the other side of the chair. "How many times have you seen the Reaper?"

I hesitate, weighing my answer. "Once before tonight." Before he can reply, I ask, "People normally don't see him, right?"

"No." For several seconds, he studies me, head cocked. "Humans normally don't possess such an ability."

"Yet you do?"

He shrugs. "Perhaps I'm like you."

Shifting my weight to my other foot, I peruse the soft golden color wafting lazily around him. "You can...see things you shouldn't?"

His lips part, and his eyes glint with interest. "Something like that."

As desperate as I am to conceal my truth, I've never met anyone else with an ability like mine. *Magic* is what others would call it, if they knew—although I hate referring to it as that, because it's artificial. The little information I have on my ability, magic, and the fae comes from my father's teachings. Most of it I read about in his personal journal after his death.

Even by telling this guy I've seen the Reaper, I've revealed too much, but I didn't realize until now how freeing it is to admit it aloud to someone—someone who gets it.

But that someone is a *gangster*.

Fear pricks at my neck. In the wrong hands, this information could get me killed.

Until I know what his intentions are, playing aloof might be my best option. He doesn't need to know about how I got my ability.

"And who exactly are you?" I ask. Under my breath, I add, "Other than a kidnapper, abuser, torturer, and Sirius knows what else."

"*Other* than all those aforementioned labels?" His eyes flick to the blade in my hand, then back to my face. I blink, waiting for him to continue. When I don't respond, his smile grows. I hate the way my stomach tingles at the sight. "I'm a Nightcrawler."

"No shit." I steel my shoulders, standing taller. "A gangster."

"Among other things." He smirks, and my cheeks heat.

"A gangster who criticizes my vocabulary," I mutter.

"You shouldn't judge."

"Take your own advice, buddy." I shake my head in disbelief. Turning, I scan the door. How the hell does it open? "You said you were letting me go."

"After we talk."

Dread fills me. I face the gangster, tightening my grip on the knife. He gestures toward the chair. But there's no way I'm sitting back down. Now I understand why he doesn't seem worried about me being free of the ropes or wielding his knife. Wherever we are, it's Nightcrawler territory. I'm not getting out of here unless he wants me to.

I swallow the lump in my throat. "And what does Silver City's most notorious gang leader want with me?"

"For now?" His eyes gleam with interest. "Well, I only want to talk, *soul-seer*."

> *"...IN MY TWENTY YEARS OF STUDYING HUMAN AND FAE BEHAVIOR AND PATTERNS, IN BOTH NATURAL AND CONTROLLED ENVIRONMENTS, I'VE BEGUN TO IDENTIFY THE TRAITS ASSOCIATED WITH VARIOUS SOUL-SHADES. THOUGH MUCH RESEARCH IS STILL NEEDED, I'VE DETERMINED THE MOST COMMON SHADES ARE THE PRIMARY COLORS."*
>
> -EXCERPT FROM THE PERSONAL JOURNAL OF DR. CLAUDE FOSTER, DIRECTOR OF FAEOLOGY AT MESMERIC LABS

CHAPTER 6
FANTASIA

I scan the Phantom, trying to interpret his intentions.

Soul-seer.

The word rings in my head.

Is that what I am? There's a name for me? Are there more like me?

My father told me that the ability to see soul-shades was a gift to be cherished. Something secret—special. But after his murder, I tried to stop paying attention to it. At first, this was nearly impossible. Everyone has a fog of color surrounding their body. They come in all hues—bright and dark, weak and strong. After a while, I suppose I grew desensitized to seeing them. A soul-shade is a part of everyone—an extension of them. Like an arm or a leg. Except for big crowds or extremely vibrant hues, I'm fairly good at ignoring them.

But a *gift*, my ass.

My stomach rumbles, and I sigh. On instinct, I reach for my phone and am surprised when my fingers brush against the device. I tug it out, looking at the time. A few hours have passed since I started chasing after the patrons—the now likely *dead* patrons, if the Reaper finished what he started.

The bar's closed.

I have missed calls from both Mellie and Reed. My finger hovers over the latter's name, until I realize I have no service here.

Wherever *here* is.

"I really don't feel like talking. Can I get out of here now? I'm hungry and tired." *And for a gang leader, you're not that frightening*, I want to add, because part of me finds it entertaining to irritate him. But it's best not to press my luck.

He drags his gaze to the knife still in my hand, then lifts a brow and raises his hands placatingly. "It's a friendly conversation, I assure you. If you don't mind—" He mimics throwing the blade on the ground.

"No." I hit the button on the knife's handle, flipping it shut, and then tuck it into my back pocket. "I'm keeping this." With my other hand, I pull out my phone and quickly find an app for recording. I hit a button, and it beeps with confirmation. "And I'm recording this conversation. If anything happens to me, I want them to know it was you, the fucking Phantom of the Nightcrawlers—Packing District, Southside."

His lips quirk. "If I did something to you, don't you think I'd dispose of the evidence, too?"

I see the illogic behind my tactic, but I don't care. Like I told him, I'm tired. It's been a helluva day, and I want this to be over with.

On cue, my stomach rumbles again.

His eyebrows rise. He reaches into his pocket and pulls out a crinkled, flattened protein bar. It looks as if it's lived in his pocket for some time, has been sat on a few times too many. He hands it to me, and I hesitantly accept.

"I'm not thanking you for this."

"Fine. Okay." Laughing, he shakes his head as I peel open the wrapper and devour the whole bar in two massive bites.

I swallow and wipe my mouth.

"You're a shitty gang leader. Giving me a weapon and feeding me."

His answering smile is subtle—shy almost. My stomach dips, and I scowl.

"I only brought you here to offer you an opportunity." My ears perk up when he says, "A *paid* opportunity, Fantasia."

I swipe my clammy hands on the front of my jeans. "It's Tasia."

"Okay. Let the record state that you, Tasia, are a soul-seer. A human one, at that. Which is—"

"Wait!" I growl at him as my thumb fumbles to stop the recording. If something does happen to me—although if he were going to harm me, he probably already would've—I don't want anyone knowing about my unwelcome ability. The one I should *not* have. I shove my phone into my pocket. "You were saying?"

He crosses his arms, raising an eyebrow. "I need your help."

"Doing what?"

"Like I said, you can see the Reaper. And you mentioned the mens' auras tonight."

I squeeze my eyes shut, thinking about my parents. "They had grey soul-shades."

"And that's abnormal?"

My eyes fly open. "I thought you could see them too," I say accusingly.

He strokes his chin, glancing at the door, then back at me. "I can sense impending death another way."

The fist around my heart tightens. "How?"

He taps his nose. "Scent."

"So...you're a soul-*sniffer*?"

The Phantom frowns at me. "No. Is grey an abnormal color?"

"Yes," I say. "A colorless aura would indicate a soul is preparing to leave its body." Colorless. The grey appearance, the absence of color, indicates a soul on the verge of fading away. "But those men were alive."

The Phantom runs a hand through his hair, pacing the small space.

"And you can see all soul-shades?"

"Yes." I've never noticed a person who didn't have one.

"I need to find the Reaper. If he's feeding on people close to death, we can find anyone with a grey soul-shade—"

"You can save them?"

"—and lure him in. You are the perfect person to assist me. This opportunity, if you choose to accept, will be on a need-to-know basis."

"Wait." I tuck a loose strand of hair behind my ear and ponder his words. "I haven't accepted shit yet. And I want answers before I entertain whatever your offer is."

"You didn't let me finish." Halting in place, he turns and smiles widely at me, and it's so charming, so disarming, that it's hard to believe he's a kidnapping asshole. "You don't need all the information, but I will give you this." He reaches up to scratch the back of his head, and my stomach tightens when I get a glimpse of a tattoo on his right forearm—intertwined vines and flowers in dark ink etched into his deeply tanned skin. "I have reason to believe the recent string of deaths around the Packing District has been caused by something unnatural. I believe something else is going on."

My attention snaps back to his face. "Why do you care?" I ask skeptically.

"I care about the city."

I snort. "If it weren't for you and your little worm minions—"

"Worm minions?" he asks, face scrunched.

"If it weren't for you guys, the city would be in fine order. It's your fault we've had an uptick in crime. First the dreamdust. Now the—"

"What do you know about the dust?" he asks, eyes narrowed and voice cold. He steps closer, and I instinctively back up until I hit the wall.

"It's *your* fault for the mass addictions that killed thousands." The Nightcrawlers were the ones responsible for creating and distributing the drug—all for profit.

The Phantom pauses, his jaw going slack before he clenches it tightly and shakes his head. He turns toward the brick wall, letting out a huff of disbelief.

When he finally speaks, all he says is, "Wrong."

"The details don't matter. If it weren't for the Nightcrawlers, the Silver Scouts wouldn't need to have such a massive presence." *My parents might never have died. And I wouldn't live in constant fear of my own stupid ability.*

The Phantom looks much too young to have been in a leadership position all those years ago, when the dust first hit the streets, but it doesn't matter. Whether it was him or someone else, the Nightcrawlers are all the same to me. Selfish, uncivil instigators of mayhem.

The air leaves his lungs in a long, slow whoosh as he turns to face me. "You have no idea what you're talking about."

"So you're a law-abiding citizen?"

His mouth opens, and then he clamps it shut, fury blazing in his eyes. "We have more important things to discuss than my civil disobedience to a corrupt political system that takes advantage of the working class."

"What the hell does that mean?"

"We have more important things." Cracking his knuckles, he says, "The Reaper is a type of fae meant to ferry souls to their final resting place. However, I have a working theory that he's consuming souls for power rather than releasing them as he should."

My skin prickles. "Releasing them where?"

He holds up a hand. "Beyond."

"Your sarcasm isn't appreciated."

"It isn't sarcasm. And the minor details don't matter."

"They do to me."

"Simply put, when you die, you're dead for good. Your soul is no longer identifiably human. It's more...energy than anything else. And it settles back into nature."

"How the hell do you know this?"

"Doesn't matter."

I grit my teeth. "So you think the Reaper is behind the deaths?"

"I don't know—reaper fae can only consume the souls of those who have died."

"Wait..." The gears in my mind spin. "Those men—they were

alive when the Reaper took their souls. So how is that possible?"

"I don't know." The Phantom runs a hand over his face, and the sight of his skull tattoo reminds me of *who* I'm in cahoots with currently. "I was wondering how he was able to consume a living soul, too."

"I've only seen grey soul-shades around people who are...no longer living."

"Which leads me to believe that something—or someone—is causing peoples' souls to die before their body does."

"How?" I whisper, shivering at the implication.

"It's too coincidental that he is simply in the right place at the right time," the Phantom mutters, more to himself than to me. "I believe their deaths were unnatural. I can sense death. And you can *see* it." A beep comes from his pants. Sighing, he pulls his phone out. His eyes dart across the screen before he stuffs the phone back into his pocket.

My blood pounds in my skull. This is an opportunity for me to get some answers, to find out more about what happened to my parents. I work to stay collected so he won't pick up on my excitement and take advantage of it. Right now, he needs me. I have the upper hand, and I would like to keep it that way.

"Wait—how the hell do *you* have service down here?" I snap.

"Jammer." He points to the pocket where my phone sits. "Blocks your service. Doesn't affect my phone."

"You can't keep me down here forever."

"No," he agrees, squinting at me.

"So, what, you want me to find people with grey soul-shades and bring them to you before the Reaper gets them or something?"

His jaw tenses as he levels me with a piercing stare. "Not exactly."

"You can sense them, too. Why don't you do this yourself?"

Hesitating for a moment, he runs a hand over his jaw. "I juggle a few...operations. I don't have time to stalk people all day on a whim."

I scoff. "And you think I do?"

"That's what you were doing when I found you. Was it not?"

"I was trying to work," I say through gritted teeth.

"And how much does this job of yours pay? A thousand silvers a week?"

Less.

Way less.

I think of Fredrik's lack of a tip, of how I'm lucky if I've walked away with five hundred silvers by the end of each week.

"Something like that," I grumble.

"I'll double it."

My heart trips over itself. "Two thousand silvers? Per week?" I'm surprised my tone comes out steady when my insides are wobbling.

He frowns. "Is that not enough? Three thousand?"

"Th-three thousand?" This time I fail at keeping composed. My eyes widen, and I stutter. "That's...that's a big chunk of change."

He smirks. "So you'll do it?"

"I didn't say that." I pause, chewing on the inside of my cheek.

Three thousand silvers is a life-changing sum of money. Might not afford me Sweetcreek real estate, but it's more than enough to get my own apartment in the Packing District.

But what would I do when the job ended and the money ran out? It sounds like I won't be able to keep my bartending job while searching for grey soul-shades. And I know Jeremiah well; I doubt he would take me back if I up and quit on him.

After the Phantom is finished with me, I'll be forced back into poverty, without my job at The Rising Star to fall back on.

There's no way I can risk that.

But then I think of my parents...

My lungs constrict.

As much as I loathe the *gift* my father gave me, I did love him fiercely. The loss of my parents left a gaping hole in my life—one I've never been able to come to terms with.

Mostly, it's the lack of answers surrounding their deaths that plagues me. And I also don't get why my father injected me with artificial magic at all.

For a long time, I figured his execution was related to that. But if that was the case, I'd be dead, too.

Right?

I don't like the way the Phantom knocked me out and dragged me down here—even if it was to protect me from the Reaper—nor do I love how his crony tied me up. I'm not ready to team up with this gangster and get involved with the city's criminal underworld. Most of all, the prospect of purposely acknowledging my ability terrifies me.

"No," I finally say. "I just—I can't do it."

I'd rather go back to my job at the bar, pretend like today never happened, and move on with my life.

"All right."

My body goes still. I'm surprised he agreed so easily. "That's it?"

He grins at me, scooping up his leather jacket and effortlessly slipping it on as he strides toward the door. "It is. Go home. Think about it."

His knuckles rap out a quick rhythm on the door, and it creaks open. The Phantom nods at whoever's on the other side, then gestures for me.

My feet are like cement blocks, refusing to move. "Aren't you gonna bag me or something first?"

He gives me a quizzical look as he runs his fingers through his hair. "Bag you?"

"You know"—I gesture toward my face—"throw a black bag on my face so I can't see your headquarters."

When he laughs, it's rich and hearty. "You mean hood? It's a hood, not a bag. And no. These aren't our headquarters. Just a connection of old tunnels beneath the city."

"Oh," I say lamely. "Okay then."

"You have a healthy imagination."

"Maybe you're just a shitty gangster." I shrug a shoulder.

He gives me a charming, amused smile, and my stomach twists. "Come on," he says. "Let's get you home so you can eat and think about my offer."

Finally, my feet follow my brain's instructions and begin moving.

"Oh, and don't you have a boyfriend looking for you?" he asks.

My cheeks flush as he throws my words back at me.

"Yes. Reed," I mutter.

Other than when I first woke up down here, I haven't thought about Reed. And when the Phantom offered me that large sum of money, I definitely didn't think about the future it could afford me and Reed.

Because we don't have a future.

There's no guilt, no sadness with that realization. It's the brutal truth. We've remained with each other out of convenience—neither having a good enough reason to end things. Sometimes having *someone* is better than having no one, even though I've never fully let him in.

The Phantom leads me through the snaking tunnels, up a rickety set of stairs, and to another door. He opens it and steps aside, gesturing for me to pass. The soft glow of a streetlamp spills in, along with a blast of humid air.

Finally, an exit.

My shoulder brushes his chest as I step past him, and I jerk away. My eyes lock onto his jacket. He looks stupid wearing that in this heat.

Sexy, but stupid.

I shake the thought away.

"I'll check in on you soon. See if you changed your mind."

"Don't bother," I mutter.

"See you soon, Tasia," he whispers with a chuckle.

As I step out into the swampy air of the street, the hum of a slumbering night greets me. I turn to ask the Phantom one last question. But only a ruddy, weathered brick wall stands behind me, no door—or man—in sight.

Blinking a few times in confusion, I reach out a hand and run it along the wall, searching for a seam or a knob. Within the textured ridges of the brick, I find no cracks or hinges indicative of an entrance.

Dread fills me.

That's how they've evaded the Silver Scouts so long. They have magic. But *how*? The Phantom has a soul-shade. He's human. He doesn't have the brutal, ethereal beauty I've heard fae possess. He's certainly attractive—but in an entirely human way.

Then again, *I'm* human and possess magic.

I have a sudden memory of my father coming home from work frazzled, his lab coat in disarray as he squatted down beside me and told me everything was going to be okay.

The softness of his words were at odds with the sharp needle as he pricked my arm, injecting me with something.

My chest grows hollow with grief. Even after all this time, I miss him.

Frowning, I shoot one last glance back at the wall before striding down the street toward my apartment, trying to shake the new fear settling deep in my bones.

> *Citizen Confinement and Perimeter Security Directive*
>
> *Silver Edict #2*
>
> *"In accordance with the directives set forth by the Ministry of Public Safety, it is mandated that no citizen be permitted to breach the city's protective walls, entering the Wilds..."*

CHAPTER 7
ARCHER

Two days go by without another sighting of the Reaper.

Wiping the sweat off my brow, I quickly navigate the maze of tunnels deep beneath the city, inhaling the dank stench of soil and sawdust. Deeper in the tunnel, loud voices yell over each other, and I head toward the sound.

"—she was just standing there, man. Then her eyes glazed over and her whole body shook. Like a seizure, but she was standing!" a voice bellows. "Then she just—she just slumped to the ground!"

I arrive at one of the main tech rooms. Godric stands facing the door, next to our hacker, Pixel and two men.

"Just dropped, man. Dead as a rock," says one of them.

"Rocks are not dead," Pixel mutters, pushing her glasses up her nose. Her shaggy, feathery hair is freshly dyed—a bright red this time. She's always changing it. "It's too early for this," she mutters.

"They sure ain't living though, man," one of the lower-rank Nightcrawlers says, elbowing her in the ribs.

Pixel winces.

"Excuse me," I say. Everyone pauses, their eyes flicking to me. I stare down the guy who elbowed Pixel. "Don't ever touch a lady without her consent."

"Who?" The guy glances around, then points at himself. "Me?"

"Yes. You."

"Bro," the guy next to him whispers, his eyes wide. "That's the Phantom."

"Oh shit," the first guy says. He strides toward me, extending a hand. "Sorry, man."

I ignore his offering, crossing my arms instead. "Don't apologize to me. Apologize to her."

Pixel rolls her eyes, a blush overtaking her pale cheeks. But when the guy apologizes, she stands a little taller, squaring her shoulders and giving him a polite nod. "Apology accepted."

"I like the red," I tell her. Her cheeks flame even brighter, and she covers her mouth before turning away from me. I meet Godric's eyes. "Resume."

Godric clears his throat, amusement dancing in his expression. "You heard the boss."

We listen attentively as the guys pick up where they left off, giving their eyewitness accounts of a dead body they found this afternoon. The city has always had its fair share of unsavory events, but we're all concerned about the increase in violence and deaths lately.

My teeth clench so hard I fear they'll crack. After a few more nods and exchanges, Godric thanks the trio and excuses them. The men scurry past without a word. Pixel gives me a shy smile, mouthing *thanks* as she heads to her station in the corner.

It's a massive, ergonomic setup with a wall of monitors, several high-powered towers that hum with quiet intensity, and a snake nest of wires. My eyes roam the screens. Some of them display camera feeds of the city streets. Some of them run lines of code. It's impressive how Pixel can keep track of so many information sources at once. She loves her tech, though, and she's good at juggling multiple tasks.

I'd go crazy stuck down here in the tunnels, with no fresh air or sunlight, just staring at screens. We'd get nowhere without Pixel, so I'm glad she enjoys it.

I uncross my arms, striding over to Godric. We clasp each other's right forearm in greeting, then quickly pull apart. I jerk my chin toward the door.

"What's that about?"

"Another one last night." He runs a hand down his face. "Out of the blue. No apparent cause of death. Her body just shut down—violently, I might add—right in front of them."

Sofia's face flits through my mind, and a pang of grief slices my chest. Although I try to remember her as the happy, vibrant girl she once was, I can only see her in those final few weeks—ill and fading away. All color leached from her clammy skin, her eyes vacant.

The grief turns to hot, visceral anger.

I clear my throat, trying to swallow the lump forming there.

"Where were they when it happened?"

"Downtown. By the bars."

Again.

I don't bother to ask if anyone saw the Reaper. They can't see through his glamour. Only Godric and I can...and apparently Tasia, too.

"They spot anything unusual right before her death?"

He swipes a hand over his mouth. "Onlookers claimed she was wasted. Running around barefoot, cursing up a fucking storm." He shakes his head and releases a heavy sigh. "Sounds like she was high off her ass. Could explain the sudden death."

I run a hand through my hair, reminding myself that she's not Sofia. "Any history of use?"

"Unconfirmed," he says. "Pixel?"

"I'm on it," she says from where she sits, clacking away at her keyboard. "Thanks to Zeke sending over the fingerprints, I've located her file within the Ministry of Records, and I just need to update my code to get through this monolith of a mainframe..." She glances over her shoulder at me. "They updated their firewalls this morning... Beautiful encryption. A shame to destroy it..." She clears her throat, her fingers working rapidly. "I have another system running her social accounts. Once I get those and her records, we'll know more."

Godric's forehead wrinkles, and I reach up, patting him on the shoulder. I know this affects him as deeply as it does me. "Zeke do the full autopsy already?"

"Nah. Sent the prints, but we're waiting on lab work," he says.

"Send it to me when you get it," I say. "You're doing good work, brother."

Godric is a good man. He joined the Nightcrawlers for all the right reasons—he wanted to make a difference and help the neglected citizens of the Packing District.

He lost Sofia, too. He gets it.

Sure, we have a hand in illegal dealings and often flout the law—and some of us even have enough blood on our hands to paint the city red—but we look out for the cityfolk. The people overlooked by the upper echelon.

People like Sofia who would've lived if things were different.

"I really need to go, Godric." I glance at the matte-black watch weighing down my wrist. "Scathe might eat the couch out of boredom if I'm not home in a timely fashion."

Godric grunts, then cocks his head. "Wait—you telling me you finally bought some fucking furniture? It's about damn time you spent some money on you."

"Well, I didn't technically buy it, but..." I whip out my phone and press a few buttons, pulling up a picture of a forest-green sectional. "It's an Yvonné. Entirely customizable. Modular. Made of sustainable—"

"Sofa." Godric snorts a laugh. "That's a fucking *sofa*, but it's a big one. I'll give you that. Now make some friends so it can get some ass."

"Crude," I mutter, giving my head a shake. "Sorry about him, Pixel."

She chuckles. "Used to it."

I have an unfortunate feeling that Godric and the bartender would get along great—if he would stop accusing her of being like her father. The thought of the sassy, scowling woman sends a zip of excitement through me. "You didn't have to tie up Tasia like that, by the way."

"Tasia? Nickname basis already?" He narrows his eyes knowingly, and his lips curve into a smirk. "I wasn't trying to hurt her. Was just doing my job, boss."

I nod. "Also," I say, lowering my voice, "I propositioned her."

Godric pats my shoulder. "Listen, I know she has a nice ass."

"You know that's not what I mean." I rub my temples.

"Sorry, sorry." He holds his hands up placatingly. "That's not who I meant when I said meet a girl."

"Regardless." I fiddle with my watch. "I proposed we work together."

His brow scrunches. "Doing what?"

"I really don't think she knows about her dad. She knew about the dust but blames the Nightcrawlers."

"She might know more than she thinks. Or she might have access to information," Godric says.

Pausing, I take a moment to consider the fear she demonstrated in the alley when I first met her. "She hates the Scouts. There's no way she'd talk openly about things that threaten her."

"Do you think you can get more information out of her?"

I stroke my jaw, hating his implication that I'm using Tasia—getting close to her to learn what she knows about her father's work. "Yeah. I think I can."

He laughs, patting me on the shoulder. "No glamour either, bro."

"I'm aware," I say. Godric can sense truths like I can sense death. But if glamour doesn't work on her, his magic might not either. "Okay, I'm going to walk Scathe. Then I'll scout the area again. Meet me downtown in about an hour?"

His frown finally softens, his lips turning up ever so slightly at the corners. "Yeah cause the mutt really needs you to walk him."

"Appearances, Godric." Having a routine—especially in Sweetcreek—is crucial to maintaining our cover.

"You walkin him? Or he walkin you?"

"Both," I mutter.

"It's been too long since I've seen that old mutt."

Scathe is not old. And he's definitely not a mutt, but I grin regardless. "And whose fault is that? Maybe if you came around more..."

He snorts. "Tell the mutt to come visit me sometime."

I chuckle. "I'll tell him."

"The ball is coming up," Godric says. "Got your suit?"

The grin melts off my face. "Hasn't exactly been my priority."

"I know, but this is important. We can find out who bought the lab."

Tightening my lips, I give a sharp nod.

The masquerade ball is an annual event hosted for the power players of the city. Though I've earned an invite for the past five years thanks to Ataraxy, my successful tech security company, this year is different. Rumor has it that Mesmeric Labs sold in a private auction and the new owner will be there.

If Godric is right, and the dust is back on the streets, this could be a huge lead. When Pixel tried to find information on Mesmeric's new ownership, she was unable to locate any records at all. Everything in their servers was mysteriously lost a few months back.

I need to attend this ball, pretend to play the game, and mingle with the people I despise.

"Got a plus-one yet?" Godric asks, a sly look crossing his face.

Glancing at Pixel, I say, "Would you care to attend with me?"

She smiles, tucking her hair behind her ear and glancing at Godric. "I can't."

"Scored her own ticket this year," Godric says, eyes narrowed. "Got a date."

My brows fly up. "A real one?"

She giggles. "A real one."

"With someone in the Ministry of Public Safety," Godric says flatly. His lips purse with disdain.

I cough, nearly choking on my spit. "That's—unexpected."

"Unexpectedly traitorous," he says.

"A Scout?" I ask, trying to keep the disbelief from my voice.

"No. He does paperwork in the Ministry Assembly Center."

"Still," Godric says. "You're dating the enemy, traitor."

An awkward tension fills the air. I wait for one of them to start laughing, but they hold each other's stares, wearing equally serious expressions.

Finally, Pixel shrugs, turning her attention back to the computer. "If you're jealous, just say so."

Godric scoffs. "I'm not jealous," he mutters.

I fight to tamp my own smirk down this time as I realize my best friend is indeed envious. Turning to Pixel, I pat her shoulder softly.

"If you're happy, I'm happy for you," I tell her honestly. "If he breaks your heart, you tell us."

"Yeah, Pixie," Godric says. "We'll fuck him up."

"Okay, Godric." She rolls her eyes at him before returning her attention to her computer. But not before I catch a hint of a blush on her cheeks.

"It's best if we attend separately," I say, striding toward the door with Godric. "The less attention on us, the better."

"So, find a date," he says, slapping my back playfully.

I pause at the doorway. "Text me if any updates come in. I'm leaving."

He grunts in response.

"Uh...guys?" Pixel's voice is quiet now, lacking the playful luster it held a moment ago. "Speaking of your cute bartender friend... Come here?"

I'm back at her side in four long strides, peering down at her multiple computer screens. She points to the largest one in the middle, and immediately I notice what she's referring to.

Another photo of Tasia. This time, she's holding a bat that has nails on it, a crazy look in her eyes.

Rubbing my forehead, I sigh. Could be worse. "How long until you can wipe this one?"

She gestures to another monitor, where fast-scrolling green code fills the black screen. "Any second now." She types rapidly, inserting a series of numbers and symbols. I might own Ataraxy, but I know very little about technology. This is why I have people like Pixel in my circle. "My concern is that they've boosted her photo twice now."

I glance at Godric, trying to process what it could mean. "Someone's taken an interest in her. Not a good one."

"They want her gone, huh?" he mutters. "Fuck. She knows something. I know it."

"Don't jump to conclusions," I say. The photo of Tasia morphs before our eyes, her features changing into those of someone unfamiliar.

"You said she was freaked out by the Scouts? Now this?" Godric gestures toward the screen, then stands up straight, cracking his knuckles. "Fishy shit."

I agree; it is odd. Of all the criminals to pursue in the city, someone's fixated on finding Tasia. They've plastered an image of her on the UIS twice now, without any real evidence or justification. She might not want to work for me, but would she want my protection? She might find that worth bargaining for.

"To my Fantastic Fantasia: Allow this journal to serve as your intellectual compass. May the essence of my spirit resonate within these written words, never leaving you solitary..."

-EXCERPT FROM THE PERSONAL JOURNAL OF DR. CLAUDE FOSTER, DIRECTOR OF FAEOLOGY AT MESMERIC LABS

CHAPTER 8
FANTASIA

The days pass as the Phantom's offer lingers in the back of my mind. I've returned to my normal life, my normal routine. After one particularly shitty night at work, I'm dragging myself up to the third floor of my apartment building, only to be greeted by the faint pounding of electronic music and the shrill tone of excited, overlapping voices.

I groan, begging under my breath, "Sirius, please."

When the entrance to my apartment comes into sight—one of

four identical metal storm doors, differentiated by the decaying 3663 identifier and a raggedy, faded WIPE YOUR PAWS welcome mat—I can see my prayers have gone unheeded.

The building's chipped plaster walls are like lungs expanding, each pulsing beat of music a violent inhale. Light seeps from beneath the door's crack.

I squeeze my eyes shut and rub my forehead, as if I can will it all away with mental fortitude. But the party isn't going anywhere. Giving up on delaying the inevitable, I twist the door-knob. The knob rattles as it spins, but it's unlocked. I shove my shoulder into the heavy door, unsticking it with a sharp jolt. The door flies open, and I almost lose my balance.

Damn latch.

"Great," I mutter as I slam the door behind me.

My entrance is muffled by the blasting music. This place reeks just like the bar.

I count to five before spinning around and elbowing my way through a small throng of people I don't recognize. My shoulders tighten and my teeth clench as I move through the living room. I'm careful to keep my eyes locked on the refrigerator across the apartment. I pass the tattered, vomit-green sofa and the rickety table currently missing its three chairs. Writhing bodies knock and jar me about, but I choose to ignore them, as if my lack of eye contact means they're nonexistent.

The rhythmic bass thumps at an unholy level, and my head pounds back in response.

With two closet-sized bedrooms and an open living space that combines a tiny living room and a galley kitchen so narrow that the oven won't open fully, the apartment barely fits the three of us who live here, let alone a dozen drunk assholes.

My two roommates—Stace and Alisha—share the slightly larger bedroom. They've been friends their entire life. I found them a few years back through an ad. When I left my foster home at eighteen, I needed a place to stay. Although I had some silvers saved up from working at The Rising Star since I was fifteen, it wasn't much. Most of my labor was paid under the table by Jeremiah, since I wasn't of legal serving age for those first three years. He jipped me, took advantage of me, but it wasn't like I had any other options. It's a damn blessing he even took a chance on me. I wasn't in a position to complain about unfair wages.

Fairness is a myth, anyway.

A private, furnished bedroom in my price range wasn't something I was poised to turn down.

Stace screeches my name when she spots me entering the kitchen, then throws her arm around my shoulders. I almost topple beneath the unexpected weight of her lean, muscular build. She's a dancer, but in her current drunken state, she's less graceful than normal.

"Please, Stace, get off me." I shove her sticky skin away, frowning at her.

She hovers a few fingers over me, one of the few girls I know that is taller than me. Her soul-shade is bright orange, vibrant, almost blinding to look at. It contrasts with her dark hair. I close my eyes and rub them, willing myself to stay focused and ignore her aura.

When I reopen my eyes, the color still grabs my attention—it's almost as annoying as the girl herself—but I focus on her face, choosing to pay no extra attention to it.

She fake pouts, her smudged eyeliner making her look comical. "Fine. Be that way."

Alisha appears, a cup in her hand, brown eyes glazed over. A soft yellow aura wafts from her body. Her curls are held out of her face by a pink floral headband that perfectly matches her dress. It hugs her curves in all the right places. She designed the outfit herself, and it's impressive.

"Get off me," Alisha mimics in a nasally voice, reminding me of *why* I don't ever compliment her to her face. "Always a bitch, Tasia."

"Takes one to know one." I roll my eyes and nudge my way past them, refusing to look at them any longer. I yank open a cupboard next to the fridge and snag a box of medicinal tea.

Lemon-echinacea flavor.

There's a niggling ache in the back of my throat. I hope it's from exhaustion and not a sign of an impending cold. Missing work is extremely unaffordable.

My mind briefly drifts to the Phantom's offer.

I fill the kettle with water and stick it on the stove to boil, then search the kitchen for my favorite mug—the one that says "Life is Ruff" with a large paw print on the side.

Ironically, despite my choice of welcome mat and mug, I don't own a dog. If we were allowed pets in the apartment, and if I could afford the time and money necessary to care for another being, surely I'd have one. I'd love a fluffy companion. Someone to love me unconditionally.

I spot the white, ceramic handle sticking up from the dirty sink, smothered in greasy pans and plates caked with crusty pasta and beans. Sighing, I curse under my breath.

Not in the mood to deal with that disaster, I scout for another mug. After a moment, I find one in a high cupboard, out of reach. As I'm debating climbing onto the counter to snag it, a pale arm with a smattering of red hair reaches up and grabs it for me.

"I got you, babe," a familiar voice says.

"Reed?" I whip around, frowning at him. He sets the mug on the counter beside me and gives me a crooked grin. "What are you doing h—" My eyes zero in on his glossy hazel eyes, his mussed up hair, and finally on the plastic cup in his other hand. "You're drunk. Seriously?"

His eyes hood as he sips from his cup. "Nahhh." He chuckles. "Maybe a little."

I scoff, shaking my head. "Unbelievable."

All night I've had to deal with drunken assholes at work, only to come home to this.

He steps closer, nudging me with his shoulder. "Lighten up, babe." He leans in to nuzzle my neck.

My skin heats with annoyance. I've been on edge with my hyperawareness to soul-shades tonight. It's as if seeing the grey shades has triggered some sort of unconscious defense mechanism, and now I physically *can't* turn a blind eye to all the other colors.

Reed's hazy fog is tinted greenish-blue, wavering between both colors.

"You sound like Alisha," I mutter, planting a hand on his chest and stepping back to keep a healthy distance between us. "Unsurprising, considering you've been hanging out with her tonight."

"Nuh-uh. Don't be like that, babe. I came to surprise you. Thought you'd be home from work, like, forever ago." My stomach roils at the bitter stench of alcohol on his breath. "Leesh invited me to hang and offered a drink while I waited. It ain't like that."

"*Leesh*?" Since when did they start using nicknames?

"Loosen up. Have a beer."

"You know I don't drink."

He snorts into his cup, his groggy eyes narrowing as he takes a quick sip. "Mmhmm."

"That's funny to you?"

"You drink at work."

"No I don't." I occasionally taste the new taps to know what I'm selling, but I don't drink it leisurely.

It's harder to control my ability when I'm under the influence. Not that I'm having any success doing that currently, but I definitely don't want to make it any worse. Plus, it's a slippery slope. One drink easily turns into two, then five, and then the next thing I know, I'm waking up in the morning with no recollection of the previous night, my body filled with leaded regret.

No thanks.

I rub my temples, taking a few intentional breaths to calm myself. My kettle whistles, the screech practically swallowed up by the onslaught of electronic music, and I flick off the stove's flame. I tear open my packet of tea, place the bag in the mug, and pour the scalding water over it.

"Here, just have some beer. It'll help," Reed says. He thrusts his cup at me, sloshing the liquid onto my shirt.

"For the love of Sirius!" I hiss, swatting the cup out of his hand. It hits the floor with a splash, and his brows rise in delayed surprise. "I'm exhausted. My throat hurts. I have a headache." None of which are being helped by the chaotic music and drunken chatter filling our cramped apartment. "I'm going to bed. Stay here and party with *Leesh*, if that's what makes you happy."

His face pinches into a frown, and he reaches out and squeezes my shoulder gently. "Sorry," he says, leaning in to whisper in my ear. "I-I only want you to have a good time, babe. You work so hard."

"I know." I pull away from him, snagging my mug of tea from the counter and blowing on it.

Stepping out of the kitchen area, I stride toward my door, only to be cut off by Stace.

"Come on, Tasia, just hang out with us for once!" she whines, sticking out her bottom lip in a dramatic pout. "We're having so much fun." Her pupils are blown wide, and I wonder—not for the first time—if she's on something other than alcohol.

"She's too good for us!" Alisha calls over the music. "Give it up!"

I turn to see her beside Reed, whose feet are still firmly rooted to the floor of the tiny kitchen. She reaches up, running her claws through his hair. He shudders, his eyes flitting shut for a moment.

My gut twists, and the urge to rip Alisha's hand away from my boyfriend rises.

But I don't.

I'm tired of dealing with them. Tired of being disrespected and belittled. Tired of my entire life, if I'm being honest.

How can I explain to Reed that I can see soul-shades? Or that I've been seeing grey ones specifically, which trigger memories of the worst moment of my life? How can I tell him that I'm tired of pretending soul-shades don't exist? That right now—with all these people, their auras, and the music—I'm incredibly over-stimulated?

I can't.

I can't risk anyone knowing about my ability, because if the wrong person found out, it could be a death sentence. Although I've known Reed since we were preteens, he's not the best person to confide in. He likes to run his mouth—especially when he's drinking. Sometimes he doesn't understand the potential consequences of his oversharing.

The Phantom knows, my inner voice reminds me.

I block it out.

"Are you coming or not?" I yell at Reed over the music, my sore throat protesting, and gesture toward my door.

When he hesitates, looking from me to Alisha, I scoff and shake my head.

"Aw come on, Tasia." He steps forward, rubbing his neck. "It's not like that. I just wanna relax and hang out, have some fun—"

"Fuck you," I mutter as I step into my room and slam the door shut.

I flick on the light switch beside my door, and the tiny room is illuminated. Someone screeches, and two faces I don't recognize peer up at me from my twin-size mattress resting on the floor. They scramble to use my blanket to cover their naked bodies.

The teddy bear my father gave me topples to the ground. It's a sad, raggedy thing with matted brown fur and a missing eye.

"Give me that!" I step forward and snatch the bear before they can soil it with their disrespect. "Get out of my room!"

The curly-haired man's glaze flicks between me and the girl in bed beside him. He shoots me a sheepish grin. "You can join us if you want."

I exhale a deep breath. "Get. Out."

With unhurried motions, the couple stands and re-dresses. I close my eyes and count to a hundred, snuggling the bear to my chest. When they finally leave, I slam the door behind them.

The past few days have been too much. I need a release.

Grabbing my mixed-media notebook and artist's toolbox, I sit on the floor. The single lamp casts warm shadows over my art as I flip through the notebook. A myriad of faces and objects stare back at me as I search for the next empty page.

Once I've located it, I snap open the toolbox, and pull out the package of oil sticks. Some colors have been worn down to nubs, but I don't have the funds for new ones. I snatch a black nub, the most heavily used color of all. My hand hovers above the paper, tracing air circles before landing on the page. I approach my work lightly, since I can add layers and blend later.

Soon, the emotions take over, and the art drowns out the rest of the world. Engrossed in my work, swapping out colors, I'm overcome by a surge of anger. I start applying more pressure to the pastels, making the colors more intense. The textured page absorbs the force. Each stroke in this gritty battle demands energy, force, and attention.

With the absence of blending sticks, I use a sock to vigorously blend the colors. By the time I'm done, my stained fingers ache. My wrist pulsates with pain. Chunks of oil pastels are caked beneath my fingernails. Despite being both emotionally and physically drained, I'm pleased. The final product gives the impression of being made with meticulousness rather than forcefulness.

Using oil pastels is different from painting with acrylics or watercolors. It's not really *painting* at all, in my opinion. It's tactile, requiring a certain amount of force. Pressure is necessary for creating art.

I can relate.

I choose to see *life's* pressures as opportunities to be transformed into art, too.

When I finish, I study those recognizable gold eyes staring back at me. Just like the process itself, the man on the page possesses a brutal beauty.

Loud screams of excitement come from the living room, and the noise comes crashing into me, jarring me from my peaceful state.

I snap my art book shut, stuffing it and my toolbox into the closet. My head is a little clearer now, my breaths steadier, but somehow I'm no happier, despite finding artistic release.

My door slams open, and a couple practically falls through, colliding with me.

"Oh shit, sorry," the girl says, laughing.

They barely spare me another glance before tumbling into my bed together.

I'm tired. So tired of this.

"Forget this shit." Snatching my teddy bear from the floor, I clutch it to my chest with oil-pastel-stained fingers, willing the blooming tears not to fall. My phone and keys to The Rising Star are still in my pocket, so I exit my room and cross the living room, fleeing from the apartment. No one tries to stop me.

The tears break free when I'm bolting down the rickety stairs. They're not tears of sorrow or even anger. My bone-deep exhaustion forms these tears, and as each one slides down my cheek, it's a reminder of how devastatingly exhausted I am of this life. And how soul-achingly alone I am in it.

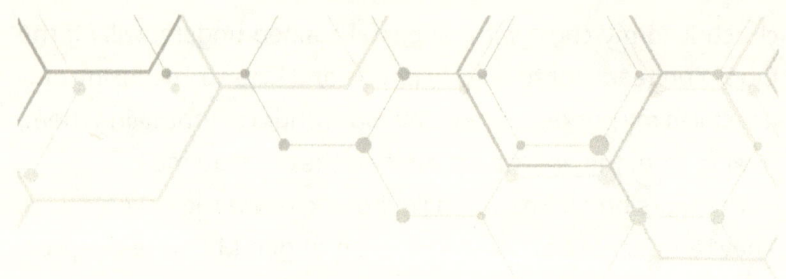

CHAPTER 9
ARCHER

The crooked, faded numbers of apartment 3663 stare at me as I raise my knuckles to knock.

I am *not* stalking Tasia.

Just because I've followed her home a few times, it doesn't make me a stalker. My intentions are truly to protect her...and maybe gather intel while I'm at it. But after that second photo of her went up on the city's UIS system the other day, I'm more than a little concerned. With all the crime around the Packing District, I find it unusual for the focus to be on one ordinary, blonde bartender.

Well, ordinary as far as anyone else knows.

I yawn, stifling it with the back of my hand. Godric and I stayed up all night, roaming the city in search of the Reaper. For better or worse, we had no luck.

Taking a deep breath, I steel my shoulders and rap on Tasia's door.

"Coming!" a high-pitched voice calls.

A few seconds later, the door is yanked open, and a tall raven-haired woman with sleep-crusted eyes and barely any clothes on greets me.

"Oh," she says. Her hands fly up and smooth back her hair, and her eyes widen. "How can I help you?"

She plasters on a toothy smile. She's a cute girl, but she stirs nothing in me.

Not like Tasia does.

I clear my throat, shaking the inappropriate thought away.

"I'm looking for Tasia," I say.

"Oh." The girl's smile drops, and she glances over her shoulder. "Come in."

She holds the door open wider, allowing me to step inside. The place is trashed, with cups and cans everywhere. Stains litter the aged carpet. It reeks like a gym bag in here.

"I'm Stace," the girl says. Shuffling past me, she flops down on the sagging couch, which groans under her weight. She picks up her phone and presses a few buttons. "Tasia's not here. Slept somewhere else last night. I texted her, though."

I stand awkwardly in the doorway, glancing around the place

with disdain. It takes me back to the apartment I grew up in—with Ma and Sofia—and I hate the mixture of nostalgia and guilt that rises with the memories.

"Make yourself at home," Stace says, waving a hand around.

I skeptically eye a stool that sits by the kitchen bar. Would it be worth it to wait for Tasia?

Deciding to remain where I am, I cross my arms and scan the apartment. The place is small—it'd be a tight squeeze for even two people—but based on the varying sizes of shoes by the door, I'm willing to bet more than two people live here.

Sofia, Ma, and me—and oftentimes Godric as well, whose own parents would go on benders and accidentally leave him locked out—stuffed ourselves into a two-bedroom apartment about this size downtown when I was a boy. Those were deplorable circumstances that I remember all too well.

But through it all, our place was always clean and neat. Sofia made sure of it. She always looked out for Ma, taking as much off her shoulders as she could.

I'm shocked it's been such a challenge to get Tasia to accept my offer. The money I'll pay her would surely get her out of this environment.

"How long until she's back?" I ask, glancing at my watch.

Stace shrugs. "I dunno."

"Any idea where she is?"

"I dunno."

I'm about to depart when one of the doors off the living room flies open and a shirtless man steps out. His reddish hair sticks up in all directions. He scratches his chest, yawning obnoxiously. When he spots me, his mouth clamps shut and he goes rigid. A curvy, curly-haired woman crashes into him from behind.

"What the hell, Reed. Move." She pushes past him, wrapping her raggedy robe tight around her body.

Reed.

The boyfriend.

My chest squeezes for Tasia.

"Where's Tasia?" I ask Reed, narrowing my eyes at him.

He glares back. "Who the hell are you?"

"I asked you a question."

He scoffs, crossing his arms and leaning against the door-frame of the bedroom. "Yeah, about *my* girlfriend."

My eyes flit from him to the girl beside him—who closes her eyes and shakes her head.

"It's interesting that Tasia thinks so highly of you," I say. "All things considered."

"You have no idea what you're talking about." His face turns as red as his hair. "Who the hell are you? And why is my girl chatting about our relationship to you?" He straightens, squaring his shoulders.

"Maybe if you spent more time with her, you'd know why."

I move toward him until we're practically chest to chest. I don't often like to use my glamour outside of work, but at times like this, it comes in handy.

Keeping my eyes locked on his, I ask in a low voice, "Where is Tasia?"

He blinks a few times, indicating the persuasion is working effortlessly.

"I don't know," he mutters.

He doesn't *know*? She could be in danger. The Scouts could've picked her up. And this jackass is sleeping with her roommate instead of looking for her.

Something I haven't felt in a long time—*fear*—crawls through my veins.

"Tasia deserves better than you," I say, tightening my jaw. Then I turn to the girl at his side. "You deserve better than this moron, too."

She gives me an appraising look, then strides past me. I turn, catching Stace staring at me from the raggedy couch, her mouth hanging open. "I think I'm in love," she mutters.

The other girl snorts as she rifles around the kitchen cupboards, searching for something.

Well, if Reed is the type of man they keep around, it figures it wouldn't take much to win them over. I offer Stace my most charming smile and step closer, until we're about a foot away from each other. Then I lean down, peering into her wide, green eyes.

"Stace?"

"Yes?" she asks breathlessly.

I can practically see the hearts dancing in her eyes. Too easy. I'm not sure I even *need* to use my glamour. But I do anyway.

"Clean this place up. It smells atrocious."

She smiles up at me and throws her phone down on the couch. Before I'm out the door, she's gripping a black trash bag and stuffing cans into it.

I have to find Tasia before the wrong person does. The need to protect her is impossible to ignore. I could tell myself it's because she reminds me of Sofia, but it's more than that. I'm drawn to her, and despite Godric's skepticism, I truly believe she's innocent in whatever war her father quite possibly started within the city.

CHAPTER 10
FANTASIA

Bright light assaults my eyelids, turning them orange, and I flinch awake with a groan.

"What the hell, TayTay?" Mellie's familiar voice—warm, with a hint of a smoker's rasp—pulls me from my slumber.

"Morning," I mutter.

I blink a few times, allowing my eyes to adjust to the brightness. The exposed metal ducts and beams of The Rising Star's ceiling stare down at me. The cobwebs and dust clinging to the piping sway gently in the meager breeze from the air condition-er.

Sitting up in the booth, I stretch my arms over my head. My back screams in protest, pissed that I slept on a slab of stiff wood. The only thing that preserved my neck was the teddy bear I snagged last night. It's not as soft as it looks; it's gotten a little lumpy with old age.

"You look like shit." Mellie's eyes roam my face, and she barks a laugh before plopping down on the bench across the table from me. "Again."

The wood creaks under her shifting weight, the noise echo-ing through the room. It's strange—almost peaceful—being in here pre-opening, without the clamor of patrons and terribly repetitive jukebox music. Even the reek of sweat and beer is minimal, blanketed by bleach and an herbal cleaner that smells of lemongrass and a little too much oregano for my liking.

"You gonna tell me what the hell you're doing sleeping in the freakin bar?"

I shake my head. "Not really." My voice comes out raspy, and I frown at the realization that my throat aches still. The sub-par rest surely didn't help fend off the cold I'm battling. My hand flies up, rubbing my neck as if that can ease the pain inside.

"I have a perfectly good couch upstairs." Mellie narrows her eyes at me. "I'll try not to take offense that you chose a stinkin bar booth instead."

"You have Axel," I mutter.

Mellie's hazel eyes soften, and she reaches across the table for my hand. "Just because I have Ax doesn't mean I don't have room for my friend." She gives me a squeeze before dropping my hand and pushing up from the table with a sigh.

My bear tumbles off my lap, and she reaches down to pick it up, chuckling. "This old thing is lumpy as hell." She holds it up by a paw, shaking it with a look of feigned disgust. "Could use some more stuffing."

I snatch it from her. "Hey! Be nice to Beary. It's the only thing I have left from my dad." That is, besides his journal. But no one needs to know about that.

"Beary?" She snorts.

"I was eight," I mumble. "Leave me alone."

She strides toward the bar, plugging in the small coffee maker and scooping in a hefty helping of ground coffee. "Still take it black?"

"Yup." I give her a genuine smile, and she cocks her head, grinning in return. "Thanks, Mel."

"You got it."

I clear my throat. "Thanks for covering for me last night, too."

She fills the coffee maker with water, snapping the lid shut and flicking the machine on. It rumbles to a start, popping and snapping as the water heats up.

"I'm not gonna ask, but at least tell me you're being safe—that you're not up to some bullshit." She plants a hand on her hip, piercing me with a motherly gaze. I grin at her sass. She's only a couple of years older than me, but having Axel and going through the messy relationship with Jeremiah has certainly matured her beyond her years. "I mean it, TayTay."

I open my mouth to defend myself, to inform her that I'm not up to anything, but she raises a hand, successfully silencing me from across the room. Still gripping my bear, I stroll over to the bar and plop on a stool in front of her.

"I'm safe," I assure her.

The lie rings out in the air between us, but based on the way Mellie grabs two mugs for our coffee while humming under her breath, I don't think she picked up on it.

When it comes down to it, *am* I truly safe? I'm lost, a bit unhappy, and wholly over my life in many ways. I don't think I've ever truly been safe.

I simply exist, slowly creeping toward my demise.

Mellie pours our coffee. She adds a heap of sugar and cream to one mug, then slides the other mug of straight black coffee across the polished bar to me. I grip the ceramic handle, raising the mug in thanks.

"Drink up and get out of my bar, girl." She grips her coffee cup and peers at me. "Respectfully."

"Sure." I blow on my coffee, eagerly waiting for it to cool enough to chug. My throat still aches, but the heat might help.

"You been painting?" she asks.

I give her a confused look. "Hm?"

"Your fingers." She points at my mug, and I follow her line of sight, noticing the dark stains on my fingertips and nails.

I bite my lip. "A little. Yeah."

Though I did wash my hands, I was so disoriented last night that I didn't take the time to properly scrub them. Oil pastels can be a bitch to get off skin. They're messy and greasy. But that's also part of why I like them so much. My art and I leave marks on each other, a reciprocal exchange.

My eyes wander to the Wanted poster on the bulletin board behind the bar, where Archer's semi-accurate face stares back at me. Mellie turns, presumably to follow my gaze.

"Five thousand silvers." She exhales audibly, turning back to me as she shakes her head. "Could you imagine?"

"You'd turn him in?" I trace the handle of my mug, avoiding her eyes.

"In a heartbeat."

I blow on my coffee harder, trying to hide my frown. "What if he wasn't guilty?"

"Not my problem." She chuckles. "You know what I could do with that money?" When I don't reply, she continues. "He's for sure guilty though. Those Nightcrawlers are the cancer of our city..."

I zone out as she continues to rant about their involvement in the city's crime world. A sickening sludge works its way through my gut. I definitely can't open up to Mellie about meeting Archer. About his proposition.

"You with me?" She waves a hand in my direction. "Well...whatever." She sips her coffee before deciding the temperature is acceptable and taking a bigger gulp. "You're worrying the shit out of me."

I stifle a chuckle, running a hand through my knotted hair. The strands are thin and damaged—bleached to hell and back. "It's just...boyfriend and roommate drama."

She grunts, going through the motions of preparing the bar for its ten o'clock opening: grabbing a box of limes and lemons, locating the cutting board and knife, scrubbing her hands, and slipping some latex gloves on.

"I never did like Reed," she mutters under her breath. "He's immature as hell. You deserve better."

"I've known him since we were twelve, Mel."

"Doesn't mean he's not an asshole."

"He has a lot of good qualities."

"Doesn't mean he's good for *you*." She points the knife at me. "You shouldn't be with him out of obligation."

"It's not—"

"Or worse, out of comfort." She raises a brow and returns to chopping.

"Yeah, yeah." Nine years I've known him. Two years we've dated officially. I thought we'd grow closer, that our love would grow stronger.

I *do* love Reed. I do.

But I'm still waiting for it to blossom into something...more.

Is Mellie right? Am I with him out of comfort? Is it because he was the one I'd cry with at night, after our foster father beat me? Is it because of a sense of misplaced safety? Being with him—as infuriating as it is at times—is predictable, which, in this chaotic world, is saying something.

While I watch Mellie work, the Phantom's offer flickers through my mind. Three thousand silvers a *week*. It's a temptation that presses closer with each breath I take. I could get my own place. Maybe then, Reed and I would have space and privacy to explore our *more*.

But do I even *want* more with him?

I sip my coffee.

It doesn't hurt that the man handing me the opportunity is handsome as all hell. An image of his boyish grin and untamed dark-blond hair flits through my mind. With those tight jeans, tattoos, and leather jacket... *Nope. Don't go there, brain*. I'd never be disloyal to Reed, for one. For two, he's a freaking gang leader.

Bad news.

I rub my eyes with the heels of my palms and groan, ignoring Mellie's curious gaze. What I need is to take control of my own life—to not give in to pretty promises and false temptations.

Patting my pockets, I locate my phone and slip it out. I press the button to turn it on, but the screen stays black. A sorrowful reflection of my face stares back at me.

It's dead.

The phone, and, in a sense, me. A part of me died the night I lost my parents, and pieces of me keep dying each day I'm stuck in this life. I'm alive in body—my heart beats in a steady rhythm—but my soul is wilted.

"Helllloooo?" Mellie waves a gloved hand in front of me. "Did you hear me?"

"What?" I snap my attention to her and chug the rest of my coffee now that it's officially at an acceptable temperature. "Sorry—I was zoned out."

"No shit." She snaps her gloves off, tossing them into a trash bin behind the bar. "Go get some rest." She reaches into her pocket, yanking out a set of keys and tossing them onto the bar. "Take my couch. Hell, take my bed if you want. Just go get some sleep."

"Mel." I shake my head, touched by her kindness. "I appreciate that, but I can't—"

"Nuh-uh." She puts her hand up. "Axel's getting picked up by his Nana soon. You'll have the whole place to yourself."

"He's up there by himself?"

"What would you have me do?" Crossing her arms, she juts her chin out. "Jeremiah's a good-for-nothing piece of—" She swipes a hand over her face, a stress line deepening on her forehead. "Ax is sick—again—and Jeremiah refuses to take him. Says he can't afford to get sick."

Rich, coming from him.

"Shit, Mel." I chew at my bottom lip as guilt blossoms inside of me. Even though I have nothing to be guilty for, I can't help but pity her in this situation. "Why don't you go be with him? I'll take your shift this morning."

She scoffs, narrowing her eyes at me. "Have you seen yourself today?" She clucks her tongue. "I don't think so."

I shrug. "It's not like I have anything else to do. Your son needs you."

Mellie shifts her weight, her attention wandering toward the upstairs. "Fine," she relents. "It's not like I'll have enough money either way." She pauses. "And, girl? You *owe* me."

Using Mellie's bathroom, I brush out my white-blonde hair and tie it up in a tight bun. A few tendrils fall free, framing my face. Rummaging through her makeup, I locate a few products to help liven me up. Her rich brown foundation is too dark for my creamy complexion, so I forgo that. Instead, I slather on some dark, winged eyeliner. My favorite lipstick is still tucked into my pocket from yesterday, so I apply that, too.

I tuck my bear safely away in her bedroom and try my best to scrub away the oils staining my fingers. Eventually, I give up, leaving them slightly tainted with color.

Thirty minutes later, I trudge back to the bar. I'm still dressed in my work uniform from last night—jeans and my bar tee. The hem is stiff with old beer, but it could be worse.

At least there's no vomit on it.

"Thanks for this," Mellie says, leaning in and kissing me on the cheek. She pulls back and points at the underside of the bar. Various fruits sit in their respective cubbies on a shallow ledge. "Garnishes are prepped. Ice is fresh. And I tapped a new keg of Sharp Wing." She jerks a thumb over her shoulder toward the back room. "Jeremiah texted and said he'd drop off clean towels later, but don't hold your breath." She rolls her eyes. "Fran is coming in for closing. She'll be here at four."

"Sounds good."

"Oh, and the good bat is missing—the one with nails." She takes a second to assess me with narrowed eyes before shrugging. "You look much better, by the way—awake."

"Something like that," I mutter, plugging my phone charger into an outlet behind the bar.

"Hey." She gently grabs my elbow, forcing me to look at her. "I only agreed to let you cover my shift because it seemed like you needed a distraction. But we aren't done talking. If you need me to take over, just shoot me a text. Ax will be fine on his own for a little bit."

I pull Mellie in, giving her a quick hug. "Thanks for this," I whisper. "I'm fine. Go take care of your boy."

The first two patrons come in shortly after opening. A soupy green fog wafts around one of the men, while a blue cloud radiates from the other. I force a smile onto my face.

"Welcome to The Rising Star," I say, infusing extra enthusiasm into my voice.

"Mornin, miss." One of them gives me a wide smile, tipping his head. "Where's Mellie at? She okay?"

The concern in his voice is touching. These men must be a couple of her regulars. I haven't met them before, but they appear much more bearable than Fredrik and my other unruly evening regulars. Lucky her.

"She's good," I say. "Her son's sick, so I'm covering for her."

"Shame." He scratches at his red beard. "Hopefully the lil man feels better soon." He holds out a hand. "I'm Kyle, by the way." I clasp his hand and shake. He releases me and jerks a thumb over his shoulder. "This is my brother, Bruce."

Bruce supplies a quick wave and a bashful smile before averting his eyes to the floor.

"Tasia," I say with a nod.

They order a pitcher of beer, pick a song on the jukebox, and plop down into seats at one of the high-tops. Thankfully, they chose one of the few rock bands I actually like. They talk animatedly with each other, flicking complimentary peanuts into their mouths and bobbing their heads. Every so often, one of them lets out a rumbling burst of laughter.

The vibes are good. Chill. I'm appreciative.

I busy myself with wiping down the bottles that line the mirrored shelves behind the bar, keeping an eye on the door and the pair by the jukebox.

The time slowly melts by. An hour into my shift, I'm getting antsy to talk to Reed. The more I replay in my mind what happened last night, the hotter my cheeks blaze with anger. It's clear, after two years, that the two of us are going nowhere.

My fingers instinctively reach for my phone, until I remember it's charging a few feet away. I unplug it and turn it on. Only a couple of messages from Stace come through, asking where I am. I sigh and stuff my phone into my pocket without replying.

I bring Kyle and Bruce a new pitcher of beer a short while later. I keep my eyes downcast, not wanting to interrupt their good mood with my pity party.

Smack.

My body jolts forward as a large hand lands on my ass.

The pitcher slips from my hand, crashing to the floor.

"What the *fuck!*" I yell, stooping down to pick up the largest shards of glass. Gods forbid one of these assholes cut themselves on my watch.

Kyle laughs. "You could use a little more meat on ya, girl."

Gone is the polite man from earlier. Now his voice is slick like oil, his tone taunting. It sends a wave of unease through me.

Great.

He can't hold his liquor.

I've met plenty of jerks who get handsy and rude when drunk. I don't care if he's Mellie's regular, he's getting cut off.

I stand, careful not to cut myself with the broken glass. That's when I catch sight of a small plastic bag on the table, smaller than the size of my palm. It's a quarter of the way full with a glittering grey substance.

"You need to get your shit and get ou—" The words die on my lips when I catch sight of Kyle's soul-shade. No longer a pea-green soup hue, it has faded into a smoky-grey.

He stands, advancing on me like a predator stalking his prey. I slowly glide backward, not wanting to turn my back on him but also not wanting to get wedged between him and the wall. Bruce, who wears a wide expression of alarm, jumps up, his stool clattering to the ground behind him.

"Hey, Kyle," he says, gripping his brother by the arm. "Maybe we should—"

Kyle turns, swinging a fist at his brother.

Bruce ducks at the last second, barely avoiding the impact.

"I swear to the Gods," Bruce says to me, his voice rising an octave, "he is *never* like this. I don't know what's gotten into him today."

My eyes shift to the left, to where the bar stretches along the wall. If I can get to my bat, I'll gain the upper hand. When my eyes return to the brothers, my gut sinks. Bruce now stands beside Kyle with a blank face, all of his alarm and fear gone.

A smoky grey fog surrounds his frame, too.

Blood pulses in my temples, and my hands shake. Something about the situation feels wrong.

So wrong.

Words from my father's journal blur through my mind. Only the dead have grey soul-shades. This is impossible, yet it keeps happening.

I take a step to the side, ready to bolt away from them. Screw the bat; I'm going out the door.

But they both lunge before I can make a move, and a scream rips from my throat.

CHAPTER 11
ARCHER

After leaving Tasia's apartment, I hustle downtown to check The Rising Star. It's the only other place I've seen her go during the past few days. If she's not there, I'm out of luck.

I arrive at my destination a short while later and push the bar's rotting door open. A bell overhead chimes with my entrance, but it's quickly drowned out by a woman's scream.

My spine turns to ice as I quickly locate the source of the terror.

Two aggressive men loom over Tasia, who's on the floor between them.

"Hey!" I yell. My head pulses, red coloring my vision.

In three long strides, I make it to them.

With a surge of protectiveness, I clock the taller one square in the face. My fist lands with a sharp *crack*, and pain explodes across my knuckles. The force causes him to stagger back, and he topples into the jukebox, rattling the old machine. His body thuds to the ground, out cold.

"Tasia!" I say. "Are you—"

The other man jumps on me from behind, wrapping an arm around my neck. I'm only caught off guard for a moment, though. Quickly, I reach up and press my fingers into the pressure point at his wrist, causing him to yelp and release me.

Like his friend, he's sloppy, untrained. Slow.

Spinning to face him, I quickly chop his throat with the side of an open hand, causing him to choke. I use the advantage to kick my foot out, sweeping his legs out from under him. He loses balance and slams into a table, releasing a strangled cry before rolling onto the ground.

I lean down, pressing a knee against his chest, holding him in place.

Then I smell it.

Death.

The scent is bitter, cloying.

The man beneath me gasps for air, holding his neck with one hand and beating on me with the other while making a slew of desperate noises.

Leaning forward, I inhale the sweet scent. It calls to me, stirring something inside of me. I lock the urge away, refusing to acknowledge it.

I growl, turning toward Tasia. "You need to get out of here."

Despite the tears streaming down her face, she seems fine.

She rises to her feet. Inhaling deeply, she squares her shoulders, standing tall.

"No," she says with a surprising calmness.

She shifts into a staggered stance and lifts her fists. I raise a brow. The sight of her—fierce and determined, not a victim, in spite of being attacked—unravels a sense of pride deep inside of me.

"Tasia," my voice comes out raspy. I clear my throat and shake away the mesmerizing hold she has on me. Death's scent calls to me, reminding me of our urgency. "You need to go. Now."

"Fuck that. I'm not going anywhere."

I sigh at her foul language and stubborn attitude, but I don't have time to argue. It's only a matter of time before the Reaper scents the deaths, too, and comes to reap these souls. Godric and I wanted to find him, but not like this. Not with Tasia here.

"Fine," I say, going for option number two.

I jump up, leaving both men on the sticky bar floor. Gripping Tasia by the waist, I toss her over my shoulder.

"Hey, asshole!" she screams, pounding on my back as I bolt for the door. As we pass the table, she stretches out and swipes something off it, but I can't tell what it is. "We can't leave them like this!"

"We have to."

"Their souls turned grey!"

I had a feeling that was the case. Pushing through the door, I exit and step onto Pub Path. "Exactly why we need to move. The Reaper will be here any second."

"No!" she screeches in my ear. I exhale heavily and grit my teeth, picking up my pace. "That is *exactly* why we need to stay!"

When I don't respond, she swings her arms and kicks her feet harder. I wince, gripping her tightly so she doesn't wiggle loose.

Continuing to ignore her ruckus, I reach into my pocket with my free hand and pull out my phone. I quickly locate Godric's name and press the dial button. I put the call on speaker, keeping my eyes forward as we navigate the street. Luckily it's not as crowded as the evenings.

Part of me feels incredibly stupid to leave behind the dying men. The Reaper will be upon them soon, and I might've just given up the chance to gain insight into what's going on around here. But my instinct was to get Tasia out of there.

Protect her.

I'm already responsible for the deaths of two women; I refuse to be responsible for another.

"What is it?" Godric's voice rings out, crisp and urgent.

"Go back and save them!" Tasia yells, drawing eyes from a passerby.

Her little fist slams into my spine with much more force than I would have expected, and I grunt. She has more fight than both those men combined.

"Is that the bartender?" he asks. "What do you need?"

"The Rising Star," I say, losing my breath...and my patience. "Hurry. The Reaper."

I end the call and shove my phone into my pocket as Tasia continues to yell and struggle against me.

There's no sense in arguing with her. My energy will be put to better use getting us the hell out of here. I stick to alleys and side streets to avoid curious gazes while Tasia continues to kick and pound like a toddler throwing a tantrum.

It's very unlikely anyone would intervene, but it's better to avoid attention as much as possible. Some noble-hearted citizen might call the Scouts.

A few streets over, I find the abandoned building I'm looking for.

Stepping inside, I maneuver through the maze of rooms in the dark like a pro, careful not to step on the rotting planks or gaping holes that lead to the floor below. It's pitch-black, and all the windows are boarded up now, but it hasn't always been this way. I've been here so many times that I can get around by simply counting my steps.

Tasia complains the whole time. I ignore her, keeping my grip tight as I step up to a wall that hides a secret passage. My hand roams across the crumbling wallpaper, searching for the hidden button. When I find it, I press it.

A piece of the wall pushes inward, and I step into the passageway. Before me, a staircase spirals downward. Right now, I can't see it, but I know the layout by heart.

"Where the hell are we?" Tasia asks.

"Almost there."

The tunnels beneath the Packing District are the last remnants of an ancient underground fae city. The land was long ago bargained away to the humans who built Silver City atop the ruins. Shortly after, an iron wall was erected around the perimeter. When the fae breached the wall back when I was young, it was reinforced and infused with salt.

I'm pretty sure the salt and iron can't really ward off the fae—that's just a myth the fae fed to the humans—but the wall seemed to work well enough...until the Reaper showed up.

We bounce down the steps, and Tasia's breasts press against my back. My cheeks flush, but then she starts cursing again, causing me to flinch.

"You sound like a banshee," I mutter.

"And you sound like an asshole."

"Mature."

"Says the kidnapper. Again with the kidnapping!"

At the bottom of the stairs, I push a door open with my hip. We're greeted with dim light and the scent of earth. I blink a few times, letting my eyes adjust.

The tunnels are like arteries running through the city's underbelly. Just as our own arteries carry blood away from our heart, these tunnels carry secrets away from the city's heart.

This is one of the lesser-used passageways down here in the Underground. The illumination comes from small bulbs attached to cords that dangle from the ceiling every so often. Although the Nightcrawlers work to maintain the electric wires, we've not done much else. The pathway, made of packed dirt, is framed with wooden beams and lined with doors leading to vacant rooms.

I kick the door shut behind me and plant Tasia on the ground.

She stuffs something into her pocket and immediately runs for the door, kicking up a small cloud of dirt in her wake. When she realizes there's no handle, no way to exit from here, she launches into a curse-filled tirade.

"You said you'd protect them!" she yells hoarsely, then coughs and rubs her throat.

I frown. "I'm protecting *you*."

At that, she goes quiet, and her cheeks turn pink. "I don't need your protection," she whispers.

Maybe she'll change her mind when I tell her the Scouts are searching for her. But for some reason I don't want to alarm her. And Pixel is on top of things, so it might not even matter, but if someone wants to find Tasia as desperately as they seem to, she might truly need my protection.

"Does your throat hurt?" I ask.

She stares at me with narrowed eyes before nodding, continuing to rub her throat. "A fuckton."

"We really must work on your vocabulary," I say.

"You're gonna get me fired." Reaching up to rub her temples, she begins pacing. "What the hell is wrong with you?"

I stare at her, aghast. "Two guys attacked you, and you're worried about losing your job?"

"Wouldn't be the first time men have used violence to get their way," she mutters. "Won't be the last."

Sorrow slices my gut. Suddenly, I want to know the name of every person who ever hurt her, so I can make sure they never do it again.

"It's fine. I don't love bartending anyway," she says quickly, brushing off the previous comments she made as if they're nothing.

"Good. Then you'll accept my job offer." When she shoots a glare at me, I can't help my responding smirk.

Then I can keep her close. Make sure no one bothers her again. Problem solved. Everyone wins.

She steps forward, planting her dainty hands on my chest, and shoves me backward with more force than I would have expected. I stumble, and my eyes widen as my back crashes into the dirt wall. My smile grows.

I think I like her aggression.

"What the hell are you smiling at?" she asks.

I shake my head. "You're stronger than you look."

"And you're stupider than you look if you think *kidnapping* me is the way to my heart."

"Good thing I'm not trying to win your heart. Just your assistance." I chuckle. "And I view it as life-saving, not kidnapping."

She pauses, studying me. "You don't want *me*. You want my ability as a soul-seer." Before I can respond, she says, "When someone's soul-shade turns grey, the Reaper comes for them. Because they're dying."

"I surmise that is the case, yes."

"Not a question." She glares at me. "I'm processing aloud."

"All right. Process away."

"So, I can essentially sense death," she mutters, "and you can also sense death...but in another way?" When I don't reply, she sighs. "*That* was a question."

"You're awfully hostile."

"I know," she says, catching me off guard. She inclines her chin. "I'm sorry." She sighs. "These last few days have been a lot. I found a dead body, got assaulted at work, and got kidnapped *twice* by a gangster."

And all things considered, she's handling the situation well. She's right. I did sort of kidnap her, even though my intention was to help. The profanities she's been hurling my way are deserved.

"You have nothing to be sorry for," I mutter.

"For what it's worth...I *am*." She takes a deep breath and glances away.

An awkward silence stretches between us. Something tells me she doesn't apologize often, and somehow, that makes her effort more meaningful. I rack my brain to think of something to say—anything to dissipate the weird energy.

"Yes," I say, answering her earlier question, "I can sense death another way."

"Do you sense it right now?"

I give her a puzzled look. "Well, no."

"Good." Her lips tilt into a small smile. "That means *I'm* not dying. Which would mean the Reaper wouldn't come for me, right?" She crosses her arms.

"Technically, no. He only reaps the souls of those who are

dying."

"Then *how* did you save my life? It sounds like I wasn't in any danger. If you hadn't come for those drunken men, the Reaper would've. And if I'm perfectly alive, he couldn't have claimed my soul."

"Ah, Tasia. You are forgetting the small fact that you can *see* him." I rub my forehead. "All bets are off. Normally, humans can't see the Reaper in his death-form. You seeing him puts you at risk."

He uses a glamour to hide himself, so—considering she's immune to mine—I'm not exactly surprised he's visible to her. I can't imagine that a reaper fae with his notoriety would take kindly to a *human* watching him siphoning off souls.

"Are you *sure* that's not just your excuse to keep kidnapping me?" she asks with a sly smile. This time, her voice holds a teasing tone rather than its earlier animosity.

My heart picks up its pace. Is she flirting with me?

Unsure of how to respond, I simply say, "Quite frankly, no."

She snorts. "But you think this will make me want to work for you..."

"Not exactly. I think it will, however, keep your stubborn self alive." I squint at her. "And I think you'll want to work *with* me sooner than later."

I open my mouth to tell her about the wanted photos right as her phone buzzes. She yanks it out, glancing at it.

"Nice," she says, grinning. "I've got service down here. I'm getting the hell out of this place."

Her eyes skim the screen, and slowly her smile fades. Her face goes dark. She tilts her head up to look at me.

"Please," she says, "explain to me why my boyfriend thinks I'm cheating on him with, and I quote, 'some broody, blond asshole with too much ego, leather, and stupid finger tattoos'?"

I'm debating how I want to answer when Tasia bursts out laughing. Slowly, her eyes roam my body, her smile growing. When her gaze meets mine, a charged energy passes between us. Her laughter subsides, but the amusement lingers.

I raise a brow. "You find this humorous?"

Once again, her reaction is surprising.

"It's the whole all-black leather vibe you have going on." She gestures toward me. "It's way too hot."

My cheeks heat at the unexpected compliment. I glance down at my fitted pants, boots, and leather jacket. My typical uniform.

"Thank you," I say, biting back a grin.

"No." She snorts. "I mean, it's as hot as Satan's balls, and you're wearing *that*." She cocks a brow. "But yes, it's also hot in the other way, too."

This time, I can't fight the smile that forces its way onto my lips.

We hold eye contact for a beat, neither of us speaking. The intensity in her coy, pale-blue eyes sends heat through my spine, and it's almost too much. The air between us grows thick and heavy.

She breaks eye contact first, and even in the dim light, I notice the pink dusting her cheeks.

It's adorable.

I lean back against the wall, crossing my arms over my chest, and try to appear unaffected.

"I went looking for you at home before I stopped at The Rising Star," I say.

She glances at her phone again, and her brow pinches.

"Reed was with Alisha, wasn't he?" Her face falls. "The really pretty girl with the big boobs and curly hair?"

My jaw tightens, and I nod.

She sighs, looking back down at her phone and angrily punching out a message. My gut tightens. I expect her to start crying or yelling, to let out some sort of emotion, but she simply shakes her head.

"So, when can I start?" she asks after a beat.

"What?"

"Don't make me repeat it."

I'm normally not such a dunce, but something about her brash attitude and ability to laugh in the midst of dark situations has me at a loss for words.

"When. Can. I. Start?" she says, enunciating each word slowly.

This time, I'm the one who bursts out laughing.

"Shit," she says. She clears her throat, then winces, rubbing at her neck. "I didn't realize I said anything funny."

"I just—you're not what I was expecting." I run a hand through my hair. "I figured you'd be livid about your boyfriend and roommate."

"I am! And I am seriously annoyed that you knew and you weren't going to tell me." Shooting me a glare, she starts tapping her foot. "But damn." She rubs her chest mindlessly. "Weirdly, I'm kind of relieved." Her body relaxes as she lets out a long breath and leans against the wall across from me, staring at a spot above my head. "Reed's a good guy, but he was never truly invested. I mean, come on. He didn't text me at all last night or this morning. Not until *you* showed up all barbaric, apparently, calling him names and ordering my roommates to clean up."

She glances at me and chuckles.

"That isn't quite how it happened." I check that my phone volume's up so I won't miss Godric's call. "And I beg to differ that Reed is a *good guy*. Good guys don't make their partner feel like they're not 'invested.' They certainly don't sleep with their roommates, either."

Tasia seems intelligent enough. Surely, deep down, she knows this already.

She holds my gaze, as if she's studying me, and then her features soften into something indecipherable until finally she swallows and looks away.

"Well, I would've paid to see that." She looks down at her phone again and groans, kicking at the dirt. After stuffing her phone back in her pocket, she says, "Speaking of pay, I just officially lost my job." Her eyes flutter shut for a brief moment. "At least the timing works out. Since we're going to work together and all that, can I at least get your real name?" She levels me with a dark stare. "Not your vague-ass gang name. It sounds as stupid as the Reaper. You two could be related with those names." She snorts. "*Phantom.*"

"I didn't choose that name." The Scouts dubbed me the Phantom—for my ability to go undetected in the city. To them, I'm more myth than man. A specter. A legend.

In reality, thanks to the glamour Godric and I cast, combined with Pixel's hacking skills, it's fairly easy to go about unnoticed. Having an alias makes it even easier. "I agree—it's not my first choice."

"Then give me your real one."

I swallow, holding her stare unwaveringly. "Names hold power."

"Exactly." She lifts a brow, crossing her arms. "And you know mine."

Stroking the scruff on my jaw, I contemplate the repercussions of acceding to her request. There's a chance she'll need to know my real name anyway, especially if I take her to the masquerade.

"Fine," I say, noticing the sparkle in her eye. "Archer. Archer Acciai."

"...THE MANIFESTATION OF GOLDEN-HUED SOUL-SHADES IS EXCEEDINGLY RARE... EXTENSIVE IN-VESTIGATION SPANNING TWO DECADES SUBSTANTI-ATES THAT GOLD TONES DENOTE AN INTRINSIC QUAL-ITY OF PURITY... DOES THE SOUL-SHADE INFLUENCE THE INDIVIDUAL, OR IS IT THE INDIVIDUAL'S QUALI-TIES THAT SHAPE THE SHADE?"

-EXCERPT FROM THE PERSONAL JOURNAL OF DR. CLAUDE FOSTER, DIRECTOR OF FAEOLOGY AT MES-MERIC LABS

CHAPTER 12
FANTASIA

Archer's phone rings, and he excuses himself, jogging further down the tunnel to take the call.

Archer Acciai.

I like that a lot better than the Phantom.

Despite being only one or two floors underground, it's like

an entirely different world down here. It's quiet, away from the bustling city above.

The rough, earthy tunnel stretches off into the distance until it disappears in shadow. I squint, noticing that it branches off in a few places. This appears to be a complex system of caves held up precariously by brick archways and sagging beams. But the modern lighting throws me off.

Agitation blazes through me, but I subdue it with a sigh, plopping onto the floor. I've been in much shittier positions in my life, and although I'm annoyed at being manhandled and carted off like a child, I'm not fearful. Oddly enough, despite his barbarian tactics, Archer's presence puts me at ease.

In fact, him worrying about me is a huge turn-on. Hell, Reed didn't even care that I ran off in the middle of the night. Yet Archer, a virtual stranger, has come to my rescue twice in a few days. His methods may be questionable, but based on that golden haze around his body, he's truly doing what he thinks is right.

Craning my neck in Archer's direction, I subtly try to eavesdrop, but he speaks in a hushed tone. I pick at some of the reddish-brown clay beneath me.

Wiping my hands on my jeans, I turn my attention back to my own phone. My most recent message from Jeremiah stares back at me:

Bossman: Your fired.

Leaning my head back, I exhale heavily. The adrenaline has finally settled, and in its place a numbness has taken over.

The thought of leaving The Rising Star makes my head a little lighter.

No more serving Fredrik and dealing with his condescension. No more getting slapped on the ass by drunken twats. No more worrying about what fights will break out during my shift. No more stressing about whether or not I'll earn enough tips to justify the exhaustion.

And damn, I *am* exhausted.

I smirk as my thumbs dart out to compose a message to Jeremiah. I'm putting the nail in my coffin. But after what happened this morning, and with Archer's generous offer dangling in front of me, I can't pretend to care anymore.

Me: YOU'RE* fired.

Bossman: No, YOU are.

Me: Yeah, I'm aware.

I chuckle when three little dots appear, indicating Jeremiah is forming his response. Quickly tapping his contact icon, I hit "block" before he can say anything further.

Mellie will be pissed, if she isn't already, but I'll talk to her later.

When I glance up at Archer, he's leaning a shoulder against some exposed brick and watching me with a curious expression. His phone is pressed to his ear, and every few seconds, he opens his mouth and says one or two words.

We continue to watch each other. Ever so slowly, his mouth curves up in an amused grin.

I fight the urge to smile back, reminding myself that I should be pissed off—or at the very least, annoyed. But still, only numbness settles inside me.

That and a migraine.

Massaging my temples, I try to relieve some of the tension there. It's probably due to the pile of hair on my head. Reaching up, I give the elastic band a few tugs until my hair falls free and cascades in jagged waves around my shoulders. A few white-blonde pieces fall into my face, and I blow them aside.

Sneaking another look at Archer, I catch him watching me with a heated gaze. When our eyes meet, he straightens up and quickly turns away, putting his back to me.

Mindlessly, I finger the lump where the small baggie sits in my front left pocket. Luckily, I was able to snatch it up as Archer caveman-carried me out of the bar. It's gotta be dreamdust.

I'm tempted to pull it out and examine it, but I don't know if that's safe. I've heard that even the smallest of inhales can get you high off your ass. It's allegedly infused with magic that causes you to think you're dreaming—which causes you to act like a real jackass. Even having it on me is unsettling.

I snatch my phone back up and open the message chain from Mellie.

Mellie: What the hell!!!!!!

Mellie: I just dropped the towels off. Where the hell r u?

Mellie: Girl, he's gonna fire u.

Mellie: Hello?

Mellie: U ok?

Mellie: U better be ok. When I find out ur ok, I'm kicking ur ass.

Heat blossoms in my face as embarrassment and guilt finally make an appearance. At least it's a step up from the ice-cold numbness I was experiencing a moment prior.

Another notification pops up, this time a text from Reed. I groan, tossing my head back against the wall behind me. My eyes shutter, and I take a few deep breaths, steeling myself. I guess he did me a favor by cheating on me—he gave me the nudge I needed to finally end things between us.

Reed: I'm at the apt. Waiting for you.

Reed: It wasn't what it looked like, I swear.

Rolling my eyes at the cliché of a line, I keep reading.

Reed: Nothing happened. Promise.

Reed: I hope you know that I love you so much, Fantasia.

I frown at his usage of my full name. My father was the only one who ever called me that—*Fantastic Fantasia.*

Without hesitation, I shoot Reed a message, letting him know that we're over. Maybe I'm a coward for ending things over text, but I'm more of a coward for letting things drag out as long as they did.

Mellie was right. Settling for comfort is a terrible option, especially when it's really not comfort at all...only a distraction from discomfort.

I also text Mellie, letting her know I'm fine, that I will explain everything to her soon.

Before anyone can reply, I power my phone down, stand, and stuff it into my pocket. Brushing the dirt off my jeans, I stride toward Archer, who finishes his call and swiftly pockets his own phone.

"Sorry about that," he says, rubbing the thin layer of scruff on his chin. His mouth is in a tight line, his forehead wrinkled. "Godric...took care of the bar."

I squint at him. What the hell does that mean? "Took care of the men?"

Archer gives a sharp nod.

"Like, he killed them?"

"They were dead when he arrived."

My eyes widen. "The Scouts?"

"Weren't called. No one else knows what happened."

No wonder Jeremiah and Mellie didn't say anything about the men being drunk and knocked out—or *dead*. Archer's friend got there before they did, apparently.

Fuck it. Let them think I simply abandoned my bar shift. I definitely don't trust Mellie enough to tell her the whole truth, because that truth includes Archer. She'll only see the price tag on his head.

I rub my eyes, processing.

"Why are your fingers stained?" Archer asks suddenly. Before I can reply, he grips my hand in his, inspecting my fingers. "Is this...paint?"

Snatching my hand back, I groan under my breath. "Oil pastels." Without giving him a chance to reply, I ask, "How'd they die?"

"To be determined." He pulls out his phone, punching out a message before pocketing it again. "We have someone on it."

The baggie in my pocket grows heavy. I'm certain the drug I found has something to do with their deaths.

"I found a—" I say at the same time Archer says, "We have a problem."

We both pause, staring at one another.

After a beat, I say, "You first." My inquiry can wait. The men are already dead, and the drugs aren't going anywhere.

"You sure?" He quirks a brow.

"A problem sounds pretty fucking ominous, so yeah, I'm sure."

He shuts his eyes and sighs—likely because of my offensive language, *oops*—but he chuckles. When he returns his attention to me, his face is serious.

"The night after we found that girl in the alley..." He shifts his weight, stuffing his hands into his jeans pockets. "A photo of you went up on the UIS."

My heart skips a beat or two. For a second, I can't speak. "Of me?"

He nods, holding my gaze. "We got it down...but another one went up a few days ago."

"Why was I on the UIS?" I ask, my voice small and hoarse. The Urban Information Screens only share shit that the city finds important. If I'm up there, then that means I'm in the public eye. And I have a feeling it ain't for anything good.

"Wanted..." He swipes a hand over his jaw, shaking his head slightly. "For murder."

My body jolts. "For...*murder*?" I yell. He winces, an apologetic look crossing his face. "Murder?"

Fear like I've never felt before floods my chest, and I begin pacing, trying to catch my breath.

No. No. *No.*

This isn't happening.

I've never harmed anyone in my life, let alone murdered someone!

"Why?" I ask, throwing my arms up.

"I don't know," Archer says, his voice low and soothing. "The first photo was of the night we met. The second photo was of you with the bat...chasing those men down the alley."

"I didn't kill them!" I whirl on him, my pulse rising. "The fucking Reaper did!"

"They can't see him, Tasia."

"So they blame *me*? Without any proof or evidence or anything?! What about *you*? You were there both times. And if someone was watching me, taking photos, then surely they saw when you..." I wave a hand toward him. "You know."

"I—" His cheeks turn pink, and his eyes shift to the side. "I don't matter. *You've* made an enemy of someone. Someone powerful."

"How the flying fuck did I possibly do that?" My throat aches, and I clear it a few times to alleviate the pain. "I go to work. I go home. I go to work. I go home. Rinse and repeat. Every fucking day!" Glaring at him, I raise a finger in his face. "I swear to the Gods, if you scold me for my language right now, Archer Acciai..."

The bastard grins. It doesn't last long before his somber expression returns, but I saw what I saw.

"You're safe," he says.

"Safe?" The Scouts are going to kill me—just like they did my parents. And there's nothing I can do. I'm well and truly screwed.

"Stay with me, and I'll protect you."

Freezing, I simply stare at him for a few moments, trying to gauge the implication there. The only thing that keeps me from laughing in his face is the fact that *his* wanted photo has been in my bar for as long as I can remember, yet he's evaded the Scouts.

"I'm not dying," I say. "I'm not letting the Scouts get me."

"They won't get you. My team intercepted the photos and took them down the moment they went wide."

"But what if someone saw them before then?"

He shakes his head. "All photos of you in the city's system have been altered." He opens his mouth to speak before clamping it shut so tight that a muscle in his jaw twitches. There's more he's not saying—I can tell by the way he's fighting his own words—but I don't press him. After a few seconds, he says, "If you stay with me, I *can* and will protect you, Tasia."

The way he says it sends a bolt of heat through my body. The heat only intensifies when he continues to stare confidently, unwaveringly into my eyes.

"Fine," I say hoarsely. "If I have to choose between you and the Scouts, I choose you."

"I'll need you to trust me."

"That's a big ask."

"Whoever wants you has resources. I'll need you to trust that I have your best interests at heart and can keep you safe. You'll need to do what I say."

My eyes roam over his body's gilded aura. That damn golden soul-shade leads me to trust him...as much as I possibly can. "Why do you care?"

He breaks eye contact, glancing away on a big inhale. "Like I told you before. You're valuable to me."

I sigh. "My *ability* is."

"If that's easier to believe, we'll go with that."

"So when is my first payday?" I ask.

Archer's face transforms from tight and angular to soft and

carefree as he bursts out into full-blown laughter.

I frown. "It's not funny."

"No, no. It's really not." He shakes his head, giving me a lopsided grin. "Your attitude changed fairly quickly, is all."

"My situation has changed." I narrow my eyes at him, crossing my arms.

His eyes flick down to my chest, pausing there for a moment too long.

"Eyes up here, asshole."

His attention quickly snaps back up to my face. Pink tints his cheeks as he scratches the back of his head sheepishly. "There's a—"

"If you're one of those leering pervs, I'm out."

He reaches out, pointing a tattooed finger toward me, and I slap his hand away.

"Don't touch me."

"No," he says, chuckling. "It's a—"

Something tickles my collarbone, and when I reach up to brush it off, my fingers make contact with something fuzzy.

"What the hell?" I pluck the thing off of me.

Holding it up, I see way too many furry, dangling legs.

A scream bursts from my raw throat as I fling the creature as far away from me as humanly possible. I jump onto Archer, wrapping my legs around his waist and my arms around his neck. A shudder goes through my body as I cling onto him.

"Is it gone?" I whisper into his neck.

His body shakes, and I pull back to see that he's wearing a huge grin. He's *laughing* at me.

"It's not fucking funny," I say.

He squeezes my hip, and his touch sends electricity through my body, sobering me up. My cheeks burn. Disentangling myself, I let go of him. When my feet hit the dusty floor, I take a few steps back, putting space between us.

I wipe my hands aggressively on my jeans and shudder.

"Yep." Archer stuffs his hands in his pockets, rocking on his heels and laughing. "I was trying to warn you."

I glare at him. His laugh turns into a fake cough.

He leans casually against the wall across from me. The soft, golden light from the overhead bulb gilds him like a piece of framed artwork. Something flutters in my chest, and I walk in the opposite direction of the spider—and him.

"Try harder next time!" I call over my shoulder.

"You didn't have to chuck the poor little guy."

"*Little* my ass." Fire shoots through my chest, and I grit my teeth. I'm not even afraid of spiders; it just scared the shit out of me. "That thing was *huge*—stop laughing!"

He quickly catches up with me, and I stop to face him. Though he's stopped laughing, his eyes still twinkle with humor.

"You're more afraid of a harmless little spider than you are of the Scouts hunting you down."

"Not true," I say through gritted teeth.

"Sure seemed like it."

"You're an ass."

"Sorry, sorry," he says, chuckling again. "I'm not trying to be..."

I turn toward him, planting my hands on his chest and shoving him up against the wall. "You are infuriating, Archer Acciai!"

His smile grows.

"What is possibly funny *now*?"

He shrugs a shoulder. "I rather like the way my name sounds on your lips."

Exasperatedly, I throw my hands up and continue walking.

"I'm suddenly jobless, homeless, and single. Your fault—all of it—by the way. Not to mention there's a fucking bounty on my head now! And you're thinking about *that*?"

There's no way I'm headed back to the apartment where both Reed and Alisha are. Something tells me someone might end up with a fist in their face—and it won't be me. Plus, my roommates would surely be the first ones to turn me in if they saw my photo blasted on the UIS.

Archer kicks at the dirt underfoot with the toe of his boot, his features pinched together. "No—sorry. I don't laugh often, but with you..."

"Me what? You find it easy to laugh at my pain?"

"That's not it at all." He gives me a sidelong glance. "It's just that, despite everything going on, being around you makes me forget the horrors of this city."

"Well...shit." That weird, warm tightness spreads through my chest again. I don't admit it aloud, but I sort of feel the same way.

Even though my biggest fear is coming true—the Scouts are after me—somehow I'm not afraid.

Not with Archer by my side.

"EXCLUDING INSTANCES OF EXCEPTIONAL RARI-TY—GOLD SYMBOLIZING PURITY, BLACK DENOTING MALEVOLENCE, AND GREY INDICATING DEATH—SUB-TLE HUE VARIATIONS APPEAR TO CORRESPOND WITH MINOR VARIANCES IN INDIVIDUAL PERSONALITIES, OFFERING MINIMAL SUBSTANTIVE INSIGHT. UNVEIL-ING THE INTRICATE NUANCES BETWEEN SHADES AND PERSONALITY TRAITS NECESSITATES AN EXTENSIVE LONGITUDINAL STUDY..."

-EXCERPT FROM THE PERSONAL JOURNAL OF DR. CLAUDE FOSTER, DIRECTOR OF FAEOLOGY AT MESMERIC LABS

CHAPTER 13
FANTASIA

I have no idea where we're going, but I follow Archer, opting to lean into the whole trust thing.

We emerge from the tunnels a short while later, and the rumble of cars on the road reverberates down the alleyway. Somewhere out of sight, a man sings out of tune, the words slurred. I squint against the sudden onslaught of midday sunlight. Turning, I'm relieved to see that the metal storm door we just pushed through is still in place, surrounded by weathered brick. Maybe I was confused when I thought the door disappeared last time.

"Where the hell are we?" I whisper, peering around the alley. I don't recognize the buildings.

The cement path before us is long and wide, littered with rubble and broken glass. It leads to the street, and it reeks of rot—urine and feces baking in the sun. Muggy air grips us tight in its fist, the tall buildings refusing to let a breeze through to clear it out.

Bile rises in my mouth, but I bite it back.

"A few streets over from The Rising Star," Archer says.

"Downtown," I mutter.

Between us and the road, a couple of makeshift tents are clustered together between trash bins, pressed up against the exposed brick, and a handful of half-conscious people are lying about. Junk is strewn all around—old shoes, empty food containers, broken furniture.

"Where are we going?" I ask.

"Somewhere safe, to eat and rest and figure out a plan."

"This doesn't look safe," I whisper.

A weathered man grins toothlessly at me from where he sprawls next to a shelter made of blue tarp and stacks of bricks on the dirty cement. He winks, catcalling me and lifting an amber bottle in my direction.

Unease swirls in my gut.

Automatically, I scoot closer to Archer, wrapping my hands around one of his firm biceps. He tenses briefly under my touch before relaxing.

"Be patient," he says, placing his hand atop mine and giving it a reassuring squeeze. "We're going to my house."

I nod, accepting that I'll figure it out when we get there.

"Gods," I mutter as I almost trip on a piece of trash. "This place is a dump. I can't believe they live like this."

Archer's stride stutters, and he gives me a sidelong glance. "I'm sure they feel the same."

"They ended up here because of their own actions." I wave my hand around, gesturing toward the beer bottles and needles that lie on the ground in surplus.

He halts and glances down at me, brows pulled together tightly.

"So that inherently means they must enjoy living like this?" The hardness in his voice catches me off guard. "Are you saying they deserve to spend their entire lives like this because of a bad decision or two somewhere along the line?"

"That's not at all what I said."

"You implied it," he says in a low voice.

Frustration heats me from the inside out, and my fingers automatically tighten around Archer's bicep. He winces when my nails dig in. I make a face and loosen up but don't apologize out loud.

"Don't put words in my mouth," I say. "Please." We walk a few steps in silence, and then I add, "No one in the PD deserves the shit they're dealt. But here we all are. Best we can do is make better decisions with the few choices we have. Being born into poverty isn't a valid excuse for letting your entire life go to shit."

"Nice vocabulary," Archer mutters, and I roll my eyes.

"I grew up in foster care not too far from here. I could've easily ended up rotting away in an alley, too." I used to choose the *easier* path—using alcohol, drugs, and sex to numb myself. Had I not chosen to sober up and throw myself into work and art, I could've easily ended up in this alley.

Or worse, dead in a ditch somewhere.

I don't have much—and working for it was hard as hell—but I chose the harder option for myself.

"You're speaking from a place of privilege."

"Privilege?" I mutter, yanking on his arm to make him stop again. I unlink myself from him, leveling him with a serious stare. "My parents were murdered, I was abused in foster care for years, and I almost ended up on the streets myself. How is *that* privileged?"

He returns my stare without any hint of emotion. "Why didn't you end up here?" he asks, voice low.

"Because I chose not to."

"What did you choose instead?"

I think for a second. "Working."

"And you don't think that's a privilege?"

"Work is exactly what it sounds like. Money isn't just handed to me. I earn it. I learned to spend my time—and my money—wisely." And I chose art over drugs. Oil pastels over drinking.

"Many of these people don't have the choice of working. They don't have the strength to *choose* to live differently." He sighs, giving me a look that can only be interpreted as disappointed. "Your resources and opportunities might not have been ideal, but you had access to more than most."

"I understand where you're coming from, but I still *chose* the hard path."

"Not everyone has the opportunity, or the *strength*, to choose." His voice cracks, and he clears his throat. His mouth twists into a wounded grimace. "Your strength, Tasia, is something I admire greatly about you. I sensed it the first night we met. I'm glad you were able to take a different path, but you're greatly mistaken if you don't view it as a privilege."

He strides away, his shoulders slumped more than usual, leaving me with a lump in my throat and fire in my cheeks.

For a second, I watch him go. Then, without the lens of judgment, I re-examine the alley. Now, rather than seeing people who chose drugs or drinking, chose not to work, or chose the "easy way out," I see it in a new light.

What if Jeremiah hadn't taken a chance on me?

What if I hadn't had Reed's friendship?

What if Stace and Alisha hadn't let me room with them?

Moreover, what if any one of *these* people here in the alley had had the same opportunities I did? What I said to Archer earlier is true: we're all one decision away from a different life. But we can only make decisions based on the resources and opportunities given to us.

And *that* is the true privilege.

The realization sends an earthquake of guilt and gratitude through my body.

"You're right!" I shout, my voice hoarse. Archer stiffens, straightens his shoulders, then turns to look at me. I jog to catch up to him. "You're right. I'm—sorry."

"Don't apologize to me. Just try to give grace to your neighbors."

My cheeks heat further, and I nod. "Did you struggle?"

"No," he says, glancing away. "Someone close to me did."

"Did they find their way out?"

His gaze meets mine, hardening. "They died."

My heart drops. I open my mouth to reply—

"Not you again, asshole," someone says abruptly. A man shuffles up to us, his dark hair greasy, his face streaked with dirt, and his white tank stained with sweat. A dusky blue hue encompasses his body. "I toldya, I'm not coming home with ya, boy."

Archer's demeanor shifts. His muscles relax, and his face softens into a look of amusement. "Remy."

"Asshole."

I glance back and forth from the two men. "Aren't you going to scold him for his language?" I ask Archer.

He chuckles but doesn't say anything, only reaches into his jacket, pulling out a few silvers and placing them in Remy's hand. At first, the man refuses, but Archer insists.

"You need to eat," Archer tells him. "You're all bones and sarcasm these days."

Remy mutters to himself, frowning. He gives me a slow once-over. "Finally got a wife?"

"Nope," Archer says.

"Shame. Got good birthing hips, this one."

I gasp, not expecting that comment. "You—"

"Remy," Archer says before I can lay into the man. "Apologize to the lady."

Remy scoffs. "Ain't no way. That's a compliment."

Archer steps forward, jaw clenched tight, and leans close to Remy. "I said, *apologize* to the lady. Now."

Remy's face goes slack, his eyes glossing over. He turns to me. "I'm sorry, ma'am."

Archer adjusts his jacket, stepping back and giving a nod. "Thank you."

Remy nods, shakes his head, then resumes scowling. "I toldya, I'm not coming home with ya, boy."

My brow scrunches. "Uh...?" I stare at Archer. What the fuck was that about? "You have weird friends," I mutter.

Archer ignores us both, reaching into an inside pocket of his jacket and pulling out a phone. He hands it to Remy. "Been looking for you so I could give you this. Call me if you need me. Godric and I are both programmed in there." He pats the man on the shoulder. "Stay out of trouble. I'll be back tonight."

Remy curses at Archer as we walk away, but he keeps the phone. Archer chuckles under his breath.

I can't stop stealing glances at Archer. There's a lot to unpack from that interaction.

"Who's Remy?" I ask as we head toward the street.

Archer sighs, running a hand over his scruff. There's an extended pause, as if he's debating what to say. "Just a man who made some bad decisions and hasn't had an opportunity to make better ones. Yet."

"He's someone special to you," I guess.

Archer sucks in a sharp breath. "He's Godric's father." There's a moment of quiet contemplation before he goes on. "They pretend otherwise, but there's years of resentment built up between them. Remy's been an addict—alcohol, narcotics—since Godric was young. He never wanted to be a dad."

"You visit him though?"

For a second, I don't think he's going to respond. Then he gives me a long look. "I'm helping him—and a few others."

"Other addicts?" I say softly.

He nods.

"The person you lost—they were an addict, too?"

A deep furrow appears in his brow. Staring straight ahead, he shakes his head. "They deserved better," he says through clenched teeth.

"Who?" I ask.

He doesn't reply, but anger radiates from him like steam from a manhole. Whatever I said—whatever he thought I was implying—seems to have triggered him. But I don't think it's me he's mad at.

After a few more steps, he lets out a long sigh.

My eyes flit to his face, but he shakes his head subtly without looking my way. I wait for him to respond, but when he doesn't,

I return my attention to the path ahead.

A scrawny cat scurries past, and I squeeze Archer's arm, tugging him to a stop. Whipping around, I squint, trying to locate its little calico frame, but it's already long gone.

After a few moments of watching silently, hoping the little guy will poke his head out, I accept that he won't be making another appearance.

When I turn back to Archer, I catch him studying me.

"What?"

"Do you have any pets of your own?" he asks, his soft tone surprising me, especially after the strange, tense encounter we just had with Remy.

"I wish."

His eyes crinkle at the edges as he grins. "You like dogs."

"Wild guess?"

"I saw your doormat."

I chuckle. "Always wanted a dog. Never had one."

He *hmphs*, kicking a pebble as we turn out of the alley and step onto the sidewalk beside one of the main roads.

Cars and bikes whiz by, and our conversation immediately ceases as we're surrounded by a cacophony of accelerating engines, aggressive honking, and loud chatter.

Archer jerks his head at a parking garage across the street and starts jogging toward it. I follow him.

A few cars honk at us as we weave through the congested traffic, but we make it to the enclosed garage unscathed.

We cross the pale concrete floor, our footsteps thundering loudly in the mostly empty space. There are a few dozen cars parked here, but no people. We bypass the first ramp and head for an elevator that's tucked off to the side. Once we're inside it, Archer punches the button for the fifth floor while I fan myself.

"It's not even summer and I'm sweating my tits off," I complain.

This earns me a chuckle. "You have a car?"

My parents had one, but it was repossessed by the city when they died, since I was too young to take over the lease. When I got old enough to drive, I never even bothered to learn. But I couldn't afford a lease even if I wanted one.

"Nope," Archer says, once again offering me nothing. He grins, staring straight ahead as the elevator carries us upward.

"Okay then," I mutter. "Keep your secrets."

Again, he chuckles, running his fingers through his mussed-up hair.

The elevator doors *ding* open, and he strides out without looking back. I scurry behind him, struggling to keep up with his quick pace. We pass a few weathered vehicles that have seen better days and a couple of newer, shinier cars that likely belong to Sweetcreek folk who work here in the city's heart.

Archer leads me to a sleek, matte-black motorcycle parked in a secluded corner.

My feet turn to stone, and my mouth drops open. "We're riding *this* thing?"

He shoots me a lopsided grin. "Is that all right with you?"

"Uh, hell yes."

Right as I'm about to ask if he has a helmet, he hits a button near the rear of the seat. The seat pops up, revealing a storage space. He pulls two helmets out, handing one to me. I eagerly accept it.

"This is so cool!" I say, giddy with excitement.

Butterflies erupt in my stomach, and I bounce between my feet, unable to contain myself.

Archer chuckles heartily as I place the helmet over my head. It's so heavy that I feel like a bobblehead—about to tip over.

My helmet slides a bit to the side, and he frowns. "Take it off for me?"

He sets his own helmet down on the bike, and I do as he says, handing mine to him. He peers inside it, scrutinizing it for a moment before fiddling with something I can't see.

"Here." He steps close to me, lifting the helmet up and over my head. He situates it gently, ensuring it doesn't slide anymore.

The heat from his body radiates toward me, and I catch a whiff of his scent—musky and masculine, like leather, but with a soft undertone of something earthy. All the little hairs on my arms stand up. My eyes lock onto his. He holds my stare, not making a move to step back.

"How does that feel?" he murmurs.

"Good." The word comes out raspy, so I clear my throat. "Better. Thanks."

Quickly, I flick the visor down, hoping to cover the flush that's aggressively taking over my face. Stepping back, I eye his motorcycle. It's all black—Archer's preferred aesthetic apparently—with round, curvy lines, and thick, sturdy tires. Modern, new, and definitely fast by the looks of it.

"So no car, huh?" I ask.

"It's easier to navigate the city like this," Archer says.

I quirk a brow. "You mean easier to outrun the Scouts?"

His responding grin is wholly mischievous.

My gaze shifts from the bike to him, and I'm grateful for the tinted visor in front of my face, because now I can gawk at him, fully and unabashedly.

He's damn sexy next to his bike, dressed in all black, with his tousled dark-blond hair and tatted fingers. His jeans, leather jacket, and combat boots make sense now—protection from the road, should he crash.

It's less about style and more about safety and practicality.

A knot forms in my stomach, and I find myself unexpectedly worrying about his safety. I hope he doesn't ever have to put his denim and leather to the test.

"Looks expensive," I say awkwardly, trying to fill the silence.

He bites his lip and glances away, rubbing the back of his neck as if he's embarrassed. The response is so cute and innocent, so not what I expected, that laughter bursts out of me. I shake my head, then laugh even harder at how the weight of the helmet slows my movement down.

He grins, and his features come alive. My breath stutters, catching in my throat. Sirius save me, he is damn handsome.

He doesn't respond to my comment, so I quickly turn away from him, saying, "Put your damn helmet on."

He does as I tell him. Then he swings a leg over the bike and settles onto the seat. He presses a button and squeezes the handles, and the engine purrs to life. Unlike some of the motorcycles I've heard roar past, this one isn't very boisterous.

"Get on!" he calls over the bike's seductive hum.

Gingerly, I throw a leg over the bike and plant my ass as far back as I can possibly get without falling off the seat. I clutch the back of his jacket in my fists.

His body shakes with laughter. He releases the handles, reaching back to grab my wrists. Then, tugging my hands around his body, he plants them on his abs.

"Keep your arms around my waist and hold on tight!" he yells. "And scoot forward so you don't fall off!"

Gritting my teeth, I slowly move forward until my body is flush against his. I tighten my arms around him and lean forward. His belly expands with a deep breath. Then all the air rushes out, and he goes still.

"Ready?"

"Yes!" I call back.

"Hang on tight!"

Before I can gather my thoughts, the bike vibrates to life and takes off, shooting through the parking garage.

"Oh my Gods!" I shriek with glee as I squeeze him even harder.

My head grows heavy with the inertia.

He slows for each turn, weaving us down the ramps and out onto the main road. The world whizzes past as he accelerates. The hair peeking out from the bottom of the helmet whips around my face, getting knotted. I can only giggle.

Adrenaline courses through my veins, and my heart pounds so frantically that I'm convinced Archer can feel it against his back.

Gods, I've never felt like this before.

So alive.

So free.

So untouchable.

I squeeze myself against him, giving him a silent thanks for this small gift.

"Perhaps if I had chosen the field of thanatology rather than faeology, I could better prepare my family. Alas, I have not chosen to study death. Instead, I've chosen a study that shall lead me to my death."

-Excerpt from the personal journal of Dr. Claude Foster, Director of Faeology at Mesmeric Labs

CHAPTER 14
FANTASIA

The bike hums along at a leisurely pace as we wind through a sprawling park. Verdant land stretches out for what seems like forever on either side of us, vibrant and thriving under the care of the district's gardeners.

Thick trees tower overhead, their trunks as wide as my kitchen and their branches casting shade over the road. Gardens filled with flowers I've never seen before dot the landscape in a riot of color. Sprinklers shower the plants in a cooling mist, droplets sparkling in the sunlight as we pass.

"You live in Sweetcreek?" I mutter. I guess I didn't take him literally when he mentioned his *house* earlier. "Of-fucking-course you do."

Between the rumble of the bike and the helmet muffling my words, the question is lost into the void.

But it's a bit surprising, honestly, considering his lecture in the alleyway earlier. I swear, for a moment it felt like we were kindred spirits—both furious about the city's shortcomings, how the PD is neglected, and how the citizens suffer because of it.

But in reality, Archer doesn't care. He's living free and easy out here in Sweetcreek. As a Nightcrawler, he's already part of the problem—they're notorious for causing havoc around the city—which means he's partly responsible for the increase of Silver Scouts. The Nightcrawlers step all over people—and probably each other—desperate to climb out of the hole the rest of us get left in.

I'm willing to bet he's not originally from Sweetcreek. In his mind, he likely thinks he worked his ass off to get here, but my perception is that he shit on his own people to become the very thing most of us hate.

"Well, shit. Being a gangster pays!" I shout.

The scenery gradually becomes less green as rows of connected homes, separated by garages, come into view.

Archer expertly maneuvers the bike into the driveway of a cinnamon-colored brick townhome. When he parks and turns the bike off, the newfound quiet is almost deafening.

After we detangle ourselves from the bike, we take off our helmets. I hand mine to Archer, then work my fingers through my knotted hair, trying to untangle the mess. He fiddles with the compartment beneath the seat, tucking the helmets away.

I inhale deeply, relishing the fresh air. The scent of blooming flowers soothes and delights me. Leaves rustle softly in the breeze, creating a gentle, peaceful melody. A few birds chirp in the distance. The earth-toned houses on either side of the street are nestled into the greenery, their pristine lawns softened by the natural beauty surrounding them. The neighborhood is well-maintained and carefully cultivated.

It's serene, idyllic, as if the very air is inviting me to slow down and enjoy the simple beauty of nature. The complete opposite of the Packing District. Somehow, we're still in Silver City, but it's like an entirely different world. No armed Scouts walk the streets here, from what I can see. No drunkards stumble around midday. In the distance, a dog barks. Children's laughter carries on the breeze.

The district is exactly how I remember it from my childhood. The nostalgia is almost overwhelming, and I find myself lost in memories of picking ashberries in the field with my mom and dad. We could never afford to live here, despite Dad's government job at the lab, but we sure loved visiting and pretending we lived here.

Smiling, I glance down at my fingers, almost expecting to see them stained purple. I had so much fun trying to wipe berry juice on my dad's face as a child. He'd pick me up, throw me over his shoulder, and tickle me until I couldn't breathe.

"Tasia?" Archer's voice caresses me back to the present. "Where'd you go?"

Heat spreads across my cheeks as I turn to face him. "Nowhere."

He squints, giving me a contemplative look before shrugging. "I called out to you a few times, and you didn't respond."

This time, I'm the one who shrugs.

"You had a goofy grin on your face," he says. His gaze flits to my mouth, lingering there a second before moving back up to my eyes.

"I was just...remembering something."

"Anything worth sharing?"

"Not with you." I step away, putting some space between us and crossing my arms defensively. "We're not friends"

Archer's body goes rigid. Regret washes over me. But it's true. We're *not* friends. He runs the Nightcrawlers. He lives in *Sweetcreek.*

He's on top of the world, a rich kid who grew up and wanted to rebel so he joined the Nightcrawlers. We live in two different worlds.

Something akin to hurt flashes across Archer's face. A muscle in his jaw tics, and he glances past me distantly.

I think of how he gave Remy money. How he helps the addicts. How he himself lost someone he cared about, and I sigh, reconsidering my attitude. If he were here, Dad would tell me to treat everyone with kindness, especially those who don't seem to deserve it, because deep down, they're the ones who need it most.

"My dad..." I take a deep breath, finding it difficult to form the words. Though I think about my parents daily, I never speak about them with anyone. "He was a great guy. My mom was sick all my life—mentally. She wasn't really there most days. Dad did everything for us. He was my superhero." I chuckle. "I told him that once when I was little, and he started calling me Fantastic Fantasia. Said *I* was *his* superhero."

Archer's face softens. When he doesn't say anything, I continue. "He was a good guy, and he'd do anything for the people he loved." When I blink, an image of him on his last day—frantically telling me to hide—pops up in my mind. My throat gets thick, and I swallow the grief down. "He was murdered. Unfairly and unjustly."

"Tasia..." Archer says softly. He reaches up and rubs the back of his neck, his face stern. "About your father—"

"There you are, Mister Acciai!" says a high-pitched voice, making me jump.

Archer's gaze locks onto something behind me, and he strides past me, saying, "Excuse me. I'll be right back."

Turning, I catch sight of an older lady hobbling across the street, her wild mane of grey curls bobbing around her head. She smiles warmly at Archer.

"Nice to see you, Mrs. Vannickle," he says.

"Sure it is." She grips his arm tightly. "A minute to spare for your elders?"

"For you?" He pats her hand gently. "Always."

Folding my arms in front of my chest, I remain next to the bike. They cross the street and walk two houses over, into the driveway of a cherry-wood townhouse, where another elderly lady stands at the trunk of a car.

He says something to Mrs. Vannickle, but I'm too far away to make out what words are exchanged. Whatever he says causes her entire body to soften, and she claps him gently on the bicep and nods her head. The three of them laugh and carry on a conversation for a while before Archer reaches into the trunk, pulls out a couple of paper bags, and treks toward the house.

I frown at the unexpected tenderness he's displaying. Guilt builds in my chest. I shouldn't have snapped at him. Maybe I *should* trust him—take his gold soul-shade more seriously.

Soon, Archer and the old lady return to the car for another round of groceries. As if he can sense my gaze on him, he looks my way. I freeze, offering him an awkward wave. He holds up an index finger, indicating he'll be just a minute. I give him a thumbs-up, which seems to satisfy him, and he heads back into the lady's house with her groceries.

Boredom and curiosity get the best of me, and I casually stroll toward his bike. I locate the button to pop open the compartment and press it. The lid opens, and I peer into the storage area. What else does he store in here?

"The hell you doin?" a gruff voice says from behind me, and I squeal, jumping back from the bike and spinning around.

A tank of a man crosses the yard, coming straight toward me. He's almost as tall and wide as a doorframe, with thick muscles straining against his T-shirt. The leash he's holding goes taut as a blur of black fur barrels toward me.

I put my arms up, screaming when a pair of hefty paws hits my chest and knocks me backward onto the grass. Then I'm being assaulted by a slobbery tongue.

"Scathe!" Archer yells.

I can't help the giggles that escape as I battle to get out from under the massive dog, who whines excitedly.

"Stop, stop," I gasp out between laughs, trying to shield myself from the onslaught of sloppy, wet kisses.

"Scathe, heel!" Archer commands from beside me.

The dog jumps off me.

Pushing myself up onto my elbows, I use the hem of my shirt to wipe slobber off my face. With the dog at his side, Archer stands glaring at the bodybuilder-man. They exchange words, but I ignore them, my eyes widening as I get a good look at the oversized creature with onyx-colored fur and piercing ice-blue irises.

"You okay, Tasia?" Archer asks, worry wrinkles marring his forehead. He extends a hand, which I accept. "I'm so sorry. Scathe is—"

"I'm fine." I wave him off, squatting down to pet Scathe's neck. His tail thumps happily in the grass. In a baby voice, I say, "He just wants some loves, doesn't he?" I glance up at Archer. "Is he a Belgian Shepherd?"

"Eh." Archer cups the back of his neck, glancing at his dog. Scathe whines, and Archer shakes his head, scowling at him. "Something like that."

The muscly man grunts. He steps beside Archer and Scathe, glowering down at me. "She was busting into your bike."

My cheeks heat as I stand. "It wasn't what it—" I pause. Gods, I sound just like Reed. *It wasn't what it looked like, I swear.* "I've never seen a motorcycle up close. I was just curious."

The stranger narrows his eyes at me, and I swear the man doesn't blink once as we have a silent standoff for a good thirty seconds.

Archer laughs in spite of his friend's harshness, and all the tension leaves my body. Unfazed, he treks toward the house, waving us after him.

"Don't touch his shit," Archer's friend says. He shoots one last glare at me, slamming the compartment shut, then joins Archer.

I jolt, backing away from the bike. "Okay, grumpy," I mutter.

Archer laughs with his friend as they head toward his house, and I hesitate to follow. When they reach the front door, Archer pets Scathe, then glances back, giving me a reassuring smile. My heart squeezes. The lazy golden glow hovering around him seals the deal for me, and my feet move on their own accord. I cross the lawn and ascend the few stout porch steps to his front door.

As we step inside the house, we're greeted by a charming entryway with a small bench, extra dog leashes hanging on a hook, and what I assume is a closet door. The spacious, open-floor plan allows me to see through the house and out the sliding glass doors all the way to the large, fenced-in backyard. My attention snags on the only piece of real furniture: a sofa sitting awkwardly against one of the walls, still adorned with a price tag. Ripped cardboard lies scattered around it, as if someone recently unboxed it and put it together.

Shifting my gaze to the left, I check out the modern kitchen, which boasts an array of shiny appliances and an impressive amount of cupboard space. The staircase, tucked into the far side of the kitchen, curves out of sight as it ascends to the second floor.

I guess he's just moved in, since everything is so fresh, pristine, and downright bare.

Archer kneels beside the dog and unhooks the leash, hanging it on the hook by the door. His face takes on the cutest grin as he scratches the dog's neck animatedly.

"That's my good boy. Daddy wubs you."

I stifle a laugh. "*Daddy*?" I mouth to his friend, whose lips quirk in response.

After a minute, Archer turns his attention to me, beaming. "This is Scathe."

Reaching down, I mindlessly scratch the dog's scruff. "No shit." Archer makes a huffing sound. "Sorry—I know. *Language*," I say before he gets a chance.

At this, the stranger makes a humored noise under his breath.

Archer gestures toward the guy. "And this is Godric—a good friend."

The name sounds familiar, and I mull it over in my mind for a moment before gritting my teeth and saying, "You're the asshole that tied me up."

"And you're the asshole who was going to get us all killed by freaking out in front of the Reaper."

I squirm, hating the amount of information he has on me. But clearly he can also see the Reaper, which is telling. If Archer trusts him, I suppose I should, too. Not like I have a choice.

"Touché." I nod at Godric. "I'm Tasia."

"I know who you are." Godric gives me a curt nod in return, all traces of his previous amusement gone.

Taking a moment to study the man, I notice the cobalt hue around Godric's body. I'm still not sure what the colors mean—Dad was killed while he was still studying the personality traits associated with different shades—but these days, I'm relieved when a soul-shade is anything but grey.

Godric clears his throat, and I quickly avert my eyes so I'm not staring at him like a weirdo.

I turn to Archer instead and am mesmerized by the movement of his body as he sheds his leather jacket and bends down to untie his boots. My eyes hungrily roam his dark T-shirt that hugs his toned chest. His fingers nimbly work the laces, and his forearm muscles flex as he pulls off his boots one at a time. Among the plethora of ink script and detailing, I catch a glimpse of the name "Sofia" on the tender skin of his inner left arm.

My traitorous stomach churns in an unusual and unwelcome bout of jealousy.

The heat of Godric's gaze bores into my side. I straighten up and turn toward the main space before he can call me out for ogling Archer.

"Nice sofa," I say awkwardly, trying to alleviate the tense energy swirling through the room.

"Thanks," Archer says. "It's a customizable Yvonné. It's made from sustainable materials and is entirely modular."

I blink at him.

"It's a sofa," Godric and I say at the same time, in the same tone.

This causes Godric's stoic demeanor to crack. He starts to laugh but quickly smothers it with a fake cough. "I'll be out back with the mutt."

He crosses the living room and opens the sliding glass door, letting Scathe dart through the house and out into the yard to chase after some birds.

"Are you gonna take that tag off?" I ask Archer once we're alone, nodding toward the sofa.

"I've been meaning to. I just..." He shrugs a shoulder, his face reddening.

"Did you just move in or something?"

"No." He frowns, mindlessly rubbing at the back of his neck. "I've been here a few years."

"Then where's all your stuff?"

He glances at his sofa, then back to me, shrugging. "I have plenty of *stuff.*"

I snort.

"I have a house, clothes, my bike, and Scathe," he says. "It's all I need."

Yet he's apparently rich as hell and lives in Sweetcreek. It doesn't add up, but I'm not here to interrogate my new boss.

I cough, rubbing my still aching throat. He frowns, his eyes tracking the movement.

"So what'd we come here for?" I ask.

He scratches his chin, and my eyes are drawn to his thick fingers and the ink that lines them.

"You need a place to stay." He waves a hand around the open space. "Welcome."

My heart drops. "Here? With you?" I laugh incredulously. "You don't even have furniture." I'm not counting the couch.

"It's a two-bedroom, two-bath, with plenty of space..."

"Hell no."

He studies me for a beat, the heat of his golden eyes burning into me. "You are incredibly stubborn." Then he bursts out laughing, running a hand over his face and stepping closer to me. "I'm trying to offer a solution here." He stretches out his arms, giving a dramatic shrug, as if he's at a loss. "It'll make it easier on us both."

I eye the open space again, considering how peaceful it'd be to live here—away from Reed, Stace, and Alisha and their incessant partying. And it would put distance between me and the Scouts; they frequent the city center, where the majority of the crime is, not Sweetcreek.

"I need you to answer something first," I say, trekking over to his sofa and perching on the armrest. He watches me like a hawk.

"Sure. Anything."

"Don't say that unless you mean it."

"Fine. Anything I'm comfortable answering," he amends.

"Were you raised here? In Sweetcreek?"

He presses his lips together, contemplating his answer for a beat. "No," he says softly. "I was born and raised in the PD." My eyebrows fly up. I'm surprised—not at his answer but at the fact he's giving it to me so freely and honestly. He rubs his jaw and glances away. "Right by that alley we popped out of today."

It inspires me to know Archer grew up like me but managed to claw his way out of the worst part of the city to build a better life for himself. We hold each other's gazes for a moment. A sense of kinship, a mutual understanding, blooms in the space between us.

"Fine," I say, slapping my thighs. "I'll live with you since you're so desperate for a roommate. What's the catch?"

He inclines his chin. "Catch?"

"Yeah. I can't afford rent on a place like this, not even with the salary you'll have me on."

"No catch."

"Oh come on. I'm not taking a handout. And I'm not owing you shit."

I'd be a fool to be indebted to anyone—especially some guy I don't even know.

He pauses, his eyes twinkling with amusement. His glances past me, toward Scathe and Godric outside, then back to me.

"Be my date," he says, "to an event this weekend."

"An event?" He nods, and a slow smile overtakes my face. "Archer Acciai, are you asking me out?"

His cheeks flush as he scratches the back of his head and looks away. "It's—I—we can—"

"I'm only teasing you," I say, chuckling at his apparent nervousness. "Yes. I'll be your date."

"Obviously it's not a real date. Think of it as work."

My heart drops. "Yes. Yes of course." I force a smile. "Your *fake* date."

He winces, giving me a bashful look. "When you say it like that—"

I cut him off by raising my hand. "Say less. I'm in."

My dad used to say that if something seems too good to be true, it probably is. But damn it, maybe it's my time to finally catch a break. Despite my skepticism about Archer's intentions, I'll take what he's offering.

A smile forms on his lips, but he runs a hand over his jaw as if trying to stifle it. Pushing off the wall, he strides past me. Our arms brush, and all my little hairs stand up. I suppress the shudder that runs through me at the contact.

Turning to watch him go, I try not to ogle. But those jeans fit him just right. Everything, from his pristine posture to his dangerous, confident gait, lights me up from the inside out.

Heat blossoms on my cheeks, and I'm glad he's not facing me.

Sirius save me, living with a man like him just might kill me.

CHAPTER 15
FANTASIA

There *are* two bedrooms.

But only one bed.

Archer forgot to mention that part. He and Godric left in a rush, before they could give me a tour, so I decided to explore on my own.

"What the actual fuck," I say as I stare into the only fully furnished room in the house.

I inhale, breathing in the musky, masculine undertones. Unlike the bright, generic aesthetic the rest of the house has, it's dark and homey in here. The walls are a deep teal color, matching the accents woven into the earthy-brown area rug. Thick drapes are pulled over the windows, letting a small amount of light seep into the room.

The large bed rests on a wooden frame in the center of the space—perfectly made up to match the rest of the room's earthy accents.

My attention turns to the furniture across from the bed—an armoire and dresser made of some sort of unfinished wood. Both appear old and worn, albeit sturdy.

The top of the dresser is an organized chaos of various objects and photos.

Stepping forward, I reach for one of the frames closest to me.

Two people are in the photo, but my gaze lingers on a younger, softer-looking Archer. He can't be any older than fourteen. His dark blond hair is the same as it is now, falling messily onto his forehead, but missing are the tattoos, scruff, and muscles. Instead of a penetrating stare, he wears a wide, toothy smile.

An ache builds in my chest. What happened to turn this soft, happy boy into such a menacing man? What inspired him to join the Nightcrawlers?

Beside him stands a taller, broader boy with a baseball cap pulled low over his forehead, as if he's avoiding the camera. But I recognize his rich coloring and scowl—Godric.

My eyes widen as surprise flashes through me. They're just boys here. No skull tattoos mark the backs of their hands, identifying them as Nightcrawlers. Apparently, they were friends before joining the gang.

And the mystery of Archer deepens.

There are a couple of photos of an even younger Archer with a brunette woman, who I'm assuming is his mother based on how she's holding his hand in one photo and carrying him in another.

My eyes bounce around the other photos, finally catching on what appears to be the most recent one. In it, Archer is tall, broad, filling out with muscles. He has a light dusting of hair on his chin. He still has that happy twinkle in his eye. Despite being the most recent photo, it's still clearly more than a few years old, considering Archer doesn't have any ink in it yet. He looks to be maybe eighteen or nineteen at most.

There's a pretty, doe-eyed girl at his side—around his age maybe—with a matching grin and shaggy, light-brown hair. His arm rests around her shoulders, and on her other side stands a smirking Godric.

There's another photo of Archer with the same girl, and in this one, she's sticking her tongue out at him as he gazes adoringly at her.

My stomach twists. Who is she? Who is she to Archer? Envy gnaws on my insides. Whether it's a romantic relationship or friendship, whatever is between them seems so beautiful and loving.

I put the photo of them back where I found it, careful not to disturb his other keepsakes. Guilt heats my cheeks. I'm snooping through his things. Asshole or not, Archer deserves his privacy.

I might not like the guy very much, but he did open up his house to me. I can respect that.

The top drawer of the dresser catches my eye, and I pause, realizing I didn't bring anything with me.

My work jeans are crusty with beer, and my shirt is damp with sweat. It's been a long day. My throat still aches from not getting proper sleep.

I could use a shower and a change of clothes. Considering I don't know when Archer will be back, or when I'll get to pick up my own stuff, I figure I might as well make myself comfortable.

Pulling open the drawer all the way, I chuckle at how damn neat the man is. It's an underwear drawer, and all of his garments are folded, stacked, and color coded. Not wanting to be any more invasive than I already have been, I snag the first pair of boxer briefs from the stack and shut the drawer.

Striding to his closet, I flick on the light and quickly snatch the first hanging T-shirt I see, without spending too much time being nosey.

I make my way to his attached bathroom, sighing in relief at the sight of soap and a towel on the long bathroom counter, placed between two sinks.

After a long, much too hot shower—Archer can clearly afford the utility bills—I dress in his stolen boxers and black tee. The name "Ataraxy" is written across the front, and the material is well-worn, making it comfortable.

Unsure of what to do with my dirty garments, I pull my tube of lipstick and phone out of my back pants pocket, then fold my clothes in a neat stack—out of respect for Archer's tidiness—and place them on the floor out of the way.

Shaking out his towel, I hang it up to dry.

Then, I curl up in his bed—exhausted and starving—and fall into the best nap I've had in ages.

A door slams somewhere down below, rousing me from my sleep. Sitting up and rubbing the sleep from my eyes, I slip out of bed and step into the hallway.

"Archer?" I call out.

It's eerily dark. Night has settled over the city. A sliver of moonlight peers through the hallway skylight. I glance up at the sky, surprised to see a smattering of stars.

It's always too bright to see them in the PD.

When Archer doesn't respond, I slowly creep down the stairs and peek my head into the kitchen. The smell of something delicious wafts toward my nose, and I start salivating.

Mustering up all my bravado, I flick on the kitchen light, expecting to see Archer—hell, maybe even Godric.

But only a lone brown paper takeout bag sits on the island counter. An excited Scathe sits wagging his tail on the floor beside it.

"Hey, good boy!" I bend down to scratch his neck and ears. "Where's your daddy, huh?"

A piece of paper on the counter beside the bag catches my eye. Standing, I stride over to it, snatch it up, and skim the words:

Tasia,

I didn't want to wake you. This soup and tea should help your throat. Please continue to rest and make yourself at home. The bag on the floor is also yours. I hope I got the right supplies.

Be back soon,

Archer.

P.S. The chicken is for Scathe.

My stomach flutters, and my lips stretch into a smile. Not only did he notice I wasn't feeling well, but he cared enough to send me something to help. I don't remember the last time anyone went out of their way to make me feel better.

My eyes linger curiously on the cloth bag sitting beside the island. I hadn't noticed it at first. Giddy excitement bubbles up.

"Your daddy is secretly a good guy, huh?" I ask the dog, my smile still firmly in place. "He can be an asshole, but I think he's a secret softie."

The *Phantom* is definitely nothing more than a persona. Each day that I see more and more of the real Archer, the better I understand his soul-shade.

"You better not tell him I said that," I tease Scathe.

He whines, which I interpret as a sign of agreement.

I hum to myself as I pull out the items in the bag —a container of soup, a cup of tea, two salads, and a plate of chicken and rice. Everything's in sealed, unmarked beige containers. Biodegradable by the looks of it.

Opening the soup, I take a big inhale, and my mouth waters. It smells divine—some sort of veggie-and-herb medley. Scathe whines loudly, pawing at my leg.

"Oh, you're hungry?" I ask him in a soft voice.

He sits back and releases a single yelp.

Holding up the chicken plate, I ask, "Is this supposed to be for you?"

Panting with excitement, he does a little tapping dance with his front paws and spins around in circles.

The chicken appears to be unseasoned. It's cut into small bites and rests on a bed of white rice with some plain, steamed broccoli and carrots on the side.

"Enjoy," I tell him as I set the plate on the floor.

Scathe licks my hand, then turns his attention to the meal, devouring the food with gusto. I follow suit, drinking my tea and slurping my soup without hesitation.

Once I'm full, I turn my attention back to the cloth bag, eager to see what Archer dropped off. Probably clothes or something.

When I open the velcro closure and peer inside, I choke on my spit. "What the hell?"

My eyes widen as I pull out the items.

A twenty-four pack of colored pencils. A box of crayons. Two good-sized sketch pads—the exact textured, heavyweight paper I prefer to use. Blending tools in different sizes and shapes:

tortillons *and* color shapers *and* kneaded rubber.

And a pack of a hundred high-quality oil pastels in a heavy wooden box.

A feeling unlike anything I've ever experienced zips through me. Gratitude. Awe. Surrender.

Clutching the heavy box of pastels to my chest, I squeal and bounce on my feet like an excited child. Scathe keeps me company as I set up on the floor and dive right in.

Gods dammit. Archer is really living up that gold soul-shade of his. That might be worse than him being a savage, selfish gangster, because his goodness gives me a sense of hope I haven't had in a long time. And with hope comes the ability to get hurt.

Something tells me that Archer Acciai is way out of my league.

CHAPTER 16
ARCHER

I stare at my front door and run a hand through my hair. What did I get myself into?

"You good?" Godric calls from my driveway.

I turn, giving him a nod. He stands next to his SUV with one hand on the door.

"Yeah," I say. "Thanks for the ride."

He's been pestering me about Tasia—or rather, chastising me about letting her stay in my house—since I brought her here yesterday. As my oldest and most trusted friend, I respect his opinion. His concerns aren't unfounded.

I still haven't told Tasia the truth about her father. She'll think I'm using her, keeping her close to learn what her dad knew, which is exactly what Godric wants me to do.

It's what I *should* do, if I were a smarter man maybe, but I can't bring myself to use her like that.

In my eyes, she's not Claude Foster's daughter. She's just Tasia. A cute, foulmouthed bartender with a sassy attitude and an inclination to get caught up in things bigger than her.

I never meant to lie to her, but at the end of the day, a lie of omission is still a lie.

"Hey." Godric steps up next to me, placing a hand on my shoulder. "You can stay with me if you need to."

Shaking my head, I finally reach for my doorknob. "I'm good."

"You didn't have to bring her to your house."

"She had nowhere else to go."

He raises a brow. "Are you sure you aren't going soft on me?"

"She had nowhere else to go," I repeat, voice flat.

"A girl like her will drive you insane. When you need a break, you know where I live."

"What do you mean 'a girl like her'?" I challenge.

Chuckling quietly, he withdraws his hand. "All that ass *and* sass? You'll either end up in her pants or in an asylum by the time you two are done with"—he gestures toward my door—"whatever the hell this even is."

"Watch your mouth, *brother*," I growl, getting into his face. "Don't talk about Tasia like that."

He smiles, looking as smug as ever. "That's what I thought."

I grunt, backing up. I should've known he was trying to provoke me. It's his favorite thing to do these days. "There's nothing going on."

"You might have the power to smell death, but I can scent sexual tension a mile away. And you two are rife with it."

"Considering you've been around us for a whole five minutes, I have to disagree with that sentiment."

"Five minutes is all I needed." He smirks. My jaw aches from how tightly I clench it. "You're already this wound up, and it's only gonna get worse. Might as well fuck her and get it over with."

"For the love of Gods," I hiss, rubbing my forehead. "Sofia would love your mouth these days, brother," I add sarcastically.

"I bet she would," he taunts, winking.

"You—" I bite down the curse I know he's trying to goad out of me. "She was practically your sister."

"Fuck no she wasn't. She was *your* sister, and if you think I ever once thought of her like that, you're a fucking idiot."

Instead of letting him rile me up, I take a deep, steadying breath and respond with an, "Enjoy your solitude."

We both need it.

I have no idea what to expect with Tasia staying with me. I'm sure she noticed I've been gone all night and day, and even though her opinion shouldn't matter, I do care what she thinks. I feel guilty for leaving her on her own for so long. Hopefully she was able to distract herself with the art supplies.

Godric chuckles, offering me a "Good night and good luck," and retreats across my yard toward his parked SUV, his shoes squishing atop the freshly watered lawn. I watch his broad shoulders disappear into the darkness. The moonlight glints off his vehicle as he drives away, and I turn back toward my door.

When I enter my house, I'm greeted by silence. Exhaling heavily in gratitude, I drop to a knee and untie my boots. Though I'm envious Godric is going to spend extra time in the greenhouse—time I could use to recharge and ground myself as well—I didn't have it in me to abandon Tasia another night. I was hoping to see her at least for a minute when I dropped off the food last night, but I couldn't stay. Not when my team was down in the city center working to find the truth about these recent deaths.

Groaning, I swipe a hand over my face. Godric thinks it's sexual tension between me and Tasia, but he doesn't even know the half of it.

Good ol' regular tension is more like it. I need to tell Tasia the truth about her dad's possible connection to the recent spate of deaths...and soon.

I rise, shucking off my leather jacket and hanging it beside the door, and notice Scathe hasn't come to greet me like he usually does. He's uncharacteristically quiet today.

Frowning, I stride into the kitchen. I flick the switch beside the stove, and a pale light illuminates the kitchen counter.

There's a pile of neatly stacked trash beside the sink—the takeout boxes in a paper bag. I rub my neck, and some of the tightness immediately subsides at the confirmation that Tasia ate the food I dropped off last night. It was...specially made to help her beat whatever cold or illness she's been fighting.

My gaze snags on the art books I got her. One of them lies open on the floor. I crouch beside it. A portrait of Scathe stares back at me. My breath catches as I take it in. The color of his eyes is slightly off, his appearance more exaggerated than real life, but it's an incredible piece.

She has real talent.

My fingers itch to sift through the pages, see if she's worked on anything else, but it feels wrong. Though I'm no artist myself, art seems...personal to me. I'd rather her choose to share it with me of her own accord one day.

Quietly making my way upstairs, I head to my room. The door is cracked open. I gently push it open the rest of the way, and sure enough, I catch sight of a sleeping Tasia.

The room is almost pitch-black, but my vision is enhanced enough that I can make everything out with ease. Tasia is curled up in a ball on the bed, the sheets pulled up to her chin, with Scathe pressed against her back.

She looks so peaceful, so soft and innocent in her sleep.

Her mouth is relaxed, not held in the tight line it's usually in. The lines of her face form a serene expression, as if she's found solace in her dreams.

My heart rate picks up slightly, an unusual warmth blossoming in my stomach.

Scathe flicks his eyes open. The vivid orbs of icy blue glow in the dark as his admonishing words fill my head.

You left her all alone. She's scared, worried, confused, and surprisingly, still thinks highly of you despite you running away!

Shame heats my face, my throat growing thick. I slowly nod in agreement.

I know, I think, using our connection to mindspeak. *I'll do better*.

Fix it, Scathe tells me. He yawns, his eyes shutting as he nestles closer to Tasia. *I like this one. Fix it.*

Rooted in place, I stare at Scathe as he snuggles against the human girl I'm unraveling over.

It's curious that the hound took to her so quickly. Normally he's indifferent—at best—around humans.

And now, despite *our* soulbond, Scathe is at *her* side—protecting her, it seems.

My brow furrows. How in the Gods' names has she won him over so quickly?

Shaking the odd feeling off, I stride to the bathroom, intending to grab a few products so I can shower in the spare bathroom. A pile of folded clothes on the floor snags my attention.

Considering the state Tasia's apartment was in when I was

there, I'm surprised to see how neat she is—organizing her trash and dirty laundry. Chuckling softly to myself, I scoop up her clothes so I can wash them for her.

Something falls out of one of the pockets, hitting the ground with a soft swish.

I bend to pick it up. My fingers skim the package, and I freeze. *No.*

My blood goes cold.

Fury works its way through my veins—whispering at first, getting louder and louder until my skull throbs with its screams.

Just the sight of the powder—a grey dust with silvery specks—in the small baggie brings an indescribable ache to my heart.

Squeezing the bag in my fist, I try to process how I missed the signs of Tasia being on the dust.

I missed them in my sister, too, until it was too late. In hindsight, I should've known. Should have seen the way her smile slowly faded. The way her liveliness dimmed out. The way she stopped enjoying our moments together—instead becoming lost to her own mind.

Sofia's face pops into my mind. Not the bright, beautiful, smiling girl I adored, but the girl with dull eyes. The girl with the faded pallor of someone too far gone.

One night she took too much.

Her scent in those final moments had a soft hint of anise that grew stronger by the second. But by the time I smelled her impending death, it was too late.

Always too late.

Sniffing the air, I begin to pace, my heart beating erratically as I try to figure out what to do with this revelation about Tasia. I'm relieved to detect no sickeningly sweet scent of imminent death.

Maybe it's not too late for Tasia to quit. She doesn't seem as hooked on it as Sofia was.

But that does little to quell the roaring in my ears.

I grip the edge of the bathroom counter, steadying myself, taking one breath at a time.

My heart rate comes down, finding a baseline. With one last lengthy exhale, I walk back into the bedroom and lean against the wall across from Tasia, watching her sleep, outraged that she brought the dust into my home but also deeply concerned that I almost didn't catch the signs.

"I can't do this again," I whisper. "I can't lose someone else."

A short while later, Tasia wakes and mumbles something to Scathe. She plants a kiss on his head. The tender adoration there almost dissolves my anger, but I glance away, fingering the baggie in my hand. Reminding myself that Tasia can't be trusted.

Not if she's on the dust.

My phone buzzes, and I fumble with it, quickly turning the vibration off so it doesn't disturb her. Zeke's name pops up.

Zeke: The bodies from the bar tested positive for an unknown substance. Matches something I found in a few others.

Zeke: Would've found it sooner if my labs weren't messed with...

Frowning at my phone, I text him back, letting him know we'll talk in person. Then I delete the messages before swiping out of the thread and stuffing the phone into my pocket. If Zeke's work is being messed with, I guarantee it's being done by someone powerful with something to hide... Maybe even the same someone trying to scare—or harm—Tasia.

It's almost a guarantee that whoever it is will be at the masquerade.

Tasia screams, and my heart stops.

Something soft but firm hits me in the face. I stagger backwards. The pillow she threw at me rests at my feet. I pick it up and toss it back onto the bed.

"What the hell is wrong with you?" she asks, her voice a few octaves too high.

She sits up in bed, the blankets pooling around her lap, and puts a hand on her heart. The soft glow of light from the bathroom leaks into the room, illuminating her. With her wild blonde hair framing her bare face, she looks like an angel.

My jaw clenches as I finger the baggie in my hand.

"Archer? Is everything okay?"

I take a deep breath, trying to find the words.

When I don't reply, she says, "Why the hell are you watching me sleep?"

"To ensure you don't die," I whisper.

"What?" she asks, genuine confusion infused into her tone. She pulls the blankets up higher and scoots back against the headboard, looking around the room. Then she pats the bed beside her, beckoning for Scathe to join her.

He obliges, the traitor, giving me an annoyed look.

This is not fixing it, he says.

"Stay out of this," I mutter, mindlessly running a hand through my hair.

"Excuse me?" Tasia eyes me cautiously, as if *I'm* a threat now.

Shutting my mouth before I make the situation worse, I hold up the baggie of dreamdust.

Her eyes widen, and she stands, abandoning the blankets. Scathe is quick to jump out of bed and join her—glued to her side.

"Shit," she mutters, a guilty look crossing her face. "I forgot about that."

"How do you *forget* about carrying drugs around in your pocket?" I say, working hard to keep my voice steady.

Her eyes narrow at me. "I never use my front pockets—only the back ones, for my phone and lipstick—" She crosses her arms. "Why the hell are you going through my shit?"

"I wasn't—"

"And why are *you* of all people so bothered about it? Isn't your little gang the one responsible for distributing that crap in the first place?"

Running a hand through my hair, I avert my gaze. She truly doesn't seem to know that *her* father was the one responsible for creating dreamdust.

Whoever hired him did also hire the Nightcrawlers to distribute it on the streets, but that was before I took over. We stopped doing that years ago. It's one of the main reasons I bothered glamouring my way through the ranks, Godric at my side.

In my rage after losing Sofia, infiltrating the drug ring and dismantling it from the inside was one of the few actionable things I could do to affect change. By shutting down the distribution, I could protect the people, prevent others' loved ones from becoming addicts and wasting away.

And it worked.

Until now.

Godric is right. The dust is back.

"Are you okay?" Tasia asks, her voice full of concern.

The baggie of dust is heavy in my hand, a weight that will never be shed.

I thought Tasia was different. That she was strong-willed.

Instead of explaining any of that, I grit my teeth and tell her a different truth: "I do not allow drugs in my household."

She flinches.

Disappointment, anger, betrayal—*something*—must show on my face, because her forehead wrinkles and she tilts her head to the side, studying me.

"You think I'm using?" she asks, her voice barely more than a whisper. Her expression holds something akin to hurt. "Even after our talk in the alley?"

Do you think I would keep it from you if she was? Scathe says. He yawns. *Don't project your own trauma onto others, Archer.*

I swear the hound narrows his judgmental little eyes. Glaring at Scathe, I don't bother to respond. He trots out of the room, likely to give us some privacy.

On his way out, he shoots one last message to me: *She's right—you* can *be an asshole.*

"We'll talk about your attitude later!" I call after him.

Frowning, Tasia looks from the doorway to me but doesn't say anything else.

"I found the drug with *your* belongings," I tell her. "Of course I think you're using."

"Well, jackass, I've never touched that shit in my life." Setting her jaw, she crosses her arms.

I don't know if I'm more relieved by her admission or by the fact that her fiery attitude has returned.

My shoulders relax a fraction. I open my mouth to reply, but she cuts me off.

"I found that at the bar. It belonged to the two men you *rescued* me from." She puts air quotes around *rescued*. "I honestly forgot it was there. Meant to give it to you."

She shrugs and fiddles with her septum piercing.

Maybe in her mind, it isn't a big deal, but for me, it opens floodgates of memories I've tried long and hard to keep buried.

She briefly spares me a glance, then turns back to the window, chewing her bottom lip. "If the Scouts found me with that..."

"They didn't."

I know what she's implying, though. Dreamdust is infused with magic. Lab-made or not, it's highly illegal. She could've been arrested for petty possession.

Stepping up beside her, I gently tug the curtain from her hand, letting it settle back into place over the window. I reach beside the bed and turn on the lamp.

She squints as the bright glow illuminates the room. Her blue eyes are rimmed in red, and she blinks back tears.

"What's wrong?" I ask her, concerned.

"I forgot I had that on me, swear." She glances down. "They could've killed me..."

A few moments ago, I was downright furious with her, thinking she was hiding an addiction—using in my house. I was filled with rage, sorrow, and a fear of my own, at the thought of finding her like Sofia.

I couldn't tear my eyes from her for more than a second while she slept, desperately hoping the scent of death didn't come.

But I had it all wrong, and now, I find myself concerned for a whole new reason.

I'm the one betraying *her*, by accusing her unfairly and causing her stress when I promised she'd be safe here.

The urge to protect her, to fix her pain blossoms in me fiercely and suddenly.

"Hey," I say softly. "You are *safe* here. With me."

I reach for her, then let my hand drop, unsure if she'll welcome my comfort. She's terrified of the Scouts, and that fear apparently runs deeper than I first assumed.

Tasia sniffles a few times, blinking away the tears before they can fall. Then she clears her throat, squaring her shoulders. I can recognize a mask sliding into place when I see it.

Her strength, her fierceness, she uses them to conceal something that's been shattered deep within her soul.

"They killed my parents," she says detachedly. "In front of me." Her eyes leave my face, finding something behind me to settle on. "It's not something I'd like to rehash."

"*Fuck,*" I whisper, the guilt once again finding its way into my bones.

She snaps out of her fog, giving me a weird look. Slowly, an amused expression replaces the distress that was there a moment prior. The corners of her lips tilt up ever so slightly.

"What?" I ask.

A chuckle bubbles out of her.

"Archer Acciai, you just swore at me," she says in a sassy tone.

"It wasn't *at* you," I correct.

After a beat, I return her smile. Despite the grim nature of our conversation—of the shadows of our past haunting us—my body relaxes in relief.

Her eyes scan my face. They settle on my lips, and she blinks a few times, her own smile growing even wider.

"Why do you hate cursing so much anyway?" she asks.

After a second, I answer her with an unbridled honesty that catches me off guard. "My sister." She tilts her head in curiosity, so I continue. "My ma died when we were young..." Tasia's eyes fill with pity, crinkling at the corners. "She wasn't much of a maternal figure for us. She was...often occupied."

She worked the streets at night, often choosing to stay with her clients long after the job ended—preferring their fancy apartments to the rundown one she shared with her kids. One night, she left and didn't come back. We thought she'd left us for good until the city showed up, telling us she'd died. Natural causes, they said.

It wasn't looked into any further. And Sofia and I were too focused on staying alive to make any inquiries. Or maybe it was that we didn't care, considering it was easy to believe Ma had simply left us finally.

"My sister, despite being only a few years older than me, raised me," I continue.

Tasia plops onto the bed, swinging her feet off the edge, while

I lean against the wall. I'm growing lighter by talking about Sofia with someone other than Godric.

Lighter, but also irritated with myself at how easily the words are pouring out.

"Are you still close with her?" she asks. "Your sister?"

Pressing my lips together, I shake my head. "She died. Over a decade ago."

When I was sixteen and she was barely eighteen.

"We've both lost our families," she mutters, shaking her head. "That's a pain I understand." A comfortable, sorrowful silence stretches out between us before she says, "You were lucky to have a sister who loved you, who took you in and cared for you."

I don't bother asking who raised her since I already checked out her background—Fantasia Foster, ironically, a foster child.

From what I read, accusations of abuse and neglect were leveled against a few of her former foster families, but nothing ever came of the reports. I can only imagine what she had to go through.

"Yeah," I agree. "I *was* lucky. It wasn't easy, but I was lucky. We could've easily ended up on the streets in the PD, but Sofia worked her ass off."

She glances around my room. "Seems like you made out all right."

"Seems like it."

"If the trick to getting out of the city is to join a gang, guess I'm on the right track?" she says.

"You're not part of the Nightcrawlers," I tell her. If I can help it, she'll stay far away from the others. My circle is trustworthy, but that trust only extends so far, and I don't need Tasia getting caught up in the messes I so often clean up.

Her eyes flick to the skull tattoo on my hand, then back up to my face.

Twisting one of the rings around my finger, I glance at the photo on my dresser—the one of Sofia, Godric, and me.

Her line of sight follows. "That her?"

I nod.

"She's stunning," Tasia whispers.

"She was." I clear my throat. "She tried her best to be the ma we never really had. Raised me to be polite. Well-mannered. Decent. Scolded Godric and me anytime we cursed. It stuck for one of us." I chuckle, shaking my head. Godric was always a handful growing up. He spent most nights at our house, seeking refuge from his own unstable family. "I try to be a decent man, in her honor."

Tasia narrows her eyes as if trying to make sense of something. She hums to herself, then stands, mumbling.

I'm not sure what exactly she says, because I finally register what she's wearing. I'm wholly encapsulated by the sight of her in my shirt. It swallows her whole, the bottom of it falling mid-thigh. Colored ink sprawls across her left thigh. This piques my interest. I'm studying the design—a watercolor butterfly with its wings wrapping around her leg—when she yawns, stretching her arms up overhead.

Heat builds at the base of my spine as her shirt rises and...

"Are those my boxers?" I narrow my eyes accusingly.

She glances down at herself, her cheeks reddening.

"I didn't go through your shit," she quickly says.

Fighting the primal instinct to stare at her—to do much more than just stare—I pry my eyes away and spin toward the dresser.

Her going through my stuff is the absolute least of my worries.

"I'll wash your clothing," I tell her, my voice rough.

After all, that was my intention initially. Not to snoop, not to find dreamdust—which we still need to have a conversation about—and not to embark deep into the bowels of our emotional turmoil.

I stuff the baggie of dreamdust into my pocket before tugging open one of my dresser drawers. Without looking, I pull out a pair of sweatpants and toss them onto the bed, battling the urge to sneak another look at Tasia.

My throat bobs as I swallow thickly. Scooping up her dirty clothes from the bathroom, I navigate out of the room without looking back.

"Archer?" Tasia calls, sounding unsure.

"Yes?" I say, pausing.

"Thanks for the...food and the tea. I feel a lot better."

I don't turn to face her. I don't want her to see the stupid grin forming on my lips. "Glad to hear it," I say, working to keep my voice steady.

With that, I make my way out of the room. Downstairs, Scathe stretches out on my new Yvonné, eyeing me judgmentally.

Told you so, he says.

"We'll talk about it later," I grumble.

Leveling him with a pointed look, I pass by, heading into the laundry room. I put Tasia's clothes in the wash, set the cycle, and turn my attention to my phone. I locate Godric's number and press the call button.

He answers with a grunt after the first ring.

"Hit your limit?" he asks.

"You were right." I pause, licking my lips and steeling myself for the words I'm about to say, knowing they'll affect Godric as deeply as they do me: "The dust is back on the streets."

Silence, then he roars into the phone, "Fucking *knew* it, man!"

"And it's worse than before."

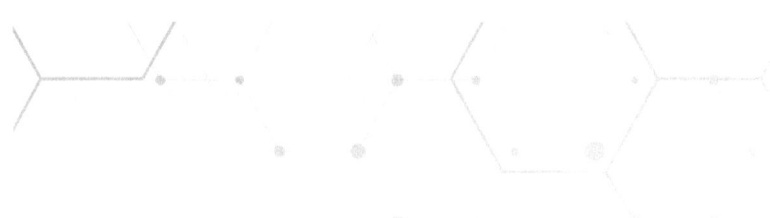

"...mRNA magic can be transmitted to individuals through delivery methods beyond injection, such as ingestion, water distribution systems, and other channels. I'm dubious as to the ethics of such methods..."

-Excerpt from the personal journal of Dr. Claude Foster, Director of Faeology at Mesmeric Labs

CHAPTER 17
FANTASIA

I throw on the sweatpants Archer gave me, rolling the waistband a few times so they stay up.

A clean, earthy scent surrounds me, and my stomach clenches in response. It's surprisingly comforting, and now I'm distracted by thoughts of him.

Great.

That's what I get for using his soap, wearing his clothes.

Downstairs, the house sits empty. It's quiet, other than the rhythmic swooshing of the washer. Archer is nowhere to be found.

"Looks like he left us again, bud," I say to Scathe as I open the fridge. Inside I locate what looks like a beet salad.

A quick sniff confirms it is. I don't have beets often. They're expensive, like many non-native veggies—imported from across the Jacarinan Sea.

Curling up on the couch with the pup, I nibble on some beets. They're surprisingly good.

I go to pick one up to offer it to Scathe, but then I hesitate. "I don't know if you can have these, bud."

I pull out my phone, and a quick search tells me that beets are fine for dogs in moderation. With a smile, I hold the veggie out for him. He sniffs it hesitantly before gulping it down.

"You gotta chew, dude."

Scathe whines in response, pawing at me. Chuckling, I give him a couple more beets.

"Does your daddy always leave you alone?" Scathe whimpers, giving me the saddest puppy eyes. "Well, you got me now, bud. We can be lonely together."

The front door clicks, and I whirl toward it in time to see it open. A moment later, Archer steps over the threshold.

Scathe bolts to the door, wagging his tail and spinning in circles. Archer loves on him, and then the pooch darts back to his place beside me on the couch.

Archer gives me a weary look. I don't know what he's been up to, but it almost seems like the last hour aged him a few years.

His hair is messy, sticking up in random places like he's been running his hand through it obsessively, and there's a haunted look in his eyes as he studies Scathe and me.

With a sigh, he settles onto the arm of the sofa, crossing his arms and ankles. Thanks to his short-sleeved shirt, most of the tattoos on his arms are visible. On his left inner forearm, Sofia's name stands out in bold letters. A cluster of somber flowers surrounds the inscription, serving as a tribute to her memory.

He said he wanted to make her proud, be a decent man.

Ironic that he joined a gang in order to do so.

However, I can't help but think that Sofia *would* be proud if she was here. He's the type of man to assist elderly ladies with their groceries, help homeless addicts fight their addictions, give a stranger a place to stay when she's on the run from the authorities.

My heart squeezes. When did I stop being bitter toward Archer for knocking me out—kidnapping me like a helpless damsel? When did I start thinking of *him* as a good guy?

We sit there in silence for a bit until Archer slides off the armrest and settles onto the couch beside me. He sheds his rigidness, his body deflating as he rubs his eyes with the heels of his hands.

"Long day?" I ask.

"Long day," he admits. He turns toward me, grimacing. "I left in a rush yesterday...there was another body found. I had to meet with my crew." My heart drops. "I didn't mean... I'm sorry I left..."

"Don't worry about *me*." I wave off his struggle to apologize, and his jaw softens in what seems to be relief. Of all things he's dealing with, I should be the least of his concerns.

Under the weight of his intense gaze, I divert my eyes downward, finding solace in the velvety softness of Scathe's plush fur. My hand glides gently along his neck, and he releases a satisfied sigh.

"The last few bodies that were found..." Archer starts, slowly articulating his words as if he's calculating how he wants to reveal what's coming next. "They had an unknown substance in their blood."

This grabs my attention. I study him. Where is this going? I'm grateful he's finally discussing things with me.

"Dreamdust hasn't been on the streets in a while, and I'm hard-pressed to believe it's a coincidence that there's been a resurgence alongside an uptick of violence and sudden deaths."

I nod, keeping my lips tightly pressed together to prevent myself from blurting something out and interrupting him. There's a hollowness in his eyes; they lack their usual luster, and my chest tightens at how he appears so vulnerable.

So exhausted.

"I'm not sure how much you know about the dust—" He pauses, waiting for a response, and I shake my head, giving him a shrug. I only know it's addicting as hell. Dangerous. "Usually, it's a slow death. Those who get hooked continue consuming higher and higher quantities until they either overdose or quit only to suffer deadly withdrawals. There are no support systems in place, no conversations about how to get help."

"Because it's banned?" I whisper.

He nods. "Possession of magic is an executable offense."

My neck prickles. I'm all too familiar with that edict. "So even if they tried to get help, they'd be killed," I murmur. How fucked up.

"Precisely." A muscle in his cheek tics, and he glances away, taking a few deep breaths. "That's how I lost Sofia—we wanted help for her but couldn't get it. She ended up overdosing."

My lungs compress, the ache in my chest so deep, so acute.

"I'm sorry," I whisper, at a loss for what else to say.

He sets his mouth in a grim line, shaking his head. "My Crawlers and I kept it off the streets for a while. Thought it was gone for good..."

"But it's being redistributed?"

He shakes his head. "If this is what's causing the insurgence in violent outbursts and deaths, then it's different than the original. The drug's original creator—" He goes still, shutting his mouth. His eyes dart away, then back to my face. "There was only one person with the know-how to make this drug, and he passed away a while ago. The formula was never located after his death. It was heavily investigated. We eliminated the remaining supply."

"Why did he make it in the first place?"

He shrugs a shoulder. "Theory is that he was corrupted. Payrolled by someone. We never caught wind of who or why."

"How long was it off the streets?"

"Almost ten years."

"Then how is it back now—if the creator's gone?"

"It's possible whoever payrolled the original project recruited someone new to take over—perhaps it took them this long to figure out how to manufacture the drug. If they had to start from scratch without the original formula, it could explain the lapse in time *and* the differences in the formula."

Archer runs a hand over his jaw, scratching the scruff there and staring at the floor between us. I get the sense there's more he's not sharing, but at least he's communicating with me finally.

Confiding in me.

"So the dreamdust *is* connected to the grey soul-shades?" I ask.

"Has to be," he says. "Like I said, there's no such thing as coincidences. This drug appears to have accelerated effects due to magic. Perhaps more potent than the original. Deadlier."

"So someone takes the drug, and their body begins shutting down, which is why their soul-shade turns grey so suddenly? They're dying the moment they find a high?" But that doesn't make sense. They're still *living*.

"I sent the dust out to get cross-referenced with the most

recent body we found. I'm waiting on confirmation before speculating further."

"What do we do?"

"Cut the head off the snake," he murmurs. When I don't reply, he glances up at me. "We never found out who payrolled the drug in the first place—or why. It's beyond time we shut whoever it is down."

Scathe yawns and stands, trotting over to the back door. On cue, Archer strides to the door and slides it open, letting the dog disappear into the moonlit yard.

"Anyone who can afford to hire a faeologist for private formulas has a disposable income," he says, "so it's a safe assumption they're in a position of power here in Sweetcreek."

My heart stutters at the mention of a faeologist. Is *that* why my dad was killed? He was a good guy. If he was propositioned to make something so horrendous, he would've declined. Maybe he refused the wrong person.

I sit up taller, refocusing on Archer. "My dad worked in the labs," I say, "before the Scouts took his life without trial."

Archer swallows a few times, his gaze locked on the floor again.

Closing my eyes, I take a deep breath. The last thing I remember of my dad alive that night was him yelling at me to stay hidden. His face was uncharacteristically somber. And shortly after, he was gone, his soul consumed. Those days were a blur, and I've worked hard to block them out until now, not wanting that shadow to follow me.

If we can figure out who the faeologist is, who hired him, maybe we can uncover the truth of what happened to my parents—why they were wrongfully killed by the Scouts.

"I think my dad turned down someone powerful. It got him killed."

"Tasia—" Archer runs a hand through his hair as his lips tighten into a grim line.

He opens his mouth like he's going to speak, then shuts it. He does this a few times before shaking his head.

Finally, he looks me straight in the eye and says, "For what it's worth, I'm sorry you lost your family."

Waving a hand, I play it off as if I'm unaffected. But my gut swirls with a renewed grief.

A lump forms in my throat, and I have to swallow a few times before I can talk again.

"How can I help you?" I ask, remembering that I'm supposed to be *working* for him, technically. "Didn't you hire me for this?"

"Everything I said before about the Reaper is true. We need to find him, rid the city of him." He cracks his knuckles, slowly pacing the length of the living room. "I'm wondering if the uptick in grey soul-shades is what attracted him to the city again..." He hesitates. "If Zeke confirms the dust is connected to the deaths, we can use your power to find the grey soul-shades before the Reaper does, just like we were planning to do."

He clears his throat and stops pacing to turn and face me. "The event we're going to at Splendor Hall? It's for Mesmeric Lab's newest venture. I've heard rumors it's under new ownership, too."

Archer mindlessly twists the ring on his thumb.

At the mention of my dad's old place of employment, my chest tightens.

"We can use your ability," he says, "if you feel comfortable, of course, to determine who is morally sound versus who might be corrupt."

Corruption? At the lab? Dad's journal never mentioned anything about corruption. Instead of admitting I don't know what the different soul-shades mean, I say, "Can we go get my dad's journal from my apartment?"

I should brush up on his notes if I'm going to be expected to actively pay attention to soul-shades.

Archer scratches his chin, shifting his weight. For a second, he almost appears nervous. "There will be many of the city's influential at the event, not just those associated with the lab." He pauses. "And yes we can go. Tomorrow?"

"Please!" I say. I may not see the full picture yet, but I understand why this event is so important now. All the power players will likely be there, in support of the lab. I glance at Archer, trying to imagine him among the uptight, wealthy city leaders, and a giggle escapes me. "Wait—how the hell are *you* on their roster, Nightcrawler?"

He grimaces, tugging at the collar on his shirt. "They don't know me as Phantom. They know me as Archer Acciai from Ataraxy, my tech security company."

With a frown, I glance down at the shirt I'm wearing, processing this revelation. Is *that* where he gets all his wealth from? Or is the company just a front for his gang dealings?

"I didn't take you as a tech guy."

"I'm not," he says sheepishly.

"Then how the hell are you in— You know what? Never mind." I chuckle when I realize I answered my own question. His business *is* a front. Probably a way to launder his dirty money. Hell, he probably has hackers stealing it. "Wait a second. Are you rich because you steal?"

"I'm *not* rich." His cheeks turn red. "It's not like that."

I giggle into my hands, giddy at the idea. "You're a freaking thief!"

"We only move money from the corrupt, the large corporations who prey on the low-income folk. It's not stealing—it's taking their money back and using it for things like rent, medical bills, education... I don't keep it for myself." He speaks with such conviction, such passion. I shouldn't have teased him about it.

"You owe me no explanations," I say softly. My heart swells at what he's openly shared with me. He's still blushing, and his eyes avoid meeting mine, so I change the subject and take the spotlight off him. "Aren't I supposed to be in hiding? What if someone recognizes me at that event?"

"Ah." He stands, adjusting his pants. "It's a masquerade, luckily."

My brows shoot up. Something about that sounds...oddly appealing. I can be anyone I want, for once. The excitement wanes when I think of my wardrobe options. "I have nothing to wear."

He stares at me, his forehead crinkling. "I'll have some dresses picked out."

"Dresses?" My nose scrunches. "I'd rather go nude."

Archer's eyes flare with heat. "I'm not sure the attendees would appreciate that."

"Loosen up, gangster. I'm only kidding."

With that, I stand, patting him on the chest.

I head to the kitchen with my empty salad container. "We still need to talk about this living arrangement, though...unless you plan to share a bed."

Archer's responding laugh catches me off guard. It carries through the house, a hearty sound, sending electric tingles dancing across my skin.

"I'll sleep on the couch," he says.

"The bed's big enough to share, and I don't bite," I tease.

This doesn't scare him off like I expected. Instead, he smirks and says in a low, raspy voice, "What if I'm into biting?"

"Archer Acciai, are you *flirting*?" A shiver runs through me at the implication. I know I should look away, put some distance between us, but I'm locked in, magnetically drawn toward him.

He takes a step forward, and I do the same, until there's only about a small space of charged energy between us. The air between us crackles in anticipation.

"Of course not," he says. "Just stating facts."

"Totally platonic facts, right?"

"Right."

"Friends share beds all the time. We can do it, too."

Archer's eyes fill with a fiery determination. "Oh, so we're friends now?"

"We're whatever you want us to be. Friends, yes," I babble, melting under the heat of his presence. My gaze drops to my toes, and my hair falls into my face, shielding me. He reaches up, pushing the strands out of my face and tucking them behind my ear.

My heart jackhammers so intensely that I fear it's trying to break through the surface.

My Gods, the sweet gestures are too much. It's just an innocent *touch*—barely even a touch—yet I haven't felt this turned on in so long.

I clear my throat and take a risk. "You know, in case you're interested, it's normal for friends to fuck." I'm done with Reed. I'm a single woman with needs. Might as well make my interest in Archer clear.

"I wouldn't know," he murmurs, his eyes flicking to my lips.

"I could show you, if that's what you want."

His brows shoot up, and a dusting of pink tinges his cheeks.

A little voice tells me to shut up, to not drag this out, but my desire takes over, pushing me to follow the temptation. "We've both had a long few days. Maybe we can distract each other...as friends."

"I'm not sure that's a good idea, Tasia." But despite his words, he studies me with heated interest. "I might ruin you for every other man."

Oh.

Yes. Ruin me. Please.

His words send a bolt of heat straight to my core. *There's* that bad-boy attitude I knew Archer possessed deep down. And my Gods, he reserves it for the bedroom. That thought makes me downright giddy. My damn *need* for him is impossible to ignore. It takes everything in me not to jump on him and tackle him right here in the kitchen.

Before I can reply, he sighs, taking a few steps back. "I should shower and get to sleep. On the couch." He reaches down to his jeans to adjust himself.

Despite his topic change, I know this energy between us is affecting him too. But he sighs, runs his hands through his hair, and heads to the stairs. At the bottom step, he pauses and turns to me. "Do you mind if I use the shower in my room?"

"Really? You're just... That's it?" I struggle to regain my composure. Going from the intense flirting straight to...whatever *this* is has given me whiplash. It feels awfully like rejection. "Why would I? This is *your* house after all."

He pauses before heading up the first few stairs. Before he's out of sight, he turns to look at me. "I'll be quick so you can get some rest, too."

I stand there awkwardly, blinking through the fog of lust.

There's no way I imagined the heavy flirting and attraction coming from Archer's side. No way.

Maybe I'm brave, or stupid, or my hormones are holding me hostage, but once I hear the shower turn on, I decide to take a risk.

I'll make it clear to Archer that I want him, that I want this—whatever *this* is. Sex. Distraction. Pleasure. Because at the end of the day, with all the dark shit out there in the world, why should we deprive ourselves of the few things that feel good?

I sneak up to his room. Quietly, I shed my clothes and burrow under his covers, sitting up against the headboard. I'm buzzing with excitement and lust as I wait for Archer to finish his shower.

Maybe this shouldn't happen. He should be off-limits. This could make everything a thousand times more complicated than it already is. While I sit and wait, I go through all the reasons why I shouldn't do this, but despite all of the reasons why this might be a bad idea, I can't stop wanting it. Wanting him.

There's plenty of time for me to change my mind, but I don't. I'm going through with it. If he doesn't want this, or if he turns me down, obviously I won't pursue it any further, but I'm going to make *my* interest very clear.

A few minutes later, the shower shuts off, and my body hums with nervous energy.

I'm doing this.

I haven't been intimate with anyone besides Reed in years, and even then, the last year has been entirely inactive. The prospect of sleeping with Archer fills me with a newfound energy.

Archer exits the bathroom, his wet hair pushed back and a towel tied low around his hips. He flicks on the lamp beside the bed, and when he sees me sitting here, he sucks in a breath and goes still.

"Tasia..." His eyes roam my bare shoulders. Hunger fills his expression. "What are you doing?"

"Showing you *how* friends can share a bed," I tease. My bare collarbone and shoulders peek out from beneath the blanket. That should be enough for Archer to realize what I'm implying. "And...other things."

He stiffens, clutching the towel tighter. "Don't play with me," he growls. "I know you think I'm a nice guy, but even nice guys have limits."

"I'm not asking you to be *nice* right now, Archer." *Destroy me,* is what I want to say. *Wreck me. Make me beg.*

He comes closer, but then his footsteps falter. Muscles in one of his cheeks twitch. "This isn't a good idea."

"Let me make you feel good," I whisper. "You deserve it."

He grips the towel tighter in his fists but then exhales heavily and relents. The towel drops, and my pulse thrums at the sight of him, hard and ready. It sends a tingle of want through me, but I stay put, forcing myself to wait in eager anticipation, to see what he'll do.

He rips the covers off, then crawls across the bed until he's hovering above me. My eyes roam the decadent curves and lines of his muscles, taking in the plethora of ink marking his tan body. His fingers reach up, gripping my chin and forcing me to meet his gaze. He leans forward, and for a moment, I think he's going to kiss me.

"This attraction can't change anything," he whispers across my mouth. "Can't distract us."

"Won't it?" I ask weakly. "You want me just as much as I want you." I reach up, gripping his hardness to prove my point. He groans, and his fingers tighten on my chin.

"Tasia."

I begin to move my hand, stroking him with purpose. His eyes shut, and he leans his head back, his breathing growing ragged.

"Tell me you don't want me, and I'll stop," I whisper, leaning forward to nibble on his jaw. "Tell me no, and I promise to listen."

Instead of replying with words, he claims my mouth with his own. The kiss is hungry, passionate, overwhelming. He grabs me by the back of my thighs, tugging me down so my back hits the bed beneath him. Then he leans down on his forearms, caging me in.

My legs spread of their own accord, welcoming him. The head of his length nudges my dampness. I writhe, beckoning him in. He doesn't move, just hovers there, as if fighting some internal battle.

I know this is dangerous, but I can't resist. Not when the hard lines of his body press against my soft curves so perfectly. Not when I've never felt more alive than I do in this moment.

I scoot down, lifting my hips, trying to take him in.

He groans again, placing his head on my shoulder. "We can't."

Abruptly, he sucks in a ragged breath, pulling off of me. His eyes rove over my naked body, which lies ready and willing, pliable, on his bed. He swipes a hand down his face, looking torn.

After a moment of silence, he snatches up his towel and jerkily wraps it around his waist.

"I shouldn't have let it get this far," he mutters. "I'm sorry."

"What the hell?" I ask, more confused than angry. "What happened to you ruining me for all other men? I'm ready. I'm consenting. Ruin me, asshole!"

Tears prick my eyes. If I thought he gave me whiplash before, it's nothing compared to now.

The hell did I do wrong?

"Tasia..." His brows draw in as he frowns. "Did you ever think that maybe *you* will ruin *me* for all other women? Maybe *I'm* not ready to be destroyed." He clears his throat, adjusting his towel. "I just...I don't sleep with my *friends*. I can't. It's not who I am."

My cheeks flame, and I clutch the blankets around my chest, covering as much as I can. "I'm sorry—can we just forget about this? It was...I was..." I babble nervously. "Seriously. It won't happen again. I was just...I wasn't thinking. And I don't want to ruin our...newfound *friendship*."

"I'm sorry." He closes his eyes and grimaces, his inner turmoil bubbling to the surface. "Regardless of this thing between us, just know, no matter what happens, I always protect what's mine."

"Yours?" I squeak out.

"You work with me," he says, voice low. "You're in my house. You're my friend. You're under my protection. Like it or not, you're mine to take care of, and I take that very seriously."

I suppress a shudder at his possessiveness. It's thrilling and unsettling at the same time.

Just take care of me then! I want to yell. *If I'm yours, come claim me!*

He grabs his clothing and exits the room, carefully shutting the door behind him and leaving me speechless. What the *fucking fuck* just happened? I fan myself, trying to cool down after that interaction.

I want to scream in frustration.

Without the lust clouding my thoughts, I replay our interaction just now. Of course the guy offered to sleep on the couch and asked to use his own shower. He didn't want to make me uncomfortable. And of course he won't make a move on me while I'm supposedly working for him and staying with him. He doesn't want to take advantage of me.

He doesn't want to risk the already fragile relationship we have.

Archer might be the first man I've ever met that thinks with his actual head instead of his dick-head.

I'm left turned-on, confused, angry, and embarrassed. I raise my fingers to my swollen lips, tracing them. The memory of his kiss lingers, and it leaves me desperate for more.

Mostly, I'm a little heartbroken at the realization that maybe I *am* a bad influence on Archer.

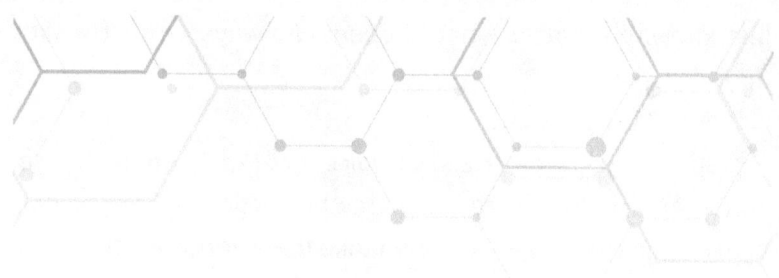

> *"THE FORTHCOMING PHASE OF RESEARCH, CONTINGENT UPON FUNDING, WILL EXPLORE HOW SUBSTANCES INFLUENCE OR ALTER SOUL-SHADES. PRELIMINARY RESEARCH INDICATES NO DISCERNIBLE EFFECT FROM ALCOHOL OR COMMON ILLICIT SUBSTANCES. HOWEVER, THE INQUIRY PERSISTS: WHAT EFFECTS MIGHT MAGICALLY INFUSED SUBSTANCES YIELD?"*
>
> -EXCERPT FROM THE PERSONAL JOURNAL OF DR. CLAUDE FOSTER, DIRECTOR OF FAEOLOGY AT MESMERIC LABS

CHAPTER 18
FANTASIA

Godric drives us to the Packing District in silence. Archer and I sit together in the back seat of the SUV, with what feels like an ocean of space between us.

Last night, Archer slept on the couch, and when I came downstairs in the morning, he silently made me some coffee—black, just how I like it—and a couple of eggs. Then he presented me with my freshly washed and folded clothing and kindly asked if I had everything I needed.

He's the most infuriating, tempting, motherfucking *gentleman* I've ever met.

Neither of us have brought up what happened last night. And stubbornly, I decided I'm not making another move until he does. If he wants to pretend there's nothing between us, fine. But I'm not risking another brutal rejection. And I can't stand feeling like I'm the one corrupting him.

We pull up outside my apartment complex, and Archer immediately opens the door.

"What're you doing?" I ask.

He glances up toward the building, then back at me, brow furrowed. "Helping you get your stuff."

"I don't need your help," I say, a little more harshly than I intended. *Smooth, Tasia.* I take a deep breath and try again, in a softer voice. "I only need to grab a couple of things, but thanks."

Mostly my dad's journal and the bear he left me. Maybe a few pairs of pants and my makeup. Archer's clothes are surprisingly comfortable, and if I'm not going to be leaving the house anyway, I'm fine to lounge around in sweatpants.

Music and laughter filter out of the open windows and into the night. Archer's jaw tightens as he glances toward the upper floors.

"I'm fine," I say. "I'm a big girl."

Godric snickers from the front seat. I meet his eyes in the rearview mirror, casting a glare at him. His snickering turns into a cough, which he covers with his hand before turning his head away.

"I know you can handle things on your own, Tasia, but it

doesn't mean you have to," Archer says. He glances around the parking lot, clearly on edge. "Pixel hasn't seen your photo around again, but it doesn't mean you're in the clear."

"You're the one who said I'd be fine," I say, apparently not as over last night's rejection as I'd like to pretend.

"If you stick by me," he says.

"Just stay here... *Please*?"

He hesitates, then gives me a sharp nod and relents, shutting his door. "If you're not down in fifteen, I'm coming up."

The protectiveness in his tone causes me to grin despite myself. I lean across the back seat, placing a hand on his leg. He stiffens, staring at the place I'm touching him.

"I appreciate that, Archer. I'll be quick."

"I mean it," he says, his voice low and raspy. "I won't let anything happen to you."

I protect what's mine. The words he said to me last night echo in my mind and have me throbbing with lust again. My heart squeezes. Tamping down the mixed emotions, I exit the car and make my way to my apartment.

Just a few days ago, this was home. For better or worse, it's no longer home. It never was, really, but now, even less so.

Sucking in a deep breath and smoothing down Archer's shirt, I climb the stairs and enter the apartment.

Warm air blasts my face, ripe with the stench of sweat, sex, and alcohol, and I almost gag. People mingle in every inch of the apartment. I haven't missed this at all. Music thumps loudly from a speaker by the couch. Only the dull light over the stove is on, barely illuminating the place.

Stace stands at the counter, bent over as she snorts something, her thick raven hair hiding her face like a curtain. Disappointment courses through me, then relief when I notice the powder is white and not a sparkling grey. A few people are packed into the tight space around her, chatting.

She quickly finishes her line, wiping her nose as she straightens. Her eyes meet mine, and a smile stretches across her face.

"Tasia!"

"Hey," I say, giving her an awkward wave.

The people in the kitchen grow quiet and turn to stare at me with disconnected expressions. I glance around the apartment, finding a few familiar faces. Alisha is nowhere to be seen, but Reed sits on the couch, sipping out of my favorite mug and chatting with a pretty redhead.

Guess I'll have to come back for that mug.

Or maybe I'll just buy a new one now that I'm going to be making real money.

Gritting my teeth, I steel my spine and keep my head up as I confidently stride past Reed into my room.

I open the door and flick on the light, exhaling a relieved breath when I discover there's no one in here. Shutting the door, I make quick work of gathering my things, snagging a duffle bag from the closet. I stuff in a couple of old band tees, an extra bra, a few pairs of jeans, and some underwear. Then, on top, I place my artist's box containing all my oil pastels, pencils, and blending tools. Thankfully it's small enough to fit.

The tools Archer gifted me are much higher quality, but I paid for these supplies with my own silvers, and I'm reluctant to leave them behind.

Hopefully I'll find time to paint again soon, to relieve stress.

Lifting the worn, tired mattress an inch off the ground, I feel around with my other hand until I locate something hard. I pull out my dad's journal, hugging it to my chest. The scent of paper, ink, and worn leather soothes me, reminding me dearly of my dad.

Even after all this time, this smell invokes the image of him. His soft blue eyes lined with wrinkles gifted from decades of smiles. His dark brown hair, speckled with hints of ashy grey.

He was my rock because my mother was so distant—mentally empty and emotionally cold. She always kept us at arm's length, so he had to take on three roles, that of mother, father, and scientist.

Striding to my tiny window, I peer out into the night, clutching the journal as if I'm holding my dad close again.

A tear streaks down my cheek, so I squeeze my eyes together to fight against the onslaught. It's no use. My eyes well up, and I clamp them shut, sliding to the floor as the tears fall.

Every few seconds, another memory of my dad passes through my mind. The tears fall harder and faster until I'm sobbing.

A minute later, I'm an ugly, snotty mess, but the release is cathartic.

The door bursts open with a bang, and I gasp. My head snaps up as I wipe at my cheeks.

Archer stands there, his chest rising and falling with vigor. In his black leather and biker boots, and with the ink lining his neck and fingers, he looks like danger. His messy hair and the menacing expression on his face tie it all together.

My stomach freefalls.

"Tasia?" he asks, gasping for breath. He shuts the door and moves to kneel beside me. "What happened?"

"What?" I sniffle, wiping the moisture from my cheeks.

"You're crying."

As he stares at me with a pained look, I smile through the tears. Despite his outer appearance, this man is so soft and sweet on the inside.

I grip my dad's journal even tighter. "Bittersweet memories," I say.

"I—" He hangs his head, running his hand through his hair, then exhales loudly. "You scared me. I thought something happened."

"I've been up here for like five minutes... I thought we agreed on fifteen?" I say, chuckling at his overreaction.

"Yes, but I saw you crying, and—"

"*Saw* me?" My smile fades, and I squint. What the hell does that mean?

"Through the window," he says sheepishly, lifting his head.

I glance at the window, frowning. We're three stories up. I passed by the window briefly, but there's no way he could have seen me from the parking lot.

As if he can sense my confusion, he says, "I have *really* good eyesight."

For a second, we sit there in silence.

"Okay, weirdo," I finally say. When he gives me an apologetic grin, I burst out laughing and playfully whack him with the journal. "I told you I'd be fine."

He reaches up, cupping my cheek and using his thumb to wipe away a lingering tear. "I know," he murmurs. "You can have someone care about you without it making you weak, you know. You're still strong and independent, even when I check on you."

My breath catches in my throat. I peer at him, processing his words. "You saying you care about me, gangster?" I whisper.

"I guess I am."

He smirks, his eyes flicking to my lips. I've never had someone care about me like this. I've never felt *worth* it. But something about Archer makes me feel calm, safe, and...appreciated. He's the first person to know about my ability—to know *me*—and even though he initially asked me to work for him, I think he cares for me beyond that.

He hasn't once made me feel used. He's barely even brought

up my ability as a soul-seer. In fact, it was *me* who asked how I could use my ability to help him.

My chest swells with affection, and I bite my lip. The warmth of his palm on my cheek heats me to the core, and I lean into it, reveling in his tenderness.

His smile grows, and he shifts closer to me.

Kiss me! I want to shout. *Kiss me, Archer Acciai!*

Suddenly, he drops his hand, pulls me into his chest, and wraps his arms around me. I let my dad's journal clatter to the floor and give in to the hug, embracing him back.

Appreciation surges through me.

He shifts from a kneeling position to sit on the floor next to me, but he doesn't loosen his grip. His arms tighten around me, and I follow his lead, straddling him and wrapping my legs around him. I try not to focus on how perfectly we fit together, how hard his cock is growing beneath me, as I bury my face in the crook of his neck, inhaling deeply. His earthy, masculine scent—with a hint of musk and ash—is a balm to my frayed nerves. I smile involuntarily, my lips skimming the tender skin on his neck.

My hips move, grinding against his hardness.

Fucking hell.

He shudders, then stills, murmuring, "Fantasia."

The sound of my full name falling from his lips sends butterflies careening through my stomach. But instead of pushing for more, or letting carnal instinct take over, I melt into the embrace and let him hold me, there on the floor.

His breath tickles my earlobe, eliciting goose bumps. I can't help but imagine how good that heat would be in other places. One of his hands slides up my back and starts rubbing in small, circular motions.

"Tasia?" Reed's slurred voice cuts through the moment, spoiling something sacred.

For a moment, I forgot where we were. I lost track of time and space. I certainly did *not* hear the door open.

Disentangling myself from Archer, I glance up to see Reed standing in my doorway, face red and features pinched with irritation. I stand up, and Archer joins me, resting his arm protectively around my shoulder.

"What're you doing here, Tasia?" Reed asks, keeping his eyes locked on Archer, who pulls me tighter against him.

My body relaxes. I'm grateful Archer came up to join me. Facing Reed doesn't seem as emotionally draining with him by my side. In fact...looking at Reed is like looking at a stranger now.

"I live here," I say, my voice void of emotion.

He scratches the back of his head, turning his attention to me. "You haven't returned my—" His eyes flick to Archer's hand, and he goes silent. "Holy shit." He steps forward, then seems to think twice and goes still. "What the fuck you doing with a motherfucking Nightcrawler, Tasia?"

"Language," Archer mutters. The humor he uses when he scolds me is nowhere to be found. With Reed, his tone is flat, unamused.

"You know excessive swearing is a sign of limited intelligence?" I say to Reed, quoting Archer.

Archer's body shakes in silent laughter beside me. Reed blinks. His eyes dart back and forth between Archer and me. He must really be an idiot—or incredibly drunk—because he staggers forward, reaching for me.

Archer tugs me closer, angling his body so I'm behind him. It's protective—not possessive—and my Gods it does something to my insides.

"I suggest you leave the lady alone," he says, his voice deep and low. It's a warning, no doubt, and it sends chills up my spine.

How could I have ever thought a man like Reed was attractive? He's immature, inconsiderate, and selfish. Archer, on the other hand, is the epitome of *hot*. The way he considers my needs, checks on me, stands up for me.

My legs go weak for a moment, and I have to force all thoughts of my attraction to Archer to the back of my mind.

"That's my girlfriend," Reed sputters.

"You sure about that? Because it certainly wasn't *your* name she was screaming when she came on my cock last night."

My mouth drops open, and I blink a few times in shock. Heat burns low in my stomach at his implication. Reed has no way to know it's a lie, and it's going to make him wild with jealousy. Despite how sweet Archer is, I'm learning he has a spicy side to him too.

Too bad he won't actually share that side with me.

"That's our private business, *honey*," I say through gritted teeth.

Archer chuckles, sliding his hand from my shoulder to my waist and giving my hip a squeeze. It sends a bolt of lightning through my core. I work to keep the reaction off my face.

Sirius above.

He's pretending.

We're just friends.

It's just pretend.

I keep repeating those words in my mind, trying to restrain the horny beast inside of me.

"You're right, *honey*," Archer says back. I glance up at him and catch him smirking at me. He winks, and I almost melt.

"Reeeeeeedy boy," a feminine voice says. The pretty redhead from the couch appears beside Reed. She places a hand with long, pointy fingernails on his shoulder, giving it a squeeze. "You're keeping me waiting."

I snort. "Classy, Reed."

My chest tightens in jealousy for a brief moment, but then Archer's fingers caress my hip. His presence grounds me, and any remaining affection for Reed that was trying to flicker back to life is lost again.

"Hold on, Rebekah," Reed says, his mouth tight. He shimmies out of her grip, pointing at me. "You broke my heart, Tasia. I fucking love you," he slurs. "We're not over."

"Tasia?" Rebekah asks.

"My girlfriend," Reed says.

"You have a girlfriend?" With a small gasp, she turns her attention to me, her nostrils flaring in surprise. She backs away from Reed, putting a hand up. "I'm so sorry. I didn't know..."

My stomach warms at the empathy in her tone. "We're not together."

She chews her lip, glancing around the room. "You live here?" she asks, as if she's piecing it together.

"Yeah, sort of," I say. Not anymore.

Her face twists into a frown. She turns to Reed, slapping his shoulder. "You brought me to hook up at your ex's place? While trying to win her back?"

Reed rubs his face. "I didn't think she'd be here," he mutters.

"You didn't think at all!" she says, a bitter-sounding laugh escaping her.

"Just—just give us a fucking minute, Rebekah."

"You're an idiot," she says. She gives me a sad smile. "*You* clearly upgraded. I could use some pointers."

Before I can reply, she turns and storms out of sight.

"Dammit, Tasia!" Reed slams his fist into the doorframe, and I flinch.

Beside me, Archer's body goes rigid. Slowly, he untangles himself from me and stalks toward Reed.

"Raise your voice at another woman, and I will ensure you

never have a voice to raise again."

The danger in Archer's tone stirs something deep inside of me.

Bending forward slightly to get on the same eye level as Reed, Archer says, "Now, apologize to my lady."

I don't miss the way he says *my* lady, and I have to work to keep the stupid grin off my face.

Reed's body jerks, and then he nods slowly, as if in a haze. He turns his attention to me, and for the first time I notice how blown out his pupils are. The last bit of my heart breaks for the little boy I once knew, for the man he grew into. I'm not shocked he's on drugs, but I am disappointed.

As much as I loathe Reed these days, I don't want to lose him entirely. Not to his own poor choices. At least the fog of teal wafting around him tells me he's likely not on the dust.

"I *am* sorry, Fantasia," Reed says, his face hauntingly hollow and his voice flat. "So sorry."

He turns back to Archer, who says, "Now leave us."

Reed nods, turning and leaving without any fuss.

The whole exchange has been bizarre, and I stand there wondering what the hell just happened.

Archer whirls toward me. He reaches out to cup the back of my head in both hands, and then his fingers tangle in my chronically messy hair. "Are you all right?"

His eyes scan my face, as if he's desperately trying to read me. I'm tempted to pull him to me again, to place my lips against his this time. I want to push him down on my mattress and tear his leather jacket off. I want to feel his bare skin against mine.

Instead, I pull free of his touch and force a smile.

"I'm fine," I choke out.

The intensity of his stare tells me he doesn't believe me, and his forehead wrinkles in protest, but he simply nods.

I'm not necessarily lying... I *am* fine.

But I'm also not naive. I know Archer's comments and affections were just for show—first to comfort me, then to get Reed off my back. He came to offer me reinforcement against my ex.

Just because he doesn't want to see me hurt, it doesn't mean he wants me.

I am *fine*, I tell myself.

Just realizing how unexpectedly and hopelessly attracted to Archer I am.

CHAPTER 19
ARCHER

Unlike Godric, I've never glamoured someone into killing themselves. But Gods above and below, when I saw the way Reed spoke to Tasia, I was close.

This woman deserves the world and more. How she ended up

with a douche like Reed will never cease to baffle me. He royally screwed up by letting her go, but I'm damn happy he did.

Too bad I refuse to take advantage of her misplaced attraction. I refuse to be a rebound, someone she gets off with, then moves on from. I'm an all-or-nothing man, and I refuse to only have pieces of her.

One day, when I have her, it will be every ounce of her.

But I have to push that thought aside for now. Right now, I need to get her out of here. Once her ex is gone and my emotions are in check, we finish gathering up her things and head for the door.

Just as we exit the apartment, Stace grabs Tasia's arm. I suppress a growl, stepping in close.

"It's okay," Tasia says with a sigh. She shakes her arm free. "What do you want, Stace?"

Their other roommate, the curly-haired girl with a permanent scowl, pops her head out of the door. Then she emerges and closes the door behind her, joining us in the stairwell and crossing her arms. She has what appears to be dried paint all over her shirt and arms—hues of green and blue. I sniff the air. Acrylic.

"No—eff this," Tasia says, her voice hard. The absence of her usual swearing surprises me, and my brows rise. She might consider me a criminal, but I'm apparently influencing her positively. My chest swells with pride.

"It's important," Stace says. "Please?" She juts her lips out in a pout, and her blown-out pupils make the expression seem overexaggerated.

Tasia hesitates, glancing back and forth between her roommates.

The painter-girl sighs, uncrossing her arms. "I didn't sleep with Reed," she says, then narrows her dark eyes at me. "Can you go or something?"

After a few moments, Tasia jerks her chin toward me in what I interpret as a subtle "go on" movement.

I nod, shifting her duffle bag higher on my shoulder, but before I leave, I move toward Tasia's roommates. Glancing at each of them in turn, I say, "You will not harm Tasia in any way. You will look out for her, always."

The women go blank, blinking a few times before nodding in assent.

"Archer," Tasia whispers, tugging my arm. "Stop being weird." I pull back, giving her a wink.

I've been quite liberal with my use of glamour around Tasia. Not once have I made an effort to conceal my own abilities. In fact, she knows I can scent death before it happens. Yet she never asks questions, never acknowledges it. It's sad that she's stifled her own magic out of shame and fear, and it's almost hurtful that she's so willing to ignore mine.

Maybe one day she'll ask, and I can give her my truth.

For now, I let her pretend with me. Pretend we are both normal, that we're not two walking death sentences in a city full of people trained to despise us.

Her brow wrinkles in confusion, and she shakes her head. She hands me her father's journal and shoos me away. "Go. Give me five."

"I'll be downstairs," I say. Leaning in, I give her a quick kiss on the forehead. She stutters, blinking up at me.

I can't help but smirk at the fact that I caught her off guard.

Once I've descended the stairs, I hide in the shadows of the stairwell, using my enhanced senses to listen to their conversation.

Even though the women are successfully glamoured and the ex-boyfriend is off the premises, I don't feel comfortable leaving Tasia alone.

"I have somewhere to be," Tasia says, her voice cold enough to freeze fire.

"Fine," Alisha says. "Then go. No one is forcing you to stay."

"Stop it!" Stace says, then sighs. "That's not— We were worried about you, Tasia. You didn't return my messages."

"I've been busy. Don't really have time for drama."

"Drama?" Alisha says, scoffing. "I never hooked up with Reed, by the way."

There's a pause. Tasia's heart rate picks up. I hate that such an ignorant boy could cause such a strong woman so much pain.

"I don't care," Tasia says. I sense an inherent honesty behind her words. She pauses, her heart rate slowing back down. "I'm with someone else now, anyway."

"Yeah, the Crawler. We saw."

"Alisha, stop being a bitch," Stace hisses.

"I'm not *being* anything," Alisha replies.

"Look, Tasia, you should probably lie low for a while," Stace whispers. "There's a reward for turning you in."

"What?" Tasia's breathing increases again. "What do you mean, *a reward*? I was on the UIS again?"

"Again?" Stace's voice holds a hint of confusion. "There were flyers with your face on them—downtown."

"They're offering five thousand fucking silvers," Alisha adds.

Shit.

I stiffen, quickly locating my cell phone. My fingers fly as I shoot off updates to Pixel and Godric, telling them to get teams on the streets—*now*. Sometimes flyers pop up around town with Godric and me on them, but our faces are normally unrecognizable, so we don't worry about it...but if Tasia's roommates recognized her on the flyers, it's only a matter of time before someone else does.

"Why haven't you turned me in?" Tasia whispers, confused.

I sift through the sounds of their autonomic nervous systems, checking for anything amiss, anything that might alert me to lies or fear or nervousness, but I detect nothing of the sort.

"Because you're one of us," Stace finally says. Fabric rustles, as if one of the women is pulling in another for a hug.

"Even if you hate us for no reason," Alisha murmurs.

"Oh, I have reasons, but we're not hashing them out now," Tasia says. I bite my lip to keep from chuckling. She clears her throat. "Thanks? I mean, thanks. Really. I guess I owe you."

"Just pay your rent until we get a new roommate and we're even," Alisha says.

The trio chuckles awkwardly, and the energy between them seems to lighten. I relax a bit. My abilities aren't a foolproof way to tell if someone's lying, but most average humans aren't trained in regulating their body's systems, so I assume the women's intentions with Tasia are honest.

Five thousand silvers is enough for most people to rethink their friendships. It's a mystery why they've not turned Tasia in, considering how strained their interactions seem to be, but I don't know enough about their history to speculate.

Their apartment door whines open, and a few people spill out, talking loudly. Tasia tells her roommates goodbye.

"I'm serious," Alisha says. "Pay your rent!"

Gripping Tasia's bag tightly, I jog toward Godric's SUV, open the trunk, and place everything inside.

"I sent out a message to the Crawlers. They're posting up around the city like you asked, boss," Godric says.

"Don't call me that."

He chuckles.

"Thank you. Now I need to recharge," I tell him. "We have to stop by the greenhouse."

"With her?" he asks.

I nod, and he meets my eyes in the rearview mirror before raising a brow and smirking. "Too much exertion, heh?"

I flip him off, and he howls with laughter before saying, "What would Sofia thi—"

I slam the trunk shut to muffle his smart comment.

When Tasia approaches, I lean against the SUV and run a hand through my hair, acting casual as if I've been here the whole time. After all the glamouring I've done tonight, I'm stretching my energy thin. Relying on my heightened senses to keep an eye on Tasia tapped into the last of my reserves.

My magic isn't endless. Just as my body requires food for fuel, my abilities need to recharge with fuel of their own.

"Let's go," Tasia says, emerging from the stairwell.

I open the back door for her, and she tilts her head up, giving me a soft smile. "Thanks."

She slides in, and I go around to the other side of the vehicle. When I enter, she gives me a questioning look. "You're a menace, you know that?"

A laugh bursts out of me. I'm not sure what I expected her to say, but it wasn't that.

Instead of replying, I take a risk and reach for her, palm-up. She bites her lip, looking from me to my proffered hand. Godric starts the engine and pulls out of the apartment complex. Finally, she accepts my hand, interlacing our fingers and scooting closer. The warmth of her skin radiates through my hand, sending an excited tingle through my veins.

It's such a simple, innocent gesture, but it's so full of meaning that it inflates me with joy.

The rest of the world melts away. It's just me and the woman who makes me smile in a city that breeds misery.

"Hey," Tasia says after we've been riding in silence for a few minutes. "Where are we going?"

We wind through the city, steel and brick buildings blocking our view on either side. Instead of going north, to Sweetcreek, we've gone deeper downtown.

"My place."

I rub the back of her hand with my thumb, hoping she doesn't choose now to press me for answers.

Exhaustion is seeping into my bones, and with the added threat to Tasia, we need to be prepared. I don't want to risk driving all the way to Sweetcreek to recharge. Not when I have my greenhouse close by.

Tasia's gaze burns into me, but I glance out the window.

I hope this is the right choice.

"It's where we grew up," Godric says, coming to my rescue.

I exhale in relief.

"You're brothers?" Tasia asks. "You don't really look alike."

Godric snorts. "No. Not in blood or name, anyway." The leather of the steering wheel creaks as he squeezes it. "Brothers in bond."

"Trauma bond," I mutter.

"We both lost our families young," Godric says. "In a way."

His father is still alive but essentially lost to him.

Tasia doesn't respond, but she grips my hand tighter. Since her parents were taken from her, she can relate. In a way, our losses connect us all. Did her roommates choose not to turn her in because they, too, know what it's like to be born into greed and sin, to have to battle their way daily toward a better life? Sure, I glamoured them, but that was after they chose to talk with Tasia instead of calling the Scouts.

All of us from the Packing District understand what it's like to simply survive rather than *live*.

Tasia pulls out her cell phone, using it as a light to illuminate her father's journal. She flips through the pages carefully. A few minutes later, she gasps.

"What is it?" I ask.

"Nothing," she mutters. "Or—I don't know. I think it's nothing." She points at a page toward the end of the book. "Here. What do you think this means?"

I read the words.

The city's heart beats to the rhythm of forgotten songs, but the symphony lies within. Remember, all that glitters is not silver. I shall lay bear the truth in the end.

"Was your dad a musician?" I ask, scanning the lines.

She shakes her head. "No. His mother was. He named me Fantasia after her. My name means 'musical composition' or something like that." She sighs, snapping the journal shut. "I just can't help but feel like there's a message I'm missing. Songs... Symphony... He's trying to tell me something." Sighing in frustration, she turns to me. "Am I going crazy?"

"Of course not, Tasia."

"It's probably nothing," she mutters, then snaps a photo of the page before stuffing the journal back into her bag.

A short time later, we pull into a poorly lit alley. Further down the alley is an entrance to the Underground. Normally I can see it from here, but with my magic running low, my eyesight has been reduced to that of a regular human. It's not a comfortable feeling—I waited too long to recharge.

"You're safe," I tell Tasia again, just in case she needs to hear it. "I need you to stay with Godric. He'll take you up to my ma's old apartment."

She whips her head around. "You're leaving me?"

I grit my teeth. "I need to take care of something."

"I'm coming with you."

"No," I say firmly. "Go with Godric."

"You can boss Reed and my roommates around all you want,

but that shit won't work on me, Archer Acciai."

Godric stifles another laugh from the front seat. "For real."

"What?" she asks, turning her scowl on Godric.

"Nothing," he says. "Come on, let's go, sassy. Leave your stuff. We'll come back for it."

She starts to protest, her lips turning down into a frown. My chest warms at the realization that she *wants* to be by my side. But I need to recharge, and I need to do it alone.

"I'll be quick," I promise. Godric turns, giving me a nod before exiting the vehicle. We've worked together long enough to read each other. He's giving me the go-ahead. All is clear.

"Look, Tasia," I say. I want to be up front with her, but I don't have the energy to dive into details right now. "I need you to trust me." I pull her hand to my lips, planting a kiss on her skin before releasing it. "Stay close. Stay out of sight. And don't tell anyone where you are."

"Someone is searching for me," she whispers. "They're gonna find me."

"No they won't."

"I don't know what they want from me." She glances out the window into the darkness.

Godric opens her door, and she steps out, giving me one last long look before following him out of the alley and to the apartment building's front door. I trust he'll keep her safe. I own the entire building, and no one else lives here. Rarely does anyone even go into the building, since the lobby looks derelict. But even if someone did, the stairs and elevators are warded—unusable to anyone except Godric, me, or anyone of our blood. Who knows? Maybe one day Godric's father—Remy—will take up my offer and move in.

One can hope, after all.

Taking a deep breath, I exit the SUV and head deeper into the

SHADES OF SILVER CITY

alley. I reach out and touch the brick wall. With my weakened vision, I have to fumble around to search for the door.

A few seconds later, I finger the latch and slide it open, pushing the door and stepping inside. The stairs take me two stories down into the earth.

The Underground.

The room I emerge into is bright, humid, and filled with greenery. It's not anything to boast about, just a moderately sized room filled with plants. I take a deep breath, inhaling the pungent, floral aroma. Beneath my feet is dark-brown, fresh-tilled soil.

Grow lights hang overhead. They're on a self-regulating timer, to mimic the sunlight. Sprinklers are arranged in rows, keeping the plants watered and the air humid.

A variety of pothos, ivies, and monsteras crawl around the room, their vines and leaves twisting up the walls and interlacing with one another.

A sense of relaxation eases through me, drawing me deeper into the room.

It's not enough. I need to be closer. I need *more*.

The quicker I can close everything out, the quicker I can replenish my stores. That's part of the reason I didn't want Tasia here with me—she would be a distraction. I need to be alone for this.

I shed my clothing until I'm fully nude and take a seat on the warm soil. Closing my eyes, I steady my breathing and find my inner peace. In a way, it's sort of like meditation.

The city leaders think the iron-and-salt walls are the most efficient tool for keeping fae out, but really, it's the lack of nature. Fae need nature to recharge.

The steel, metal, and glass buildings do enough to repel magic on their own, and most fae avoid the city by choice.

I continue inhaling and exhaling deeply. Each breath seems to bring me back to life, and my magic courses through my limbs. A pulsating tingle works itself through my body, from my head down to my fingers, then down my legs to my toes.

There's another reason I didn't want Tasia here with me. It's because her magic is artificial and seems to come at no cost to her. If she were here, I don't know how she would react. I fear she would look at me differently...that instead of seeing our similarities like she does now, she will only see our differences.

> *"THE BEHAVIOR OF ARTIFICIAL MAGIC WITHIN HU-*
> *MAN HOSTS DIFFERS FROM THE NATURAL MANIFES-*
> *TATION OF MAGIC IN FAE HOSTS... THE ARTIFICIAL*
> *MAGIC APPEARS TO DEMAND LESS MAINTENANCE;*
> *HOWEVER, CONSTRAINTS EMERGE AS POWER LEVELS*
> *ESCALATE."*
>
> -EXCERPT FROM THE PERSONAL JOURNAL OF DR.
> CLAUDE FOSTER, DIRECTOR OF FAEOLOGY AT MES-
> MERIC LABS

CHAPTER 20
FANTASIA

Godric leads me to an elevator that takes us up ten floors. When the doors open, the hallway we enter is dimly lit. The worn carpet has a mix of geometric patterns and stains. I wrinkle my nose as the scent of mildew and dust invades my nostrils.

"Where the hell are we?" I whisper, not wanting to raise my voice and shatter the eerie silence. Archer said this was his mother's old apartment, but this place is hauntingly empty. Not a soul to be found.

The only reply I receive is the groaning of old pipes. Godric gestures for me to follow him further down the hallway. I hesitate, glancing around at the rows of doors before shuffling after him.

At the end of the hallway, he stops, and we enter one of the rooms. Inside, he flicks on a light, and I glance around, taking in the sight of a cluttered but clean apartment not much different from my own.

Books are scattered on every surface—the coffee table, the two-person dining table, the long counter that separates the living room and kitchen.

The fridge is covered in papers and pictures. I stride toward it, viewing the various images of Archer at all ages. Many of the images have Godric, Sofia, and the dark-haired woman I saw before—his mother—in them.

Godric remains near the door, fiddling on his phone. After about twenty minutes of perusing the photos and books in tense silence, I turn to him.

"We grew up here," he finally says, shoving his phone into his pocket. His face is rigidly impassive, as if he's suppressing his emotions. "My parents left when I was young, so Archer's family looked after me."

It doesn't feel appropriate to ask where his parents went, so I nod, offering him what I hope is a sympathetic look.

"We both loved Sofia," he says as he pulls a photo off the fridge. Longing fills his eyes as he stares at the image. "In different ways."

The door creaks open, and Archer steps inside the apartment. His hair is even messier than usual, and his shirt is rumpled. Frowning, I scrutinize his unbuttoned jeans.

"You left us for a quickie?" I say, narrowing my eyes. It was meant to come out as a joke. There's no way I believe Archer would hold my hand one minute, then leave me to spend time with someone else...

Right?

A sharp, annoying pain pierces my stomach.

Archer gives me a tight-lipped look as if to say, "*Really?*"

My eyes travel downward, to his unlaced boots, covered in dirt.

He glances down, then quickly slides his boots off.

"Where were you?" I ask.

"The Underground." He brushes past me, into one of the rooms beyond the kitchen. "I'm changing really quick. Then we can go."

Okaaaaay.

I raise a questioning brow at Godric, but he turns away from me, striding to the window and focusing his attention outside.

Whatever Archer was up to, it doesn't concern me, so I plop onto the sagging sofa and browse through more of the books on the coffee table.

The Lost History of Silver City

What Lies Beyond the Wilds

The Science Behind Magic

"Interesting reads," I mutter.

There's no dust or grime in the apartment, and it smells like dried herbs, which leads me to believe that Archer spends more time here than he does his house in Sweetcreek. It would explain why his house is so bare and empty.

I have plenty of stuff, he said.

A thin, unlabeled leather spine peeks out from a stack of books on the coffee table. A weird sense of familiarity crawls up my spine.

I glance over my shoulder. Godric is still at the window, his back to me. Quietly, I slip the thin book out from the stack and examine the cover.

Everything around me fades away.

I go still, blinking a few times, as if that will clear away the image before. My veins go cold, and an uncanny feeling swallows me whole.

It looks identical to the journal I left in Godric's car. I flick through the pages, immediately recognizing the handwriting.

Dad's.

Unlike the journal I have, which is filled with scientific speculation, words of wisdom, and rational advice, this one is filled with formulas, scribbles of nonsensical numbers, random words, and tons of scratched-out bits.

Without hesitation, I stuff the journal under my shirt, jumping to my feet. I turn, bumping into Godric's broad chest.

"Gods!" I scream, almost losing my balance.

"No—just God*ric*." He backs away, not bothering to steady me, his brow furrowing. "You okay?"

"Fine," I say. "I just...need a minute."

Without waiting for him to respond, I bolt out the apartment door.

"Where are you going?" his voice carries down the hallway.

I run until I hit the elevator, then start jamming my finger into the button rapidly.

Nothing happens.

"Fuck," I say. Pulling the journal out of my shirt so I can continue running, I turn and locate the stairwell. "Double fuck!"

I burst through the storm door, taking the stairs two and three at a time. My lungs threaten to explode as I spiral downward. When I finally hit the first floor, I double over, catching my breath.

Attempting to quiet my sharp gasps, I listen carefully. The

stairwell is silent.

Either they're not following me, or they somehow got the elevator to work and are already waiting in the lobby. I've been a fool to trust Archer. What was I thinking? He has one of my dad's journals.

He *knows* who my dad is. How could he not? The title page literally says "Dr. Claude Foster" in big letters. And I've mentioned my dad was a faeologist.

Like Archer said before, there is no such thing as a coincidence.

Stupid. Stupid. Stupid!

Sucking in another big breath, I grip the journal and bolt from the stairwell, rocketing straight for the lobby door and out onto the street.

I glance around, ensuring I'm in the clear before rounding the corner into the alley.

Archer knocked me out once before; I wouldn't put it past him to do it again. When I reach Godric's SUV, I yank on the door handle. To my dismay, it's locked.

Cursing under my breath, I kick the tire angrily. My foot bounces off the rubber, making my toes throb with pain.

I'll have to leave the other journal.

"Tasia," Archer says from behind me. "What's wrong?"

"Stay the fuck away from me," I say, turning to face him. The alley is dim, save for a little yellow light seeping in from the streetlight, and it's blocked in on three sides. A dead end. The only way out is the way I came in—past Archer.

"I never meant to keep it from you," he says. His voice is strained, a little desperate even.

For a moment, he sounds so broken that I give him the benefit of the doubt. He has his own abilities—he's never kept that a secret from me—so what if my dad experimented on him, too?

Maybe his possession of my dad's journal isn't nefarious at all...

"You knew who I was," I say, taking a gamble to try and uncover his intentions. "When you met me."

"Yes—no." He takes a few hesitant steps toward me. I stay rooted in place, to make it clear I'm not afraid of him. "Not at first. I found out shortly after we met."

"You knew my dad?"

"No. I knew *of* your dad." He glances over his shoulder, toward the street, then back to me. "Can we please go inside and talk? I wanted to tell you...but it's not safe out here."

"Why do you have his journal?" I ask, my voice breaking.

"Let's go inside."

"No!" I find my voice this time, saying louder, "Tell me why, Archer."

"Because your dad is the one who created dreamdust."

If I thought my heart had been ripped in half before, it's absolutely obliterated by this damning statement. I almost lose my grip on the journal, but then I squeeze it tighter, until my fingers ache enough to distract me from the emotional pain.

"No he didn't," I whisper. "Why would you say that?"

"Tasia..." Archer steps toward me. "Please listen to me." When I hear how sincere, how sorrowful his expression is, the truth sinks in. "He was the original designer of the drug."

"Is that why he was killed?" My mind races with possibilities and explanations. No. It doesn't make sense. "He worked for the city. The city funded his studies..."

"I don't have answers for his—"

"Then why do you have *this*?" I wave the journal in Archer's face.

"Because I wanted to find a cure, Tasia. My sister was hooked. No one had answers. I couldn't fix it—even with my abilities." Turning away, he runs a hand over his face and walks in a small circle. "I thought if I found who created the drug, I could find an antidote."

"Did you?"

"No."

Archer stops pacing. He faces me. He throws his hands up in defeat.

"I found more questions than answers."

"That's why you're so upset about the drug being back..." Pieces start to come together, filling the gaps in my mind.

"We thought we got rid of it all. Claude was—he was unable to make more. I had his only journals."

"Except one," I add, gesturing toward the car where my dad's other journal—the one with information about *my* magic—sits.

Archer goes silent, glancing away and scratching the back of his neck—something he does when he's nervous or uncomfortable, I've noticed.

"Wait," I say, my rage building. "Is this why you got close to me? To take the journal? Search for answers?"

"No—" He groans. "This wasn't supposed to happen." After a few seconds of silence, he sighs. "I'm the one who brought that journal to you after I found it." He says it so quietly that I almost convince myself he didn't say it all.

The journal did show up randomly one day at my foster home—two years after my parents' deaths. I assumed my dad had left it for me but that I'd somehow overlooked it in my grief. I thought it was his way of explaining everything, making it easier for me to live with what he'd done to me. I was young, so I never questioned how or why. I even speculated that it might've appeared by magic, like what he'd infused me with.

"It showed up two years after his death," I say stupidly. I was ten.

"I was sixteen," he says. "Young and reckless. I broke into his lab—stole his work. His research didn't help me find an antidote to the dust. I still lost my sister that year."

The air drains from my lungs as I process this new information. "I'm sorry, Archer." A few beats pass. "Why did you bring that journal to me? Specifically?" I whisper.

"Because...the first page said: 'To my Fantastic Fantasia—'"

"'—everything begins with a...dream,'" I finish. The air whooshes out of my lungs as that dedication takes on new meaning.

"It wasn't too difficult to figure out who Fantasia was."

But I still don't understand why Dad would have dedicated his soul-shade research to me. Why he would have injected me so young. Why he seemed to anticipate his impending death. Nothing makes sense.

"Do you think—"

A white light from behind Archer blinds me. I flinch, putting my hands up and squinting. Two pairs of metallic boots make their way into sight. The light is too bright to allow me to look directly at them, but there's no mistaking the Silver Scouts.

Time slows. I forget how to breathe.

"Fantasia Foster, AR 362, under direct order of the High Chancellor, you're under arrest."

"I HAVE A HIGH LEVEL OF CONFIDENCE IN THE STABIL-
ITY OF MY mRNA FORMULA, TO THE EXTENT I WOULD
ASSERT A WILLINGNESS TO ADMINISTER INJECTIONS
TO PERSONS OF PERSONAL SIGNIFICANCE. HOWEVER,
SUCH A SCENARIO REMAINS PURELY HYPOTHETICAL,
DUE TO THE ETHICAL AND LEGAL RAMIFICATIONS..."

-EXCERPT FROM THE PERSONAL JOURNAL OF DR.
CLAUDE FOSTER, DIRECTOR OF FAEOLOGY AT MES-
MERIC LABS

CHAPTER 21
FANTASIA

"**G**entlemen," Archer says, the epitome of nonchalance.

I squint against the light, keeping my hands up in front of my face to block as much of the beam as I can.

Archer takes a casual step forward, and the Scouts swing the light onto him.

"Stay where you are!" one of them says.

"Put the light down," Archer says in a commanding voice.

My mouth drops open. I'm tempted to yell at Archer, tell him to stop being a fucking idiot before he gets us both killed, but I'm too afraid to speak.

The Scouts obviously don't relent. They step closer.

"On your knees, now!"

"Drop your weapon," Archer says, his voice wavering slightly.

"By order of the High Chancellor, we are authorized to shoot on sight if you are uncooperative."

At this, Archer gives me an indecipherable look. Putting his hands up, he slowly drops to his knees. "Stall them, Tasia." His voice is calm, steady. "Don't worry about me. They won't shoot *you*. Stall them."

"I said shut up." One of the Scouts steps forward, hitting Archer in the head with his weapon.

The air catches in my throat, and I gasp as I watch him topple over and hit the cement with a *thud*. Every fiber of my being begs me to run to him, to check on him, but the persisting memory of the Scouts killing my parents keeps me rooted in place.

They *can* and they *will* end a life if they choose.

I stay frozen, careful not to even breathe too loudly, for fear of offending the Scouts. I'm already under arrest; there is absolutely nothing I can do to avoid being taken in. Archer can't possibly know they won't shoot me unless he believes they're intent on bringing me in *alive*.

The light is finally lowered, and the Scouts make their way toward me with iron cuffs. I notice they both have prominent soul-shades—one a bright orange, the other a translucent blue-green.

It shocks me that their soul-shades aren't black—the color of evil. Not for the first time, I wish my dad would've finished his research, so I would be able to understand the differences in color. The Scouts are inhumane, and I refuse to believe they're anything less than evil.

"What am I under arrest for?" I ask in a high-pitched voice. "I didn't do anything."

"Shut it," one of the Scouts spits.

"How much does the city pay you to turn on your own people, huh?" I glare at them. "Does it feel good? Working for the wealthy and shitting on your neighbors for a few silvers? Your friends and family proud of you? Fucking traitorous—"

"Don't make me shoot you."

"You won't." Then, playing with fire, I say, "You're supposed to bring me in alive."

"Don't even bother reading her rights," the Scout says to the other. "Just cuff her."

"What about the guy?" He nudges Archer with his boot.

"Don't fucking touch him!" I growl.

"He only wants the girl. Leave the—" A strangled cry rips from his throat.

The other Scout whips toward his companion. The lamp on his helmet spotlights a large, black beast that has its fangs buried deep in the first Scout's leg.

In a flash, the beast releases its grip and lunges toward the other man. A *bang* echoes through the night as the Scout fires his weapon, but the animal sinks its teeth into his arm, unaffected.

As quickly as the commotion started, the alley grows silent again. Both the Scouts are slumped over on the ground. Their chests still rise and fall, but they're out cold.

I carefully step back, not wanting to instigate the beast.

Too late.

It pounces, and I scream, closing my eyes.

I wait for the pain to come—the savage puncture of teeth.

Giant paws land on my chest, and something wet swipes my cheek. I flick open my eyes to face the beast, only to find that it's—

"Scathe?" I whisper. "Holy shit."

I drop to my knees, wrapping my arms around the Shepherd's furry neck and inhaling his sweaty canine scent. After a brief thanks, given in the form of *good boys* and pets, I take the Scouts' weapons and slide them under Godric's SUV, out of reach, and crawl over to Archer.

Placing two fingers on his wrist, I check his pulse.

It's strong and steady.

Thank Sirius.

Tears stream down my cheeks as I pull his head into my lap and brush his bangs to the side. There's a gnarly lump on his temple and a bloodied gash cutting across his forehead.

My stomach quivers with rage, but I swallow it down.

"Scathe," I whisper. "Where's Godric? Can you get Godric?"

His ear twitches, and for a second, I'm convinced he can understand me. But when he looses a low whine and steps up to us, nudging Archer's hand with his snoot, I lose hope that he understood my request.

I glance at the Scouts. How long will they be out for?

I need to get Archer out of here. We're stuck in a dead-end alley. I don't have the keys to Godric's SUV. Maybe if Archer has his phone on him, I can find Godric's number and call him.

Patting down Archer's leather jacket and jeans, I locate his phone. Using his thumb to unlock the screen, I open the contacts and scroll down to Godric's name. I press the *dial* icon and let the phone ring.

No answer.

I call twice more.

Nothing.

I shoot him a quick text, letting him know it's an emergency and Archer's been hurt.

Scathe whines again, nuzzling Archer's cheek.

"I know, buddy," I say. "I know."

"Tasia?" Archer's croaky voice says.

"Oh shit! Thank Gods."

Coughing, he struggles to sit up. "Language."

When he meets my eyes, humor twinkling in his expression, I don't hesitate; I launch myself at him, wrapping my arms around his neck.

"Thank the Gods," I repeat, burrowing my face into his neck. We're both sweaty messes, but I couldn't care less. "Your dog saved me."

"I told you you're safe with me... With *us*." His hands splay out against my back, holding me in place. "We got you."

We pull apart, and he stands, reaching down to pet Scathe. "Thanks, bud."

"He b-bit them," I stammer, pointing at the Scouts with a shaky hand. "They just...dropped."

"Good."

"How?"

"He's not a Belgian Shepherd." Archer clears his throat, sharing a glance with his dog. "He's a...rare breed with a toxic venom."

Scathe lets out a happy bark in response.

A thousand questions run through my mind. I swallow down that information for now. We can come back to it later. After all, I've seen weirder things in this city. "Archer...this is my fault. Stace and Alisha—they warned me there's a bounty on my head."

"I know." He grimaces.

"Someone knows we're here. We led them to your mother's. I'm so sorry."

"The building is warded," he says. "You're safe...inside."

"Warded?"

"It's a—type of magic. Like glamour for objects instead of people."

"Yeah I figured it— The hell is a glamour?" I mutter. "No wonder your gang goes undetected through the city. You guys use magic. Do you work with the fae?"

"Not exactly." Archer hovers over the Scouts, checking their pulses. Then he pulls back, stroking his chin repetitively. "My glamour didn't work," he mutters. "It should've. I've recharged."

So *that's* how he's been getting everyone to do what he says. Holy shit. My eyes widen. Except...if he can force people to do what he wants...

"Archer Acciai, have you ever glamoured me?"

He turns to me, blinking a few times as if processing my question. "I tried once—the night we met."

My shoulders relax. "You felt wrong, couldn't go through with it?"

"No—you were immune."

I snort a laugh at the unexpected answer. The Scouts' prone bodies sober me up real quick though, a grimness taking over again. "Like them?"

"No." He shakes his head. "Different. Unless they have magic—which I doubt—these guys must've already been glamoured...by someone else."

"Uh, who else can do that? Kinda rare, right? In a city full of *humans*?" I take in the rich golden aura around him, reminding myself that he *is* human, after all. Fae don't have soul-shades. At least not ones we can see. My dad was certain.

"You'd be surprised," he mutters.

"Can Godric glamour?" I ask. Archer gives me a look of surprise. I take that as a yes. "Speaking of, I tried to call him."

Archer reaches for his phone, glancing at the screen with a

scowl.

A brick drops into the pit of my stomach. "Would Godric—would he turn me in?" I ask, unsure.

"Never." But Archer's features tighten in contemplation, which does little to settle my nerves.

"He said he loved Sofia..." If he knows who I am, who my father is, he likely blames my father for Sofia's death. "What if he wants retribution? What if he takes it out on me?"

"I trust Godric with my life, Tasia."

"He knew we were here. He can glamour. He likely hates me. Archer, I'm no detective, but that sounds like means, motive, and opportunity to me."

"Never..." Archer runs a hand through his hair, sharing a look with Scathe. The two engage in some sort of unsettling, silent conversation. After a few seconds, Archer breaks into a run, beckoning for me to follow.

We enter the building and head straight for the elevator. Archer pushes an unlabeled button. It turns black, then lights up with a green glow.

Well shit, that would explain why I couldn't get the damn thing to work earlier.

When we get to the tenth floor, we sprint down the hallway to find Archer's old apartment door wide open. Books lay scattered around chaotically, and pages flitter across the ground, as if someone has just strewn things about.

The small table is broken, the two chairs on their sides.

"Godric?" Archer calls out.

I notice a pair of shoes peeking out from behind the kitchen counter. "Over here!"

We rush toward the kitchen. Godric's on his back. Blood gushes from his abdomen.

"Shit," I say. Instinct takes over, and I grab a hand towel from the counter, pressing it to his wound. "I thought you said the building was safe!" I snap at Archer.

"It should've been," he growls. He whips out his phone, calling someone and barking out instructions.

When he hangs up, I give him an apologetic look. "Guess he wasn't the one who turned me in?"

Archer sighs, rubbing his brow. "I need to let the guys up. The elevator is only supposed to work for us." He gestures at himself and Godric, confirming my earlier suspicion. "Stay here. Scathe will stay with you."

He pauses long enough to give his dog a serious look, then jogs out of sight. Scathe whimpers, licking my hands as I hold the towel against Godric's wound.

"For such a vicious creature, you're a softie," I whisper. "Just like your daddy, huh?"

Scathe's blue eyes twinkle with mischief as he lays down beside Godric. With Godric's wide frame taking up most of the floor, the three of us barely fit in the narrow kitchen.

"You've lost a lot of blood, my friend." My eyes wander to the fridge, finding the photos of Archer and his family. There's no father figure to be found in any of the photos. Nor are there any girlfriends. It's only Archer, Godric, Sofia, and their mother. "I hope for Archer's sake, you're okay, you big brute." I sniffle, trying to hold back the tears. "You're all he's got." My voice cracks.

Scathe whines, lifting his head to nuzzle my hands again.

"In here!" Archer yells from the hallway. I turn my head, using my shoulder to dry my face while keeping my hands on Godric's wound.

A flurry of boots pound into the apartment, and everything moves in a blur. Archer pulls me off Godric and into his arms, hugging me tight to his chest. We break apart to watch a couple of Nightcrawlers put Godric on a stretcher, stabilizing him and toting him out of the apartment.

A guy with a lime-green mohawk, which somehow almost perfectly matches his soul-shade, and a half-dozen jingling bracelets turns and salutes us, saying, "We'll bring him to Doc's. He'll be fine. Strong pulse. Superficial wound. Looks worse than it is, boss."

I notice this man doesn't have the gang logo on his hand, like the two carrying Godric's stretcher.

Archer gives him a responding nod and says, "Call me the moment he's awake, Zeke."

I stare at the spot in the kitchen where Godric was lying. The off-white tile is stained bright red. The pool of blood is so large that I don't know how Godric could possibly be okay.

"Someone's coming to clean it," Archer murmurs in my ear. "He'll be okay."

I vaguely register myself nodding. He takes my hand, even though his friend's blood stains my hands, and he leads me to the bathroom.

"I dropped the journal," I mumble. When Archer doesn't reply, I repeat myself, staring at the toilet. "I dropped the journal."

"It's okay." He squeezes my hand.

Letting go, he reaches over to turn on the water. He checks it every few seconds, and when it's a temperature he approves of, he turns to me and askes, "Clothes on or off?"

"What?" I frown.

"You're in shock, Tasia. I'm not letting you leave like this." He glances at my hands. "Let me get you cleaned up. Clothes on or off?"

"Off," I murmur.

He nods, working efficiently to pull my shirt over my head. He fiddles with my bra, struggling to unclasp it, but I don't help him. I don't want to touch it and stain it. It's stupid, but it's all I can think about.

After he successfully removes my bra, he works the button of my jeans. But there's nothing sexy about it. Nothing in Archer's expression tells me he's enjoying this. He's careful not to touch my exposed skin, and he keeps his head down, staring intently at the floor.

"I need you to lift," he says.

"What?"

He gives my pants a tug, and I realize he means I need to lift my foot. I oblige, one foot at a time. I repeat the movement as he slides off my panties.

When I'm fully naked, I step into the shower. Archer sheds his leather jacket, shirt, and pants, joining me a moment later wearing only his boxers.

Once I'm standing beneath the spray of water, staring at the spiral of red twisting down the drain, the tears fall.

I stand there and cry as Archer washes me. Once he's done, he slides down into the tub and pulls me into his lap. The water sprays over us as he hugs my naked body tight to him. The skin-on-skin contact is amazing, comforting. It's an intimacy I've never experienced before, and it makes me sob harder.

I cry because I'm fucking exhausted and overwhelmed.

Because I thought my dad was the good guy, but I didn't know him at all.

Because I wanted there to be meaning to the magic he injected me with...but I'm nothing more than a subject for his studies.

Most of all, I cry for Archer and all he's lost—and for Godric and what he almost lost.

CHAPTER 22
ARCHER

"I'm fine, brother," Godric says for the tenth time. "Your girlfriend is fine, too."

"She's not my girlfriend," I mutter.

"You sure about that?" Godric side-eyes me, and I face forward, continuing to walk through the tunnel. The packed dirt muffles our footsteps, but our voices echo and carry through the tunnel.

"What are we, twelve?" I ask.

Godric barks a laugh. I'm glad he's able to heal faster than regular humans. It's probably why he's alive despite losing so much blood last night.

"You like her."

I grunt.

"You *really* like her." He snickers again. The only reason I let him tease me is because I'm so damn happy he's up and fine. "When's the last time you got laid, brother?"

"You know I don't sleep around," I growl.

"It's fun. You should try it."

"I'm not like you."

"Ah, that's right. You need connection and love and all the fluffy feelings to get off." I elbow him, and he stifles a laugh. "Do you cry and tell your dick *I love you* when you masturbate?"

"Shut the hell up, Godric."

"Holy shit, I got you. I finally got you riled up. *She* is your weakness."

"Not all of us lead with our dicks," I mutter. "Some of us actually have brains and morals."

Godric coughs, then chuckles. "You know, both your pulses skyrocket around each other."

"Have you considered maybe it's because I'm stressed out?"

"Is that what they call *aroused* these days?"

"Good Gods," I mutter. "Glad you're feeling better, but you're pissing me off. Yes, I like Tasia. Now leave it alone."

Godric snickers. "That's the first honest statement out of your mouth today."

Once again, he's trying to provoke me. Normally, it doesn't bother me, but today my self-control is weak. Yesterday's attack roused a dormant fury inside me. I'm sick of always doing the right thing only to end up losing the people I care about.

If something were to happen to Godric...or Tasia...

"You still don't remember anything?" I ask, switching to a more comfortable conversation.

Godric grunts. "Nothing new. Only what I told you. Heard the door open. Thought it was you or Tasia coming back. The room went dark. Woke up at Doc's."

"You didn't hear or see anything else out of the ordinary?"

"Like I said, nothing."

Soon, we reach the end of a tunnel, and I push open a metal storm door. Muffled cries fill the dark space. I reach around, searching for the string I know dangles above. When my fingers brush against it, I give a tug, and dim light washes over the room. Two men, bound and gagged, sit in the middle of the space.

The foul stench of sewage assaults my nose. One of them has apparently soiled himself. Without their Scout uniforms, they look weak and pitiful. They sit there glaring at us in nothing but their briefs. Neither is particularly built, and both have pale skin, as if they never see the sun out of uniform.

"Pathetic," Godric mumbles. He steps toward one of the men, ripping the gag out of his mouth.

The man immediately spits, and Godric backhands him, drawing blood.

Bending forward, Godric says, "Tell me your name."

"Roman," the man says, dazed.

"And your partner?"

"Paul."

Godric turns to me, a smug look on his face. "Minds are pliable again."

"Hmmm." I consider this for a moment.

Stepping forward, I level my gaze with Roman. "Who gave you orders to arrest Fantasia Foster?"

The man opens his mouth to speak, but nothing comes out. His eyes widen as he tries to say something again. He can't. It's as if the glamour hasn't fully worn off... Or perhaps it's not glamour at all but something more powerful keeping the men from speaking.

"Fae?" I ask Godric. "Or artificial magic?"

"Whatever it is, it's strong as fuck."

I can't imagine the fae would enter the city to glamour a couple of Scouts into hunting a random bartender. There's something missing here... Artificial magic seems more likely, especially considering how corrupt the city's elites are. I wouldn't put it past the High Chancellor in particular to find a way to use magic in his favor.

And there's only one place that manufactures magic: Mesmeric Labs.

It all leads back to the lab. The dreamdust, Tasia's magic...

When I went back to the alleyway yesterday, the Scouts were still knocked out, but Godric's SUV had been broken into. Tasia's dad's journal was gone, stolen along with the one she dropped in the scuffle.

Perhaps they assume she knows something about her father, or maybe they think she's a risk. That she might expose them. It could explain why they want her out of the equation.

Even if these men were glamoured to stay quiet, Godric should be able to use his ability to sense the truth. We might be able to work around it.

I turn my focus to Roman. "Where were you before arresting Fantasia Foster?"

"Mesmeric Labs," Roman responds.

My jaw tightens, and I lean against the wall, watching with rapt attention as Godric takes over the line of questioning.

"With Paul?"

"Yes."

"Were you injected with something?"

"No."

Godric and I exchange a look.

"Who was the last person you talked to at the lab?"

Silence.

"What was the last thing you remember?"

The Scout blinks a few times, as if he's puzzled. "I—I don't know."

"Who are you working with?"

More silence.

Godric takes the gag out of Paul's mouth, glamouring him into obeying his commands, then repeats the same line of questioning.

We get the same answers.

"Come on, Godric," I mutter. "We're going to Mesmeric."

Leaving the men behind in the makeshift dungeon, we head back to Nightcrawler headquarters to get set up for a nighttime escapade.

Two hours later, I'm tightening my grip on the gas canister as we trudge through the tunnels, away from the inner city and toward the outskirts.

"You sure this is the right thing, boss?" Godric keeps pace with me, his voice gruff.

I hate that he calls me that, considering it's a title I didn't technically earn. It could've just as easily been him leading the gang. He's always been stronger than me, physically and mentally. I've been kinder, more patient, but that's gotten me nowhere. All it's gotten me is a fridge decorated with memories.

"I'm sure," I say.

"It's barely gonna make a dent. Most of the building's fire-proof."

"It's not about burning it down. It's about making a statement, showing them they have enemies—and we're powerful, too." Powerful enough to get past their guards and onto their precious property. Brave enough to take a stand and openly show opposition. "Sometimes, to cut the head off the snake, you need to smoke it out first."

Godric makes a contemplative noise. "You're gonna be late for the shit in Sweetcreek."

I don't care about being late to the masquerade. I'll get there eventually.

"It's now or never."

I focus on the sloshing sound of the gasoline, willing time to go faster. We could've taken the streets, but with the Scouts out for blood, I didn't want to risk it. Someone already made it past my apartment's wards. I can't even guarantee the Underground is safe anymore, but it's safer than the streets above.

"You good?" Godric asks.

I'm a coiled spring filled with tension, but I swallow it down, keeping my focus on the winding tunnel before us. "All good."

A short while later, we emerge from a warded door and step out into an alley. Behind us, the entrance to the tunnel disappears from sight. Glancing around, I examine the dark alley before trudging toward the main road. It's a quiet street on the very edge of the city. The area is mainly open space and government buildings, such as the Ministries, which are mostly empty tonight.

The lab sits straight ahead—a two-story building with a row

of smokestacks toward the back and a distinct lack of windows. An electric fence runs along the perimeter, and there is a small, shack-like building serving as a check-in point by the street.

My phone buzzes, and I glance down at the text.

Pixel: Cameras are offline. You're good.

Nudging Godric, I show him the message before typing out one of my own.

Me: Did T get the dresses and shoes?

Three dots appear and disappear, and then Pixel's response comes in.

Pixel: Affirmative.

I sigh in relief and stick the phone back in my pocket. If Tasia doesn't want to go tonight, I'm not going to force her. This morning, she seemed back to her normal, dynamic self. She swore she would go with me to the ball but was fairly uncommunicative otherwise. When I tried to talk to her about last night, she brushed it off like it was no big deal.

I hate that she stuffs her emotions down so deeply and won't talk to me about how she's truly doing.

Godric and I make our way toward the security shack, sticking to the shadows as we cross the street. Godric and I move forward, ready to glamour our way into the property.

I grit my teeth, clutching the gas can and reminding myself *why* I'm doing this. Tasia and Godric could've been taken from me too easily last night.

I've been too dismissive of the threats facing the people closest to me...too passive in ensuring their safety. What's the point in trying to cause the least amount of harm possible when it ends up hurting me and mine?

A Scout exits the shack. "Name and purpose," he says. I swiftly step toward him. "What do you—"

"*Quiet,*" I say. "Eyes on me."

The Scout's face goes slack, and he stares at me expectantly. Godric steps around us, entering the shack to take care of any remaining Scouts.

"You will not remember anything from tonight," I say, digging deep into my reserves to instill the glamour. The deeper it runs, the more magic it requires, and the more drained it leaves me. My next instruction is lighter, less taxing on me. "Leave and go home. Now."

The Scout nods, walking away in a dazed state. A moment later, his companion exits the hut doing the same. They both walk down the street without looking back.

Then Godric must hit a button or something, because the electric gate slowly wheels open, and he exits the shack.

"Let's go," he says.

I hand the canister to him and watch as he douses the ground with gasoline, creating a trail up to the lab. The building is made mostly of steel, to protect the chemicals and experiments inside, undoubtedly, but a good chunk of the front offices are made of wood and glass.

Once Godric has emptied the container, he backs up, joining me a good distance away from the building. He pulls a pack of matches out of his back pocket.

"Wait." I reach out, stopping him from striking the match.

Every time I blink, I see Godric lying in his own blood on my ma's kitchen floor. I see Tasia's shell-shocked face as she stands before the Scouts. I see her crying in the shower over wounds I can't see.

I see the look on my ma's face before she left the apartment for the last time, never to return.

I see Sofia's face, pale and gaunt, as she seizes from too much dreamdust and fades from the world.

And then, it's as if the pipes inside me burst, letting out the rage I've stifled down. This lab and its drug are not taking anyone else from me. Whoever is behind it will pay dearly.

Red fills my vision as I snatch the box from him. I strike a match, holding it up in front of my face. I stare at the flickering flame, and its heat reaches out as if it's itching to burn something to the ground.

Tasia's sobs in the shower last night gutted me.

"Never again," I mutter.

Her father might not have hurt her physically, but he hurt her nonetheless. Everything vile in this city can, in some way or another, be traced back to Mesmeric.

With zero remorse, I toss the match. The moment the flame kisses the spilled gas, it ignites into a roaring monster. Heat bursts over me, gripping me with its intensity. Fire explodes down the slick line, ready to consume the building.

"Come on!" Godric yells. He tosses the canister into the grass, and we break out into a run.

We barely make it across the street when the explosion rocks the world behind us, the blast forcing us to the ground. Debris clatters all around us. I cover my head with my arms. My ears ring, and I glance back at the inferno.

What did I just do?

I never get my hands dirty.

Ever.

Not even after losing Sofia. But the thought of losing Tasia, too? It shattered something crucial inside of me.

Godric is the first to get up. He rushes to my side. His mouth moves rapidly, but I can't hear what he's saying. A persistent, high-pitched tone reverberates through my skull. A sharp ringing.

Flames burst up into the night sky, reaching for the stars and consuming the front of the lab. The sight is so bright that I'm forced to squint.

What did I do?

My gut sinks as the gravity of the moment settles in.

What bothers me most is not that I did it, but that I'd do it all over again.

For her.

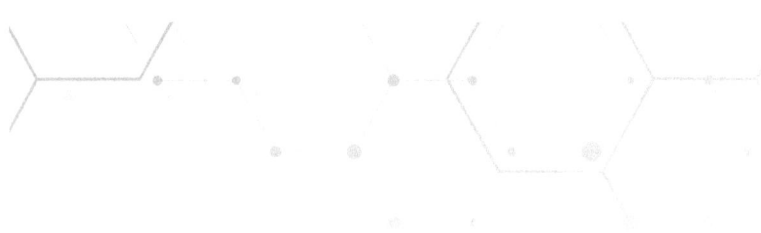

"...HUMAN PERCEPTION IS LIMITED TO THE STAN-DARD SPECTRUM OF COLORS AVAILABLE—BETWEEN 400 NM TO 700 NM. I HAVE YET TO UNLOCK THE ABILITY TO PERCEIVE ELECTROMAGNETIC RADIATION BEYOND MY ORDINARY RANGE, BUT THE FAE HAVE SOUL-SHADES, AS DO ANIMALS. THEY ARE SIMPLY IM-PERCEIVABLE BY THE HUMAN EYE."

-EXCERPT FROM THE PERSONAL JOURNAL OF DR. CLAUDE FOSTER, DIRECTOR OF FAEOLOGY AT MES-MERIC LABS

CHAPTER 23
FANTASIA

When I agreed to work for Archer, I thought we'd be out in the Packing District, scouring for soul-shades or something dramatic. I pictured us fighting the Reaper, knocking that shadowy fucker back to the Wilds or whatever realm he crawled out of.

I did *not* think I'd be sitting in Archer's house getting ready for some bullshit ball a day after almost being arrested by the Scouts, a day after seeing Godric almost die on the floor. I will never forget how his ribs expanded and deflated beneath my palms, his breathing coming in shallow gasps.

My heart hasn't slowed its pace all day, and I'm still jumping at every sound. Honestly, I think I'm on edge because Archer isn't here. Scathe's around, though, which is the *only* thing settling my nerves.

Taking a deep breath, I lean closer to the bathroom mirror and apply another coat of lipstick. It's an expensive matte shade called Black Cherry—Mellie gifted it to me for my birthday last year—and it's so dark it's almost black. It, combined with the winged, smoky eye makeup, contrasts sharply with my pale skin and hair, making for an incredibly dramatic look.

I might feel like shit on the inside, but at least I can use my makeup as a mask to help me hide.

A trio of sharp raps on the bedroom door causes me to jump.

"Sirius A!" I call out, my hand flying to my chest. I take a few breaths to quell my pounding heart. "Already?!"

Archer said he wasn't going to be here until ten to pick me up, and it's only—

I glance at the time on my phone.

Oh.

10:00 p.m. on the dot. The event starts at eleven. I was told this by Pixel when she dropped off dresses for me. A midnight masquerade.

Cursing under my breath, I adjust my nose ring and dart out of the bathroom.

"Give me ten more minutes," I say as I whip open the bedroom door. "I'm almost..."

I forget what I'm going to say as I catch sight of my fake date for the evening.

Archer leans against the wall across from my door, ankles crossed.

He wears the most elegant suit I've ever seen up close. His black jacket is adorned with textured beading, perfectly accented by a gold vest and matching bow tie.

My cheeks heat as I ogle the way the fabric hugs his strong thighs and tapered waist just right. Everything is fitted—not too loose, not too snug—as if the outfit was made just for him.

"Hey," I say breathlessly. I get a whiff of something like gasoline and smoke—it's faint but prominent enough to make me curious. "Why do you smell like you just came from a bonfire?"

His face darkens, but he doesn't reply. He runs a hand through his carelessly styled dirty-blond hair. My eyes linger on the dark ink marking his neck and hands. Something's different about him tonight.

There's an air of danger about him.

Squinting, I notice that his soul-shade is a little richer than normal. A honey-gold, rather than the bright, iridescent gold it normally is. I frown. Are the lights playing tricks on my eyes?

Or am I perhaps misremembering the hue? It's still gold, after all.

"Tasia?" he mutters.

Our eyes connect, and my mouth dries out. His gaze bores into my soul, heating me from the inside out. For a moment, neither of us says anything.

His eyes slowly roam my body, and his forehead briefly wrinkles in confusion before he quirks a brow.

I can't stand the intensity, so I cross my arms and break eye contact in favor of scanning his body again. He holds something shiny in his hand, but I can't quite make out what it is.

"What are you wearing?" he asks, his voice low.

The deep baritone rumbles down my spine.

"I lost track of time," I say. "All I have to do is change and fix my hair. I'll be quick."

I spin around and step deeper into the room, but his fingers gently skim my wrist. There's nothing aggressive about it, and he doesn't grab me. Based on the tenderness in his touch, he only means to snag my attention, and it works.

Pausing, I turn back around to face him. His nostrils flare, and he licks his lips before looking away.

"I meant...*what* are you wearing?" He gestures toward my outfit, and I look down. "Did you go through my things again?"

Embarrassment floods my face as I realize I'm dressed in his boxer briefs and another one of his shirts.

Then I remember that the few items I packed got stolen from his friend's car. I incline my chin and shoot him a challenging look. "What else was I supposed to wear?"

He looks taken aback. "I sent you clothes."

That he did. Or rather, he filled the closet in the guest room with a plethora of brand-new items. Smoothing my hands down the shirt I'm wearing, I meet Archer's gaze. "You can return them." His forehead wrinkles again, but I continue before he can misinterpret the meaning behind my words. "I don't feel right accepting a bunch of stuff I don't need. I have my own, perfectly good wardrobe at my apartment. Use that money on someone who needs it."

His face softens. "I'm sorry."

"It's fine." I shrug, not wanting to make the guy feel bad when he's going out of his way to help. "We can get the rest of my shit after the masquerade or something. Or tomorrow. Whenever you're free."

I forgot to look for my bear.

He nods, scanning me again. "Whenever you want, Tasia."

As his line of sight drops down to my bare legs, his lips tighten. He runs a hand through his hair and turns away, swallowing thickly.

"I didn't mean to make you uncomfortable," he says in a gruff voice. "You can wear whatever you want of mine."

The last thing I need is to be further indebted to Archer. But I don't tell him that—he'd have a counterargument. Instead, I touch on something that might resonate with him.

"You understand what it's like, right? Coming from nothing?" I know he does. I saw the apartment he was raised in.

His head jerks up, and he stares at me for a second before giving me a sharp nod. "I do."

"So you get why it's weird for me—living here?" I wave a hand around. "And accepting so much stuff I really don't need?"

He runs a hand over his jaw. "Trust me, I do."

A look of regret crosses his face, and I realize something.

"It's why your house is so bare, isn't it?" I ask softly.

A small, disbelieving laugh bursts from him. "Maybe we understand each other better than we'd like to think we do."

We study each other for a beat, and my hands grow clammy as his eyes dart around my face, as if he's desperate to read the words written beneath my skin.

"Yeah," I whisper. "Maybe." I clear my throat. "Hey, why the hell do you have such a fancy-ass couch though? Of all things."

"I bought it at an auction."

I can't help but laugh at the sheepish look he gives me. "An auction?"

"A charity auction."

"Oh." I cock my head, seeing him in a new light. "Charity for what?"

"Supporting educational rights of foster children," he mumbles. "So, about the clothes. I'll return them. We'll get the rest of your stuff tonight."

I figure the conversation change is purposeful, so I don't push, but his kindness warms my heart.

Twisting something in his hands, he says, "I came to give you this."

He lifts an arm, dangling something from a single out-stretched finger.

"Is that a *mask*?" I ask stupidly, squinting at the gilded item in his hand.

"Yes." He clears his throat, meeting my gaze again. "It should match your dress. Scathe said you might like it."

"Scathe?" I laugh. "Okay, weirdo."

Accepting the mask from him, I run my fingers over the ma-terial. The mask is divided into two distinct halves. The first is adorned with a shiny gold surface and black detailing, while the second half has a matte-black finish with gold detailing.

The top edge of the mask, just above the eyeholes, curves up-ward in a graceful manner, forming an elaborate, asymmetrical butterfly design.

It's captivating. Elegant. With a touch of whimsy.

My eyes widen. "Wow, this is..." I whisper. The words catch in my throat.

Breathtaking comes to mind.

But it's also so not...*me*. It's much too fancy, expensive.

Maybe it can be me, though, just for a single night.

I turn away, mostly to try and hide my silly, budding smile. He chose a *butterfly*. For me. It can't be a coincidence, since he saw the tattoo on my leg the other night. My symbol of growth. Transformation. Freedom.

There's no such thing as coincidences.

I'm absolutely not this girl—the type to get glammed up, to go on fancy dates, to burst with giddiness at the attention of a handsome man—but I can't help the flutters that erupt in my stomach.

And handsome isn't even the right word for him. It's almost sinful how downright sexy he is, all dressed up.

"Thanks," I say, lifting the mask. I tamp down my smile as I try not to openly ogle him.

He gives me a coy smile, then turns and heads down the hallway, leaving me to finish getting ready.

Twenty minutes later, and my dress is on. Saying I'm out of my depth is a massive understatement. It's the fanciest piece of fabric to ever touch my skin. The dress is the color of the starless sky. Delicate straps adorned with black flowers descend into a backless top and a plunging V-neck in a risqué manner I'm not used to.

It's revealing, seductive, but at least I have a small chest, so I don't run the risk of something popping out.

The cinched waist accentuates my hips, while the billowing skirts cascade into a captivating bell-shaped mass of tulle. Ebony flowers are scattered across the fabric. The absence of color accentuates the allure, all its beauty derived from the layered textures. My hair falls freely down my back in gentle waves.

My heart hammers as I step into the hallway. Shaking out my hands, trying to brush off the nerves, I take a deep breath and head downstairs to join my not-date for our outing.

ARCHER

When Tasia enters the room, I swear to Sirius I forget how to breathe.

I'm in the kitchen, leaning against the island and having a conversation with Godric, when she descends the steps and enters my line of sight.

I trail off mid-sentence, forgetting what we were discussing.

All the oxygen whooshes from my lungs, and my head swims.

Bringing my fist up to my mouth, I bite down on one of my knuckles to keep from saying something stupid that will make Tasia uncomfortable.

Sirius knows I've already done enough of *that* lately.

Luckily—or unluckily, depending on the perception—Godric whistles sharply, catching Tasia's attention. He motions with his finger for her to twirl. Her cheeks flush, but she obliges with an eyeroll, giving him a shy smile afterward.

It sends a bolt of jealousy careening through my bones.

When her eyes meet mine again, she appears to shrink, ducking her head, as if trying to make herself smaller. She fiddles with one of the straps on the dress and keeps glancing down at herself nervously.

Gods, she is indescribably beautiful. The dress shows just enough skin to incite temptation without being gaudy, and her makeup is as bold as she is.

Except...her usual confidence is nowhere to be found.

I frown as I take her in.

"What?" she whispers, wrapping her arms around her midsection. "Do I look stupid?"

Blinking a few times, I try to process how on earth she could ever assume that.

Scathe, from where he lies in the middle of the room, angles his head toward me.

You're in over your head, buddy. Are you prepared for this?

I fight the urge to glare at him.

"No—not at—" My voice is hoarse, and I don't know if I'm replying to Tasia or Scathe at this point.

Reaching for my cup of water on the counter beside me, I gulp it greedily, unsure of what to say. I quickly turn to the sink, busying myself with refilling the cup.

"You look hot as shit," Godric says.

"Wow—thanks," Tasia replies hesitantly, as if she's caught off guard by his attention.

That makes two of us.

Whirling around, I catch them both staring at me.

I raise a brow. "What?"

Tasia's smile wavers. Godric presses his lips together tightly as he gives me a wide-eyed look I can't decipher.

I admire Tasia's appearance again. She looks like a work of art. Perfectly made-up. Impossibly beautiful.

My skin overheats, and I'm fighting a hard-on like a twelve-year-old boy seeing a nude woman for the first time.

She certainly is beautiful, but I can't help but notice her slightly slumped posture, the way she fiddles restlessly with her skirts, how she keeps double-checking the dress.

This isn't her.

Tasia is most comfortable in pants and an old T-shirt. Hell, she's probably more comfortable in a pair of my old boxers.

And what truly makes her breathtaking is her sassy, unshakable confidence.

I hate that it's missing.

Clearing my throat, I finally say, "You look better in jeans."

Immediately, I know it's the wrong thing to say, because Godric groans, and his hands fly up to his face.

Tasia squints at me for a second. Then her face falls.

Shit on a stick, you suck at this, Scathe says. *This is too painful to watch.*

With a yawn, the hellhound rises and trots out of the room.

Language!

Piss off, he says.

As I stand there trying to come up with a way to explain what I meant—that she looks stunning but shines the brightest when she's *herself*—Tasia starts chuckling. When it turns into full-blown laughter, Godric and I look at each other in confusion.

"Tasia," I finally say, "that's not—"

"Makes sense. I *feel* better in jeans." She shakes her head. "This is downright bizarre."

The knot in my chest unravels, and my shoulders finally relax a bit.

"You look unreal," I say, "and I mean that in the most complimentary way possible—"

"No." She waves a hand to cut me off. After a few more seconds of laughter, her posture becomes sturdier, and her hands relax at her sides. "Seriously, it's okay. I'm glad I look better in jeans, 'cause jeans are my jam. There is no way in deep hell I could manage a look like this on a regular basis."

She winks, and my brows shoot up.

I discreetly adjust my pants, trying to hide the effect this woman has on me.

When I first met her, this attraction came out of nowhere, quietly and subtly at first. Now, it's roaring toward me like a rabid hellhound, and I'm at its mercy.

Once I'm able to think coherently again, I reach for my duffle bag on the floor beside the counter.

"Here," I say, pulling out a pair of black satin gloves and handing them to her. "These are for you."

She immediately slides her hands into them, smiling.

"Thank fuck," she says. "I didn't do my nails." I sigh, pinching the bridge of my nose. "Don't get your panties in a bunch, Archer. I'll watch my mouth when we get there."

Godric smirks at me, and I'm tempted to flick him off, but that'll only make me look like a hypocrite.

Honestly, I'm just thankful Tasia's feeling more like herself.

Locating my own pair of gloves, I pull them on, covering my

Nightcrawler tattoo. A bit of ink spills out of my collar, still visible, but it's nothing identifying. Merely art.

Next, I pull out my switchblade and open my jacket to stick it in the holster beside my gun.

"What the hell?" Tasia says. "You're bringing a gun to a masquerade?"

I nod. "Of course."

"What if someone gives you a hug and feels it?"

I laugh. "I don't *hug* people."

Except...that's a lie, because I hugged *her*. The memory of her body in my arms, her soft skin, sends another bolt of lust downward.

It's going to be a long night at this rate.

"What if you bring someone home with you and they undress you only to find you're packing, and not in the way they expected?"

Frowning, I ask, "Why would I bring someone home with me?"

Her nose scrunches. "To fuck them?"

Before I can respond and tell her I will not disrespect her like that, even if she isn't my *true* date, Godric starts to laugh. It's not his normal short-lived laughter, either. It's a full-bodied, contagious sound that fills the kitchen with life, booming off the walls.

It's been so long since I've heard that sound that I can't even be annoyed.

"Arch doesn't *fuck*." Godric eyes Tasia appreciatively, and a burst of fire spreads through my chest again. I subtly slide over a few inches, attempting to block her from his line of sight.

Godric's eyes sparkle with mischief. He sidesteps me, leaning in closer to Tasia, whispering, "But if that's what you're looking for, I can help with—"

"I'm sure you enjoy tying up your victims and pounding them

into their next life, but no thanks," she says without missing a beat.

Red sparks flare to life in my vision as I turn my narrowed gaze to Godric. He gives me a sly wink, clearly enjoying the emotions he's riling up.

"Not your girlfriend, I thought," he teases.

"What?" Tasia asks, peering over his shoulder.

"Nothing," I say through gritted teeth. "Godric was just apologizing for his uncultivated manners."

Godric turns back to Tasia. "Sorry for being forward." He covers another laugh with a cough. "I'm sure Archer might make an exception...for you."

I sigh, giving Tasia an apologetic look. It's been a long while since I've seen this playful—infuriating—side of Godric. It's bittersweet. I'm glad it's returning, but now is also not the time.

Tasia smiles sweetly, and a bolt of desire goes through me once again.

"I assure you, I enjoy pleasure in all forms," I say, letting her interpret my words however she chooses. Then I clear my throat, veering the conversation back to what we were discussing earlier. "Godric, follow up with Zeke. See how much it'll cost to expedite the results. I'm sick of waiting."

We've had no updates from the medical examiner on whether the substance in the last victim's body matches the dreamdust. It's been a few days, and that's beyond long enough.

"Yes, boss," Godric says, pulling out his phone immediately.

Tasia watches me carefully—excitement, intrigue, and joy playing out on her face. After a moment, she averts her eyes, rubbing her arm nervously.

"Let's do the damn thing," she says.

I offer her an arm. "Shall we?"

I've always wondered if politicians have souls. Now I'll get to find out.

> *"Color is associated with electromagnetic radiation of a certain range of wavelengths visible to the human eye. The spectrum visible to humans is much more limited than what is available to the fae."*
>
> -Excerpt from the personal journal of Dr. Claude Foster, Director of Faeology at Mesmeric Labs

CHAPTER 24
FANTASIA

Splendor Hall is twenty minutes north of Archer's house in Sweetcreek. Godric is driving us in his SUV, which has freshly repaired—and reinforced—windows.

When we got into the vehicle, Archer slid into the back seat beside me instead of sitting up front with Godric, and the resulting flutters in my stomach caught me off guard. His presence has me on high alert. I've never been so attuned to someone before. Every time he shifts, my breath hitches. It's as if my body is secretly hoping for contact with his.

After what we've been through the past few days, there's no going back to being just *friends*. At least not for me. Pretending to be his date—when I want nothing more than to truly be his date—is excruciating, and the event hasn't even begun yet.

Neither man has said a single word for the entire ride. I stare out the window, watching the colorful houses and landscapes whiz by. It's so...empty and quiet in this part of the city. Unlike the PD, which is filled with constant ruckus and chaos, the streets are mostly deserted, the yards empty.

This is eerie.

Turning to Archer, who's staring straight ahead through the windshield, I study his profile for a moment. As if he can sense the heat of my gaze burning into him, his eyes snap to mine. The wrinkles lining his forehead slowly soften, and his lips curve up slightly on one side.

I twist my hand in my skirts and wiggle around, adjusting myself in the seat.

Archer's soft expression morphs into a frown. Leaning in so his breath tickles the shell of my ear, he says, "Nervous?"

I shake my head.

"You'll be great." The heat of his breath causes all the little hairs on the back of my neck to prickle, and I try to repress an involuntary shudder.

As if I wasn't already nervous, now I'm a wreck.

"Just relax and let me take the lead," he says. "Will that help?"

His scent—natural, manly, with a subtle hint of smoke—fills my nose, and my insides begin to melt.

The air between us crackles, and suddenly, the back seat is much too small. We're too close.

He pulls back slightly to scrutinize me, but he's still leaning into my space.

The car jerks, and we jolt to the side as Godric swears under his breath. Archer's arm flashes out, and he braces himself against my door so he won't crush me with his muscular body.

"Sorry bout that!" Godric calls back with a chuckle.

There's humor in his voice, but I'm too distracted to wonder if his swerving was intentional. I'm busy being caged in by Archer. Instead of releasing me, he remains there with his right arm reaching across me. His jaw clenches, and he gives me a concerned look, his golden eyes roaming my face.

"You okay?" he asks.

"Yes," I whisper. My heart thumps rapidly.

We stay like that, staring at each other, for an extended minute.

My cheeks flush. Why is he not making any move to pull back? His eyes flick to my lips, then back up. Heat builds in my stomach, blossoming lower and lower. I freeze in anticipation of his next move.

"What're you doing?" I finally mumble.

His brows rise. "Waiting for you to let go of me."

It takes me a second to realize I have him in a death grip, my hands clutching onto his biceps.

"Sorry," I mutter, releasing him.

Smiling softly, he settles back into his own space and adjusts his jacket. If my cheeks weren't already blazing before, they're flaming now.

When we pull up to the hall, my lungs squeeze. Massive spotlights illuminate the property. The angular building, made mostly of dark stone, stretches wide and tall. It has a steepled roof made of iron and sits atop a small hill. An abundance of stairs stretch from the street up to the entrance.

In the distance, beyond the hall, a section of the wall separating Silver City from the Wilds is visible.

My heart thumps in overdrive, and I lean closer to my window, desperate to get a better look. The wall has the same grim, dark coloring as Splendor Hall, almost blending into the shadows completely, and it stands at least a dozen stories high, running as far as the eye can see in each direction.

I never stray near the wall. I've always heard it's where the majority of Scouts roam, on the lookout for fae enemies who might attempt to breach the barrier.

Shuddering, I tear my eyes away from it. "I didn't realize we'd be so close to the wall," I mutter.

Godric snorts, his eyes meeting mine in the mirror. "A reminder of what the hall is for—worshiping our wonderful Council and the High Chancellor himself, for protecting us from the treachery beyond." Sarcasm drips from his words.

"I hate these events," Archer mutters, rubbing his jaw as Godric drives us closer to the entrance, where all sorts of well-dressed, masked folks climb the stone stairs. "But now that the lab's destroyed, we can see who's really behind the endeavors at Mesmeric."

We come to a complete stop at the curb. Godric puts the car in park.

"What?" I scrunch my nose. "Destroyed?"

Archer and Godric go silent, exchanging a look in the mirror. "It...burned down," Archer says. Godric makes a noise in his throat, and Archer's cheeks turn red. "I burned it down."

My eyes just about pop out of my head. "*You* burned it down?"

"Not entirely. Just a portion." He scratches the back of his neck nervously. "We have a plan. Tonight is a fundraising event for Mesmeric—or, it was supposed to be. Without a lab, there are no experiments. There is no dreamdust—so we theorize."

"But they'll just build a new lab," I say, not following.

"Exactly," Godric says.

"They need a lab," Archer says. "It'll be expensive, but those who are most invested in the lab's...research will ensure the appropriate funding is there." Archer looks contemplative for a moment. "We track the major funding, we can follow it back to those with ties to the lab."

"Why burn it down, though?" I ask. "Why not just track who donates at the event tonight?"

"It's a threat." Godric laughs. "Sweetheart—"

"Don't *sweetheart* me in that condescending tone, you asshat."

Archer chuckles, shifting in his seat and watching me with rapt attention.

"Sorry, *Tasia*," Godric mutters. "Those who fund the small events like this are mostly people with means who hope to get in the good graces of those with true power in the city."

"Those with...personal attachments or a true stake in the lab will need it built as soon as possible," Archer says. "They'll donate quickly and generously, under the guise of serving the city."

"Why exactly does it matter?" I ask, eyeing a woman with a gorgeous teal dress and a peacock-feathered mask as she walks past our car, headed toward the stairs. Her soul-shade blends with her outfit almost perfectly.

"Eyes on the enemy," Godric says. "That's why it matters."

"There will always be another lab, more dreamdust, more experiments." Archer sighs. "It will never end, unless we can find those at the top."

"And then what?" I ask.

He purses his lips and glances away. "Cut the head off the snake."

"I gotta move," Godric says. "Can't park here."

Archer pulls out our masks, handing me mine before pulling his own on. I'm careful not to mess up my hair or makeup as I slip it into place. The butterfly stretches up on the left side, reaching a few inches higher than the right. I was worried the asymmetrical design would make the mask heavier on one side, but the thicker material on the right balances the weight distribution.

His mask is much simpler than mine. Its coloring is black and gold like mine but is entirely matte, understated. It covers the top half of his face, leaving his defined jaw and soft lips exposed. I've never noticed before how beautifully sculpted his face is. Yeah, he's handsome. Hot. But with his mask putting the bottom half of his face on display, he looks downright beautiful.

Like he's on a mission to break hearts.

When he catches me staring unabashedly, his face slowly lights up. He breaks out into the smallest, cutest grin, and Sirius save me, I practically melt.

Something flutters in my stomach, and heat builds in my core again.

How can this powerful, dangerous, *asshole* of a man be so fucking *cute* at times? A gangster who helps out old ladies and blushes.

For a moment, I let myself forget that he's already turned me down once. Instead, I wonder what it might be like between us if this date were real—if I could act on my attraction to him. Before Reed, I had plenty of enjoyable encounters. But during the last year or so of my relationship *with* Reed, that side of me died. Even before that, since the beginning, our intimacy was a monotonous routine—something done out of requirement—lacking the passion, lust, and spontaneity that's suddenly begging to be released.

I yearn to hike up my dress and straddle Archer—masquerade ball be damned.

"If you two are done eye-fucking each other back there..." Godric says.

He presses the button, and the locks disengage. Archer breaks eye contact, smoothing his hand down his thigh and straightening his posture.

Godric glances at me in the mirror, and I flick him off before opening the door and jumping out, nearly tripping over my feet.

And I'm in *flats*. At least Archer had the sense not to subject me to heels.

"I was supposed to open the door for you," Archer says as he rounds the vehicle with a scowl.

Once we're on the sidewalk, Godric drives off, leaving us alone. As I watch the plain black SUV depart, I notice the windows are incredibly tinted from the outside, making it impossible to see the driver. Good.

"So you're courting me?" I ask.

He glances around, likely to ensure no one is listening to us, then leans in so only I can hear. "For tonight, I am indeed."

His low, furtive tone sends a shiver up my spine, and I narrow my eyes at him, stepping back. "Stop whispering in my ear."

His golden eyes light up in amusement, and he holds an arm out. "May I?"

I once thought his eyes and soul-shade were the same bright, rich hue. But now, there's no mistaking the fact that his soul-shade is definitely darker than his eyes...and darker than it was before.

It unsettles me briefly, but I shake it off.

Reaching up, I wrap my arm around Archer's bicep and try to ignore how solid it is in my grip. And how warm his body is next to mine... How good he smells...

"This is going to be a long night," I murmur. His body shakes with silent laughter.

As we head toward the stairs, my limbs grow heavier and heavier. There are so many people around. I scan the various soul-shades, searching for grey. Everyone is surrounded by color, but that does little to ease my panic.

My lungs tighten, and suddenly there's not enough air out here.

"I can't do this." I stop moving, squeezing Archer's bicep even tighter. "The Scouts are still—"

"They're not here," Archer murmurs. "And they won't recognize you."

That absurd thought does little to calm my anxiety. "A mask isn't going to keep them from recognizing me, Archer." It's nice to be able to use his name openly for once, because here, he *is* Archer.

Not the Phantom.

"Not only that. But they're not searching for you *here*."

The implication of his words hits me. I'm just a low-life bartender who wears stained shirts and curses too much. Tonight, I'm done up and mingling with the city's finest. I'm hidden in plain sight.

He places his hand on mine, giving me a brief squeeze that only makes me more nervous. "You're not alone. We're doing this together."

"Yeah, but I don't belong here."

"And you think *I* do?" he murmurs. "Then you don't know me at all."

Swallowing the lump in my throat, I take a deep breath. My hands shake as we continue walking. Archer reaches out to cover my hand with his, giving me comfort.

Whether it's intentional or not, it works.

CHAPTER 25
FANTASIA

We climb the stairs, keeping some space between us and all the other couples, throuples, and larger groups headed inside for the evening. Though the sun has set a while ago, it's still warm, and the humidity threatens to melt my makeup off my face. I'm tempted to speed up—to get into the air conditioner that awaits us inside, and get this over with—but based on the slow, nonchalant pace of those around us, it's not the Sweetcreek way.

Archer and I don't speak during our ascent. The confident energy radiating off his body is enough to keep me moving. But once we get to the glass doors separating us from the hall's interior, my hands begin to shake even more. My legs go weak, and sweat lines the back of my neck.

Glancing up at the intimidating building makes it worse. The entire front is made of opaque glass. I can see my reflection perfectly. Although the girl standing before me is gorgeous, I can still see the regular Fantasia Foster underneath the mask, the makeup, and the expensive fabric draped over my body.

The girl whose parents were executed by the Silver Scouts.

The girl who grew up in foster care and was repeatedly abused by the same men who were supposed to protect her.

The girl who's worked in a bar since she was a teen, serving the aimless alcoholics of the inner city.

The girl whose boyfriend cheated on her and disregarded her emotions.

I don't belong here.

I won't fit in.

I'm tempted to turn and bolt down the stairs—away from all this nonsense—but Archer releases my arm, steps ahead of me, and pushes the door open.

"Tasia," he says softly. "After you."

Cool air washes over me the moment I step inside the venue. The door softly closes behind us, and Archer approaches me from behind. He draws me in, pulling me tight to his side.

"Hey," he murmurs. When I glance up at him, he's staring down at me, reverence and adoration simmering in his gaze. He reaches up to trace the skin beneath my mask. "You are absolutely gorgeous."

"Right back atcha, handsome," I say, smiling softly.

"I'm serious." His eyes roam my face. "Any man would be lucky to have you at his side."

My heart thumps wildly. As I wait for it to calm down, I study the deep honey-colored hue around his body, and I realize that maybe he truly doesn't belong here either. As cruel and lawless as people think the Phantom is, and as rich and arrogant as people probably think Archer Acciai is, he is none of those things.

To me, he's simply Archer.

The man who's protected me, fought for me, and made me feel safe and seen for the first time in my life.

Longing swirls in my stomach, and it's suddenly so strong that it aches.

The lights flicker and go out, and I gasp. Archer tightens his grip on me as frantic muttering echoes through the hall.

A voice comes over the loudspeaker, effectively silencing us all.

"Thank you, citizens of Silver City, for joining us tonight in honor of Mesmeric Laboratories." The lights flicker back on, but this time the illumination is a dim, red hue. I blink a few times, letting my eyes adjust. "As you may have heard, there was an unfortunate event this evening, rendering a portion of the labs useless. We thank all of our patrons, vendors, and donors for being here, and we implore you to consider the implications of our loss. Our community is only as strong as our weakest, so we must work to rebuild as one."

Polite applause rings out, and I glance at Archer, trying to follow his lead. The soft expression he wore a moment ago is gone. His jaw is set tight. Without a word, he leads me toward the ballroom.

I blink again, taking in the sight of Splendor Hall. A wide hallway adorned with chandeliers leads to an open ballroom. Flowing fabrics cascade from the ceiling down to the walls, where they're tied to either side of the hallway.

Everything—the hallway, the ballroom, the twirling people and their excessive gowns—are bathed in a deep red hue.

If the masks weren't enough to keep our identities mostly hidden, this new, eerie lighting helps. It's aggressive and sensual, but it muddles the dozens of soul-shades around the room. Instead of vibrant, glowing colors, everyone has a barely noticeable fog wafting around them.

"Archer," I whisper, panic gripping me once again. "I can't make out any soul-shades in here."

He glances down at me. "The lighting?"

I nod.

"I'll get Pixel on it."

"She's here?"

He nods, scanning the ballroom. I assume he's searching for her.

On the dance floor, couples and groups dance elegantly, practically floating around one another in perfect sync. It blows my mind how they can twirl so fluidly in their billowing layers and teetering heels. A slow, lazy beat plays loudly but crisply throughout the ballroom, dictating the pace of the dancers.

Massive chandeliers made of jewels and gilded chains hang above the dance floor, and off to the sides, more excessive drapery trails from the ceiling, down the walls, and all the way to the floor. It'd be overstimulating if it weren't for the fact that all the textures, layers, and adornments bask in the same red glow.

Servers carrying trays of beverages mingle with the crowd. They wear identical, bland dresses with high necklines and skirts that skim the floor, and their masks have dark feathers on them.

When one of the servers offers up a tray to us, I politely turn them down. Archer follows suit.

"You can drink," I say. "Not that you need my permission."

He laughs softly, his eyes still darting around the room. "Not while I'm working."

I exhale in relief. There's something comforting in knowing he'll be sober tonight, too.

My gloved fingers dig into Archer's arm, and I observe his face expectantly. Soon, recognition flares in his eyes, and his shoulders relax subtly.

"I'll be back," he says, releasing my arm. "Pixel."

"Okay." I stand there stupidly, watching him stride away. "I'll just...be over here," I mutter to myself.

Across the room, a short woman wearing an owl mask and an incredibly revealing dress greets Archer with a wave. Archer doesn't slow his pace as he approaches her. He breezes by, and she turns and follows him. They make their way toward the curtains on the side of the room and out of sight.

My heart squeezes, and a flood of disappointment washes through me.

What the hell am I supposed to do now?

Eyeing a three-tiered table full of elaborate finger foods on the opposite wall, I begin striding toward it. Snacking never hurts. It'll keep my hands busy and my mouth full. Hopefully that will keep me from saying something stupid or looking like a lost lamb.

Two mini muffins later, my stomach protests, flipping itself inside out.

Damn nerves.

Sighing, I slowly stride along the perimeter of the dance floor, watching the revelry while trying not to draw any attention to myself. I square my shoulders, keeping my head inclined and my pace Sweetcreek-slow so I fit in.

The shattering of glass—barely audible over the loud music—snags my attention. Flinching, I whip toward the direction of the noise. No one around me seems to have noticed it. They are all too busy with their own conversations or dances.

An obviously drunken trio shimmies past, much too close to me, giggling as they stop to pepper each other with sloppy kisses. One of their elbows accidentally juts into me, and I scowl. They don't even acknowledge me, too lost to the sauce.

"Fun times," I mutter, stepping away. I thought I'd gotten away from this uninhibited lifestyle by coming to Sweetcreek, but apparently they indulge as much as the inner city folk do.

I used to be just like them—letting alcohol lead me.

When I first quit drinking, I had a constant nagging voice in my mind, telling me to find a drink. Take a sip. Just one.

It took at least a year of me fighting that voice to get past the craving. And now, I find it easier and easier to stay away from alcohol—especially when I see how ridiculous it makes people.

Striding through the room, I find a less populated corner to stand in.

Nearby, a woman with a long braid and a sparkling fish-shaped mask leans forward, snorting something off another woman's cleavage.

I'm about to turn away, to give them some space and privacy, when I realize the woman's breasts are covered with a glittery substance.

Not glitter.

Dust.

It's almost indecipherable in the single-hued lighting.

My hands grow clammy, and suddenly I'm wishing I could see their soul-shades, to determine with certainty that the color is still there. But I have no way of knowing.

"Come on, Archer," I mutter, needing him to hurry up with Pixel so she can get the lighting situation fixed.

My feet move of their own accord, drawing me closer to the

women.

"Hey!" I yell, but they don't seem to hear me.

I grab my skirt so I don't trip, and then I rush toward them.

"Stop," I say, planting my hands on the woman in the fish mask and pushing her away from the other's breasts.

My foot must land on her skirt, because there's a loud ripping noise, and we both tumble to the ground.

"What in the Gods' names is wrong with you!?" says the woman standing above us, who wears a fox mask. Powder still glistens on her chest. She lends a hand to her friend and pulls her to her feet. "Lennia, is this another of your lovers?"

I'm surprised when she turns her angry pout toward her friend, crossing her arms.

"No!" Lennia says. She scrutinizes me. "I mean—I don't think so."

The first woman slaps Lennia so hard that her fish mask flies off, clattering to the floor. I almost feel bad...until I remember they were doing dreamdust. Their recklessness is going to get them killed.

Rising from the floor, I say, "You shouldn't do the dust." They both turn to me. Lennia stoops to get her mask. "It's tainted," I say, taking a risk.

"Dust?" Fox-mask looks me up and down.

"Dreamdust." I point to her breasts.

"Cocaine?"

"It's— You're doing coke?" I ask, dumbfounded.

She ignores me, gripping Lennia's arm. They rush away from me, shooting me pissed-off glances as they put distance between us.

The air leaves my lungs in a rush, and I smooth down my dress. I'm just on edge. I'm being a fucking idiot.

At least we were out of sight from most people. No one seems to be paying me any mind. With a sigh, I head back toward the snack table.

I make it three strides when someone sidesteps me, stopping me in my tracks.

"My, my, my," a man whispers in a low, sensual voice, leaning down so his face is next to mine. "What a lovely little butterfly you are. Please, do me the honor of enjoying a dance with me?"

I take a step back.

His height is similar to Archer's, and he has a broad chest and muscular physique. It's impossible to make out the exact color of his hair and eyes in this lighting, but they both appear so dark that I speculate they must be close to black.

The mask he wears shines, and it looks heavy as hell. At each of his temples, the mask curves up into sharp horns.

Unease courses through me. Taking another step back, I offer the man a polite smile. "I'm a bit tired. Perhaps another time."

"Tired?" he asks, leaning closer. "Perhaps you're reserving your energy for more remarkable tackles?"

Frowning, I fight the urge to take another step back. "You've been watching me?"

Glancing around, I try to locate Archer, but to no avail.

"Your date is rather busy at the moment," he says. Then his mouth tightens and his eyes harden. "If that's who you're searching for."

I shake my head. "No." I'm about to clarify that Archer isn't my date, until I remember that he's *supposed* to be. "I mean, yeah, but he'll be right back."

"I wouldn't be so certain about that, Fantasia."

My heart skips a beat. "How do you know my name?"

He smiles, leaning in to say, "I make it my mission to know everyone of import in my city."

I almost snort but hold it back at the last second. There are over ten million people spread throughout Silver City.

My city? Who the hell is this guy, the High Chancellor? No, it can't be. The Chancellor is an old, weathered man with a cane. I've seen him on the broadcasts.

"Impossible," I say.

"Then I make it my mission to know all the *soul-seers* in my city." He winks, holding out a leather-clad hand. "So, what do you say, Fantasia? Join me for a dance?"

CHAPTER 26
FANTASIA

I reach up and accept the mystery man's hand. He knows who I am—what I am—and something tells me running won't do anything for me.

In the moody lighting, I can't see what color radiates from his body, but based on his arrogant demeanor and the way he called Silver City *his* city, I'm willing to bet he's an important man. Surely he wouldn't do anything to me here.

We walk to the very center of the dance floor. People scurry out of our way.

The man draws me in closer, and for a moment, we stand there with our bodies unbearably close, just observing one another. A nervous laugh bubbles out of my mouth.

His head tilts to the side, and the corner of his lips quirks. "Something entertaining?"

"I can't dance," I choke out.

"Follow my lead," he says.

Before I can protest, he pulls my arms up around his neck and plants his strong hands on my waist. Our bodies gently touch as we sway, and I'm not sure if I'm annoyed or grateful that the music has slowed to something that barely warrants movement.

Glancing around, I notice most of the dancers are moving similarly to us, albeit much more closely—more intimately—with their fronts fully flush against one another. One woman nearby rests her head on her dance partner's shoulder.

Thankfully, the man makes no move to pull me closer.

"What do you want?" I whisper through the lump in my throat.

"The lights are nice, no?" he murmurs. His body goes still for a second, before a low, quiet chuckle escapes him. "The red is harsh—bold enough to make a statement. Powerful."

He tilts his head down, giving me a knowing look. I try to ignore how beautiful his face is. How decadently sinfully his body moves against mine.

My cheeks heat. I hate my involuntary response to him.

"Yeah, I get it," I mutter, scanning the room over his shoulder, hoping to see Archer.

The man's body vibrates as he laughs again. Then he stops moving. One of his hands slides sensually up my spine until it grips the back of my neck beneath my hair. His fingers bite into my skin—not enough to hurt me but enough to send a searing bolt of danger through me.

"The red eats up all other colors—the predator of the

color wheel. Perfectly concealing even the most vibrant of soul-shades." Leaning forward until his lips brush over mine—not a kiss, more of a promise—he says, "Tell me, pretty butterfly—"

"Get the *fuck* away from her," Archer says from behind me, his voice low and threatening.

Sweet relief floods my veins.

The strange man releases me. "Why, hello, Archer *Acciai*."

Archer tugs me to him. His warm, firm body presses against my backside as he wraps an arm protectively around me. I shudder, relaxing into his touch.

"Arlo Osiander," Archer spits. "Finally, I can put a face to the notorious name."

"I'm impressed with your little show at the lab tonight." The mystery man in the horned mask winks. "Didn't think you had it in you." Archer makes a deep grumbling sound. The man chuckles. "No worrying. We shall keep that our little secret."

Then, not sparing Archer a glance, he stuffs his hands into his suit pockets and turns on his heel, gliding into the crowd.

Releasing me, Archer spins me toward him and cups my chin, bringing my gaze to him.

"Are you all right?" His eyes roam my body, as if he's hunting for some obvious damage.

"Yes," I whisper.

"Tasia," he says gently. "You're shaking."

He pulls me off the dance floor and into a private room beyond the curtains. Leading me to a chaise, he guides me to a seated position, then kneels in front of me. He looks like a fallen angel, with his dark mask and shining hair, his fierce scowl and tattoos. And even though I can't see his aura in this lighting, I know it's there, as golden as ever.

He's the perfect mixture of light and dark. Of purity and danger.

The emotions his presence evokes in me are so intense that I turn my gaze to the floor.

"Look at me," he says quietly.

Static runs through my veins, and I oblige, facing him. "Who was that?"

Archer opens his mouth, then shuts it, running a hand through his hair and messing up the perfectly styled waves.

"Arlo Osiander is just a rich bastard with a mysterious past. I've never actually met the guy, but I hate him more than anyone."

"Why?" I ask.

"He's up to something. Snatching up property around the city—specifically, outbidding *me* on every property I try to purchase. And I'm pretty sure he has half the Ministries in his pocket, considering I can't get permits for any of the shelters I'm building downtown." Archer grits his teeth. "It's like the guy is out to get me. And worst of all? He's good at hiding his tracks digitally. Pixel only *just* got a photo of the man recently."

"He knew *me*," I say. Was he using me in an attempt to get to Archer, since they have such a sordid rivalry going on?

Archer growls, glancing over his shoulder. "What did he say?"

"Nothing, really. You got there before he could say anything. Why did you interrupt, anyway? And don't tell me it's because you hate the guy. I very well could've gotten information on him."

He cups my jaw. "Is seeing another man's lips on yours not enough of a reason?"

I bite my lip to keep my mouth shut. My cheeks heat, and I'm glad he likely won't notice my blush in this lighting. Arlo wasn't kissing me, but I'm sure that's what it looked like to Archer.

"You're right," I say. "That might ruin our cover. Can't have someone else kissing your date."

"Tasia," he murmurs, stroking the bottom of my mask with his thumb. "It's not some *date* I care about. It's *you*."

My breath hitches, and I search his expression, trying to decipher the intentions behind his declaration. Slowly, my lips lift into a smirk. "You're jealous."

"I don't want anyone's lips on yours," he says. He slides his hand to the back of my head and pulls my face to his until our masks touch at the forehead. "Anyone else's but mine," he whispers, his warm breath fanning across my lips. Butterflies erupt in my stomach, and before I can formulate a response, he presses his mouth to mine.

His lips are soft but firm. They don't linger long. When he starts to pull back, I reach for him, fisting my hands in his shirt and pulling him back to me.

This time when our lips meet, there's less hesitation. Fire erupts beneath my skin, and it's as if I'm floating and burning at the same time.

I encircle my legs around him. With ease, he reverses our positions so he's on the couch and I'm straddling him. Our kisses grow fervent, and I moan into his mouth. Each second that passes, he hardens between us.

After a few intense minutes, the kisses slow, until we're tenderly making out. When we pause for air, we're both breathing hard.

"I can't stop thinking about you," he says. His lips meet mine again, and I breathe in his smile. "Since the moment I met you."

My heart stutters.

This is more than a hookup.

This is more than mere attraction.

I don't know exactly what it is... It's just *more*.

But...the memory of him turning me down when I laid myself bare for him is still a raw wound.

I pull back.

"Archer..." I sigh. "I'm not making a fool of myself again."

"You're never a fool," he murmurs, tenderly stroking my back in lazy circles. "I want you more than I've ever wanted anyone before."

"I feel the same," I whisper with sincerity.

His body tenses, and then he relaxes. "Then it's settled."

"What's settled?"

He pulls me to his chest and gives me a warm embrace. I've never known a comfort as warm and secure as Archer's arms. Tears prick at my eyes, and I rapidly blink them back, not wanting to smudge my makeup. Allowing my body to relax, I hug Archer back, reveling in the feel of his arms around me.

"What's settled?" I repeat.

Giving me a soft squeeze, he whispers, "You're my date tonight."

I pull back and chuckle. "With the way my lipstick is smeared all over your mouth, I doubt anyone would contest that."

"No, Tasia, you're my *real* date." He pauses. "If you want to be."

I nod. "I fucking want you, Archer. I don't know how much clearer I can be." Reaching up, I grab his hair in my fist, yanking his head back and forcing *him* to look at *me* this time. "More than just a date. More than just tonight. I want *you*."

His eyes gleam with lust and mischief, and I lean forward, peppering kisses on his jaw and neck, leaving my mark. He groans, pressing his hips up so his hardness rubs against my core. My dress pools around us, with only my underwear and his pants between us. The friction teases me deliciously.

"Do you want me?" I whisper in his ear.

"So badly." He groans.

"Tell me you want me. That you want this." Gesturing to the space between us, I unzip his pants and pause, waiting for his confirmation.

When he says, "I want it," I hurriedly work his boxers, gripping his thickness and pulling him free. "I want to feel all of you."

Spurred on by his dirty words, I tug my underwear aside, lining him up with my entrance. I don't want to waste time with foreplay. I've been craving this for so long that I'm ready for him just from making out—something that's never happened to me before.

His fingers grip my hips. "Tasia, wait," he mutters. He holds me in place, preventing me from sinking down on him. "I won't *fuck* you."

My heart drops. If he's about to reject me again with some bullshit excuse about preserving our friendship—or worse, about me *ruining* him—I'm done.

"I'm clean," I rush out. "And I'm on birth control."

His lips curve up with humor. "Good, me too. But I mean I don't *fuck*," he repeats, his eyes searching my face. "It's all or nothing with me. Be mine. Tell me you're mine."

"You sentimental asshole." I chuckle, squirming over the cock he's currently preventing me from riding. "Are you telling me you only make love or something?"

"I'm saying I won't share you, Tasia. If we do this, you're ac-knowledging that you're mine and only mine. That you're in this all the way with me."

"What happened to you saying you'd ruin me?"

A smile crosses his lips. "I don't need to *fuck* you to ruin you."

"Come on then, Phantom, show me what you got. Or are you all talk?"

Fury blazes in his eyes. He grabs my hips tighter, and I wiggle, rubbing my slickness on his thick head, begging him to enter me. "Say the words, Tasia."

"Fine." I lean forward, nibbling his earlobe. When he grunts with pleasure, I move to his neck, biting the skin there just enough to elicit a sharp intake of breath from him. The asshole did say he liked biting, after all. "I'm *yours*, Archer Acciai. Only yours, and all yours."

"Yes you are." He pulls me down, sheathing his raw cock inside of me. I gasp, and a blazing warmth spreads through my veins as he fills me.

Gripping his shoulders, I begin to move, sliding up and down as he thrusts steadily beneath me.

He fits so perfectly, so snugly, and he's hitting that place inside that causes my eyes to roll back.

"This is *my* pussy," he says, moving one of his hands up to the back of my neck. "Only mine."

"Yes," I gasp in agreement. With the sensual red lighting, the near-anonymity of the masks, and the seductive music playing around us, the pleasure is enhanced. Another strong bolt of arousal shoots through me at the realization that anyone could walk in on us.

"What if...someone walks in..." I pant as I ride him.

His breath hitches, and his thrusts increase. "You'd like that, wouldn't you? If someone pulled that curtain aside and walked in to see you bouncing on me."

His words send me over the cliff. I clench around him, finding release faster than I ever have in my life.

"Archer!" I cry, leaning forward and wrapping my arms around him. I go limp for a moment as I recover from the tsunami of pleasure.

"We're not done yet, baby."

In a swift movement, he picks me up, making me gasp in surprise. He turns me around and pulls me back down onto him, with my back to his chest, so I'm facing the curtain that leads to the ballroom. With a gratified huff, he lifts my skirts up to my waist, exposing the area where our skin meets. If anyone were to walk in, they'd see everything.

"We can give them a show," Archer whispers in my ear.

Dirty, dirty man.

He holds tightly onto my hips, dictating the pace as I ride him. Our skin makes obscene sounds as we enjoy each other. My head falls back on his shoulder. His thrusts grow deeper, faster while he pounds into me from beneath.

"I thought you said you don't fuck," I say through the fog of pleasure.

"I don't," he says, his fingers reaching for my clit as his other hand reaches up and wraps around my throat, squeezing it just enough to hold me in place against him. "I *claim*."

The beginning of another release flutters deep inside me. "Don't stop," I beg. "Please."

"You feel that?" he whispers sensually in my ear as one of his hands does wicked things between my legs while the other tightens around my throat. "This isn't sex. It isn't fucking. It's a promise. A promise to always worship every inch of you, to leave you breathless, trembling, and captivated." I clench around him, but my heart squeezes too, as his words take this union from mere physical intimacy to something...more. "I'll ruin you for every other man because I will *devour* you, Tasia. I'm claiming every part of you. The moment I entered you, I became a part of you, and you a part of me."

And then I'm crying out his name again. His words, mixed with the way he grips me aggressively while somehow still tenderly cradling me against him, make my orgasm more intense than anything I've experienced before.

The things I would do for this man...

He gives me a minute to come down from the aftershocks, but before he can readjust us again and continue to take charge, I stand. When he slides out of me, I immediately mourn the loss of his flesh against mine. It's like I'm missing a crucial piece of my essence.

I pull my lipstick from the inside pocket of my dress and apply a fresh coat, giving him a sly grin. "My turn."

"I'm not done with you, baby." His voice is stern, but he has no idea how demanding *I* can be, too.

"I said it's *my* turn." I drop to my knees between his legs. "Hold my hair."

He arches a brow and leans back against the sofa. His hard, glistening cock stands at attention between us. Before he can ask for clarification, I seize his shaft and guide it to my mouth, swirling my tongue around the tip. "Hold my fucking hair. Don't make me ask again."

"Yes, ma'am," he says, smirking as he lifts my hair away from my face. I keep eye contact while licking him gently, then sink my mouth down around his shaft. He exhales heavily, his body shuddering beneath me as I swallow him to the back of my throat. "That's my girl," he mutters.

I work him rapidly, until *he's* the one desperately moaning beneath me. "I'm gonna come," he hisses. "Tasia."

I hum in acknowledgement but continue my pace. It's enough to send him careening into the abyss. "*Yes*," he groans as his hot, thick release shoots down my throat. His hands stay tangled in my hair, and his body trembles.

After he's gone still, I pull back with a *pop*, smirking at the mess I just made of him. My dark lipstick is smeared all over the base of his shaft.

"Let *that* be a reminder of whose cock this is," I say, pointing to the territory I marked. "If I'm yours, then you, Archer Acciai, are *mine*."

"My Gods, you beautiful, wicked woman." He sits up and reaches desperately for me, pulling my lips to his in a messy kiss.

When we break apart, he gives me a dark smile. "And if Arlo dares put his lips on yours again, make sure he tastes my cum on your tongue. It'll be the last thing he tastes before I end him."

With that, he releases me, tucking himself away.

When I stand, my legs tremble, and I fear I won't be able to hold myself up. Archer is at my side in an instant, pushing my curls behind my shoulder and offering me an arm. I reach up, using my thumb to wipe away the lipstick staining his mouth, and he does the same to me.

"How do I look?" I ask.

"Like a dream," he whispers. "If beauty were a language, you'd be its most eloquent expression."

I blush, biting my lip as I glance down shyly. My Gods. "You sap! You *are* going to ruin me for every other man, aren't you?"

He smirks, leading us toward the ballroom. "It's a good thing it's you and me versus the world, baby."

We dance for a few songs before I excuse myself to pee. When I return to the ballroom, I spot Archer by the far wall, surrounded by a few important-looking men in suits. His gaze flicks in my direction, and his features relax. I send him a soft smile and a wave, at ease again with him nearby.

My legs are still jello, and the ghost of him inside me lingers. I'm oddly content—satiated.

Figuring he has work shit to do, I put up my hands in a "stay" gesture, then point in the direction of the lounge in the corner. He can come find me when he's done.

Archer Acciai is *mine*.

The thought makes me giddy.

The only open sofa is a fancy high-backed couch with soft, plush material, but it's just out of Archer's sight. I fight the urge to plop down and instead gently perch on the edge and cross my legs.

Almost immediately, a presence invades my space. Alarm shoots down my spine as I glance up.

"Fantasia," the mysterious man in the horned mask says.

"What do you want?" I stand, squaring my shoulders and jutting out my chin, showing the man I'm not afraid of him.

"Pretty, pretty butterfly. Who *are* you under that mask?"

"You already know, asshole."

"No, Fantasia. I mean under the mask you wear so well every day." He extends a hand, and his fingers graze the exposed skin on my jawline. My stomach tightens with fury, and I slap his hand away.

He leans in, undeterred, and whispers in my ear, "We all wear a mask, every moment of every day. Different masks for different situations, different people. When does yours come off? When you're all alone in the dark of night? Or do you keep it on permanently, lying even to yourself about who you are?"

I jerk away from him.

Just then, a voice comes over the loudspeaker again, talking about Mesmeric Labs and the auction items for tonight's event. I barely register it. My stomach tumbles, and I fear I might vomit.

Suppressing a growl, I say, "You bast—"

A spotlight comes on, illuminating the man before me. All eyes seem to shift in our direction.

No, *his* direction.

Scurrying backward, I quickly put a bit of space between us, not wanting to be anywhere near the large circle of light, where everyone is now focusing their attention.

The man's expression morphs into something friendlier. He waves, glancing around.

I study him in the new lighting, trying to pinpoint what exactly seems off about him.

He's not exactly familiar, but he also doesn't look like a stranger. He appears to be maybe in his late twenties or early thirties. Even in his creepy metal mask, with his haughty demeanor, the man is extremely handsome. His eyes *are* black, I notice, as they swing toward me again. The exact opposite of Archer's golden—

My spine goes stiff.

The man apparently notices, and his smile grows.

"What ever is the matter, dearest butterfly?" he whispers. It's so quiet, I almost don't hear it over the voice blaring from the loudspeaker.

"—the owner of Mesmeric Laboratories and the newest challenger for High Chancellor, Arlo Osiander!" the voice yells out.

The crowd roars, and the man before me bows, offering a few dramatic waves.

Before the significance of what I'm seeing can fully sink in, Archer reaches me. "Tasia, we need to go." His voice is a low rumble. His chest rises and falls as if he's been running.

I frown, glancing back at Arlo, who winks at me.

"What's wrong?" I ask Archer.

As he opens his mouth to respond, the lights flicker on, a bright fluorescent replacing the red glow. The crowd groans collectively. The man on the loudspeaker apologizes—says something about technical difficulties. I blink a few times to let my eyes adjust. All around us, various colors waft around the many bodies.

My stomach turns into a ball of nausea, reminding me that I hate crowds for this very reason.

"We need to go," Archer repeats, interlacing my fingers with his and pulling me away from Arlo and the majority of the crowd.

"Stop," I say. "What's going on?"

When he faces me again, he's pale. "I smell death."

A high-pitched wail rips from the crowd.

CHAPTER 27
ARCHER

"We can't just leave them!" Tasia yells, yanking free of me and stopping in her tracks.

I growl, running a hand through my hair to avoid doing something stupid like throwing her over my shoulder. We both know I'm not above doing that.

"I'm not. I'm getting *you* out of here."

"I'm not fucking leaving you, idiot!"

"Are we seriously having our first fight right *now*?"

"It's not our first fight."

I sigh. "Tasia." I shoot her a pleading expression. "Something's going on. I smell death. A *lot* of it. I need to get you—"

Another scream rings out behind us, and the people in the crowd begin jostling each other, panicking and searching for an exit.

"You need me," she says. "I can pinpoint grey soul-shades."

The sickeningly sweet scent is overpowering—more than I've ever smelled at one time. It rouses the magic deep in my gut. Something dormant, wild. Something I've never wanted to awaken.

Gritting my teeth, I bite down on my initial response. We're wasting time, and she's right. If I didn't feel the way I do about her, I'd let her help. It's not fair of me to stifle her and refuse to let her help because my heart beats a little harder for her than it does on its own.

"Fine," I say. "But stay close."

Focusing my mind, I quickly locate the mental tether leading to my hellhound.

Scathe, I mindspeak. *We might need you. Bring Godric.*

By now, most of the guests have cleared out. Only about two dozen people remain, and they're scattered throughout the room, engaging in various activities.

Or, I should say, various acts of destruction.

They all seem to have lost their minds. Fistfights have broken out, and people are violently battering one another. A few folks stand by the buffet table, sticking their hands into the food and tossing it at one another. One woman stands over a man, stabbing him with the heel of her shoe. He's long dead, his body a piece of tenderized meat.

"Oh Gods," Tasia says. She gags. "They all—their souls. *Grey*." Her voice squeaks, as if she can barely get the words out.

"All of them?" I ask. Now I realize why the scent is so overwhelming. Normally, I smell death in an isolated manner. No more than a few people at once, depending on the situation. Never have I smelled a massacre.

"We need to get out of here," I mutter. That unsettling magic inside me tries to claw its way out, desperate to get free. It swirls through me, craving release, wanting to be let out. Concentrating, I lock the cage tight, refusing to succumb. I control my abilities, not the other way around.

"We can't save them," I say finally.

I can't save them.

I ignore the guilt rising in me. It's the truth. Even though I have abilities beyond normal human capability, I'm not all-powerful.

If these people are dying, there's nothing I can do. Plus, the Scouts will be here any second.

I can't risk Tasia's life.

The woman who just murdered a man with her shoe stumbles toward us. Her pink dress is now stained with blood and food, making it look like a sort of macabre tie-dye. As she gets closer, she holds her shoe up and picks up her pace. I'm debating pulling out my gun—though I've never actually had to use it before.

With a hiss, the woman lunges.

I'm just about to throw Tasia over my shoulder when she grabs my hand. This time, she's the one who pulls me along as we run.

I'm relieved that whatever's happening isn't affecting Tasia and me.

"Wait, Archer," she says, jerking on my arm. We slow. She points to a couple of women who are beating each other beside the ballroom entrance. "Those girls...they were snorting some-thing. I thought it was dreamdust."

Frowning, I clench my jaw. "Why didn't you say anything?" I try not to snap, because it's the situation I'm angered by, not her.

"I'm sorry," she mumbles. "They said it was cocaine, so I—" One of the women, who wears a fox mask, yells something at us. Grey glitter sparkles on her ample chest. "Oh shit fuck shit."

I don't bother scolding Tasia for her colorful use of expletives. Instead, I pull her into a run again, and we exit the ballroom at full speed.

As we dart through the massive hallway, Tasia continues to curse. "It was...the dust..." she pants. "I'm sorry."

We burst out of the building, flying down the stone stairs.

Godric and Scathe run up, and we pause near the halfway mark. Tasia doubles over, catching her breath.

What's going on? Scathe says. *Is she hurt?*

"She's not hurt," I say. I rub her back in small circles. "Breathe, baby, you're okay." I turn my attention to Godric. "It's a massacre in there. Dust."

"How many?"

"At least twenty or thirty. Hard to say. They're all—"

"Where's Pixel?"

My hand freezes on Tasia's back.

Pixel.

I left her inside.

Without another word, Godric takes off running toward the building. I let him go. We both know that being around that much death is triggering for me. It could hijack my magic, awak-ening the power I've stifled for so long.

"There's something I have to tell you," Tasia says, gulping in another big breath and standing up straight. She stares past me, her eyes roaming the stairs as if she's searching for something.

"That guy—the lab owner?"

Arlo Osiander.

The insufferable cad who's been snatching up an absurd amount of properties around the PD.

Most notably the man who tried to kiss *my* girl.

"What about him?" I growl.

"He has no soul-shade." Tasia squeezes my arm tighter. "I think—" She lowers her voice. "I think he's fae."

> *"The city's heart beats to the rhythm of for-*
> *gotten songs, but the symphony lies within.*
> *Remember, all that glitters is not silver. I*
> *shall lay bear the truth in the end."*

-Excerpt from the personal journal of Dr.
Claude Foster, Director of Faeology at Mesmeric Labs

CHAPTER 28
FANTASIA

Sirens go off in the distance. Alarmed, I glance at Archer. That sound signifies the impending arrival of the Silver Scouts' armored vehicles.

"Archer..." I say, scanning the streets down below for any sign of them. Panic rises into my throat.

"I know." He grips my hand tightly.

"Archer!" a feminine voice yells. I turn to see Godric and a short redhead with a soft pink soul-shade—Pixel—exiting the building.

She runs to Archer's side. "Are you guys okay?"

"We're fine," he says. "Where's your date?"

"He left me!"

"Fucking Ministry scum," Godric growls. "I told you, if he hurts you, Pixie, he's a dead man."

The siren gets louder, drawing closer, and we all bolt down the rest of the stairs toward Godric's SUV.

We pile inside, with Pixel up front by Godric, and Archer, Scathe, and me in the back. I rip off my mask, and Archer does the same.

"Go!" Archer yells at Godric. "Get us out of here."

Seconds later, we're flying down the street, Godric flooring it.

In the chaos, I can't help but think of my dad—his final moments, which will always haunt me, but also the words he left behind in his journal.

"Arlo," I say to Archer, "he's fae."

"He owns the lab," Archer mutters. "Of course." He facepalms. "Why didn't we see it earlier?" Then, he leans toward the front seat, saying loudly, "That's why we couldn't find a record of Mesmeric's sale or new ownership. He must've glamoured his way in. Of course it's *him*!"

"It's probably how he got into your ma's apartment," Godric adds. "He has his own magic. Immunity to glamour himself, likely. He's powerful, Archer."

"That's why the Scouts were impervious to our—" Archer glances at Pixel and cuts himself off.

Interesting. Does she not know about their abilities? Right now, she seems to be in shock, staring disinterestedly out the window.

If Archer's right, and my dad created dreamdust, does that mean Arlo sent someone to steal his journals? So he could get more information from the drug's original creator?

"I bet he glamoured my dad, Archer. I'm telling you, I know my dad. He was a good guy."

His features pinch together, and he gives me a sad look. "Arlo is a new owner, Tasia. He wasn't there when your dad worked—"

"We don't *know* that. Like you said, there are no coincidences. And Arlo has a sketchy past. If it's coming out now, it's because he wants it out there. There's a reason dreamdust is back on the streets now after all this time."

"Why *does* Arlo want the dust?" Godric mutters as he cuts through someone's yard to navigate us around a traffic jam. "Why your dad's journals? *If* he was the one searching."

"Because he's looking for the original formula," I surmise. "You said it yourself; this batch is different. I mean, look at the chaos it wreaks."

The sirens grow louder, and a low, rumbling hum starts resonating through the SUV. Bright beams of light shine through the windshield. Three steel vehicles are rolling toward us. They're cold-looking, with reinforced windows and tires designed for rough terrain. A mounted turret looms atop the square frame, and I shudder. What the hell could they possibly use that for?

Instinct has me ducking down below the windows, but the vehicles shoot past us toward Splendor Hall.

"You're okay, Tasia," Archer says, rubbing my back in small circles. "You're with me. I got you."

Scathe whines, putting his paw on my leg.

I sit up straight in my seat and close my eyes, willing my heart to settle down. It's as if it beats to the rhythm of chaos these days.

That thought sparks remembrance of something my dad said in his journal.

The city's heart beats to the rhythm of forgotten songs...

My dad's words play on repeat in my mind. If the journals hadn't been stolen, I'd comb through the pages again. Read for anything I might've missed.

"Wait," I whisper, remembering that I took a photo of one of the pages.

I pull out my phone and search for the photo I took.

Dad's neat handwriting stares back at me.

The city's heart beats to the rhythm of forgotten songs, but the symphony lies within. Remember, all that glitters is not silver. I shall lay bear the truth in the end.

Dad's writing is straightforward throughout the rest of the journal. If this wasn't his handwriting, I'd almost think it was written by someone else. Something seems off about it...as if it's some sort of puzzle.

Like I told Archer the other day, the first line could be a round-about reference to me, but I don't understand what it might mean.

The second line is an ancient proverb...implying that not everything is what it appears. Sometimes looks are deceiving.

And the third line... He'll lay bare the truth? It sounds like he's admitting he'll share—

Wait.

I reread the final line my dad wrote. *I shall lay* bear *the truth in the end.*

In Dad's entire journal, I don't remember seeing a single word misspelled. He was a meticulous man. A perfectionist with an eye for detail.

"Archer," I say, frantically tapping his leg. "Look." I point to the misspelled word. "He wrote *b-e-a-r* instead of *b-a-r-e.*"

Archer squints at the page. "You think it means something?"

"It's out of character for him." I take a breath, calming my racing pulse. "His handwriting here is just as neat and tidy as the rest of the journal. It doesn't appear rushed or sloppy, so I don't think it's an accident."

The car rolls to a stop.

My head snaps up, and I notice we're at Archer's house.

"Zeke's on site," Godric says, staring at his cell phone. "I'm dropping Pixel off in the city and meeting him up at the hall."

"Keep me updated," Archer says. He opens the door, placing one foot on the ground. "I'm staying with Scathe and Tasia until we figure out what's going on."

He exits fully, holding out a hand for me. I accept it, sliding out of the car with his assistance. Scathe jumps out after.

Godric wastes no time speeding off. Clearly he has things to take care of with the Nightcrawlers.

"I need to go to my apartment," I say to Archer as we step toward his house.

"Not safe."

I knew he would say that. His first instinct is to protect me, keep me away from any harm. It's the primitive side of him. However, I've noticed I can get through to him by appealing to his logical side.

"It's a lot safer tonight than it will be tomorrow or the next day," I argue.

"After what happened at—"

"The majority of Scouts will be deployed to the hall, trying to figure out what happened. They're not looking for me while this is going on. Now is the best time to go. After this, the streets will be flooded with Scouts. I need to get to my apartment. Tonight."

He strokes his jaw, his muscles tense. "What's so important that you need to risk your safety?"

"My bear." The teddy bear my dad gave me when he was still alive. "It's the only thing I can connect to the message my dad left for me."

He nods. "Fine."

I tilt my head. "You're not going to tell me it's a stupid idea? Or that it's a reach?"

"Why would I do that?" He studies me. "If you think he left you a message, I'm inclined to believe you. It'll also be up to you to decipher the meaning, all things considered."

"All right then." I try to keep the relief off my face, but I'm glad Archer's starting to trust me as much as I trust him.

"Let me get my bike." Archer heads to the garage while I run into the house to change.

Scathe follows me like a silent shadow. His presence is reassuring.

Upstairs, in Archer's room, I exchange my dress for a pair of sweatpants and a light hoodie. It's still muggy outside, but the hood seems like a safe option if I end up needing to hide myself. Not caring to wash my makeup off right now, I throw my hair into a braid, locate some socks, and bolt down the stairs to slip into my boots.

As I head back outside, the night's events keep replaying in my mind. Everything happened so quickly. Arlo Osiander knows who I am. *What* I am.

Did he know my father?

Or worse, was he responsible for my father's death?

Archer wheels his motorcycle out of the garage. "Let's make this quick," he says. "I don't want to be on the streets long."

Scathe lets out a long, low whine that grabs our attention.

"You're not coming," Archer says.

Scathe pins his ears back and growls.

"I know." Archer pauses, and a silent stare-off ensues between them. "Okay, point made. You're right. I'm wrong." Another pause. "I'm not telling her that."

"Archer?" I say carefully, not wanting to interrupt whatever weird silent conversation he's having with his dog.

He turns to me, pink lining his cheeks, as if he's just remembering I'm there. "Scathe is..."

"Struggling with separation anxiety?" I offer when he doesn't finish his sentence.

He scratches the back of his neck. "Something like that." Then, with a frown, he pivots toward the garage. "Give me a second. I'm going to get his sidecar so he can come. He's right. His venom saved us last time. I'd feel better knowing you have both of us."

Turning on his heel, he darts over to the garage and yanks the door up. I watch the street for any sign of movement, listening for distant sirens. A few seconds later, Archer emerges, wheeling out a matte-black pod that sits on a single wheel. It has a seat inside with a protective windshield in front.

It takes him a few minutes, but he attaches it to the side of his motorcycle. As soon as that's accomplished, Scathe jumps in. Archer reaches into the storage compartment of his bike, pulling out a small helmet and attaching it to Scathe's head. It has a little visor that flips down, protecting his eyes.

It fits perfectly.

The sight is so adorable, my chest pinches.

"You have to be kidding me," I say, giggling. Even with all the darkness in the world, there are moments of utter happiness. Seeing a dog wearing a helmet is one of those moments.

Unable to resist, I snap a photo of Scathe, then bend over to give him all the good-boy loves.

Straightening, I turn to Archer and point at him. "You and I are having a talk after all this."

"I hope we have many talks," he says with a wink.

"I'm serious!" I give him a look that means business. "I've ignored your weird"—I glance around and drop my voice to a whisper—"weirdness long enough. I have questions."

"And I'll give you all the answers." He steps forward, placing a hand on my waist and dropping a kiss on my forehead. "After we get your bear."

We put our helmets on and straddle the bike. I wrap my arms around Archer's body, nestling into his back. Unlike last time, I let myself melt into him, reveling in the feel of his strong muscles, gripping him as tightly as possible. It's insane how quickly a night can go from perfect to shit.

One moment, I have this beautiful specimen of a man inside of me, worshiping me, and the next we're running for our lives.

"Ready?" he yells over the soft purr of the engine.

"Yes!" I call back.

We take off, flying down the road. Once again, a rare sense of freedom takes over my body. It's as if I'm weightless, soaring through space and time. I'm untouchable, invincible.

We slice through the night, toward the inner city. In the distance, the city's glow emerges, a tapestry of twinkling lights.

I glance at Scathe, who's staring straight ahead, his tongue lolling out. For a moment, everything falls away. I'm just a girl, on the back of a guy's bike, hanging out with him and his dog.

With each second that passes, the distant lights grow brighter and the ragged skyline grows sharper. Soon, we're winding our way through the great labyrinth of glass, metal, and asphalt, greeted by the restless city center.

Streetlights and neon signs brighten our path, and vehicles and pedestrians appear on the streets alongside us. The skyscrapers seem to swallow us up as we head deeper into the city.

We pull into my apartment complex and park. The motorcycle's hum fades into silence while I swing a leg over the side and dismount. Warmth radiates through my inner thighs, and my legs continue to vibrate.

"I'll be right back," I tell the boys as I pull the helmet off and hand it to Archer.

Scathe whimpers.

"He's going with you," Archer says.

"No," I say sternly. "You two need to stay here, in case we need to dip. I'll be quick."

Staying vigilant, I throw the hood up over my head and tuck away my bright hair. I pat Scathe on the helmet before turning to bolt up the stairs.

Tonight, the building is mostly quiet, no parties raging on. The knot in my chest loosens. Without knocking, I use my key and enter my old apartment. It's dark, other than a neon-green light seeping out of Stace's open door.

Not wanting to alert anyone to my presence, I sneak toward my room. As I pass through the living room, a shadow moves in the kitchen to my right, startling me.

"Reed?" I whisper, squinting at what looks like my ex-boyfriend's silhouette by the sink. I flip the switch on the wall, wincing at the onslaught of fluorescent brightness that washes over us. His teal soul-shade billows out around him, and I exhale heavily, relieved after everything I've seen tonight.

Reed's reddish hair sticks up in all directions. There are bags under his eyes and a stress wrinkle in his forehead.

After connecting with Archer—giving him my all—I no longer have even a flicker of attraction toward Reed.

I do, however, harbor great concern for the friend I once had.

"The hell, Tasia?" he rasps.

"What are you doing here?" I ask.

He mumbles something incoherent.

I glance at Stace's door. Did she hear me enter? When I face Reed again, his tired expression morphs into something else entirely. Concern slithers down my spine. "Are you all right?"

The whites of his eyes are bloodshot, indicating he's on something. Again.

I sigh, my shoulders drooping. Reminding myself that I can't help someone who doesn't want to be helped, I hustle to my room to grab my bear. Reed doesn't follow me, which is just as well. I don't have time to worry about him.

The small space is almost unfamiliar to me now. The bed is rumpled, as if someone recently slept there. My few remaining belongings are scattered around the floor. I kick a pair of jeans away, sifting through my clothes and blankets.

Where the hell is my damn bear?

Seconds later, it hits me. The night I slept at The Rising Star, I snagged my bear and used it as a pillow.

"Shit," I groan, fighting the urge to rub my face. All my makeup from the masquerade is still on, and I'd rather not smear it.

Pulling out my phone, I shoot a text to Mellie, asking if she's seen my bear. I wait a few seconds, and when the dots don't appear, I stuff the phone back into my pocket. I'll just have to check. If it's not there, I've lost it.

I take one last look around my room. At the lopsided mattress resting on the floor. The chipping plaster. The single window overlooking the parking lot. Compared to Archer's old apart-ment, it's depressing. He might've lost his family, too, but his apartment is filled with photos and memories. Filled with love.

This place isn't my home. I don't know where I belong, but it's not here.

I text Archer, letting him know everything is good but I need a little more time. For the next ten minutes or so, I pick up the mess in my room, double-checking for anything I might want to take with me. After witnessing the casualties tonight, my *stuff* all seems so invaluable or meaningless. So replaceable. Nothing in this room matters as much as the people around me.

Like Archer.

And he seems to thrive on caring for the people around him, protecting them. So maybe I'll just start fresh and let Archer take care of me after all.

With what feels like finality, I turn the light off and exit the room, shutting the door behind me. Something tells me I won't ever sleep here again.

> *"The ethical implications of my experiments weigh substantially on my conscience. My resolve remains steadfast, however, in the pursuit of a benevolent future."*
>
> -EXCERPT FROM THE PERSONAL JOURNAL OF DR. CLAUDE FOSTER, DIRECTOR OF FAEOLOGY AT MESMERIC LABS

CHAPTER 29
FANTASIA

A shattering sound causes me to gasp, and I whip toward the noise. Reed and a brunette girl stand bent over the counter side by side, giggling. Splintered chunks of white ceramic lay broken at their feet in the kitchen.

"Is that my mug?" I storm toward them, picking up the big pieces and confirming it's my favorite coffee cup. "Fucker."

"It's just a cup," the girl says. Her tone comes across as reassuring, rather than cruel or apathetic, but I take a deep breath to keep from cursing her out regardless.

She's right. It's *just* a cup.

Reed bends over the counter and snorts loudly. A second later he stands up, shaking his head and pinching his nose, then inhales sharply.

My stomach roils at seeing the man I once knew—the boy I thought I loved—spiraling. Without thinking, I grab his shoulder and pull him back.

"Reed—" I trail off when I catch sight of the substance on the counter. Glittering grey. "What did you do?" My voice sounds hazy, far away. I barely recognize it. "Reed, what did you do?"

"It was free!" The girl giggles. "Some guys in masks were handing it out downtown."

Reed laughs, and it's a dry, empty sound.

And then it's as if time slows down and speeds up all at once. The air around him, a faint teal hue, begins to waver, slowly desaturating before me.

It fades from a blue-green ocean to a cloudy sky.

Paler and paler.

"No," I whisper. "No. Not you, you son of a bitch!" I want to reach out and slap him for being so fucking stupid. I want to hug him, tell him I'm sorry for turning my back while he was clearly struggling. But the way the color is leaching from his soul-shade tells me it's too late.

I turn to the girl, gripping her shoulders.

"Ow!" she says. "The fuck is your problem?"

Ignoring her, I take inventory of her soul-shade—a bright, strong magenta. It seems to be holding steady. I inspect her nostrils, searching for any sign of the sparkling powder. "Did you take any of that?"

"Not yet," she says, wiggling out of my reach.

"Don't," I say, my voice as cold as a corpse. I wanted confirmation that the dreamdust was responsible for killing souls, and now I've got it.

But at what cost?

The girl goes still, studying me for a second. Whatever she sees in my expression must affect her, because she gives me a slow nod. I release her, and she pulls away, darting out of the kitchen and toward the front door, taking her bright aura along with her. I don't bother watching to see if she leaves.

I don't care.

Turning to Reed, I catch him as he leans forward to snort more of the powder.

"Stop!" I yell, grabbing his arm and yanking him back. "It'll kill you."

Reed whips toward me, a hollow smile on his face. "Tasia," he slurs. "I've missed you."

Sluggishly, he loops his arm around my waist, dragging me close to his body, but I push him away. He stumbles backward into the counter. A dark laugh comes from him, and quicker than I expect, he lurches for me, wrapping his fingers around my throat.

"Ree—" My voice sputters out as he cuts off my oxygen.

"Didn't you miss me?" he asks, his voice becoming steadier. The aura around his body is fully grey now, a depressing fog that hangs over him like a storm cloud.

It's too late for him.

I choke, my lungs burning for air.

My vision starts to go black.

It's not too late for *me*.

Using all my force, I bring my knee up into his ball sack. He doesn't double over the way I expect him to, but he does release me for long enough that I'm able to turn away and try to run.

In an instant, he catches me by the waist. I scream as he

spins us both around and presses my front against the fridge. Instinctively, I throw my head back, hoping to slam it into his nose, but I only hit air. He must've dodged me. I wiggle and thrash, desperate to break his hold.

The dust seems to have given him some sort of abnormal power or insensitivity to pain, because Reed has never been this strong. No man can bounce back from getting his ball sack hit that hard.

"Tasia? Reed?" Stace asks, her voice higher-pitched than normal. "You guys okay?"

Reed keeps his hips pressed against me, pinning me in place. His other hand toys with my throat, squeezing hard enough that I can only let out a strangled gasp. "None of your fucking business," he says, his tone devoid of emotion.

"Tasia?" Stace asks again.

"We're making up," Reed barks. "Tell her," he whispers so only I can hear. "Tell her to get the fuck out." His fingers tighten ever so slightly in warning before loosening to allow me to speak.

Stace might not be my favorite person, but she had my back when the Scouts were searching for me. She warned me. She didn't turn me in.

I can't let her get hurt because of Reed—because of me.

"Leave us alone, Stace," I croak out.

"Are you—"

"Get out of here," I say. "Give us some space for once, dammit."

"Fine," she whines, obviously hurt. "I'll be in my room."

"Get out of the *apartment*," I hiss. Hopefully she'll pick up on my tone and leave. She'll spot Archer downstairs. I don't need him to save me, but my Gods, I do appreciate him being here.

Reed pets my hair, calling me his *good girl*, and my stomach clenches violently. I swallow the rising bile while he continues to feed me a quiet mixture of sweet nothings and cruel warnings.

A moment later, Stace sighs. Soft footsteps patter away, and the front door clicks open and then clicks shut. My body slumps, relieved that she listened to me.

Reed releases his grip on me just enough that I'm able to wiggle free. Quickly, I spin around, striking his nose with my open palm.

"You bitch!" he shouts. The back of his hand whips out and strikes my cheek so quickly that I see stars and taste blood before I register what happened.

Of all the ways I thought I might meet my death, I never would've guessed it'd be in a fistfight with Reed.

I've got to get out of here, but he's blocking the way out of the kitchen. He stands there, smiling at me grimly, with blood spurting out of his nose and down his face, staining his teeth.

I quickly run through my options. He doesn't seem to be experiencing pain. Getting past him isn't likely. I could reach for one of the knives stowed away in the drawer behind me, provided I'm quick enough, or I could hop over the counter and bolt for the door.

Neither option is perfect, but they are both better than the alternatives.

We're coming, a deep, unrecognizable voice says in my head.

I'm losing it.

Deciding the knife is my best option, I shuffle backward as subtly as possible. I reach my fingers out behind me, searching for the drawer and work quickly, tugging it open, but he's too fast.

He's beside me in an instant, slamming the drawer shut and barely missing my fingers.

"Please," I whisper. I stare into his eyes, searching for any sign of recognition.

But he's gone.

Someone—some*thing*—unfamiliar, tortured stares back.

But it's not my Reed.

It hits me then, why the soul-shades turn grey despite the person being alive. Their souls are long gone, and something unnatural has taken their place, something driven forward by one thing: violence.

"I'm taking you with me, Tasia," Reed says as he steps forward, reaching for my throat again.

I duck under his hand, but he must have anticipated the move because he's ready for me. He wraps his hands around my still-sore windpipe again.

This time, his grip is unrelenting. He means what he said.

He *is* going to kill me.

I flail and fight, kicking him with every bit of power in my body. But slowly, the room around me begins to fade out. The fight leaves my body, and my limbs fall limp at my sides.

The front door crashes open, slamming into the wall so hard it cracks the drywall.

A black blur flies through the living room, clearing the counter and landing on Reed.

Scathe!

The pressure on my throat is released as Reed is swept away from me. He and Scathe collapse into the fridge. A scream rings out as the dog sinks his teeth into Reed's arm.

Still not having enough room to go around them, I pull myself up onto the counter. My body is weak, exhausted. Before I can crawl across to the other side, into the living room, strong arms scoop me up.

Archer cradles me to his chest. "I got you, baby."

He carries me to the couch, setting me down gently. I gasp, still trying desperately to catch my breath. My violated throat throbs with pain.

Reed's cries die out. Scathe rounds the counter and pads toward us, blood matted around the fur on his mouth.

"Is he..." I can't bring myself to say the next word.

Archer winces. "Not yet."

It really was the dreamdust after all. Reed is *dying*.

I squeeze my eyes shut, willing this all to be an awful nightmare.

"Tasia," Archer murmurs. He holds my chin gently in his fingers, angling my head to inspect me. "Your cheek..." His gaze roams me desperately. The muscles in his jaw become tense. He barely moves his mouth when he growls, "Your throat."

Reed must've left a mark. With the way it aches, I'm not surprised.

"He hurt you." Archer's face darkens. His fingers gently ghost over the tender skin, without actually making contact. "He *hurt* you."

Fury blazes in his golden eyes. They flicker, and his pupils dilate, darkening his irises. It's the only warning I get before his face begins to transform before me.

Unblinkingly, I stare as Archer lets out a guttural roar. His familiar face morphs into a frightening mask of pale skin stretched over bone and tendon. His cheeks hollow out, and his mouth stretches into an impossibly wide hole, gaping at me. Hungry for something. I shove myself backward.

Gone is the handsome, tanned face I'm familiar with. Gone is the man I've started to fall for.

In his place is a thing of nightmares. Haunting. Otherworldly.

A horrible noise erupts from the gaping hole that used to be his mouth. Then he bursts into action, springing up from the floor and moving into the kitchen with inhuman speed.

As if connected by an invisible tether, I jump up from the

couch, trembling as I move closer to see what's happening.

I should run.

But my morbid curiosity and terror are holding me prisoner.

Archer, who is now hovering above Reed, begins to inhale audibly, his chest expanding with the breath. The grey fog surrounding Reed's unconscious form wavers before wafting upward, like a snake being summoned by a flute.

All the blood drains from my face.

Archer sucks up the remnants of Reed's soul, absorbing it into his own body.

No.

It can't be.

Archer can't be the Reaper. I've seen them both at the same time, in the same place.

But...he's not unlike the Reaper either.

The tether holding me in place seems to snap then, and I shake myself from the daze. Adrenaline fuels me as I bolt from the apartment. Scathe whines, chasing after me, but he doesn't attack me. He keeps pace with me, as if watching over me.

I have nowhere to go.

No one else to look out for me.

I'm a dead woman running through the city.

Without stopping to think, I head toward the only other place I know to go.

CHAPTER 30
ARCHER

The beast inside of me swallows the lifeless boy's soul, consuming his energy until every inch of me is buzzing with the high. Power like I've never felt before roils beneath my skin.

When the last ounce of his essence is drunk to the dredges, I tilt my head up to the ceiling, shuttering my eyes and taking a moment to enjoy.

This.

This is what I've been missing out by ignoring the call of death.

This is my purpose. My calling. It's natural.

Wild.

Free.

Archer, an urgent voice whispers into my skull. *Archer, what have you done?*

My eyes fly open, and I scan the room, searching for the source of the voice.

Hungry.

So hungry.

For *death*.

The hellhound's perceptive blue eyes pierce me like shards of ice.

Scathe.

Don't make me bite you, you profound moron. A low growl reaches my ears as he pulls his lips back to reveal his sharp teeth. *Snap out of it!*

The high begins to simmer down, and I blink a few times.

The last few minutes come back to me. Now that I'm no longer numb, the electric zing coursing through my veins subsides, allowing the emotions to thaw out.

Guilt.

Regret.

Fear.

There is no beast inside of me, not actually. It's only me and the part of my power I've stifled for so long.

Stuck in place, I stare down at the man at my feet. Tasia's ex. Reed.

"Where is Tasia?" I ask Scathe, frantically searching the room.

The bar.

You let her go? I scold. You should've stayed with—

I'm your bonded, Archer. You are my concern.

Not wanting to argue with the hellhound, I locate my phone and dial Godric.

"Call Zeke. We need his services." I tell him to come to Tasia's, then hang up. Turning to Scathe, I ask, "Did anyone else see?"

No one is here. Scathe whines, low and dramatically. *Your face—it's normal now, but it changed. You weren't...you.*

A flicker of power buzzes to life inside of me, and instinct tells me I need to get rid of the soul I consumed. The sooner, the better. I've never done this before...never given in to the craving for death. I've always been strong enough to fight it.

Until *her.*

She is my weakness, and seeing her hurt is my undoing.

Without waiting for Godric and Zeke to show up, I dart outside and down the stairs to my bike. I situate Scathe's helmet on his head before putting on my own, and then I take off toward Ma's apartment.

My thoughts race as we fly down the streets, the buildings blurring past.

The boy would've died anyway. I didn't actually kill him—only took his soul. I can still release it into the Wilds, free him, even though he doesn't deserve it.

It's not for you to decide what he deserves, Scathe says.

Get out of my thoughts, you meddling mutt!

I'm looking out for you, he thinks. *I'm worried about you.*

Gripping the handlebars tighter and leaning forward, I propel us forward faster, weaving in and out of traffic, mindful of the extra space I take up with Scathe's sidecar.

I've always known I was different. When we were kids, it was clear that Godric's magic was simple—he could make doors disappear, create illusions, ward objects. My power seemed weaker in comparison. But it was darker. Heavier. The scent of death on the wind. The gnawing hunger in response.

I was always afraid of following the rope and finding out what was tied to the other end.

I need to find the Reaper, I think to Scathe.

You are out of your damn—

He's the only one like me. He can help.

Gritting my teeth, I pull into the alley beside Ma's apartment and shut off my bike. Without taking off my helmet, I begin pacing. The hunger lingers, and I find myself sniffing the air, desperate for a hint of sweet anise.

I need to get this out of me, Scathe. It's affecting me.

The only way I know to reach the Reaper is through death.

There's no way I'll kill someone to summon him. I can't. Not an option. Especially not with this unchecked desire inside of me. I can't guarantee I won't ache for their soul myself.

"I'm not a monster," I say, silencing the debate in my mind. It doesn't even deserve contemplation.

What do I do, Scathe?

Listen to your intuition. What does it say?

"It's untrustworthy," I mutter. "It wants more—it craves death."

Not your power—your intuition, Scathe amends.

Closing my eyes and leaning against the brick wall in the alley, I ignore the steady buzz of power and try to tap into my intuition.

Tasia is the first thing that comes to mind. I need her to be safe. Healthy. Happy.

Go to the bar, I command Scathe. *Check on Tasia. Stay with her until I can find her.*

There's no way she'll want to see me now. Plus, I don't trust myself in this state. Not until I can relieve myself of Reed's soul and subdue the ravenous beast within.

Scathe whines. *I don't—*

Please, I say to him, squatting down to scratch his neck. His back foot thumps automatically in response as he leans into the scratches. He might be more intelligent than a typical dog, but he's still a canine in many ways.

The mutt side-eyes me before relenting. *Fine.*

I take his helmet off, and he bolts away, around the corner and out of sight.

With that out of the way, I take my own helmet off.

"Okay, intuition, what do you say?"

When I first started learning about my power, I hadn't met Godric yet. My ma and Sofia were both regular humans, so they couldn't offer any insight. Things changed when Godric came into my life. Together, he and I discovered that being grounded in soil or around plants replenished our power, made us stronger.

In fact, it was the only way I knew to recharge...until now. Death makes me stronger than nature ever could.

Nature.

An idea forms, and I follow it. I felt pulled to my ma's apartment for a reason, after all. Jogging deeper into the alley, I run my palm along the brick until I locate the secret door. Entering the space, I fly down the stairs until I'm in our underground greenhouse.

The place where Godric and I recharge if we can't make it to Sweetcreek.

Something inside of me stirs. It rises higher, like bile, as if begging to come up and out of my mouth.

Then it stops.

It sinks back down into my bones.

It's not enough.

I know what I have to do. I need to release the soul into nature, where it can rest. It needs freedom. Real nature. Beyond the city.

It needs the Wilds.

"Devoting one's existence to faeology is inherently isolating. I am in a perpetual state of introspection, reflecting on the validity of my decisions, but the nuances of my research are apprehended by me alone."

-Excerpt from the personal journal of Dr. Claude Foster, Director of Faeology at Mesmeric Labs

CHAPTER 31
FANTASIA

By the time I make it to The Rising Star, I'm drenched with sweat and panting for air. Before entering, I catch my breath and take a look around to ensure Archer didn't follow me. The streets aren't that busy at this time of day, with the bars getting ready to close. Scanning the few passersby, I find a variety of different hues but see no sign of gold.

My blood runs cold.

Is Archer's soul-shade still gold after that?

How would it be gold in the first place if he's a reaper—*fae*?

Shuddering, I enter the bar. The bell over the door chimes, and Mellie's head whips up. The smile melts from her face at the sight of me. Unlike the last time I burst in here a hot mess, she doesn't run over to greet me.

"Tay," she says cautiously.

"Hey, did you get my text?" My voice comes out too high and squeaky, but I'm trying my best to stay cool. The image of Archer consuming Reed's soul sits at the forefront of my mind.

Reed is dead.

Archer is a reaper.

It doesn't make sense.

"You hear me?" Mellie asks, tossing a bar towel onto her shoulder.

My head grows light, and I try to focus on Mellie's familiar face and push away my panic. "I'm sorry—what?"

My legs move, taking me toward her. It's like I'm not in control of my body. It's moving on its own.

"I said I replied." She places both palms on the bar and leans forward. Some of the patrons lingering at the bar until last call turn toward me in their stools, and several people chatter in a booth to my left, but I pay them no attention. Fumbling with my phone, I unlock it to see her text staring back at me.

Mellie: I don't hear from u in days and this is what u say

Mellie: Yeah. I have ur bear...

Swallowing the lump in my throat, I try to force a smile. "Oh, no I didn't see it. I was already on my way here."

She squints. "You okay?"

Luckily, someone at the bar asks for a refill, so she moves to grab his glass before I can respond.

"It's upstairs," she calls to me. "You can head up and grab it."

Relief softens my tense muscles. "Thanks, Mellie."

"Make yourself at home. Axel's with his dad."

Instead of lingering, I head straight for the stairway leading to Mellie's apartment. I close the door at the bottom, and make my way up the stairs.

The overpowering stench of spoiled milk slaps me in the face. High ceilings make the studio appear bigger than it actually is, but it holds onto warm air even more than downstairs does. Three windows overlook the bar's roof and Pub Path down below. They're open, letting in the sticky late-night air. There's a daybed with a coffee table beside it. A glass of what looks like curdled milk sits there.

Gagging, I pick up the glass and walk it to the kitchenette, where I dump the disgusting mess out in the sink. I rinse the glass and leave it there.

With a sigh, I turn to survey the space. Clothing is strewn about, along with toys and various empty food containers.

I hadn't realized that Mellie's place had fallen into such a state of disarray. My heart pangs with sorrow and guilt as I realize I likely had something to do with this. Without me to help at the bar, she's probably having to work more, so she has less time to care for herself and Axel.

Spotting my bear on the floor beside the daybed, I stoop to pick it up.

"Finally." I clutch it to my chest. "I miss you, Dad."

Just a couple of weeks ago, everything seemed so much clearer. My life was lackluster, yeah, but it was my life. Oh, how everything has changed. A tear slides down my cheek, and I quickly wipe it away.

Squeezing the bear tighter, I realize Mellie was right. The old thing sure could use a good stuffing. He's lumpy as heck.

"Wait," I murmur.

Flipping the bear over and inspecting it, I search for an opening, any type of hidden pocket. I've had the ratty thing for years and never noticed anything amiss, but there has to be something I overlooked. My gut tells me to look harder.

When I don't find anything, I take a risk and give the fabric a tug at its seams. If I'm wrong, worst case scenario I lose my old bear. If I'm right...

The seam gives with a loud *rip*. Pieces of fluff fall out. I reach in, plucking out more of the white material, and my fingers scrape against something rough.

"No fucking way," I say breathlessly, tugging out the item.

It's a paper folded into a square no bigger than my palm. Rushing to unfold it, I try to steady my shaking heads, careful not to rip the paper.

Fantastic Fantasia,

I hope you find this letter before it's too late. It's glamoured to be read by your eyes only. It's not the only thing glamoured. There's much to say but not many words. The city isn't what it seems; protection is a synonym for prison, and not all is artificial. Blood is thicker than water, but blood can wash away dust.

I've made mistakes and sold my soul to the monsters. I only wanted to afford a better life for us. I had no idea what was in store.

Please forgive me, my girl.

I will love you always.

If I wasn't wholly certain this is my father's handwriting, I wouldn't believe this was from him. The syntax is different from that of his journals. And what he wrote makes little sense—

"It's not the only thing glamoured." *He* was glamoured. I knew it!

My hands shake as I read it over and over, working to decipher what it means. He's speaking in code, giving me a roundabout message in the only way he could.

A loud screech from the street pulls me out of my thoughts.

My head whips toward the nearest window. I run to it, peering down below. Even at this hour, Pub Path is well-lit by street lamps and various signs. A handful of Scouts emerge from their armored truck, charging toward the bar. People flee, yelling dramatically as they go, but the Scouts make no move to chase them. Instead they pause in front of the bar. Then they talk amongst themselves in low voices for a moment before readying their weapons.

I duck down out of sight, my heart jackhammering in my chest. Tucking my dad's note in my bra for safekeeping, I scurry toward the stairwell.

I have no idea what's going on, but it looks like they're about to raid The Rising Star.

When I'm halfway down the wooden stairs, the door at the bottom is flung open. I freeze, but luckily it's only Mellie.

"Mel, the Scouts are here," I whisper.

She sniffles, wiping her nose on the back of her hand. The way she doesn't meet my eyes causes the hair on the back of my neck to prickle.

"Mellie?" I whisper.

"Axel is sick... We—we really need the money, TayTay." Her voice cracks. "It's nothing personal."

She tosses a crumpled-up wad of paper toward me. It lands on the stair below me. I stoop down to snatch it up, smoothing out the page.

A sketch of my face stares back at me, the word *WANTED* written in big letters above my head.

When the disbelief fades, realization hits me like a sledge-hammer.

Mellie called the Scouts.

She turned me in for silvers.

"Nothing personal?" I whisper.

"If you had a kid, you'd get it."

I nearly double over from the shock.

"Mellie... I would've helped you." I would've given her my own paycheck or asked Archer for money. Something. Anything.

When she finally meets my gaze, her eyes are brimming with anger. "You left work with no word. You've been unreliable...secretive. In your own world." Mellie sniffles again, her face scrunched, as if she's fighting an inner battle.

A sharp, shooting pain pierces my heart. "Mel..."

"It's fine. Even if you didn't have your own shit going on, I need more help than you can afford. I'm sorry. Really."

All I can do is shake my head. I don't bother telling her about the job I have with Archer—the money I'm making working for him. She'd just turn him in, too.

She steps up toward me, reaching for my hands, but I pull away.

"You broke my heart, Mellie." My voice is strained.

Nodding, she glances over her shoulder. "You broke mine, too, by shutting me out. So I guess we're even?"

With that, she exits the stairwell and closes the door. The latch clicks—she's locking it behind her. Not that it matters. I'm not about to run down there straight into the Scouts' open arms.

The bell chimes as the front door crashes open, and I know it's too late.

They're here for me.

It's over.

Out the window, a deep voice says in my mind. It's the one I thought I heard before. Decidedly not my own voice.

Don't be stubborn, Tasia. Go out the window!

"What the hell?" I say. I glance at the window, goose bumps covering my arms. "Who the hell's there?"

You have about twenty seconds. Go now!

My feet move before my brain can fully process what's happening. I dart to the open window, push out the screen, and poke my head out. Down below, a lone Scout stands facing the building. He hugs his firearm to his chest, keeping his hand on the grip as if ready for action.

"Fuck," I mutter. "He'll see me."

Seven seconds. Move!

The floor vibrates as the Scouts pound up the stairs behind me. I don't have time to dawdle. I slip out onto the roof just as Scathe lunges into sight down below and sinks his elongated canines into the Scout's leg.

The man's mouth opens in a scream, but only silence escapes. He crumples to the ground, immediately rendered unconscious.

Belgian Shepherd my ass. That is definitely *not* a normal dog.

Follow the roof around the corner. Then jump.

I scurry across the shingles, heeding the mysterious voice in my head. Sirius save me, I'm losing it. After all the trauma I've endured in this life, I've finally gone and lost my damn mind.

Behind me, inside Mellie's apartment, the Scouts are yelling at one another.

Without glancing back, I round the corner of the roof, heading toward the alley. It's much narrower and steeper on this side. I don't see any way off that doesn't require—

Jump, Tasia! the voice yells.

Down below rests a haphazard mountain of black trash bags. I almost slip and fall off just from peering over the edge.

Fuck that! I think.

Jump, you stubborn tit!

The voice in my head just called me a tit. It's enough to unsettle me.

Taking a big breath, I oblige, launching myself off the roof. A shot rings out into the night as I soar through the air.

The bags soften my landing, releasing a thick *whoosh* of raunchy air. I gag.

"Run!" a shrill voice says—this one I hear aloud.

I turn to catch sight of Stace rounding the corner, with Alisha on her ass.

"We could only hold them off for so long!" Stace yells. "The dog helped, but they shot at him and he ran off!"

Scathe.

Alarm rings through me. "Shot? Is he okay?"

"Dunno!"

We bolt down the alley. It doesn't take long to realize our mistake.

"Dead end!" I yell as we draw closer to the brick wall ahead of us. Light seeps out from a window above, threatening to reveal us to anyone who might peer into the alley.

Before I crash into the wall, I halt to a stop. Desperately, I pat the bricks, searching for some sort of magical invisible entrance. Of course I find nothing.

Despite the horrifying scene I witnessed at my apartment, I can't help but wish Archer were here. He'd know how to help.

"We didn't make it this far to get fucked so hard!" Stace yells, stomping her foot.

Her anger catches me off guard. "What are you even doing here?"

"I came to get a drink with Alisha when you kicked me out," she says quickly, frantically. "Overheard the bartender call you in."

I scan the alley, looking for an escape. The only way out is Pub Path—past the Scouts. We're well and screwed.

Eyeing my roommates, I ask, "Why are you helping me?"

"Why the fuck not?" Alisha says. "Can we have this conversation later?"

I throw my hands up. "Gladly! If I have a later."

It strikes me—they don't know Reed is dead. They might turn me in if they knew. Hell, this could be a setup for all I know. Maybe they lured me out here on purpose, intending to turn me in.

"Idea," Stace says. She reaches into Alisha's jeans pocket. Alisha swats her hand, but Stace successfully pulls out what she was looking for.

A familiar-looking baggie.

It's too dark to make out the contents, but my spine prickles. "Stace...what is that?"

"Something to help."

"Is that dreamdust?" I ask, my voice wavering.

"How'dya know?" she asks, confused. "I thought you don't touch drugs."

I snatch it from Stace, desperate to keep it away from her. Enough people have fucked with this drug. I'm with Archer; it's destroying our city.

"Where did you get it, Alisha?" I whisper.

Alisha sighs. "Reed brought it over earlier. Said it's new. Got it for free. From his supplier. That's what I was trying to tell you before—he's my dealer. *Not* my booty call."

"You've been on the dust?" I whisper, bile swirling in my stomach. Reed's been *dealing* it?

"Nah, but he brought us a free sample, said it gives us power. Maybe it can help—"

A bright light washes over us, and suddenly, it's as if I'm underwater. The voices and sounds around me fade to a low buzz. I barely register any of it.

A Scout stands before us with his weapon pointed in our direction.

Not again.

I clutch the baggie of dreamdust in my sweaty hand as my mind races to solve the puzzle. There must be a way out of this. There needs to be.

Scathe isn't coming to save me this time. He could be out there on the street, injured for trying to protect me, and I need to find him. My gut tells me Archer isn't coming either...

The Scout commands us to put our hands up. Slowly, Stace and Alisha lift their hands, panic painted on their faces. It takes me all of two seconds to realize they really aren't here to turn me in. Archer must have glamoured them to have my back. If the Scouts win here, it's not just me they'll take in. It's Stace and Alisha, too.

For the first time, people are counting on me.

The Scout steps closer. "Get on your knees!"

I think of the reward being offered for turning me in. How desperate they are to find me—plastering my photo on the UIS. This Scout won't kill me. Whoever wants me wants me *alive*.

"Come get me, asshole," I say, proud of how steady my voice is.

I can't make out any of the Scout's facial features behind the bright light bursting from his helmet, but I don't need to. They don't matter. In this moment, I see the person who shot and killed my parents.

Suddenly, I'm eight years old again, crying in the closet. Staring at a murderer through the wooden slats of the door.

Except I'm no longer eight years old.

I'm not weak and fragile. I'm not hiding from the violence.

I embrace it.

"Back up," I tell Stace and Alisha. "Now!" Surprisingly, they both scamper backward. "This is for my dad, you fucker." Before the Scout has time to react, I pinch the baggie open, jerking my arm toward his face and releasing the dust into the air. I blow as hard as I can, forcing the glittering powder toward him.

He staggers backward, but it's too late. I was too close, and my aim was spot on.

He coughs, stowing his weapon to claw at his face in desperation.

"Run!" I yell at the girls. "Let's get out of here!"

They bolt past me toward Pub Path. I kick the Scout in his balls, bringing him to his knees. He goes down with a *thud*.

I pivot to make my escape, but his hand constricts forcefully around my ankle, impeding my movement. It tightens, yanking me backward. I land with a thud and find myself on my back. The Scout holds me down, leaning in and locking lips with me.

As I fight him and try to scream, he blows air forcefully into my open mouth. Something chalky hits my tongue, and I gasp and cough when I realize what he's done.

He wasn't forcing a desperate kiss.

He was blowing the dust back into my mouth.

> *"My involvement in faeology has transcended the confines of mere employment; it has transformed into a profound and enduring life passion."*

-Excerpt from the personal journal of Dr. Claude Foster, Director of Faeology at Mesmeric Labs

CHAPTER 32
FANTASIA

When I awaken, my head throbs, and my throat is dry and scratchy. Peeling my eyes open, I squint at the sight before me. It looks like there's a layer of thick glass between me and an industrial ceiling overhead. With a groan, I sit up on my elbows. The floor beneath me is hard cement.

Frantically, I search my surroundings. Sure enough, I'm in a glass cell of some sort. It's about the size of Archer's king-sized mattress. There's enough space to stretch out, but it's still cramped. The enclosure looks to be at least twice my height.

I check my pockets for my phone, and my chest tightens when I come up short. My pulse picks up, the blood pounding in my temples.

Beyond the glass cell, the room is empty. I appear to be in a warehouse of some sort. There's an unmarked door a few steps away and a few more doors across the room.

A carton of water and a plate of food sit beside me.

Greedily, and without hesitation, I open the carton and chug the water.

What happened?

I close my eyes and wince against the headache, trying to remember how I got here.

Dreamdust.

Holy shit.

I'm alive.

How am I alive?

"Hello?" I call out, listening for any movement in the distance.

Silence greets me.

When I bang my fist against the glass, I'm unsurprised to discover it's sturdy, likely shatterproof. There's a door built in, but it's almost seamless with the rest of the glass. It has no hinges, only a handle on the outside and a small food slot at the bottom. As I work to keep my panic at bay, I inspect the door closely for any weak spots. Nothing gives. I search each wall of the cage, finding nothing of significance.

"Fantasia," a familiar voice says.

Spinning around, I spot the newcomer. I didn't even hear him enter the room. I'm easily able to make out his features in the harsh fluorescent lighting. His skin is a deep olive color, his irises and hair pitch-black. A stern, formidable expression sits on his face.

His expensive tailored suit hugs him perfectly, highlighting his pristine posture.

"Arlo Osiander." My blood goes still. "The man behind the mask," I say. Metaphorically and literally.

He steps forward, hands in his pockets, until he's just beyond the glass separating us. He tilts his head down, scrutinizing me.

"You're a very difficult woman to get a hold of."

He's been trying to reach me? I frown at that. Why would—

"You," I say, stepping forward and slamming my hand into the glass in front of his face. He doesn't even flinch. A single brow rises on his face, and the corners of his lips tilt up ever so slightly. "You're the one who plastered my photo on the UIS. *You* sent the Scouts after me."

"Like I said, you are very difficult to reach."

"What could you possibly want with me? You knew who I was at the masquerade."

The humor fades from his eyes, and he frowns. "Yes, but unfortunately, due to unforeseen circumstances—"

"You mean the massacre?" I hiss. "That you set up!"

"That was not at my hand. Humans are often beyond my control, glamour excluded. They love to flout rules and make poor choices. They often destroy themselves."

"So you have nothing to do with the dreamdust?" I say, crossing my arms.

"I never said that. But I had nothing to do with the mass overdose at Splendor Hall last night."

Last night.

How much time has passed? It was almost two in the morning when I made my way to the bar. Before Mellie turned me in. After Archer took Reed's soul. A sharp pang shoots through my chest.

"See, I was hoping to find my answers in the lab," he says, "but when I didn't, I figured you might have the information I seek."

He *hmphs* to himself. "The journals were useful, but not exactly what I was searching for either."

My blood runs cold. So it *was* him behind the UIS blast and the robbery at Archer's apartment. "What the hell were you hoping to find?"

"His other studies, of course."

"What other studies?" My confusion must show because Arlo laughs.

"Useless," he mutters, shaking his head. I frown, racking my brain and trying to connect the dots. Before I can say anything, he continues, "Fitting you would find solace in my brother. You don't quite fit in with the humans, nor do you fit in with the fae."

I stare, letting his words sink in.

Brother.

"Archer?" It hits me all at once like a bag of bricks. After seeing the extent of Archer's power last night... "*You're* the Reaper."

"A reaper fae, yes, but the nickname is rather unoriginal." He sighs, pulling his hands out of his pockets and adjusting his sleeves. "I'm not the only one of our kind, clearly."

It clicks into place, why he would want dreamdust on the streets—so he can consume souls. For power. For control. For ego.

"You killed my parents," I growl, fire coursing through my veins.

"No, no, no," he says, shaking his head. "I do not *kill* anyone. I ferry souls—"

"You sick bastard!" I yell, my voice echoing through the warehouse.

The Reaper's hands tighten into fists at his sides. "Listen to me..." My stomach turns into a ball of nausea, but I don't say anything. "*If* your father is dead, it was at the hands of the city. For breaking the third edict."

Pausing, I go through the edicts in my mind. The third edict is the Prohibition of Fae and Magic. "He was a faeologist!" I say in disbelief. "Of course he dealt with magic!"

He *tsks*, his expression grim. "I'm not talking about his job."

I stare at him, trying to understand what he's implying. "Are you saying my dad was in cahoots with fae?"

"Ah," he says, tilting his head and smiling softly. "Was? No. I wouldn't say he was."

I place my palms on the glass and sneer at him. "You and Archer are despicable. You soul-sucking monsters."

He leans forward, studying me. Only a wall of glass separates our faces. "Archer, a monster?"

My brow furrows. "No shit. Taking souls clearly runs in the family."

Something similar to alarm flickers through Arlo's dark eyes, but then it's gone. "Where is he?"

"I don't fucking know. And I don't care." I slam the glass once more before turning around, striding to the other side of the cage. "Dumping my ex-boyfriend's soul—if he's not keeping it for his own power."

After an extended pause, I turn around. Arlo is nowhere in sight.

"Let me out, you fucker!" I scream.

I kick the water carton, and it hits the glass with a soft *thwack*.

He has to come back soon. If he wanted me dead, I'd be dead. He certainly wouldn't bring me water and food.

Inspecting the food on the tray, I notice it's cold. It must've been here for a while. Regardless, I do need to preserve my energy and stay sharp, so I slide to the floor, grab the chicken breast, and bite into it.

It's thick, chalky, and awful in my mouth. I taste nothing and force myself to swallow it for the sake of keeping up my strength.

What does the Reaper want with me?

As I chew, I close my eyes and rest my back and head against the glass. I sift through my brain, trying to put this fucking puzzle together.

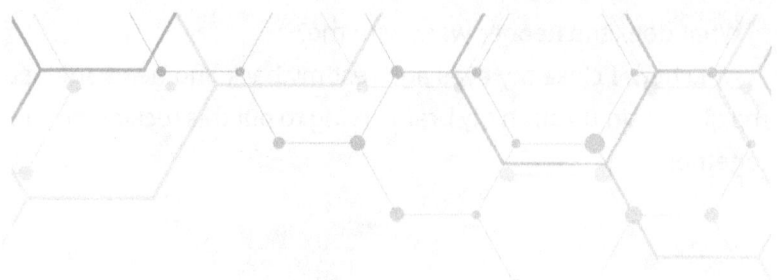

CHAPTER 33
ARCHER

Time becomes a blur.

Trusting that Scathe will watch out for Tasia, and Godric and Zeke will take care of Reed's body, I focus on myself for once. I need to release this soul before it becomes a permanent part of me.

I'm not sure what the implications of that would be, and I don't care to find out.

The soft dirt underfoot swallows the sound of my footsteps as I navigate a less-traveled section of the Underground. I follow one of the tunnels east, away from the coast and toward the Wilds. There are a few tunnels that run beyond the wall, but I seldom use them. We have no business out there.

The unsettling buzzing in my blood continues, pestering me to find another soul.

It's still hungry for more.

I take a sharp left, and the tunnel narrows into a smaller path that barely allows me to stand at my full height. My shoulder brushes against the wall. I pick up my pace.

I'm half-fae.

Reaper fae.

The irony isn't lost on me, but I truly had no idea. Godric and I have always known we were different, assumed we were part fae, but I hadn't expected *this*. And it's not like we could start a magic support group and find others like us.

As far as we knew, since fae and magic are banned, we were the only ones like us in the whole city. Two boys who got lucky in finding one another.

The dirt path begins to curve upward, growing steeper. I grab a rope that rests on the dirt beneath me and give it a tug to ensure it's still sound. Using it to pull myself up the steep slope, I walk slowly, taking small steps and moving hand over hand.

As I get closer to the surface, birdsong reaches my ears.

Eventually, the ground levels off again. Early, pink daylight seeps in from a hole overhead. It took hours to walk the distance to the Wilds—zigzagging through the tunnels. Hours of being alone with my thoughts.

Hours of hating myself.

Gripping the edge of the hole, I hoist myself up and out, landing on a bed of plush, thick grass. I lie there for a minute on my back, reveling in the soft morning sun on my face and the chattering of birds flitting in the trees nearby.

A shudder racks my body as the sweet arms of nature wrap around me, welcoming me back with warmth and tenderness.

When I get up, I glance toward the city. The wall sits a few miles away in the distance, an ominous black thing cutting off nature from the sprawling metropolis.

Sighing, I search my surroundings to ensure I'm alone. From what I've heard, fae normally don't wander this close to the city—why would they? They prefer nature to the horribly polluted metal and brick wen.

This area lives up to its name. All around me lush wilderness stretches on, teeming with flora and fauna. There are a few trails cutting through the dense foliage, but most of them are overgrown, untamed. Everything is alive with color.

Putting my back to the city, I face the expanse of nature and exhale forcefully, attempting to free the soul I consumed.

Nothing happens.

I try again, closing my eyes, focusing on Reed's spirit within me.

Once more, I exhale audibly. Then I draw in another deep breath and do it again and again.

After a few minutes, when nothing changes, I release a frustrated grunt and run a hand through my hair. I growl and start to pace.

What am I doing wrong?

According to my understanding, nature has a process of recycling souls... My intuition led me here.

"Ah, nature in its purest form is breathtaking, is it not?"

I whip around, catching sight of Arlo Osiander. He's quite out of place here in the wilderness, in his shiny loafers and fitted, luxury suit.

"Much better than that horrible concrete prison you prefer to reside in," he says.

Gritting my teeth, I think of what I could possibly say to him. But his presence is the least of my concerns right now. When the silence between us stretches on, he sighs as though he's annoyed. His features begin to change, shifting into something beyond human.

Something sinister.

His mouth widens into a gaping hole. His black irises bleed into the whites of his eyes.

Staring at me is the face of the Reaper.

My spine tightens, and I stand up taller, watching him with rapt attention.

The revelation should bring me a sense of vindication at the very least, but nothing trumps the concern I have about consuming a soul.

"You," I mutter. A plethora of thoughts spin through my mind like a hurricane. But right now, the most important thing is figuring out how to release the soul. "Help me." I'm ashamed to have to ask, but not too obstinate that I don't. "How do I get it out of me?"

Arlo's face shifts again, bones cracking as his previous features return. There's something familiar about him. Something I can't quite place.

"I'll tell you," he says, "for a price."

"Name the cost. I can afford it." It's honest, not arrogant. Whatever it is, I can pay it.

He chuckles, shaking his head. "The price is not your human silvers. It's a bargain."

Through gritted teeth, I repeat what I said earlier. "Name the cost."

I don't know what will happen if I don't release Reed's soul. Will it become a part of me? Will it feed the monster inside of me until I'm the one stuffed away—at its ravenous mercy? I'm not willing to take that chance. Keeping it inside of me isn't right.

"I'll show you how to be a proper reaper, but in return, you hear me out and cause me no harm."

"Hear you out?"

"It's a very fair price, is it not?"

"Yes," I say without hesitation. He wants me to listen to him? Surely I can do that without issue. As for causing harm, I try to avoid doing that in general, so it's not a big ask. "Fair enough."

He puts out his hand, and I eye it warily before shaking. A buzz courses through my palm and up my arm, and although I have no formal experience with bargains, I inherently know that magic has sealed the deal.

"You need to become one with nature," Arlo says, stepping closer to me. Stray brambles scratch at his pressed pants, but he seems to pay them no mind. "Find a quiet place that calls to you, and focus your mind."

I wait for him to go on, but he gestures toward the forest behind me, as if urging me to heed his advice. Obliging, I turn to face the woods and wait for a call. A tug. Something.

Nothing comes.

I choose an ash tree nearby, stepping up to it and placing my hands on the rough bark.

"Close your eyes," Arlo says. "Focus."

I do as he says, shutting my eyes and trying to summon the foreign spirit within me. Minutes go by, and my arms begin to protest the static position.

"Focus," Arlo says again. "I have quite the packed schedule. A lab to rebuild—thank you—ministries to glamour, and a pretty little soul-seer who awaits my return."

"*What*?" My eyes fly open, and my chest tightens. Whirling around, I storm toward Arlo and grip his jacket in my fists. "What the hell does that mean?"

He chuckles.

"If you touch her, I swear to the Gods—"

"You'll what, Archer?" He smirks. "We made a deal."

Instantly, the gravity of the situation weighs me down. "That was before I knew you had Tasia." I try to tighten my grip, but my fingers freeze, unresponsive. They loosen their grip of their own accord, and my body jolts back a step.

Magic.

From the bargain.

He has Tasia.

My pulse quickens.

"Alas, here we are," Arlo says. "I imagine she'll need human facilities and sustenance rather soon, so perhaps we can move along with our little lesson and I may be on my way."

My mind trips over itself trying to figure out a way around Arlo's bargain. Perhaps I can have Godric harm him for me—on my behalf. Or perhaps I can tie him up and keep him somewhere safe yet isolated. That's not technically harming him.

With more force than I intended, I slam my palms against the ash tree, closing my eyes and shutting out the world around me.

I search for the tree's soft buzz of energy, the one I find when drawing replenishment from nature. I locate it swiftly, but instead of drawing the energy toward me, I focus on expelling my own energy outward.

It works. A steady stream of spirit begins to leave me.

My vision goes black, and my hearing fades into nothing but a low hum as I force it out.

After a moment, I'm no longer forcing it. It's flowing naturally, like a steady stream. When the last of the unfamiliar soul leaves my being, I gasp for air, sucking in a big breath. All at once, my vision and hearing come back. Quickly, I draw in nature's regular energy, replenishing my magic stores.

Like the fae I am, I realize.

A boiling fury courses through me, and I turn, striding toward Arlo until we're face to face.

"I will never be a monster like you," I spit.

"You call me a monster, yet you are exactly the same as me." He gestures toward the tree I utilized to liberate Reed's soul.

"No. I released the soul to find its *peace*." He doesn't need to know it was selfish, that I did it to rid myself of the ill feeling it gave me. "I do not consume souls for my own gain."

He laughs, a surprised look crossing his face. "No wonder you fight me so." He shakes his head. "There's much you've yet to learn about your own folk."

"You're not my people."

"Am I not?" He smiles smugly. "I'm surprised your whore of a mother didn't tell you—"

Red fills my vision, and I vibrate with rage, unable to physically make a move on him. "You will not speak of my mother in such a manner," I yell.

"—about our father," he says, ignoring my outburst.

My heart stalls.

Our father.

"Shut your Gods-damned mouth," I growl.

"Archer," the Reaper sing-songs. "I'm Arlo." He places a hand on his chest and smirks at me. "Artair is our father. Archer. Arlo. Artair. You can't tell me you don't see the significance there. Quite adorable, really."

"You're *not* my brother."

"Ah, but we share blood."

Like Godric has said many times before, blood does not make brothers...but it does explain how Arlo got into my ma's apartment.

Why has he been poking around?

My temples throb in tempo to my pounding heart. What he's saying—no. It can't be true. Ma said she didn't know who my father was.

My mother wasn't the best. She was often high, incoherent, unreliable, but she wasn't a liar.

Turning, I trudge back toward the tunnel entrance, desperate to put some distance between Arlo and me. I need to get to Tasia.

"Your mother was offered safety here with us in the Wilds. Before *and* after your sister was born. She chose to keep you both in the city, knowing our plan to take it back."

"You don't know what you're talking about!" I call over my shoulder.

"Archer Acciai...you're quick to protect half your kind, but what about the other half? The half that was here first. The half whose land the city was built atop?"

"That's your plan? To destroy the city?" I laugh humorously.

"I don't need to destroy the city when it'll destroy itself." His voice fades out as I pick up my pace.

"Go to hell, you fucker," I mutter as I drop back into the hole.

If only Tasia could hear me now.

I start running toward the city. It's the memory of her contagious laugh that propels me forward, desperate to find her. Protect her. And win her back.

I fear I've lost her. And selfishly? The fear of losing her is more terrifying than any of today's other revelations.

> *"SOUL-MAGIC SERVES AS THE ANTITHESIS OF DEATH*
> *MAGIC, ACTING IN A MANNER THAT ESSENTIALLY*
> *COUNTERBALANCES AND NEUTRALIZES ITS EFFECT."*

-EXCERPT FROM THE PERSONAL JOURNAL OF DR. CLAUDE FOSTER, DIRECTOR OF FAEOLOGY AT MESMERIC LABS

CHAPTER 34
FANTASIA

The metal door slams open, sounding like thunder in the warehouse. I jolt up from the ground to catch sight of Scathe bolting toward the enclosure.

"Scathe!" I yell, running up to the glass. He whimpers. "I know, boy. I'm okay." I scan him, searching for any sign of injury. He's walking fine, and there's no matted fur or blood on him.

"How the hell did this happen?" Godric's voice booms from the doorway.

"Are you a fucking reaper, too?" I ask, narrowing my eyes at the brute.

"What?"

He's not, the voice from earlier says into my mind.

"Get out of my head!" I shout.

Scathe whimpers, lowering his head.

Sorry, Tasia. I was only trying to help.

"All right then," Godric says, blowing out a puff of air dramatically. "We're only trying to help. I'm going to get you out of here."

"That's what it just said, too," I mutter, rubbing a hand over my face. "The voice."

Godric presses his palm into the door and closes his eyes. His palm glows white.

"I'm sorry, Godric. I'm on edge. After Reed overdosed and Archer turned into a freaking ghoul and slurped up his soul like a freaking spaghetti noodle and then Mellie turned me in and I basically murdered a Scout to get away—oh, with Stace and Alisha's help, of everyone's? Not to mention thinking Scathe got shot and accidentally inhaling dreamdust, thinking I was going to die, only to wake up here and find out Arlo is the Reaper and he's Archer's brother, all on top of the weird voice in my head. I'm losing it."

I pause, sucking in a huge breath to compensate for the lack of air during my rant.

"Whoa." Godric stills, his hand pressed against my glass prison. The white light on his palm flickers. His jaw goes slack, and he stares at me with a blank expression. "You said—Archer what?"

Of course out of everything I rambled, the mention of Archer takes precedence. He's his *brother* after all. I can't blame him. "Looks like you and Archer have a third brother in the mix," I say, throwing my hands up. "The cocky lab owner."

"*Arlo*? The one making a bid for High Chancellor?" Godric

shakes his head. Keeping one hand on the glass, he runs his other hand over his face. "Fuck," he mutters, shutting his eyes again. "Where the fuck is Archer?"

"I don't know—wherever reapers go with souls?"

His eyes flick open, and the glow emitting from his palm subsides. "He's not a reaper."

"I saw it with my own eyes." Unless I'm going crazy.

You're not going crazy, Tasia. Well, maybe a little, but certainly not because of me.

"Get out of my head!" I glare at Godric. "You don't hear that?"

He pauses, glancing at Scathe, then back at me. His eyes narrow contemplatively. "What exactly does this voice sound like?"

"I don't know. Deep. Sassy. Kind of annoying."

Godric sighs and turns his attention to Scathe, who sits patiently like a good boy at his side. "Knock it off, hound."

"He's not doing anything. Don't snap at him."

"You want him to leave you alone or what?" Godric shuts his eyes again, and his palm begins to glow once more.

It takes me a minute to understand what he's implying. "No. No. Scathe isn't—he can talk?"

"Mindspeak," Godric murmurs. His hand is glowing brighter now. "Can you give me a second, please? Trying to get you out of there."

"Shit, yeah, sorry."

I focus on my own thoughts. *You can speak?!*

Woof, woof, bark, Scathe says into my mind as sarcastically as ever. *Yes, Tasia, I can.*

What the ever-loving fuck?

Scathe barks. *If Archer was here, he'd scold you for that, you know.*

A loud cracking noise grabs my attention, and I notice the glass beneath Godric's palm is cracking upward in a long zigzag.

"Back up," he says.

I do as he says, and a second later, the glass shatters, collapsing in a pile of jagged edges at his feet.

"Holy shit." I stare at the broken glass in awe. "That was pretty cool."

"Comes in handy every now and again," he mutters, brushing his hands together.

"One second," I say.

Jumping over the broken glass, I run to Scathe's side, bending down to inspect all four of his legs and paws.

Gently, I grab his soft head, inspecting his neck and scruff for any sign of injury.

I'm fine, he says in my mind.

"I heard you got shot. I was worried." I wrap my arms around his furry neck, hugging him close. "Wait," I murmur into his fur. "You're not, like, a human dude or something, right?"

"Hellhound," Godric says. "Let's get out of here." He hustles to the door, calling over his shoulder, "Explain everything. Starting at the beginning."

Why couldn't you fill him in? I ask Scathe.

No time. We just got here.

Jumping to my feet, I bolt after Godric to the door closest to the glass cell. We exit into an even larger room made of concrete with a labyrinth of pipes running overhead. Fluorescent light fixtures buzz above us, and more glass prisons sit empty around the room.

"What the hell are these?" I ask.

"Holding cells," Godric says, words clipped.

"Is this a prison?"

"No—private property."

His strides are long and confident. I figure he knows where to go, so I hustle to keep up with him. Scathe stays by my side.

How'd you guys find me? I ask him.

Scented you.

I make a contemplative sound. *Can you speak to everyone?*

Only fae.

"I'm not fae though," I murmur.

Guess you're close enough, Scathe replies. *Would've tried striking up a conversation sooner had I known you'd hear me, human.*

I might've had an aneurysm. A delirious giggle escapes me at the thought. I'm talking to a freaking dog.

Hellhound, Scathe amends.

You can hear all my thoughts?

Just the ones you don't guard.

"Well, fuck." I side-eye the hound as we burst through one final door and emerge into the bright morning sunlight. Warm air welcomes me. For once, I find it comforting. "Did you know about Archer?"

What part? That he'd lose the cool on his power for you?

"What? That's not what—"

"If you're done talking to yourself," Godric says with a low growl, "can we hustle?" He points to his SUV up ahead, parked in an empty lot.

"I'm talking to Scathe," I mutter. Squinting against the rising sun, I glance around. I've never been to this part of the city. The air carries a hint of salt. We've got to be on the east coast—near the Jacarinian Sea. The city's skyline sits off in the distance in what must be the west.

There are quite a few warehouses here, separated by concrete lots. Further east, beyond the warehouses, the city prison stands like a storm cloud, with its own wall wrapping around the property. Beyond that are deadly cliffs jutting over the sea.

I study the enormous concrete prison building one last time and shudder. At least I wasn't in there.

Arlo must've wanted me for some reason. I still can't figure out why, though.

Wordlessly, we jog to Godric's vehicle, and Scathe and I get in the back.

"Where are we going?" I ask.

"To the last place Scathe saw Archer so we can follow his trail."

As soon as I put my seat belt on, I lean over to kiss Scathe's head. "You're a good boy, huh?"

The goodest of all.

Godric floors the vehicle, and I jerk forward, slamming my hand into the passenger seat in front of me. "Good Gods, you maniac."

I turn back to Scathe. *What do you mean that Archer lost his cool...because of me?*

Scathe sits alert on the seat next to me, staring out the window. *I've known him my whole life. He's always struggled with the darkness inside of him, Tasia.*

I frown, staring out my own window and watching the warehouses whip past in a blur. We're winding through the back roads, heading toward the city.

Archer has a gold soul-shade though. How could he possibly struggle with darkness?

I didn't know the extent of it, Scathe says. *I don't think he knew either.*

Are you saying he didn't know he was a fucking reaper? I ask him.

Scathe yelps. *Why is that so difficult to believe? You thought your dad was a good man. It's easy to ignore things we don't want to believe.*

"Hey, leave my dad out of this," I say angrily.

Godric makes a questioning noise, glancing at me in the rearview mirror. I shrug, and he turns his attention back to the road.

No need for hostility, but your passion about the matter, instead of looking at the facts, proves my point, Scathe says.

Scathe…I don't want to talk about my dad right now.

The city rises up ahead of us, sunlight reflecting off the skyscrapers. The traffic gets more congested, and Godric swerves through the streets with reckless abandon. I clutch my churning stomach, willing myself not to get sick.

You should know, Scathe says, *even after you abandoned Archer, he sent me after you. To protect you.*

"I didn't abandon him," I say as we pull into a familiar alley. We're at Archer's city apartment. Godric parks behind Archer's motorcycle. Scathe's sidecar is still connected to it.

Didn't you, though? He gave in to his darkness to protect you. He put you first, ahead of his own morality. He found out a truth he wasn't prepared for, and you left him to clean it up on his own.

I unbuckle my seat belt and open the door. Scathe places his paw on my lap, grabbing my attention. When I turn to him, his icy eyes peer right into my soul, as if sending me a message beyond words.

Tasia, Archer's life mission has been to protect people. Save them from harm, not cause harm. He is not a judge or a jury, nor is he an executioner. Reaper magic or not, give him the same grace he's given you.

A knot of guilt tightens in my chest.

Did I overreact?

Archer didn't actually kill Reed. Reed killed himself, *and* he was dealing dreamdust—killing others inadvertently.

Is he okay? I ask, suddenly worried about Archer. He always seems so strong, so self-assured. I didn't realize he could potentially be struggling with his own inner darkness.

I hope so. Scathe sniffs the ground, then glances back at Godric and me. *He wasn't himself when I saw him last.*

"Follow Scathe," Godric says, gesturing at the hound.

My heart squeezes at the thought of Archer *not* being okay.

Scathe leads us partway down the alley, and Godric presses

his palm into the brick. It opens up into a hidden doorway. My brows fly up, but at this point, I'm no longer surprised.

We enter a short tunnel, then descend some stairs, finally arriving in a strange, small room. The floor is made of black dirt, and a plethora of greenery is packed into the space. It's bright, with lights hanging above all the plants.

"Where are we?" I ask.

Godric grunts, and Scathe growls at another door on the other side of the room. Godric crosses the room and opens it to reveal what I recognize as the Underground—tunnels that are simultaneously familiar and unfamiliar.

Scathe bolts down the tunnel. Godric starts jogging after him. I follow suit, suddenly grateful for being somewhat in shape thanks to my job at the bar. But even though my endurance is accidentally pretty decent, I still struggle to catch up with the duo.

After twenty minutes of running, I have a cramp in my side. I slow down to catch my breath.

"Go...on," I say, doubling over and wiping the sweat from my brow. As I do this, I notice the path here isn't as packed as some of the other tunnels.

He's here! Scathe says. *Get your ass over here, woman!*

Gulping in more oxygen, I get a second wind and push forward.

Up ahead, the tunnel bends out of sight. I grit my teeth and force myself to keep going. When I round the corner, my shoulders relax, and I allow myself to slow down.

Archer kneels next to Scathe, scratching the hound's neck. He glances up, saying something to Godric. I halt, frozen in place as I watch the interaction.

Archer's honey-gold soul-shade wafts around his body. The sight of it steals the remaining air from my lungs. Even though

I'm no longer running, my heart continues to race. He tears his gaze away from Godric and faces me. Then he stands, staring at me with a heartbreaking look of sorrow and regret.

My instinct is to run to him, kiss away his pain and fears, but I can't get my legs to move. He's half-fae. He's a reaper. He's not the man I thought he was.

Quit being dramatic, Scathe says. *He is the same man you know. Forgive him.*

Get out of my head, mutt.

What Scathe said earlier hits me hard. He implied Archer didn't know what he was—he never *wanted* to know. It's only because of me that he let his darkness out. I always knew this man was too good for me, that I'd be the one to ruin him.

I think about how he's dedicated his life to changing the city.

How he gives every ounce of energy to making the lives around him better.

How he would never purposely hurt someone, even if they deserved it.

I think of how he brought me tea and oil pastels when I was sick. How he thoughtfully picked a mask to match my tattoo. How he disrupted his entire life to protect me and make me comfortable.

How, if it wasn't for me, he might never have known the true, dark extent of his power.

No matter what his power is, he's still *my* Archer.

Fuck it.

I rush forward. He takes my cue and does the same, meeting me halfway. I launch myself into his arms, gasping for air. He wraps me up in his strong muscles. My legs latch around his waist, and he spins me around, squeezing me tight.

"Tasia," he says like a prayer. "You're okay. You're safe." He continues to mutter my name, not attempting to hide the emotion in his voice. "I'm sorry. I'm so sorry. This is all my fault."

"Archer," I whisper back. I'm still angry at him. So angry. But deep down I know he's still the man I've come to care for. The man with a golden soul-shade and a golden heart.

"Did you know?" I whisper, needing confirmation.

He squeezes me tighter. "No, I didn't." He makes a small noise in the back of his throat before nuzzling me and saying, "I knew I was different. I knew there was more to my magic—to me—but I never wanted to face it. I thought if I could ignore it..."

"That it wouldn't exist?" I whisper, knowing all too well what he means. "That *you* wouldn't be different from the people around you?"

"Yes," he breathes. "I was afraid. I think, deep down, I always knew what I was...but I was afraid, Tasia." He draws in a big breath. "I can't express how sorry I am for letting you down."

"That was your first time? With Reed?"

"Yes." His voice is thick, weighed down by guilt. "I'm sorry for scaring you, for disappointing you, but if I'm being honest, I can't apologize for what I did to protect you. I would do it again. I'll *always* protect you, no matter the cost, baby."

My stomach clenches with desire when he utters the term of endearment, and tears prick my eyes. His body nestles perfectly against mine. His strong arms hold me with ease. I can relate to his battle with his magic, with identity. His admission only softens me toward him.

Pulling back so I can see his face, I take a deep breath, then press my lips to his with desperation. One of his hands moves to cup the back of my neck while the other grips my hip, holding me flush to him.

He breaks free from my mouth, trailing kisses down my jaw and to the tender skin of my neck.

"I'm so glad you're okay," he murmurs into my neck.

"That makes two of us. You had me worried there for a minute, gangster."

"You don't need to worry about me." He squeezes my hip. "I was coming for you. I will always come for you, whether you need me to or not."

I smile as his breath tickles my skin.

When he pulls back, his expression is full of relief. He studies me for a moment before breaking out into a grin.

"What?" I ask, smiling back.

"Was there another spider?" His eyes, now filled with humor, crinkle at the corners. "Last time you jumped into my arms like this, it was to avoid death by spider."

"Oh." I chuckle. "I'm not used to you having a sense of humor."

"Only with you," he mutters.

With that, he sets me down. I bite my lip as I stare at him expectantly. Neither of us talks for a moment.

"I'm sorry for abandoning you, Archer." My eyes flick to the dirt ground. "I didn't know—I wasn't..."

"It's okay," he says softly, pulling me to his chest in a reassuring hug.

Okay, okay, I know I said forgive him, but can you guys do your makeup sex later?

"We're not having sex!" I yell.

Archer jerks back as if I burned him. His brow furrows. "I wasn't trying to—"

"Not you," I rush to say. "Sorry—your dog is in my head."

His eyes light up. "Scathe's speaking to you?"

"Yes. He saved my life, actually. Again."

Archer's amusement rinses away, and he grabs my hand, pulling me through the tunnel. "We need to make sure we're all up to speed."

"Hey," Godric says when we catch up to him. He holds up his

phone and waves it at us. "Pixel has eyes on Arlo. He's in the Ministry District, likely glamouring his way to the High Chancellor position. She'll keep us updated on his movements."

"That fucker," Archer growls.

I snort. "Did you just drop an f-bomb, Archer Acciai?"

"I've changed," he teases.

My nose scrunches and my heart pinches at the thought of Archer changing. I like him just the way he is. "I hope not too much," I say.

He squeezes my hand in reassurance, and the four of us stride through the tunnels.

"We should stop to fill each other in," Archer says a few minutes later.

Is that what the kids are calling it these days? Scathe woofs at me.

"Sirius save me," I mutter, chuckling at the hound. *You're a perv*!

Scathe barks again, and I swear he's laughing.

"Good idea. It'll give us a moment to rest and recoup," Godric says to Archer.

A short while later, we end up in what looks like a meeting area. The room is cavernous, carved into the earth, with various wooden beams helping to hold the dirt at bay. A wooden table with matching chairs sits in the center of the space, and we all grab a chair. Scathe sits at my side, his head barely reaching the top of the table.

Without wasting any time, Archer looks at me and says, "I think Arlo is my half-brother."

I wince at his disdainful tone. The news isn't any less shocking as it was the first time I heard it. "I know."

His face remains neutral. "You do?"

"He told me while I was in his little glass prison."

At these words, fury blazes through Archer's expression. He runs a hand through his dark-blond hair. "Tell me everything."

And so I do. When I finish, he returns the favor, telling me everything he's learned about the Reaper, concluding with the bargain he made.

"You can't touch him, then," Godric remarks.

"No," Archer says. "But *you* can, surely. We need to get him out of the city. For good."

"Wait," I say. "I still feel like we're missing something here. *Why* would a powerful fae want to run the city? Why would he run a lab, glamouring faeologists into making a drug that kills people? Maybe he wants to rid the city of human bloodlines and move in his own...fae."

"That's not it." Archer looks deep in thought. "The fae hate the city. They don't want to live here."

"Well, Arlo sure seems to want to," I say.

"No," Archer says, his eyes glazed over. "Bargains," he mutters. His posture tightens, and he sits up tall. "Bargains. The humans made a deal with the fae, long ago, according to the books I've read. Fae leave the humans alone so long as they stay contained in the city—leaving the Wilds untouched."

"What exactly does that mean?" I ask.

"It's a loophole," Godric says, slamming his hand on the table, causing me to jump.

Archer stands so quickly that he almost knocks his chair over. "Arlo said, 'I don't need to destroy the city when it'll destroy itself.' He also mentioned something about my ma knowing about his plan." His eyes flick to Godric, and his jaw tightens.

My mind whirls as I put together the pieces. "He also mentioned something about not causing the dreamdust mayhem at the masquerade...but he admitted to having something to do with the drug. He said that humans often destroy themselves."

"It's not coincidental," Archer says. "He's bitter about humans being on his family's old land. He's hoping they'll ruin the city themselves so he can take the land back."

"But what does my dad have to do with all this?" I whisper. "Arlo said that the Scouts killed him for breaking an edict."

"Tasia," Archer says, giving me a regretful look. "It's possible your dad simply got caught in the middle, as a faeologist who had experience with magic."

"His note implied he was glamoured," I mutter. "Likely by Arlo. To make the dust."

Godric hums to himself. "If it was unauthorized, and someone caught wind and reported your dad, he'd be executed for treason."

"So he *was* a good guy." That's enough to bring me a small sense of relief. It won't bring my dad back, but it at least explains why he did what he did. And they must've thought my mother knew about my dad's experiments with magic, even though she was mentally incapable of understanding any of his work. "If he was glamoured into creating the dust, it wasn't his fault—it was against his consent."

"Yeah." Archer swipes a hand over his jaw. "After all this time, why did Arlo choose to come after you *now*?"

"Maybe for my dad's journals?" I say. "He stole them, after all." Thinking of my dad's words, I reach into my bra, pulling out the note.

"Does it really matter?" Godric asks. "I'm ready to murder the bastard."

"He's cunning," Archer says. "We need to come up with a plan."

"Can you read this?" I ask the men, unfolding the paper and showing it to them.

"No." Archer and Godric both say. They shake their heads, looking at me curiously.

"Good. You said he's in the city still?" I ask, wheels turning. "So he doesn't know I escaped?"

"Shouldn't," Godric says.

"I don't like where this is going," Archer growls. "Whatever you're thinking, Tasia—"

"Godric," I say, ignoring Archer, "can you use your magic to put the glass back together?"

"In theory, yes."

"Take me back." Meeting Archer's gaze, I say, "I have an idea. But I need dreamdust for it."

Ignoring their protests, I rise, heading out of the room. They have no choice but to follow.

Help me out here, Scathe, I say. *Lead the way out.*

Tell me your plan at least so someone can have your back. Scathe whines, trotting ahead of me. He glances back, and I swear the beast has a glint of judgment in his blue eyes.

Fine, but you can't tell Archer. If he doesn't know my plan, his bargain with Arlo can't stop him. No harm, no foul.

Icy fear freezes my veins as I go over the plan in my head. The note from my dad had a line that didn't make sense before, but now I think I understand it: *Blood is thicker than water, but blood can wash away dust.*

Blood, as in *my* blood. Washing away dreamdust. As in cleansing the poison. Maybe I'm overthinking it, but it feels right, especially after reading my dad's journal. Plus, the Scout blew the dust into my mouth, and I never got high. I'm still alive today, with no apparent issues.

I think...I think I'm immune to dreamdust, I say to Scathe. *I can hide it in my mouth and blow it into Arlo's face. Just like the Scout did to me.*

If I'm wrong? Well, I won't live long enough to find out...

-EXCERPT FROM THE PERSONAL JOURNAL OF DR.
CLAUDE FOSTER, DIRECTOR OF FAEOLOGY AT MES-
MERIC LABS

CHAPTER 35
FANTASIA

"Tell me your plan, Tasia," Archer growls. I've never seen the man so terrifyingly angry, not even when he sucked Reed's soul down.

"Not happening," I say for like the tenth time.

Godric gets behind the wheel of his SUV and drives away, presumably off to locate Stace and Alisha, to find more dreamdust, if he's a man of his word.

I can only hope he finds them and that they have access to more.

Without my cell phone, it's not like I can call them and check on them.

Archer angrily pulls Scathe's helmet out of his bike's compartment and puts it on the hound's head. He pulls mine out next and steps toward me.

"You are absolutely infuriating, Fantasia Foster," he mutters, his deft fingers working swiftly to place it on my head and adjust it.

I can't help but smile behind the helmet's shield, knowing he can't see me. "We are equals, Archer Acciai." I throw his full name back at him sassily. "Anything you're willing to risk, I am too."

"I'm not willing to risk *you*." He turns and pulls on his own helmet, indicating the conversation is over.

As soon as we get on the bike, I eagerly wrap my arms around him.

My teeth chatter during the ride, despite the air being comfortable. Another reason I don't want to tell Archer my plan is because I'm pretty sure he'll think it's stupid. Reckless. And maybe it is, but Arlo has answers about my dad. He clearly wants something from *me*. I worry that if I let the men do what they intend, Godric might end Arlo's life before I'm able to get my own closure.

This way, I can control the situation.

I can ensure we all get what we want.

Plus, something tells me Arlo wouldn't let Godric get close to him anyway.

Unfortunately, my plan is contingent on everything working perfectly. Godric needs to find dreamdust—and fast—and meet us at the warehouse. He needs to put the glass together, with me inside, so it looks like I never left.

However, instead of sealing the glass perfectly, he'll leave it breakable. I'll have the dust in my mouth, and I'll break out of the glass, blowing it into Arlo's mouth. Just like what the Scout did to me—except in reverse.

If he doesn't die, well, plan B. Archer and Godric can tie him up. We'll keep Arlo somewhere without nature, where he can't recharge his power, and then we'll question him when he's at his weakest.

When I get my answers, they can finish him however they see fit.

You're right, Scathe says. *Very stupid plan.*

You said you wouldn't tell Archer, I say.

And I won't, but it's better if you let me bite Arlo—I'll take him down with my venom.

I sigh. *We don't know how powerful he is, Scathe. He's clearly capable of a lot. The moment he sees you, he'll disappear. You won't be able to get close.*

And you will be? he asks.

Yes, I say confidently. *He let me close at the ball—twice. Whatever he sees in me, it certainly isn't a threat.*

Scathe growls into my mind, and I shut him out, tightening my arms around Archer's waist. Despite the dangers of the bike, nothing makes me feel safer than being this close to Archer. I know wholeheartedly that he wouldn't put me in danger. Not purposefully. In fact, he's worked quite hard to keep me *out* of trouble.

A short while later, we pull up to the warehouse. Archer hides his bike around back. As we begin to scout the place out, he calls Pixel and puts her on speaker so she can keep us updated about Arlo's whereabouts in the city.

"Eyes at the Ministry of Trade," Pixel says. Clicking noises fill the air. I imagine her tapping away at her computer, hacking the various security cameras to keep tabs on Arlo. A minute later, she says, "There are no cameras near your location, boss, so be careful over there."

"Heard," Archer says into the phone. "Scathe, stay out here."

Scathe whines but obliges, sitting back on his haunches while we enter the warehouse. Soon we're in the room where Arlo was holding me. I shudder at the sight of the broken glass on the floor.

"You sure about this?" Archer mutters, his jaw tensing.

No. "Yes."

"I trust you." He reaches out, grabbing my wrist and pulling me toward him. Without warning, he presses his lips to mine. Heat blazes in my stomach as I kiss him back. I wrap my arms around his neck, tugging him as close as possible.

"Uh, guys?" Pixel's frantic voice breaks us apart. "Arlo's gone."

Archer lifts the phone, his jaw tightening. "As in?"

"He straight up disappeared. Gone. Like in the blink of an eye."

Leisurely footsteps echo through the cement building behind us, and I whip around to see Arlo striding toward us. With his impassive expression and his impeccably gelled dark hair, he looks every part the manipulative politician he is. His almost blinding beauty makes sense now that I know he's fae.

"Hello, little brother," he says in a deceptively warm voice.

"Pixel—I'll call you back." Archer hangs up and stuffs the phone away. He steps in front of me, partially blocking me with his muscular frame.

Arlo stops where he is, a few paces away, and raises his hands in what I interpret to be a calming gesture. It does the opposite, stirring up my disgust and fear.

"It's a shame you refuse to acknowledge your bloodline." Arlo *tsks*, stuffing his hands in his pockets. Despite the seemingly casual gesture, his posture is rigid, his eyes coy, like a serpent ready to strike. "Reapers can veilwalk. It'd be quite easy, and useful, for you to learn."

Arlo begins striding in a small arc around us, and Archer rotates, keeping his front toward Arlo at all times, with me behind him.

"No thanks," Archer growls.

"Shame," Arlo says. A sharp smile forms on his face. "Perhaps then you'd stand a chance at challenging me." Before Archer can respond, he continues. "Ah, speaking of challenges. I've successfully earned the backing of the twelve Ministries."

"Earned? Glamouring isn't earning anything," Archer spits.

"You say we're nothing alike," Arlo says, wagging a finger in Archer's direction. "But we're more similar than we are different. You glamoured your way to the head of the Nightcrawlers, no?"

"That's different."

"Archer," I whisper. "Don't engage. He's trying to get under your skin."

"Why would I do such a thing?" Arlo taunts. "You, missy, are highly underestimated. Claude would be quite proud to see how clever you are."

"Keep my dad's name out of your mouth." I step forward, but Archer puts his arm up, blocking me from getting closer.

Arlo's eyes flash with amusement. "You clip your butterfly's wings," he murmurs while staring at Archer.

"You glamoured him," I say, balling my shaking hands into fists. "My dad. Into making dreamdust so you can gain *power*."

"Tsk, tsk, tsk," Arlo says, swiveling around and taking a few small steps away. He sighs, then glances back at us. "Your father was the one obsessed with power. With *magic*, Tasia. He used you for one of his experiments, without fear of consequence."

"No," I snarl.

"Dreamdust was a creation gone wrong," he says. "It was meant to be a way to give humans magic for a short duration, to let them become fae themselves. Your father does not work for me. I'm only here because he brought me here—to experiment on me."

"But the glamour," I say, dumbfounded. "He said he was glamoured."

"Did he?" Arlo challenges.

"Yes," I whisper.

"What were his exact words?"

Archer gives me a quick shake of his head, presumably to warn me to stop speaking, to stop giving Arlo information, but I ignore him, desperate for the truth.

"He said his letter was glamoured to be read by my eyes only, and that wasn't the only thing glamoured."

Arlo gives me a pitying look. "Pretty little butterfly, your father was not glamoured."

My vision goes spotty as my head swirls. "What?" I croak out.

"For all his faults, your father is an intelligent man, Fantasia." He clears his throat, straightening his jacket. "He needed help, and I wanted my freedom back, so we bargained."

"What was the bargain?" I whisper.

"Power. He wanted power. I traded my power for my freedom."

"I don't understand," I say.

Archer launches himself at Arlo, only to hit some sort of invisible wall. "I will kill you," he hisses.

Arlo's face morphs into a thing of darkness. The whites of his eyes darken until they're nothing more than black shadows. His jaw cracks and stretches until his mouth is open impossibly wide, and he steps forward, inhaling Archer's wavering gold soul-shade.

"Stop!" I screech. I lunge for Archer and rip him away from Arlo. We tumble backward. Archer's head hits the cement with a resounding *thwack*. "Archer!

I frantically tap his cheek, trying to rouse him. His eyes stay shut, but luckily his breathing is steady.

"Don't kill him, please," I say desperately, glancing up at Arlo, whose face has returned to its regular, ethereal beauty. He stays rooted in place. I turn back to Archer, jostling his shoulder. "Please, Archer, wake up."

"Reapers do not kill for the harvest; they can only harvest when souls are finished with their current body," Arlo says. "He's not dead."

"You—"

"You'd be wise to remember the power you're dealing with. We might not kill, but there are many other ways we can cause pain."

"I will fucking end you, you bastard." I jump to my feet.

"Your little hero over there—" Arlo jerks his chin toward Archer's unconscious frame. "Have you ever stopped to consider his intentions? Perhaps he's the most selfish of them all."

I spit at him, but it's a pathetic spittle that doesn't even make it to his boots. Arlo gives me a mischievous grin.

"You fucking narcissist," I spit. "You're the selfish one, you—"

"I beg to differ." He steps forward, leaning in until our faces are a mere hair's-distance away. His warm breath caresses my face, and I grit my teeth. "You will not spit at me again." At his words, an icy tingle courses through my veins. I jerk backward, almost tripping over my feet.

He's trying to glamour me.

"You see me as a villain and Archer as a hero." He pauses, staring deeply into my eyes. When I don't reply, he chuckles.

"That is a dangerous, dangerous thing, little butterfly."

"Don't call me that," I say through gritted teeth.

"A hero is someone who is unwavering in their beliefs. Someone who will stop at *nothing* to do what they believe is the right thing."

I continue to glare, unsettled by the way Arlo's deep black eyes bore into my soul. "Exactly. The *right* thing."

"What *they* believe is the right thing," he says. He lifts his brows, as if he's trying to make a point. "Selfish."

"And what's your excuse? What you're doing is no different. At least Archer has a good fucking heart and good intentions!" I yell.

"Good intentions for whom, exactly? Himself? By seeking vengeance for his junkie sister? His whore mother? To absolve his own guilt?"

I snarl, wanting to punch Arlo in his deceptively pretty face. Violence isn't my go-to, but suddenly I'd love nothing more than to mark his face with bruises—so it matches the ugly inside of him.

"Nothing is more dangerous than a man seeking vengeance," Arlo warns, his playful expression slipping into something more sinister.

"And what is it exactly that *you're* doing? Filling the streets with a deadly drug so you can kill humans and feast on their souls?!" I scream. Arlo takes a step back. "For power? For control? You say a man seeking vengeance is the most dangerous, but a man craving *power* is the deadliest of all. At least vengeance is birthed from love, from passion. What's power birthed from? Ego. The need to control. The desire to be better than others. You narcissistic asshole!"

Arlo's eyes flash to Archer, then back to me. A line forms in the middle of his forehead. "That's what he told you? I feast on human souls for *power*?"

"You're despicable."

He tuts at me, then resumes pacing slowly, like a predator circling its prey. "Little butterfly, let me ask you: when a human dies, where does a soul go?"

I blink, frowning at him as I ponder the trick behind his question. It's *Arlo*. There's obviously more to his words than it seems.

"Before you say I *consume* it, let it be known that I eat food for sustenance. The same as you. I enjoy the PD's street tacos and a greasy hamburger as much as any two-legged being in this city does." He pauses, offering me a coy smile. "Or four-legged, if we're bringing that crafty little *dog* into it."

After a beat of silence, he leans in and whispers, "I am the scythe not to destroy but to sow the new harvest."

I squint. Before I can ask what that means, the air shimmers besides me and a dark shadow of fur appears in my periphery.

"He can veilwalk?" Arlo whispers, his face morphing into something akin to shock.

Take it. Scathe says urgently. *Now, Tasia!*

Without hesitation, I open my hand. Scathe drops a small bag into my waiting palm.

The dreamdust.

I don't know where Godric is, but they got the dust.

This plan might work after all.

"I'll tell you where *your* soul is going," I say. Moving deftly while Arlo is still close—distracted by Scathe—I dump the dust into my hand and blow it straight into Arlo's face before darting away from it. "Straight to hell."

He staggers back, blinking a few times as he coughs. Glittering grey dust speckles on his shirt and floats like ash onto the ground around him.

"What did you do?" he asks, alarm pinching his handsome features. His eyes dart from me to Scathe.

His breathing increases, and he shakes his head in panic.

Scathe flickers out of sight, reappearing at Arlo's side. He snarls, his white teeth gleaming with saliva as he clamps down on Arlo's hand.

"Scathe—!" I yell. *That isn't part of the plan!*

I can't risk you and Archer, Scathe says frantically. *Sorry, Tasia.*

Arlo flinches, although he's staying much more composed than I'd expect after being blasted with a deadly drug and bitten by a hellhound.

Clutching his bleeding hand to his chest, Arlo glances at Archer's body, then back at Scathe. "You'll regret that, Fantasia. Let me die, and you'll regret it." His voice warbles. Then his body flickers, fading into a shadow. "I'm the only connection to your father..." His voice fades as his body disappears from sight.

Scathe sneezes. He stands there, frozen, for a moment, watching the spot where Arlo disappeared.

Dropping to my knees, I wrap my arms around Scathe's neck and sob. I bury my face into his thick midnight fur, inhaling his canine scent.

"Sirius save me," I say, my body shaking from the adrenaline. "I can't believe that worked."

There is no remedy to the dreamdust. It works fast, and Arlo's body was already showing signs of the drug working its way through his system. Which means my plan *worked*. Arlo disappeared to lick his wounds and die in private.

For a brief second, guilt squeezes my chest, but I turn my attention back to Archer and push the thought aside.

"We need to get Archer up," I say, letting go of Scathe. I drop down beside Archer and pull his head into my lap. I check his pulse. It's still strong and steady. "Where's Godric?"

When no response comes, I glance up. "Scathe, can you wake Archer? Maybe you can mindspeak to him and get him to wake up?"

The hellhound is curled into a ball on the floor, his breath coming in quick pants.

"Scathe?"

Sliding out from beneath Archer's head and gently placing it down on the ground, I dart back toward the mutt as quickly as I can.

"What's going on?" I run my hands over him, looking for any signs of a wound. "Where are you hurt?"

A rumble shakes his body, like a growl he's trying to suppress. When I peer into his blue eyes, I notice his irises are almost concealed entirely by his pupils.

"No..." A cold sweat breaks out on the back of my neck. "Absolutely not, Scathe. Not you. Not today." The sure signs of a dreamdust high in my furry companion bring bile up my throat. Did he somehow inhale some?

Clenching Scathe's fur beneath my fists, I turn to Archer.

"Archer!" I scream. "Wake up! Archer, please." My voice cracks. "I don't know what to do." Wrapping my arms around Scathe and holding him to my chest, I mumble into his fur again and again, "I don't know what to do."

On the other side of Scathe's body, I glimpse the now empty baggie on the ground.

There's a puncture in it.

Likely from Scathe's canine tooth.

"Oh Gods, no."

No no no no no.

This is my fault.

"I can't lose you!" I cry out into Scathe's fur. "I love you, Scathe. I can't lose you."

Everything is silent, save for my sobs, as I wait for that familiar sarcastic voice to fill my head.

His panting becomes dangerously rapid. Everything in me shouts to back away from him, to get away before the dust takes hold. I've seen what it does to people—what it did to Reed.

"I'm not leaving you," I say like the Gods-damned idiot I am.

"Sirius save us both, but I am *not* leaving you."

Scathe's breathing slows, and my breath hitches. A blossom of hope opens its petals inside of me. Is he fighting the dust somehow? Is he okay?

I lean back to look at Scathe's eyes, and my heart drops when he immediately looses a predatory growl, snapping his sharp fangs at me.

"No—" My voice goes hoarse, silent, as he lunges at me.

I barely have time to lift my hands up and block my face before his teeth sink into the fleshy part of my forearm. White-hot fire shoots through me.

I scream in desperation.

While facing the end of my road, the tiny, locked box in my heart opens, and words bubble out of my mouth without my consent.

"I love you, Archer," I whisper before blinding pain consumes my consciousness.

CHAPTER 36
FANTASIA

I wake to an angelic being hovering over me. His tan skin and dark-blond hair are gilded by the bright light above him.

"Archer?" I croak, pushing myself to a sitting position.

"Don't move—"

His words are eclipsed by a sharp pain that shoots through my arm, so intense that my vision turns to spots. I bite back a scream.

"Scathe?" I moan, squeezing my eyes shut.

"The bite isn't that bad. I stopped the bleeding. His venom is working its way out of your bloodstream now. The pain will subside any second now that you're awake."

I don't give a fuck! I want to yell. I'm consumed with grief and heartbreak. My body is so heavy, it's like an anchor—and I want nothing more than to drift down to the sea floor. To drown in my sorrows.

I like a lot of things about you, Tasia, a deep, steady voice says in my head, *but that manner of talk is malarkey.*

You can hear me? I think, trying to direct it toward my furry pal.

Heard all that melodrama.

A warm, wet tongue slathers my face with saliva, and my body instantly lightens. This time when I open my eyes, it's Scathe's furry face and pointed ears hovering over me. I squint, making out his vibrant, cool blue eyes—with normal pupils.

Sorry about the wound. One might say I wasn't in my right mind.

Gasping, I sit up and wrap my arms around the mutt's neck. My left arm is wrapped haphazardly with a dark piece of cloth, but the pain is already a whisper of what it was a moment ago.

"Holy shit—you're okay." Tears streak down my face and into the hellhound's fur as I nuzzle him.

Keep that up and my fur will mat. I'd rather not entice Archer to brush me any more than he already does.

I laugh, making a snotty, bubbly sound.

Gross, Scathe says. But his voice is filled with dry humor.

Laughing harder, I release the mutt and run my hands over his neck fur—hitting the spot he likes. His back leg thumps involuntarily against the concrete floor as he leans into my touch.

Right...there... Ahhh yes.

"Tasia," Archer says. The spell of the reunion is semi-broken as everything comes rushing back to me. Archer's rich, golden eyes are filled with warmth as he gazes down at Scathe and me. "How's your arm?"

"Forget about me—how are *you*? Arlo knocked you out!"

His lips slowly curve up into a grin as he kneels down beside me. Gently, he places his big, strong hands on either side of my head, working his fingers into my hair and holding me reverently.

"Look at us." I chuckle. "We are one hell of a pair."

"You're one hell of a woman," he says.

Before I can respond, his lips descend on mine—firm and demanding. Reaching up with my good arm, I pull him closer, deepening the kiss. When I make a soft sound of satisfaction, he groans and pulls away, releasing me.

"How is Scathe alive?" I ask. As ecstatic and grateful as I am that Scathe made it through the dreamdust high, panic courses through me at the thought that Arlo might've survived, too. "How is he okay?"

Archer and Scathe share a long look, and I realize they're probably mindspeaking. After a few beats, Archer turns back to me with a serious expression on his face.

"Your blood."

"What?" I frown in confusion.

"Scathe told me your theory on immunity. We think when he bit you...your blood neutralized the magic."

"'Blood is thicker than water, but blood can wash away dust,'" I whisper as it clicks into place. It's not just immunity I possess, it's an *antidote*.

My father must've known something terrible was coming to Silver City. He was in the thick of it. How else could he have planned all of this the way he did? Injecting me with the soul-magic mRNA. The bear...the note...the journals. The puzzle he left behind.

He didn't just inject me with artificial magic, but with a solution.

I am the antidote—for everyone.

My pulse picks up.

"Archer," I whisper. "We can save them."

My thoughts race.

Dreamdust needs to get off the streets completely, but with Arlo gone and my blood as the remedy, we stand a chance at turning this city around.

Archer shares a look with Scathe, who whines excitedly.

"What are the chances?" I say. "The entire time you were looking for an antidote, it was *me* you were searching for without even knowing it."

Archer bows his head, his shoulders relaxing. For a moment he stays like that, his hand squeezing my thigh. "I always knew you were special."

After a moment, I glance around the warehouse, realizing it's still only the three of us in here. "How long was I out? Where's Godric?"

"Not long." Archer lends me a hand, helping me to my feet. "Godric got caught up in a security check in the inner city."

I had a feeling your little plan was going to go awry. I took things into my own paws. Got to Godric in time to snag the dreamdust and veilwalk back here, Scathe says.

Of course the crazy ol' mutt can veilwalk. Typical hellhound shit, I suppose? There's so many questions I still need answers to.

"You did good," I tell Scathe. "Just don't ever put yourself at risk again." Scathe bares his teeth, pinning his ears back, but I shake my head. "Nice try. I'm serious." I turn to Archer. "What about Arlo? Where'd he go?"

"Pixel's running his face through the system. She'll let us know if the cameras flag him anywhere in the city. So far, nothing at all."

"The drug was affecting him, Archer. I saw it. His pupils were blowing out; he was panicking. If he survived it..."

"Based on what we've seen, I don't think he could've." He clears his throat. "And even if he *did*, we'll be ready."

"He's a powerful fucker."

"He's also by himself," he says contemplatively. "We have the advantage of knowing what he wants. We know what he's capable of. We also have each other, and Scathe, and Godric. And Pixel." He grunts. "Zeke, too."

I nod, thinking of my two ex-roommates who proved to be even kinder than I expected, despite their prickly exteriors. Once I recover from the chaos of the past few days, I plan to make an effort with them. We might never be friends, but it doesn't hurt to try.

"We have a lot of people who would support us, I think," I agree.

Arlo wanted to take the city back for the fae. He failed spectacularly, and it's safe to say his intentions were misguided.

"We'll win, either way," I say, steeling my shoulders.

"We *will*," Archer says, his expression shining with unwavering certainty. "After we get the *fuck* out of here."

My brows rise at his cursing, and I exchange a look with Scathe.

The hellhound tilts his head, and his tongue lolls to the side as he says, *You are a bad influence, woman.*

Snorting a laugh, I shake my head. *Gods, I am so glad to have your judgmental ass back.*

Archer and I walk out of the building hand in hand. I can't help but glance back at Scathe every so often, ensuring he's truly okay. His tongue hangs out of his mouth as he trots. Slowly, my shoulders relax.

"Arlo said some things about my dad..." I pause, trying to gather my thoughts. "If my dad was truly obsessed with his work as a faeologist, do you think the dreamdust resurgence is his fault?"

Archer squeezes my hand. "I think everyone's responsible for their own choices, regardless of their personal history."

I sigh, disappointed by the betrayal from the man I've regarded so highly all these years. A new wave of grief rattles through me, shaking my bones—grief for my dad as I knew him, as I thought he was. Even if his intentions were good, his impact was awful. And if his intentions weren't good...

No.

I can't think about that.

"I still don't understand what exactly Arlo wanted," I say.

Archer leads me to his bike, then starts pulling out the helmets. "We might never know, Tasia. If I had to guess? Obsession. Vengeance, even? Maybe he was as obsessed with your father as your father was with the fae. Arlo *did* buy Mesmeric, after all. He found a way to remake dreamdust, albeit years later. He wanted your father's research—his daughter, his lab, and who knows what else."

He puts Scathe's helmet on, and the hound jumps into the sidecar.

"*Why*, though?" I ask, unsatisfied with the few vague answers we've received. And with Arlo dead, I'll likely never understand.

"Obsession is a scary thing. It causes us to act irrationally. It's like a current pulling us along, and all we can do is swim with it, hoping it doesn't drown us."

"Spoken like someone familiar with it," I whisper as I take the helmet from him and slip it on.

"I'm very familiar," he mutters, swinging a leg over his bike. "Come on, let's get some rest. We need to meet up with Pixel and Godric downtown as soon as we can."

I climb onto the bike and wrap my arms around Archer, nestling against him. Exhaustion weighs on my bones.

As we weave through the backroads toward the city, my mind wanders.

Before I know it, we're parking the bike and heading into his mom's old apartment. The place is tidier than it was before, the books arranged in neat stacks again, and the kitchen floor glistens.

I shudder, remembering the blood that stained it—and my hands—the last time I was here.

Before I can hyperfixate, Archer leads me to the bathroom. We clean ourselves up, then proceed to his bed, where we fervently and gratefully explore every bit of each other's skin. Afterwards, we cuddle, whispering our appreciation for one another as we succumb to a much-needed sleep.

The next day we head to the Underground to meet with the crew.

I hear Godric before I see him. "I swear to the Gods, Pixie, if you don't give me that bastard's name, I'll find it myself."

"Just give it to him, Pix," another man says.

We enter a room with actual flooring and walls, equipped with tons of nondescript electronics and a wall of computer screens. It's less like a cave or derelict house and more like a legitimate office. Godric has a chair pulled up beside Pixel in the corner, and he's staring at her intensely while she clacks away on a keyboard.

The prominent scent of weed draws my attention to a guy who's leaning against a wall nearby. It's the same guy from

Godric's apartment, with that unforgettable green mohawk.

"Zeke." Archer nods at him. "There's not enough ventilation down here for that."

"Sorry, boss, was just takin the edge off," he says, taking another long drag from his joint before using his fingers to snuff it out. His bracelets jingle as he wipes his hands on his skintight jeans. His eyes swing to me. "Oh shit, where are my manners? You want a hit? I can relight it real quick. If the Phantom don't mind."

Archer sighs, rubbing his forehead.

I shake my head. "I'm good. Thanks."

Godric stands, meeting us in the middle of the room. "I wasn't about to tell him to put it out. Not after the shit we saw the other night." He grunts. "Figured there's more important shit to fight about."

"Appreciate that, Ricky," Zeke says, joining us.

"Shut the fuck up with that nickname," Godric mutters.

So much for not fighting.

Zeke chuckles, reaching for a hit of his joint before seeming to remember he put it out.

My mind wanders back to the night of the masquerade. The tragedy at Splendor Hall. I vaguely remember Godric saying he and Zeke would go back and investigate. I shudder, thinking of what the scene looked like when we left. I can't even imagine how horrible it must've been at the end.

Archer frowns, running a hand over his jaw. He strides over to Pixel, and I follow him. "Anything?" he asks.

"Hey, Arch," she smiles up at him, and then her eyes shift to me. "Hey! We haven't officially met, by the way. It was kinda chaotic the other day. I'm Pixel. I'd shake your hand, but uh...kinda busy." She keeps typing even as she talks to us, and this time I can't help but laugh.

"Tasia." I nod. Her eyes crinkle at the corners when she smiles, and the warmth there eases my nerves. When her focus returns to the screen, I notice the tattoo on the back of her hand—the skull with a worm. I'm pleased to meet another important person in Archer's life. "You're the one who keeps these guys in check, huh?"

She snorts a laugh. "Not by choice."

These people are more than just coworkers. They're his family. It hits me then how Archer has a whole life I don't fully know yet. A life I desperately want to be a part of.

"No sightings of Arlo Osiander," she says, bringing the conversation back to its origin. I study the abundance of screens, trying to understand what we're looking at. A few monitors have grids of greyscale footage from surveillance cameras—real-time feeds, if the timestamps are any indication. Other screens blast lines of bright green code, scrolling faster than I can keep up with.

Archer makes a contemplative noise. "I'm assuming you have both his name and face flagged?"

"Oh yeah," she says.

I'm in awe. Something tells me she's the true brains behind many of Archer's operations. Archer is the obvious leader, Godric the brawn, Zeke the resources, but Pixel is clearly the one who ties it all together with her wit.

"Tell her to give me that ministry prick's information," Godric says to Archer. "That prick left her the night of the masquerade. She could've fucking died because of that asshole."

"Godric," Pixel says softly, giving him a long look.

"I'm with him on this," Archer says.

"He didn't hurt me," she mutters, cheeks flushing. "Good Gods, this is the last time I mention my dating life in front of you guys. You're a bunch of overbearing brothers."

Godric seems to deflate. "Yeah...brothers," he mutters, frowning.

"Okay," Pixel says, clearing her throat. "What I *did* manage to do is unseal the previous lab owner's records."

Zeke steps forward, planting a kiss on Pixel's head. "You little genius," he says excitedly into her hair. Her cheeks turn as red as said hair.

"Get off her," Godric says, jerking Zeke's skinny frame back.

Curiously, I watch the three of them for a moment. What exactly is their dynamic? It's entertaining, to say the least.

Archer, on the other hand, seems unfazed. "What did you find?" he asks.

"Well, turns out the previous owner bought Mesmeric under a shell company—a fake name. We never noticed before because it was well hidden. But...something felt off about it, all things considered. I took another look, tracing it back, and..."

"Who is it?" Archer leans forward, eyes scanning the words on a screen Pixel points to. "Artair Münryn..." He mutters something under his breath before yelling, "Fuck!" He slams a fist on the desk, and we all jolt, staring at him with shocked expressions.

"Who is that?" Godric asks slowly, seeming to sense the significance of the revelation.

"If Arlo's word is true," Archer says, running his hand obsessively through his hair and starting to pace, "I think that's my biological father. The lab's original owner."

Thick silence blankets the room. I place a hand on Archer's bicep, giving him a comforting squeeze. He softens under my touch, interlacing his fingers with mine.

"Apparently Artair died...a few years ago," Pixel says.

"Shit," I say. "So Arlo was upholding a family legacy—trying to get their land back? Maybe Arlo tried to replicate my dad's dreamdust formula and took it too far?" Maybe *that's* why the drug was so intense—so deadly when it came back. Maybe Arlo has actually been looking for the journals hoping to learn the original formula and scale it back. "What if he wasn't trying to *kill* everyone but was only trying to cause enough mayhem for the city to destroy itself and fall from within? So he and his family could take the land back? He did say he wasn't consuming souls for power, after all."

"It's making more sense now." Archer sighs. "If Artair was living in the city, that explains how my ma met him. Her clientele was high-class. Rich. Powerful." He pauses, stroking his jaw. "You know, Arlo *did* say she knew what the plan was—for them to 'take back the city.' I think you're right. Arlo was trying to follow in his dad's footsteps, and both times I've thwarted their plans."

My pulse picks up as I rush to say, "*That's* how my dad was glamoured, Archer!" I grab his arm, looking at him with wide eyes. "Arlo said *he* didn't glamour my dad, but someone must've. My dad's note implied it. It had to have been Artair. I bet his power is just like yours and Arlo's, which means he can totally glamour."

My dad didn't betray me or the city. He wasn't a bad guy, after all. He was a good guy, and an even better scientist, who got caught up with the fae, glamoured to do their bidding. Relief courses through me. I want to cry happy tears.

Is *Artair* the reaper I saw the night of my parents' deaths? Maybe it wasn't Arlo at all. He did say there were many reaper fae and that their job is to ferry souls.

"Uh, guys?" Zeke asks. "What the shit are you talking bout?"

I realize the room has gone silent. Even Pixel has stood from her computer to watch the interaction.

"There's something we need to tell you," Archer says to her and Zeke. He glances at Godric, then me, jaw tense. I nod in reassurance. "It's time."

Thirty minutes later, Pixel and Zeke are filled in on almost everything: what Godric and Archer really are, who Arlo really is, and even about my dad and the magic he injected me with. If Archer trusts these people, so do I. Plus, after everything that's gone down during the past few weeks, it's not exactly like I can ignore that side of me anymore.

It's a relief to be my true self, without stuffing parts of me down and pretending I'm normal. It's like taking off a bra after a long day—I can breathe, relax.

I'm not alone anymore.

"So, like, magic," Zeke says once Archer has finished explaining things. His eyes burn bright with curiosity. "Can you make joints roll themselves and shit like that?"

"For fuck's sake," Godric mutters, squeezing his eyes shut. When he reopens them, he turns to Pixel. "What about you? How do you feel about all this, Pixie?"

She shrugs, looking from him to Archer. "I'm really not surprised. It makes sense, all things considered." Without another word, she turns back to her computer.

I laugh, realizing just how much I like her.

We quickly shift topics, nailing down our plan to fix the dream-dust problem.

"Godric and I need to glamour the lower-level Crawlers to clean up the streets...again." Archer exhales slowly. "But this dust isn't like the old batch. The formula is different now. It's deadlier. People don't even have time to develop an addiction, considering they seem to die the first time using it."

This morning, when Archer and I woke up, we talked about my idea to protect the city from dreamdust. I remembered something my dad wrote in his journal, about potentially distributing magic through the water supply systems, and it spurred an idea.

I clear my throat, drawing everyone's attention to me. "We

think, since my blood seems to be an antidote, if we can figure out exactly how much is needed to counteract the effects of the drug, we can add just enough to the public water supply to prevent people from dying." I pause, letting them absorb the information. "We don't have the time or resources to pinpoint who will use the dust, and because death happens so fast, we need to be preventative rather than reactive. But hopefully, if we can keep the antidote in the water, it will protect people if they choose to use, until we get the drug fully off the streets."

"Zeke," Archer says. "Since you still have access to your lab, we need you to take a sample of Tasia's blood and ensure she's clean—that there's nothing else there that might cause harm."

My cheeks heat at the implication, but we already talked about this. We need to make sure this is as safe as possible, that the benefits outweigh the risks, or it's all for naught.

"We need to move fast," Archer continues. "Get this done as soon as possible, then run some tests to find out what the smallest effective amount possible is."

"Test it how?" Pixel asks, her full attention on us again. "On someone?"

"Well, Scathe agreed to let us test it on him first, since he's already gone through it once. We *know* with certainty that Tasia's blood can save him and counteract the effects. But we'll need a human test subject afterward."

"I'll do it," Zeke says, puffing up his chest.

Pixel's eyes widen. "But...what if it's not safe?"

Godric eyes them speculatively and jumps in. "Nah, *I'll* do it. Your system's already fucked up with drugs, skinny-boy."

"Oh, come on, Ricky. We both know you don't really wanna do it."

I roll my eyes. "I can barely breathe through all the testosterone in here," I deadpan.

Pixel snorts. "Now you know why I prefer computers to people."

"No one is doing anything until we test *my* blood first," I say, "so let's get on that and see if this plan is even feasible."

"You know, I think this might work," Zeke says, fingering his joint as if he's itching to light it up. "My lab tested some of the food and drinks from last night, found out someone spiked the liquor with dreamdust. It's why it hit so fast, so hard."

"What?" I ask, turning to Archer, who seems just as shocked. We're lucky Pixel and Archer didn't drink anything.

"Yeah, you can totally ingest the dust and get the same effect. I'd imagine your blood might work the same way." He flips his mohawk out of his face, bracelets jangling. "Didn't hear it from me, but official word is someone was trying to be smooth—get everyone to loosen up. Some rich asshole thought he'd get everyone high. They're calling it a tainted batch. An *accident*. But publicly? They're using this as a reason to crack down even harder on the city—blaming the tainted drugs on the PD and calling it a terrorist attack."

"Holy shit," I mutter.

"We might never know the truth," Godric says. "The best we can do is take control of this shit before it gets any more out of hand."

"Well," I say, "let's get to work."

Something tells me the city will never truly be safe. There will always be something, someone, or some *fae* trying to fuck shit up.

But with Archer by my side? I've never felt safer. And I'm starting to see the true power of his gang—his family—and how they are Silver City's true heroes.

When those in power neglect their duty to protect the city, the Nightcrawlers ensure safety—they fight back against the harm caused by greed and corruption.

Like the nightcrawler worms surfacing at night to feast on decay, they, too, emerge from the shadows, feeding on the city's waste.

In the underbelly of our tainted city, the Nightcrawlers prowl.

> "THE MAJORITY OF INDIVIDUALS EXHIBIT A PERSISTENT AND INVARIANT SHADE. HOWEVER, RECENT RESEARCH SHOWCASES A CAPACITY FOR ALTERATION AND ADAPTABILITY..."

-EXCERPT FROM THE PERSONAL JOURNAL OF DR. CLAUDE FOSTER, DIRECTOR OF FAEOLOGY AT MESMERIC LABS

EPILOGUE
FANTASIA

Two months go by, and Arlo doesn't make an appearance. Pixel stays glued to her screens, running all sorts of programs to search for his face and track the web for chatter about him. Other than rumors about his unusual disappearance during his bid for High Chancellor, nothing interesting comes up.

We successfully distributed small samplings of my antidotal blood through the public water system, which minimized the amount of dreamdust deaths, while the Nightcrawlers worked to clear the streets of the remaining dust. Other than the increased presence of Silver Scouts, and the same lingering injustices, things are going pretty okay.

"Maybe you should try to get the Ministries' backings," I say, rubbing Archer's shoulders after a long day of helping people move. He finally convinced a dozen or so cityfolk to move off the street and into his mother's old building. Glamour-free, I might add.

I'm glad the space isn't going to waste.

Now, we sit in the newly furnished lobby while the new tenants—for lack of a better term, since Archer is charging them nothing—get situated in their rooms upstairs. Cleaning, remodeling, and moving has been a massive undertaking, and we're all beat.

Archer moans, leaning his head back in pleasure as my fingers continue to knead his flesh.

"Get a room, you assholes," Godric mutters from a nearby ladder, where he screws in a new lightbulb. "We're in public."

Pixel giggles from a table across the lobby, where she curls over her laptop and types furiously.

"Shut up, jerk!" I call to Godric. "You're just jealous no one wants to touch your grumpy body."

Godric snorts. Archer shakes his head, reaching back to grab my hand. He turns his head and places a tender kiss on my palm. "What'd you say about the Ministries?" he mutters, continuing to pepper me with kisses.

"Edict twenty-four," I say. "If you get at least eighty percent of the Ministries to back you, you can run for High Chancellor."

He laughs, shifting on the couch and pulling me toward him until I sit between his legs with my back to him. His fingers begin working the knots in my shoulders, and immediately I see why he moaned the way he did.

Gods, his hands feel so good.

"Why are you wearing this?" he asks, giving the sleeve of my hoodie—or rather, *his* hoodie—a gentle tug. "It's hot out."

I shake my head. "I'm comfy. Plus, I like that it smells like you. So, Chancellor?" I tease.

He chuckles. "Who says I *want* to run for Chancellor?"

"Uh, you'd be the best man for the job, Arch. Are you kidding me?"

"She's got a point." Godric descends from the ladder, moves it over a few feet, and climbs back up to repair another light fixture. His eyes flick to Pixel in the corner, and I don't miss the way his gaze softens as he watches her work. A small smile forms on my lips. As if he can tell I'm staring at him, he turns his attention to me and narrows his eyes. "What're you looking at?"

"Oh, nothing." I smirk. "Hey, Pixel?"

Godric's gaze turns murderous.

"What's up?" she says, looking up from the computer screen and adjusting her glasses.

I let Godric sweat in the silence that stretches, let him worry that I'll make a joke about his little crush and embarrass him.

But I figure it's not my place to intervene with a blossoming love. Especially when it's one-sided.

"Wouldn't Archer be the best man for High Chancellor?" I ask instead.

Godric rolls his eyes and chuckles. I love giving him a hard time, considering he gives Archer such a hard time.

"Oh yeah," she agrees. "I tell him that all the time. He basically runs the city as it is. It would be the same job but in a more legit-imate capacity. He'd wield power to make change from beyond the city shadows."

"See?" I say, tilting my head to the side to give my boyfriend a gentle kiss. "We all agree."

He hoists me off his lap and sets me gently down beside him. His hand comes to rest naturally on my thigh. "I don't know that I'd get the backing I need."

"Archer," I mutter. "*Glamour*."

Pixel chuckles.

"I'd want to win the fair way," he says. "A legitimate challenge. With the backing of the Ministries *and* the cityfolk."

"So you *have* thought about it," I tease.

Before he can respond, the front door creaks open. I cringe at the loud noise that echoes through the lobby. That door could use some grease.

Remy slowly steps in, his face stern and unsure. He scans the room, his gaze landing on Godric before shifting to Archer, who stands.

"You again, asshole," Remy says.

"Remy," Archer says. "Language in front of the ladies."

"Finally got a wife?"

Archer looks at me and smirks. "Something like that."

Wanting to give them some space to talk, I cross the room to where the resident hacker sits. The red hair she had when I met her has faded into a strawberry blonde, and jagged bangs skim across the top of her glasses.

"Hey, Pixel," I say softly, not wanting to disturb her.

She turns, curiosity burning brightly in her eyes. "What's up, T?"

I lower my voice even further so the men can't hear. "Can you...hack bank accounts?"

She squints. "Depends."

"Not to withdraw anything," I quickly add. "But to...deposit?"

"Yeah, but why go through all the trouble of hacking for that? It might be quicker and easier to do it the old-fashioned way."

I bite my bottom lip, thinking of Mellie. The woman I considered a friend for so many years. A woman who deserves a better life than the one she's living. A woman whose son deserves to grow up strong and healthy.

But sadly, a woman who will never be my friend again. That door closed when she chose to turn me in.

"I, uh, want it to be anonymous," I say through the knot in my throat.

Pixel *mhmms* her understanding. "I'll need their name and the amount of money you'd like to transfer."

I rattle off Mellie's information, then say, "All of it. Everything Archer's paid me." I tell her the number and give her my bank account information.

Pixel freezes. She glances up at me. "You sure?"

Archer has been paying me the amount he promised, every week since the day we met, despite us being a couple. I told him I didn't want his money, but he swore he was only paying me for the services I provide the Nightcrawlers. Since I'm one of them now.

I nod. "She needs it more than I do."

"No wonder he likes you." Pixel smiles as she works. "You two are perfect for each other."

A booming laugh catches my attention, and I cross the room in time to hear Remy say, "Well, it's a good day for you, asshole, cause I'm finally coming home with ya, boy."

"Glad to hear it," Archer says, trying to conceal his pleasure. "Godric can show you to an apartment."

Godric mutters something under his breath, descending the ladder. He hesitantly strides toward Remy, and the two stare at each other with their arms crossed.

"Never mind," Remy mutters, turning toward the door. "Forget I came. I prefer the streets."

"Fucking *wait*," Godric hisses. Remy pauses with his hand hovering above the handle. "We have shit to talk about. Come on, old man."

I hold my breath as Remy lowers his hand. Finally he turns to follow his estranged son. The two head toward the elevator and out of sight.

"That's *huge*," I say on an exhale.

A fleeting look of worry crosses Archer's face. Then it morphs into a small smile. "It's something."

We're coming, Scathe says. *Be there in three...two...*

The front door groans open again with a loud *creak*. Scathe bounds in, with Zeke right behind him.

"What is it?" Archer asks in alarm. Understandably so, considering these two are supposed to be working—Zeke in the lab and Scathe downtown, keeping an eye on things.

"Gotta show ya something, boss," Zeke says with a grin. His mohawk is growing out, flopping over into his face. I don't know how it doesn't drive him nuts to constantly have green strands in his line of vision.

"Hey, Zeke!" Pixel calls.

"Little genius," Zeke responds.

"Tell me why you're here. What is it?" Archer says, using his stern voice. The one that means business. The one that sends a tickle zipping between my legs.

I bite my lip, tamping down the lust so we can show Archer what we got.

"So...don't freak out," I say.

He spins to face me, stress wrinkles on his forehead. When he reaches up to run a hand through his hair, I know we're really making him nervous.

Zeke and I share a look. I nod, and we both remove our hoodies at the same time. Zeke has a medical bandage about the size of a fist taped to his pec. It matches the one on my left inner forearm.

"What is this?" Archer asks, his gaze flitting between us. Pixel shuts her computer, joining us for the reveal. She, Godric, and Scathe knew what we planned, but no one told Archer.

I wanted to surprise him on his birthday.

Zeke goes first, peeling back the bandage to reveal fresh ink and angry, red skin. It's an exact replica of the Nightcrawler tattoo. The same one Godric, Pixel, Archer, and the others have on their hands.

"It's a symbol of solidarity. Of loyalty, bro," Zeke says, smiling at Archer. "I mean, boss. Bro-boss."

"You idiot," Archer mutters, but he's smiling too.

"Couldn't do it on the hand. Public job and all."

"Tattoo or not, you've always been one of us." Archer places a hand on Zeke's shoulder, pulling him in for a side hug. Finally, Archer turns to me, his eyes blazing. "You, too?"

"Not exactly." I bite down on my lip to keep from smiling as I pull back the bandage on my arm. Unlike Zeke, who got his tattoo done only moments ago, I got mine done yesterday. The skin isn't as irritated as it was, but the ink is just as vibrant.

"Holy shit," Archer whispers when I reveal the whole thing.

At his cursing, my laughter breaks free. "You like it?"

"I love it, baby." He steps forward, cupping my cheeks in his hands. "Come here," he mutters, planting kisses all over my face.

I told you he'd like it, Scathe says.

No, you tried to talk me out of it, mutt, I reply.

When Archer pulls back, he grips my hand gently, pulling my arm up to inspect the tattoo. "That's why you were being weird about my hoodie. You were hiding this from me, huh?"

"Yep." I grin, glancing at my arm, still pleased with how it came out.

Instead of a skull with a worm crawling out of the eye socket, *my* skull has colorful caterpillars crawling out of the eye sockets and a gorgeous butterfly—already transformed—flitting away. It complements Archer's Nightcrawler tattoo as well as the larger one on my thigh connecting them, morphing them both into something hopeful.

"So, I gotta show you something, too." Archer's cheeks turn pink as he scratches the back of his head. He reaches for the hem of his shirt, lifting it up and revealing a tiny butterfly on his hip, right above the waistband of his jeans.

I gasp, tracing the ink with my fingers. His tattoo is fully healed, as if it's been there for a while. But there's no way. I would've seen it yesterday morning when I had him naked in bed.

"When the hell did you get this done?"

"This morning." He grins adorably at me, looking pleased with himself. "Superfast healing, remember?"

"You asshole." I laugh, gently shoving his shoulder.

"You're even sassier than Scathe, you know, and that's saying something." Before I can respond, he says, "I wouldn't have it any other way."

Scathe growls, and Archer chuckles. He gently kisses the back of my hand and murmurs, "You're perfect the way you are."

"You're not really the asshole I once thought you were, are you?"

"Oh, I absolutely am." He smirks. "I'm only an asshole *for* you, never *to* you."

My smile grows as I shake my head.

He clears his throat, and his features harden into something more serious. "It's you and me, baby," he says. "I love you."

That's my cue, Scathe says.

In my peripheral, I catch the hound leaving the room with

Zeke and Pixel. But I keep my attention fully locked on Archer, on the life-changing words he chose to utter for the first time. Right here, right now, on his birthday, in the newly renovated lobby of the apartment he grew up in. With all of our friends around, after a streak of recent accomplishments in the city.

It's too perfect.

Too *right*.

I'm scared I misheard him.

"What'd you say?" I whisper, staring into Archer's kind, gold eyes. My heart flits faster than a hummingbird's wings, and suddenly all the joking and teasing melts out of my body.

I'm desperate to hear those words again.

I need them more than I need the air in my lungs.

He places his palm on my cheek, gently tilting my head back and leaning forward until his mouth hovers above mine. "I said, I love you, Fantasia Foster," he whispers across my lips.

"I love you, too, Archer Acciai." I smile into his lips, not quite kissing him yet, blinking back joyous tears.

"I hope you know that I'd do anything for you." He lowers his voice. "And I mean *anything*."

Our bodies are so close that his golden soul-shade practically wraps around me. I'm so used to it that I don't pay extra attention...until the aura wavers in color. It flickers, deepening in color until it's almost brown.

I blink, and it's gold again.

Sighing in relief, I press my lips to Archer's. I'm seeing things. It was only a trick of the lighting.

Because Archer has the kindest heart I know.

The purest soul I know.

Nothing could corrupt him.

The End...

Or is it?

Other books by Miranda Joy include:

THESE WICKED LIES SERIES
THESE WICKED LIES
THESE WICKED TRUTHS
THESE WICKED GODS (COMING SOON)

COURTS OF MALICE SERIES
A CURSE OF MALICE & MERCY
A DREAM OF FATE & FLESH (COMING SOON)
A REALM OF FEAR & FURY (COMING SOON)

SILVER CITY SERIES
SHADES OF SILVER CITY
SOULS OF SILVER CITY (TBA)

I have endless gratitude for you, dear reader. Thank you for making it this far. Thank you for giving my story a chance and for sticking with me. You keep me going.

Miranda Joy is an author from Upstate New York. She's a fan of all things magical and romantic. She believes some of the best heroes come from dark pasts and that family is more than blood. Her weakness is for characters who overcome unpleasant situations, uncover their inner strength, and find love along the way. Miranda holds a BA in English and an MFA in creative writing. When she's not scratching out notes for her next story or devouring a book, she's likely petting her dogs, doing yoga, or playing Animal Crossing.

Find her on Instagram at @authormirandajoy—she loves to connect!

www.ingramcontent.com/pod-product-compliance
Lightning Source LLC
Chambersburg PA
CBHW022242020726
47496CB00004B/1024